YESTERDAY IS GONE
... BUT THE MEMORIES LIVE ON

YESTERDAY IS GONE

...but the Memories Live On

Larry Hicks

Copyright © Larry Hicks 2020

ISBN (softcover) 978-1-7771984-0-4

All rights reserved.

Printed and bound in Canada.

Edited by Jane Karchmar

Design and composition by
Magdalene Carson / New Leaf Publication Design

This story was written to capture a part of the lifestyle into which I was born in the mid-forties. It is meant to reflect the attitudes and behaviours of some of the people from that time. The names are fictitious, but a few of the events really did happen; they have been altered for the story. The intent and purpose of this writing is to bring enjoyment to the reader, and in this I hope that I have been successful.

I want to thank those who have helped
and encouraged me in the writing of this book:

Donna Walton

Liam from Bayberry Design

Jane Karchmar

Madalene Carson

Contents

1. Uncle Charley *1*
2. Charley's Family *9*
3. A Trip to Town *19*
4. Billy Arrives *30*
5. Uncle Charley Arrives *42*
6. Bull's Eye through a Knothole *60*
7. Billy Gets Introduced to Ol' Zack *74*
8. Applesauce *81*
9. Two Little Buddies *94*
10. Target Practice *107*
11. A Buggy Ride *115*
12. A Bottle of Turpentine *132*
13. The Return of Ol' Zack *148*
14. Maw Comes Home *170*
15. A Ride with Eddie *180*
16. Storytelling *199*
17. Wild Bill *209*
18. Back at Home after the Hunt *243*
    About the Author *258*

YESTERDAY IS GONE
... BUT THE MEMORIES LIVE ON

Uncle Charley

The ringing of the old alarm clock drew Charley's undivided attention. He rolled over, reached out, and turned off the ringer.

After stretching, yawning, and rubbing his eyes, he muttered to himself, "Guess I better get up and be ready for when Harry comes tuh get me!"

Pulling back the homemade covers, he swung his legs out and onto the floor. He sat there for a moment with his head in his hands and his elbows on his knees.

His general appearance may have caused one to think this was something the cat dragged in sometime during the night.

His hair was every which way from scratching his head, and his face wore a three-day growth of whiskers. His eyes were red and puffy, giving the appearance that the night may not have lasted quite as long as he would have liked.

He also gave the impression that he didn't have a care in the world, and the truth was he didn't. He was satisfied with being just who he was. He had never entertained the idea of rising to such heights as holding the office of prime minister of Canada, or any other position of that nature. He was quite content with just being Charley.

His everyday appearance no longer bothered him, and if anyone didn't like it, well . . . there was always the other side of the road to be travelled, and you wouldn't hurt his feelings one little bit if you should decide to cross over. Plus, he lived alone, and from

Charley's point of view, how he lived inside of his four walls was nobody's business but his own.

Standing up, he again stretched and yawned, and gave his head a final scratch. Then he picked his pants up from the floor and laid them on the bed. He removed his shirt from the bedpost and laid it beside his pants. Grabbing the bottom of his nightshirt, he pulled it up and over his head, then he placed it on the bed. It would be going with him to Harry's.

Naked as the day he was born, he walked over to his old beat-up dresser. He had no fear of anyone seeing him through the window, for his neighbours were too far away, and if anyone should ever dare to peek, well ... what they'd see would most likely scare them half to death. And, if he should ever catch anyone bold enough to do such a thing ... the old thirty-thirty, which was hanging above the door, was a guarantee that they would think twice before they'd ever try'r a second time.

Charley opened a drawer and pulled out a pair of summer underwear. They were identical to the winter ones, except they were made from a lighter material and had short sleeves.

He loved their fragrance from being out on the clothesline. They were fresh and clean and they fit nice and snug, just the way he liked his clothes to fit. Charley had never cared for baggy clothes, and in his younger days he liked them to show off his manly figure. But now, his waist was well past the thirty-six-inch mark, and gravity had pulled his chest down till it was almost hanging over his belt buckle. The worst part was, there wasn't a doggone thing that Charley could do about it.

Reaching around behind him, he buttoned up the trap door, sucked in his stomach, and fastened the buttons up the front, with the exception of the one at the top. His shirt had been worn for the last two days, but it was still in pretty good condition, so wearing it another day or two wouldn't hurt. He put it on and rolled the sleeves up to the elbows, pulled on his pants, tucked in his shirttail, did up his belt, and made sure that he had fastened the two buttons below the belt buckle.

He left the bedroom in his bare feet, and if his toenails had been any longer, they would have been clicking like some old hound dog crossing a hardwood floor. He had good intentions of cutting them, but it seemed there was always something else that took priority.

Picking up the wash dish, he opened the back door and threw the contents outside. Another beautiful morning, and it looked like it would remain that way for the rest of the day. The sun was giving everything it touched a golden glow, and the sky was blue and cloudless. The air still held the chill of the night. It was fresh and invigorating, but that would pass as the sun climbed in the sky.

The grass was growing fast, and once again it was above his ankles. It had already been cut once this summer, and it looked like he would have to do it again.

This meant getting the old scythe out and putting it to work. But that would happen on another day when there was a little more time to spare.

The screen door closed with a bang as Charley put the basin back on the washstand. Using the dipper, he refilled it with fresh water, then reached for the bar of soap. After wetting it, he rubbed his hands together until he produced a rich lather. Placing the soap back in the soap dish, he worked the lather over his hands and face. When he was finished, he rinsed his face and then ran his wet fingers through his hair. After drying himself, he placed the towel back on its nail, and picked up the comb. His next challenge was to sort out this tangled mess. Dipping the comb in the water, he worked diligently till every hair was in place. Then smiling, he looked into the mirror and said, "Yuh sure are one good-lookin' ol' son-u-va-gun!"

The man in the mirror was the only one who would ever hear Charley make such a remark about himself.

Putting the comb down, he walked over to the cookstove and opened the door to the firebox. After placing some kindling, shavings, and crumpled paper in the stove, he struck a match and placed the flame beneath the paper. It quickly ignited, spreading the flame through the shavings and kindling.

He closed the door, picked up the kettle, filled it with water, and placed it back on the stove. Reaching up, he took a container from the top of the heater that had "TEA" written across the front of it in big, bold letters. He removed the lid, took out a pinch of loose tea, placed it in the teapot, and added more water.

Once a week, Charley would remove the used tea leaves. In his way of thinking, leaving them in the pot added more flavour.

Removing the lid from the back of the firebox, he placed a cast-iron frying pan over the hole. Then going to the cupboard, he opened a door and pulled out a hunk of bacon that was wrapped in butcher paper. He unwrapped the bacon and placed it on a wooden cutting board, then with a large knife carved off four thick slices. These were placed in the hot frying pan, creating that familiar sizzling sound and the wonderful aroma of bacon being fried.

He took a fork from the old wooden box that was on the table and turned the bacon. Then he adjusted the draft on the stove, hoping to obtain a more even heat. With the fire now established, he added some small pieces of hardwood and closed the stove door.

Returning to the cupboard, he lifted the lid on the old tin breadbox, and, like Charley, it was showing its age. It was scratched and dented, and most of the blue letters that read "Bread" were worn off. But it had belonged to Charley's mother and because of the sentimental value, Charley wouldn't trade it for the world.

His mother had often set him down, scolded him, and warned him of the rewards of evil. Then she would give him points to ponder in her effort to keep him on the straight and narrow. In the years that followed, there was many a time he had regretted not taking her advice.

He took the bread over to the table and cut off two thick slices. Then removed the front lid on the stove and placed an old wire toaster over the hole. He positioned the two pieces of bread on the toaster while whistling his favourite fiddle tune. Suddenly the room was filled with a wonderful breakfast odour, a mixture of homemade bread being toasted and bacon being fried.

Opening the cupboard door, he chose a dinner plate, from which the flowers were faded and had lost most of their colour. He placed a stained teacup and a glass butter dish on the plate and set these on the table; then, reaching across, he picked out a knife and spoon from the old wooden cutlery box and placed them beside the cup.

Next, he transferred the bacon to his plate and set the plate on the reservoir. On returning to the cupboard, he chose two eggs from a bowl that was just inside the door. He cracked them on the side of the skillet and dropped them into the hot bacon grease. Lifting the toaster, he dropped the eggshells into the fire. After replacing the toaster, he turned the toast and waited. Once the toast had been browned enough, he placed it on the plate and put the toaster back on top of the heater.

He put the lid over the hole and buttered the warm toast. He then spooned the hot grease over the eggs until they turned white. Charley never flipped his eggs, because he liked them sunny side up with a runny yoke. Using the egg lifter, he placed the two eggs on his plate. The frying pan he shoved to the back of the stove, and the lid he placed over the frying pan hole. Picking up his plate and teapot, he set them on the table.

After filling his teacup, he reached over and pulled the pail of corn syrup a little closer.

Seated at the table, Charley bowed his head and folded his hands and gave thanks. He said, "Dear Lord, I thank yuh for the food, Amen."

Charley enjoyed his breakfast, and, to finish it off, he used a piece of toast to sop up the egg yolk and clean off his plate. He refilled his teacup, picked up his spoon, and, using the handle, he pried the lid off the corn syrup pail. After picking up his second piece of toast, he licked the spoon clean and shoved it down into the corn syrup. While lifting it up, he twisted the spoon to keep the syrup from running back into the pail. Holding the spoon over the toast he let it spread as evenly as possible. With this done, he once again licked the spoon clean and put it down. Picking up his toast, he leaned forward, and proceeded to enjoy the last, but most delicious part of his breakfast.

When breakfast was over, Charley put everything back where it belonged. He picked up the kettle and filled the dishpan with hot water, added some dish soap, and placed the dishes in the water. He gave them a good washing, threw the water out, and dried the dishes. With his job completed, he hung the dishtowel on its nail and put the dishes back in the cupboard. After wiping the table, he turned the dishpan over and spread the dishcloth over it to dry.

"Done!" he said to himself while walking over to the stove. He took his socks from the oven door, picked up his boots, and sat down in his big chair. He pulled on his socks and then his long-topped boots, which were laced halfway to the top. He tightened the laces, wound them around the boot, and tied them. After stuffing his pant legs into the boot tops, he leaned back into the chair and closed his eyes.

How he loved his old brown chair. He had felt the need to place a blanket over it, covering the threadbare and torn places. But that wasn't a good enough reason to get rid of it. For it was the most comfortable chair Charley had ever sat on, and that made it a keeper.

He opened his eyes, reached over, and took his Bible from the stand beside the chair. Opening it to Psalm 23, he read, "The Lord is my shepherd, I shall not want . . . " He stopped reading and looked around the room. Then in a soft and sincere voice he said, "Thank Yuh Lord for give'n me so much; there ain't a thing that I need that I don't have. Thank Yuh. Amen."

After finishing the psalm, he closed the book and set it back on the stand. Again he closed his eyes and said, "Lord, I thank Yuh for this day and I pray that Yuh'll keep us safe throughout it. And Lord, please protect us in at the farm. Yuh already know, that while we 'r in there, we 'r gonna need all the protection we can get. Amen!"

Charley dearly loved his sister, Mary, her husband, Harry, and their three boys. But as sure as God made the little green apples, some kind of a problem would occur each and every time that he went in there.

He still had a clear and vivid memory of his spring visit. The boys thought they'd start a fire in the orchard to burn the dead grass, but no sooner did they get it going than a wind came up and took it out of their control. It had taken all six of them over an hour to keep it from getting into the forest, and then to put it out. In Charley's opinion, had it reached the bush it would have cleaned out at least seven townships before they could have ever thought of getting it stopped.

And how could he ever forget the time Harry's sister came to visit? Everything was going just fine until the two oldest boys, Mick and Dan, thought it a good idea to put some old dried-up thistles under her bedsheet. As soon as she landed on them, she started into the screaming. Harry jumped out of bed to see what was the matter, and in doing so, he struck his big toe on something. He hit it hard enough that it turned purple and stayed that way for about a week.

The next thing on Harry's agenda was a trip to the horse stable to get him a hame strap. Both boys got their back ends leathered but good that night, but it didn't seem to change a thing.

Then there was another time when they asked Charley if he would come and help them with the hay. Which he did, and everything was going just fine till Mick run across a snake. He picked it up with his fork and threw it at Dan. Dan was on the wagon, building the load and driving the horses.

The snake hit the top of Dan's shoulder and wrapped itself right around his neck. He immediately started to scream, dropped the lines, and jumped off the wagon. This scared the horses and they took off running. The wagon didn't get very far till it hit a good-sized rock and upended, scattering hay all over the place. But that didn't seem to matter much — the horses never halted till they'd succeeded in tearing the ol' wagon rack all to slivers. The boys didn't sleep too well that night, either, but it didn't seem to help any.

He didn't like to say no to his family when they asked for his help. But he knew for certain that each and every time he went in there, before he would ever see home again, some kind of a disaster would have definitely taken place. But he would still go, just like he was planning on doing again this morning. This time it would be for three days, and God only knows what could happen in that length of time.

His thoughts returning to the present, he opened his eyes, reached into his pocket, and pulled out his mouth organ. Wiping it on his pant leg, he put it to his mouth and started to play. This would help to pass the time till Harry arrived.

Charley's Family

Rays of sunlight were streaming through the upstairs window as Joey raised an eyelid. The sound of grates turning in the old cookstove had roused him from his sleep, and, not yet fully awake, he snuggled back into his pillow. Lying there, he let the sleepiness of the night slip away and the reality of a new day come slowly creeping in. Those few moments of transition were the sweetest of the whole night. As he lay there, he could hear the snapping and crackling of the cedar kindling, and on the morning air came the faint aroma of wood burning.

This day was starting off like all the others, but then he recalled the importance of this one. Maw and Paw were going away for three days, and Uncle Charley was coming to stay till they came back.

How he had tried to persuade his mother and father to take him with them when they went to visit Uncle Walter, but they said no, not even to town to pick up Uncle Charley. He felt both disappointed and rejected, but this boy was no quitter, and there was still time for one more try.

Joey, a thin and wiry young boy, was just entering his tenth year. He was full of energy and ready to release it at a moment's notice, but more times than he cared to think of, it had gotten him into trouble. Too many times his adventurous spirit had taken him well beyond his limits, and for this he had often paid the price. But that was yesterday; today and tomorrow still needed exploring, and he was more than willing to be the one to do it.

His hair and his eyes were brown, with a slight dusting of freckles across the top of his cheeks. He had a shy personality along with a sweet smile, and this combination had often brought him favour.

His closest buddy was half a mile away, and that meant he didn't get to see him that often, and it wasn't much fun being alone on the farm. His activities were made up of his chores and whatever mischief he could create. So he looked forward to the trips to town, or any other place that he got a chance to go; but the problem was, in this neck of the woods it didn't happen very often.

His two older brothers, Mick and Dan, were in the bed across the loft. They were rubbing their eyes and grumbling about having to get up so early in the morning. They were of the opinion that if the good Lord wanted them to see the sun rise, He would have made it happen sometime later on in the day.

Paw had just come out of his bedroom and was making his way to the head of the stairs. His pants were done up with the suspenders hanging down to his knees, his shirt was tucked in, and he was busy buttoning it up as he went by. His hair looked like he had just combed it with a firecracker — it was going every which way, but this was a minor thing to Paw, being it was early in the morning.

On passing their beds, he said, "Okay, boys, roll out, it's daylight in the swamp and times a' wastin'."

Joey knew all too well that when Paw said it was time to roll out, he meant exactly what he said. Being mindful of that, he pulled back the homemade covers and slipped out of bed. Picking up his pants, he pulled them on, then grabbed his shirt from the bedpost and headed for the stairs.

At the foot of the stairs was a large room that served as a kitchen and living quarters. Two smaller rooms ran off the back. The one on the left housed the cream separator, along with some other odds and ends. This was where the rifles were stored; they were hung on the wall, one above the other.

The room on the right contained the box stove, along with a sideboard, which held dishes and such. The pipes from the box stove ran up and along the ceiling to the chimney at the other end of the house. It was designed this way so the heat from the stovepipes would keep the upstairs floor warm in the wintertime.

Other than sleeping, most of the family activities took place in this room.

At the foot of the stairs, on the right, was the cookstove. In it, the kindling was burning at a rapid rate and igniting the hardwood. Once the fire was established, Maw could start breakfast.

As Joey was descending the stairs, he could hear the screen door slam. This meant Paw was on his way to the barn to feed the horses, and this would give him a chance to talk to Maw, one on one.

As he entered the room, the coffee percolator was popping bubbles, the bacon was sizzling in the cast-iron frying pan, and the water was starting to steam in the oatmeal pot. Everything was normal. Joey tucked his shirttail into his jeans, adjusted his belt, and then walked over to the washstand.

Picking up the dipper, he filled it with water from the water pail, and then poured it into the wash basin. After wetting his hands, he took the bar of soap from the soap dish and rubbed it until he had a good supply of suds. Placing the soap back in the dish, he rubbed his soapy hands over his face. When finished, he rinsed his hands and face. Taking the towel from its nail in the wall, he dried himself. He was now clean as a whistle and ready for breakfast.

Placing the towel back on its nail, he turned to his mother. Speaking soft and with a pleading tone in his voice, he proceeded with his case.

"Are yuh really sure that I can't come?" If he could just persuade his mother to let him come before Paw returned from the barn, maybe she could work on Paw and turn this thing around. There was still hope within him and he wasn't about to give it up.

His mother was busy kneading flour into bread dough in a big granite pan. With a flour-covered hand she pushed a few strands of hair from her face, then looking up she replied. "No! You have to stay with your brothers. Maybe the next time we go to town you can come. But this time we are in a hurry and we have to pick up Uncle Charley. There won't be much room in the cab and you'd have to sit on somebody's lap." Maw's voice gave evidence that she was getting irritated with her boy's persistence.

"Oouh . . . Maw, please can't I come?" A feeling of being left out was slowly creeping in. He usually went with them to town, even taking time off school to go. But this time it was different. Maw was anxious to get going and she was not going to allow anything to stand in her way. She was definitely not going to have Paw get upset and change his mind about going, for he was already complaining about what it would cost for gas.

"You heard your father, didn't you?" replied his mother, sounding a little impatient as she kept on working the flour into dough.

"Yah, but you could change his mind," insisted Joey, not wanting to give it up.

"That's what you think!" came the reply, her voice rising a little. "When your father makes up his mind, the devil himself couldn't change it. So you might as well get used to it — you are not going, and that's that!" The tone of Maw's voice told him the jury was out and the decision was final.

His tummy felt like ice water had just flowed through it as he realized the trip to town was a no-go. Mick and Dan were okay, and Uncle Charley was great, but it was never the same when Maw and Paw were gone. The days seemed longer and the nights were a lot darker, and there was an uneasy feeling that always hung around. He didn't know why, but it was always there, each and every time. But one thing he knew for sure, he felt safer and more at ease when they were all back home again.

If the trip to town was a no-go, then why not try for the one to Bellville?

Once again he turned to his mother, his hands in his pockets, his shoulders sagging, and his head drooping forward, trying to look as dejected as possible.

"Well then, if I can't go to town with yuh, why can't I come with yuh to visit Uncle Walter? There'd be room in the cab goin' there . . . Huh, Maw?"

"Because Uncle Walter and Aunt Beth don't have any kids, and you get bored and whiny because there's nothing to do!"

"I could play with the other kids that live there!" His head was leaning toward his right shoulder, his hands fidgeting in his pockets. He was trying to draw sympathy from Maw's heart. But it was no use. It would have been far easier to draw blood from a rock.

"You bet you could!" she replied in disgust. "The last time we tried that, you stone-pegged one of those poor boys all the way to his house, and that made his parents mad at us. Then we had to stand there and listen to his parents lecture us on how to raise kids!"

"Yah . . . but that was cuz he was pick'n on me. He said that I talked funny." Joey's head had now come erect, his fists clenched in his pockets as he went on the defensive.

"That's no reason to throw rocks at him," insisted his mother, her voice betraying her disgust.

"'Twas too . . . he was bigger 'an me," answered Joey, his voice rising as he spoke. "An' Paw always said if yuh get into it, be sure to pour it to 'm . . . and I did!"

Satisfied that he had stood his ground on that one, he paused as he thought of his next move. It wasn't long coming.

"Maw . . . I don't want to stay with Uncle Charley and Mick an' Dan—they're always bossing me around and they don't let me have any fun!" Again he was trying to find a crack in Maw's armor . . . but it was no use, because there wasn't any.

"That's because you are always getting into mischief. Behave yourself and things will go a lot better. Now . . . you are not coming with us, so have your breakfast, then go and find something to do!" Maw's voice was strong and stern, and her cheeks were beginning to turn red. The argument was over and done. Joey had lost with a TKO.

Last night he had done the best that he could to get them to give in, but it was no use. However, he thought it wouldn't hurt to try again in the morning, just in case they may have mellowed a little overnight and would reconsider the matter. But the matter was settled, and he knew it. He wasn't going anywhere, so it was time to make the best of a bad situation and get on with the day.

Anyways, Uncle Charley was coming, and there was always some kind of excitement going on when he was around.

Uncle Charley was Maw's brother, the youngest of five siblings. He lived by himself in a two-room house not far from town. Paw said he lived alone because no woman in her right mind could put up with him.

Charley was kindhearted and easygoing; it was just that he was pretty well set in his way of doing things, and that doesn't usually work very well in a double harness. Some folks were of the opinion that he was a brick short of a full load, but old Charley was mentally stable, just different. He was a big man with a bit of a tummy, and this caused Paw to say that he knew ol' Charley was on the dead level, because his bubble was always in the middle.

Joey picked up his ankle-high boots and carried them over to the stair steps. He sat down, pulled them on, and tied up the laces.

"Can you stop and ask Billy to come back and stay with me?" Again the voice was pleading, as if loneliness had already set in.

Billy was Joey's closest neighbour and his best friend. Being true buddies, they got along very well. Having Billy around would help fill the gap made with Maw and Paw being away, and he'd have someone his own age to keep him company.

"I guess we could," his mother replied, while working the bread dough. "But you boys had better be good or else there'll be fur flying when we get home!"

Maw's voice was stern, and Joey knew this was a solemn warning that held weight.

"Oh, Maw, you know we are always good," came the soft reply as he stood up and moved to the table. "I'm hungry for some porridge... can you get me some?" Joey's voice was soft and pleading as he tried to work on Maw's sympathy.

He was old enough to get it for himself, but it seemed to have a far better flavour if Maw's hands touched it.

"Hold on a minute till I get this dough off my hands," came the reply, as his mother walked over to the washstand and washed her hands. With the argument over, her voice was back to normal, and, as always, she was trying to please him.

Ol' Jake was outside looking at her through the screen door, sniffing the air and taking in all the wonderful odours of breakfast. He'd been around long enough to know that his turn didn't come till after the others were done, so he might as well be quiet and wait.

The screen door opened, and Paw entered the room. On his way back from the barn, he had stopped at the milk house and picked up some eggs and a bottle of milk. He set the milk on the table and took the eggs over to the cupboard and put them in a bowl.

"Boy, that spring water sure is cold!" he was wiping the moisture from his hand on his pant leg as he spoke, then he took a towel and dried off the milk bottle.

There was a natural spring in the milk house and it was used to keep things cool in the summertime.

The milk house was a small log building with no windows, which had been built over the spring with this in mind. Paw dug a hole beside the spring and placed an old washtub in it, then directed the water into the tub. Things like milk bottles and containers with butter and such were placed in the cold water to keep them cool. Usually a wooden barrel with salt pork was kept in the building as well.

"Why don't you spoon some ov the cream from the top ov the bottle and put it on your porridge?" suggested Paw as he pointed to the bottle. "Add a little maple syrup and yuh'll have a real treat."

Paw's voice was soft as he spoke to his boy. Perhaps he was compensating for Joey being left behind. But on the other hand, when Paw said he wasn't going there was no changing his mind.

The cream appears when milk is left overnight in its natural state. Being lighter than the milk, it rises to the top of the bottle and separates itself from the milk. There was about three inches of cream on the top of this bottle. Plenty for Joey's porridge and some left over for Paw's coffee.

Paw glanced around the room and then he roared, "Mick and Dan, are you two not out of bed yet?" the walls were still vibrating from his voice as the answer came,

"Yes, Paw, we just finished dressing and are on our way down!"

Everyone in the family knew that when Paw spoke he expected action, and the sound of two young men crashing down the stairs meant that he wouldn't be disappointed. Paw wasn't a big man, but he had a way of voicing his determination that usually got things done his way and on his terms.

Paw walked over to the washstand and washed his hands and face. Removing the towel from the nail in the wall, he dried himself. Then he sat down at the end of the table.

Before him was a plate of home fries, bacon, two eggs sunny side up, and a thick piece of toasted homemade bread with homemade butter melting all over it. A jar of strawberry jam and a bottle of maple syrup sat at the centre of the table.

Maw removed the two pieces of toast from the wire toaster, replacing them with two more pieces of bread. This process would continue until there was enough toast for everyone.

When bread was toasted this way, it had a flavour all of its own. A lid was removed from the stove and the wire toaster was placed over the opening. The heat from the coals toasted the bread and gave it that special wood burning flavour.

Maw was ready to pour Paw's coffee as he pulled his chair into place.

"I'll have a spoonful ov cream and a little sugar, if yuh don't mind," he said, nodding to Joey as he settled himself in at the table. Joey passed the bottle of milk and then the sugar bowl.

Mick and Dan had already taken their places at the table as Maw delivered their steaming bowls of porridge. Once everyone else was served, Maw sat down beside Paw.

Dan reached over and picked up the brown sugar container, removed the lid, and spooned out the sugar. When he was done, his porridge looked like it was a mountain capped with brown snow. The heat from the porridge was melting the sugar and it was running down on every side. Next came the milk, circling the base of the mound.

Picking up his spoon, Dan skimmed off some sugar-covered porridge, dunked it in the milk, and placed it in his mouth. Immediately his lips protruded as he started sucking in air, trying to cool down the porridge.

"Phew... that was hot! There is nothing on God's green earth that holds the heat like oatmeal porridge!"

Mick used maple syrup to sweeten his porridge, then added milk and stirred. As he watched the steam rise from the bowl, he said, "There, now, that should cool it down enough so that I can eat it."

Then he smiled at Dan and said, "Burn your tongue?"

"No, but I come darn close to it! Let me tell yuh, that stuff sure is hot!"

With breakfast over, Mick and Dan went to the separator room and picked up their milk pails, then left for the barn. It was their job to milk the cows, and this was required both morning and evening. They had a total of six cows, so they each had three to milk.

Many times Dan got knocked off his three-legged stool. His job was to milk ol' Spotty, and there never was a cow that liked to trail through the blackberry brush like she did. The results being she would get her teats scratched from the thorns. Dan never seemed to catch on, he would sit down grab and pull, and then kerbango! She'd kick, and Dan would go backwards off the stool, ass over teakettle in a cloud of dust. It was then he would remember to go and get the Watkins ointment and soften her teats before trying to milk her.

No matter what these two got involved in, it would always end up in some form of a disaster.

With breakfast over and the dishes washed and put away, Maw was ready for town. She changed her dress from one hand-me-down to another that she thought best suited the occasion. Her left arm was through the handles of her purse, and her hair was done in a roll that went all the way around her head. To accomplish this, her hair had been rolled upward and inward around an elastic band. When this task was complete, she placed her bandana over her hair. This was a square piece of cloth that was folded to make a triangle. Two points came down and tied under her chin, while the third one hung down the back of her head.

There was a notable air of happiness around Mary this morning, for her surroundings were about to change. She didn't see much of the outside world while living in the backwoods. So she tried not to miss an opportunity that would allow her to get out and experience it. Her butterfly attitude indicated that her daily cares were now behind her, and indeed, she was ready to be on the move.

Paw also was ready. He had traded his blue jeans and work shirt for a clean blue shirt and an old pair of brown hand-me-down dress pants. On his head was his favourite red cap. There were sweat stains where the peak and headpiece met, making that area a little darker than the rest. He also was wearing a light green windbreaker and his old, beat-up work boots. The boots were done up halfway and tied, with the pant legs stuffed into the open tops.

He stood patiently by the old pickup, softly whistling while he waited for Maw to get herself together. Once she felt everything was in order, she was ready to go.

She closed the truck door and leaned forward. Looking past Paw, she called out to the boys, giving them their final instructions. They were to put the bread dough in the pans in about half an hour. This was to make sure they would have fresh bread while she was away, and it should be raised and be ready for the oven by the time she got back. "And don't forget to wash the separator when you're done with the dough!"

"Yes, Maw," replied the boys, as they stood in the doorway waiting for her departure.

After hitting one of the many bumps in the laneway, the tailgate sprang loose and dropped down. "Harry!" said Mary. "That stupid ol' tailgate is down again!"

Harry stopped the truck and got out. His frustration was obvious as he applied a little extra force in putting it back in place.

The truck was getting old, and originally it had been painted a bright red, but over the years the sun had reduced it to more of a dull orange, the result of surface oxidation.

A Trip to Town

After closing the tailgate, Harry re-entered the truck, released the emergency brake, and moved forward. Mary asked if everything was okay, to which Harry indicated that it was as good as could be expected under the circumstances.

For a moment or two they travelled in silence. Then Harry asked if there was anything they needed to pick up while in town.

"We need a few things," Mary said, "but not too much this time. A half dozen yeast cakes, a can of baking powder, a coupla pounds of sugar so I can preserve some blackberries, a box of matches . . . oh, and did you think to bring the coal-oil can? I put the last of the oil in the lamps last night."

"Yah, I put it in the back ov the truck."

Mary turned to Harry and asked, "How much money do we have?"

"Well, these few groceries and the trip to Bellville will probably use up the twenty I got for the steer last month. I tell yuh, money doesn't last too long these days, so go easy!"

"How much do we have in the bank?"

"There should be close to a hundred dollars, that's countin' the money I got for the logs we cut last winter." He paused, then continued, "If the calves do well, we should get about another sixty when we sell them this fall. So, we should be okay if nothing happens.

"The potato crop looks good, and the garden seems to be come'n along. If you can put away some berries and rhubarb, and maybe some fruit . . . we should still have a couple gallons ov maple syrup left for the winter." He paused, as if doing some calculations, then carried on.

"All in all, things should be okay. Come fall, yuh can dry some ov those winter apples. I like the dried apple pie that you make, and if I can get a deer or two this fall, we should be in pretty good shape for the winter." Again he paused.

"A pail ov honey and one ov corn syrup, a hundred-pound bag ov flour and one ov sugar . . . a few yeast cakes . . . and we should be okay till spring."

He was looking out through the windshield deep in thought, anticipating the coming days.

"If I can get a couple ov days workin' on the road, I'll put it t'wards our taxes; every little bit helps. So be careful with what yuh buy and we shouldn't have tuh worry none."

"You know that I am always careful with our money!" Mary's voice was soft but defensive.

"I know you are," was Harry's quick reply; "it's just that we've come through some pretty hard times and I don't think that we're back on level ground yet. What yuh buy is high-priced, but what yuh got tuh sell, they want for nuthin'. And I don't want tuh have tuh go and spend another winter in a loggin' camp just tuh make ends meet!" The drop in Harry's voice betrayed his feelings. He sincerely meant what he had just said.

"I don't want you to, either!" Mary's response was quick and sincere. "We wouldn't see you all winter, except for Christmas, and then not till the camp closed in the spring. The boys are getting big but they still need a man around the place to keep them in line.

"The money we get for the cream helps pay for their clothes, but we only get it for the summer months." She smiled, then said, "If Dan doesn't stop growing he'll soon be as tall as Mick and that will put an end to the hand-me-downs."

Again they travelled in silence, their thoughts centred on their financial worries. Suddenly Harry pointed to the right side of the windshield, and when he spoke there was excitement in his voice.

"Look, Mary . . . look over there! Over near the edge of the bush, just under that big oak tree! There's a nice buck standin' there. Wish I had my rifle with me — he'd make good summer meat!"

"Oh, yes, I see him!" Mary also came alive. "They blend in so well with their surroundings that it's hard to pick them out if they're not moving. Yes . . . he is a nice one! Looks like he may still have some velvet on his horns. But that don't matter . . . he'd still taste pretty good."

"They sure do blend in . . . sometimes it takes a trained eye tuh pick 'em out." Harry paused for a second, "Remember last fall when I took the three young lads huntin' with me? We were walkin' on that old wagon road down along the river when I noticed that something didn't look right. The ground under a Balsam tree had a strange lookin' bump. When I took a closer look, I realized it was the top ov a doe's head. She was layin' flat out with her ears back, and tight to her head, tryin' not tuh be seen. I stopped and put my hand up for them tuh be quiet. Then I said, there's a deer layin' under the tree over there, and then I pointed to it. They took a look and couldn't see anything. They thought it must be an old root or somethin' like that that I was look'n at. I said no, there's a deer layin' there. She's tryin' tuh hide till we go by. They looked again and said they still didn't see anything. So I dropped down on one knee, jacked a shell in tuh the barrel, took aim and fired. Nothin' moved, so they started tuh laugh, and said I was just wastin' my bullets on an old root or a stone or somethin' like that.

"I said, no sir, there's a deer there!

"So I jacked out the empty and loaded another round. This time I took a real good aim and fired. Up jumped a big doe and took off while they were standing there leanin' on their rifles. I said, darn it, didn't I tell yuh there was a deer layin' there! I tell yuh the laughin' ended pretty quick! The smile was on the other side ov their face as they watched her run away.

"I said, don't worry, there's no use in cry'n over spilt milk. We'll wait about twenty minutes and then we'll go and get her.

"So we waited, then I told them where to watch and I went and chased her out. Bob shot her and when we looked her over she had two marks on her head. The one bullet had shaved the hair off along the top ov her head, but it didn't break the skin. The other one went through her ear. I guess the one on the top ov her head must have stunned her, and the one through her ear woke 'er up."

Harry smiled and looked at Mary, "Not bad shootin' for an old fella, don't yuh think?" Harry was looking to glory a little in his ability. "And it sure taught those young fellas tuh keep their eyes open when they're in the bush. But again, if your eye isn't trained tuh see what your lookin' at, then, it's easy not tuh see 'em."

Harry had made his point, now it was time to move the conversation forward.

"I guess I'm gonna have tuh go over to the marsh one evening and see if I can get a deer. Maybe Tom will come with me. I'll need some help to drag it outta there, and a whole deer is too much for one family this time ov the year. It'd spoil before we could get it all canned, and I don't like tuh see good meat go tuh waste. But, I'm getting tired ov eggs, bologna, and salt pork every day, so some fresh venison would taste pretty darn good right about now. That reminds me, pick up a few onions, for when I get one, venison tastes a lot better when it's cooked with a little onion."

"The only thing is, the flies will eat you alive in the evening — they've been pretty bad this year!" warned Mary.

"I'll go when there's a little breeze, and if we lay on top ov the bluff that overlooks the marsh, the wind should help tuh keep them away. At least that's what I'm hoping for."

Harry gave a little chuckle.

"That reminds me ov Russel. He said, he wouldn't mind the flies walkin' across his face if they wouldn't drag their feet . . . specially when they stroll over his lips. I guess he figured that drag'n their feet is what makes it tickle."

Once more they drove in silence, then Harry looked over at Mary, smiled, and said, "Yuh know, you're a purty good-lookin' woman, an' I'm really glad tuh have yuh for muh wife. And yuh've been a good wife; yuh work hard, yuh're easy tuh get along with, an always tryin' tuh keep me happy, 'specially when the times are tough." He shot her a glance, then placed his hand on her knee.

"Yuh know that little coal-oil lamp over at Murphy's store, the one with the flowers painted on the base? I see yuh lookin' at it every time you go in there. So why don't yuh go an' buy it today. It can't be any more than fifty or seventy-five cents, an' I'd like yuh tuh have it. Yuh can put it on the dresser and use it for a night light if I'm away!"

"Thanks, Harry. I do like it, but are you sure we can afford it?"

Mary's smile widened and her face lit up, feeling that she was important to her husband. Her voice showed some excitement as she thought of getting something that would be considered an extra. Money had been tight for a number of years, and extras were few and far between.

"Yah, it's okay!" Harry's voice was soft and gentle, expressing inner feelings that didn't surface quite as often as Mary would have liked them to, but they were still appreciated when they did.

"I know yuh like tuh get out and visit, and that's all right. Times have been tough and money has been scarce, and we don't have very good transportation, but we'll go tuh Belleville for a few days. At least we'll get tuh see some family and things that we don't see every day. It'll be a nice change."

Mary was looking ahead, smiling, taking it all in. Then she turned, and her smile faded as she spoke. "Harry . . . you have no idea how much I'm looking forward to going. Those four walls are just about to drive me crazy. I haven't seen any of the neighbours in months. Barb and Helen came over to pick some strawberries one day and that's been about it for visitors. Everybody's too busy picking berries or looking after their gardens and kids; nobody has the time to visit anymore. We should start going out and visiting on Sunday afternoons; nobody is supposed to be working anyways. And maybe we'll get some return visits before winter sets in . . . and as you know, only the men go out to visit once the snow comes. The women and kids stay in the house where it's warm, so we don't see anybody . . . maybe sometimes at Christmas."

Harry was silent while thinking on what Mary had said.

Then Mary spoke again, changing the subject. "I hope Charley is ready to go and we don't have to sit around and wait for him. The last time I talked to him about it, he didn't sound as if he was too keen on staying alone with the boys for three days.

"But anyways, he sort of has his moods ... sometimes it seems as if he's up for anything, then other times he seems to be a bit on the lazy side. I guess he's getting older now and slowing down. I suppose we all are."

"Don't you worry none," promised Harry; "he'll be up and ready. It'll give him a chance tuh tell some more stories, and you know the boys, they'll keep him busy."

Harry drove the truck up to the front of Murphy's store and stopped.

"I'll drop you off here, and then I'll go tuh the back and get the coal oil and fill the truck up with gas. I'll pay for the stuff when I come in."

"Okay, it won't take me long — there isn't very much to get."

Mary got out, closed the door, and hurried on into the store. Harry drove to the back, pulled up to the gas pumps, opened the door, and stepped out.

"Fill'r up and give me a gallon ov coal oil, would yuh please," Harry said to Shorty, while reaching into the back to get the coal-oil can.

"Not a problem," was Shorty's reply as he started to work the lever, pumping the gas up into the glass tank. On the top of the pump was a glass cylinder, and it had markings running down the length of it. The markings started at one gallon and worked their way down to ten. The markings went like this, starting at the top: one gallon, ¼ gal, ½ gal, ¾ gal, two gallons, all the way down to ten gallons. When the gas had settled at the top of the tank, Shorty removed the gas cap and placed the nozzle in the opening to the tank, pressed the lever, and gravity did the rest.

While the tank was filling, Harry casually leaned against the side of the truck.

"Hear ov anyone getting any deer round town?" He asked, looking to start a conversation.

"No, I haven't! But then, most are sorta tight-lipped just in case Blackwood might get wind ov it."

"Oh, I think he's pretty good about it," said Harry. "I don't think he'd pinch anyone if he thought they needed the meat!"

"Yah, I think you're right about that. I heard that he stopped in at the Thompson's last fall. 'Twas the middle Sunday ov hunting season, and everyone knows that you're not tuh be huntin' on Sunday. It had just snowed, and the two boys were out playing in it when Blackwood arrived. He wanted to talk to Thompson about tradin' some hounds, so he asked the boys where their father was. They looked him straight in the eye and said he's gone huntin'! Blackwood laughed and said, you boys don't know what yer talkin' about. And they said, oh yes we do know what we're talking about. We saw him take the gun and go. He's gone huntin'!

"So Blackwood told them to tell their father when he got back that he'd been there to see about the hounds. Then he got in the truck and drove away laughin'.

"Yah," said Harry, "He's sort ov a neighbourly cuss. Ol' Jake said Blackwood told him that many a time he sat at someone's table and ate venison out ov season. He kept his mouth shut because ov the kids. He said it looked like they needed the meat!"

When the tank was filled, Shorty released the lever and replaced the cap. Reading the scale on the glass cylinder, he calculated how much gas had been removed. Then he turned to Harry and said, "That was five and a half gallons at forty cents a gallon. So you owe Murphy two dollars and twenty cents for the gas and fifteen cents for the coal oil, making the total two dollars and thirty-five cents."

Shorty picked up the coal-oil can, screwed the top off, and placed it under the tap on the coal-oil drum. He filled the can, screwed the top back on, and handed it to Harry.

Harry placed the can in the back of the truck, and said, "Thank yuh, Shorty, and we'll be talking tuh yuh."

"See ya," said Shorty, as he walked back to the store. Inside, he would find something else to do while he waited for another customer. Harry climbed into the cab and drove around to the front of the store, stopped, and went in.

Mary was standing at the counter, waiting for him to pay for the things she had picked up. She had a smile on her face and the little lamp in her hand.

"Mr. Murphy knocked off ten cents, so it only cost me sixty-five!" She held the lamp up for Harry to see.

"Thank yuh, Mr. Murphy, every cent counts, and I owe yuh two dollars and thirty-five cents for the gas and coal oil," Harry said while crossing the floor to the counter.

"That'll make your bill come to three dollars and ninety-five cents," said Murphy with a smile.

"Oh," said Harry, "I'll be need'n two quarts ov oil. I'll pick it up on the way out."

"That's okay, so the new total will be four dollars and forty-five cents."

Mary said, "I picked up a can of salmon so I can make sandwiches for lunch. It was a sixteen-ounce can on sale for twenty cents, so I bought it."

"Good enough," said Harry. "And by the way, we better get something for the boys. How about a bag ov peppermints. Give us about ten cents worth."

Murphy scooped up a handful of mints and placed them in a paper bag. "The new total will be four dollars and fifty-five cents, if you please!"

Harry glanced up at the little sign Murphy had hanging on the wall for all his customers to see. It read, "I don't mind giving you credit, but please remember, IF YOU KEEP YOUR MONEY AND YOU KEEP MINE TOO, THEN WHAT IN THE WORLD AM I GONNA DO?" That little sign said it all.

Harry placed a five dollar bill on the counter as Mary picked up the bag of groceries. Murphy handed him the change, which he placed in his pocket.

"Thanks Mr. Murphy, and we'll be talking tuh yuh," said Harry, as he turned and followed his wife to the door.

Mary placed the bag of groceries in the back of the pickup. Then she climbed into the cab and settled herself with her little lamp on her lap. Harry closed his door and started the engine, "Now tuh see if Charley is up and ready."

"What time is it?" asked Mary.

Harry took his watch from the watch pocket in his pants and

turned his hand so he could read its face.

"It's five after ten. He was probably up at six, washed, shaved, and waitin' for us tuh get there."

As they pulled up in front of the house, they could see Charley watching them through the window. A moment later, the door opened and he came out, holding his packsack in one hand while he closed and locked the door with the other. He put the key in his pocket while walking to the truck. Tossing his packsack into the back, he opened the door and climbed in beside Mary.

"Mornin', Charley," sang out Harry. "And how are things this morning?"

"Not bad, considerin'!" answered Charley.

"And what seems tuh be the problem?"

"Well . . . there really ain't any problems as yet, but I suspect that before the three days are up I'll be seein' a few ov 'em!"

"Oh, Charley!" spoke up Mary, "you and the boys will have a good time! They always seem to like having you around!"

"Maybe so, but the problems will come just the same!"

"And what exactly do you expect to happen?" questioned Mary, sounding a bit annoyed with her brother.

"Hard tuh say, but in three days I'm pretty sure they'll be able tuh think ov a few things! The last time I was there, they started a grass fire that took all ov us about three hours tuh put out. If it woulda got tuh the bush, the way the wind was blowin', it probably would ov burnt down the half o' Bangor Township!"

"Oh, Charley!" responded Mary, "you're always exaggerating — it wasn't half that bad!"

"Maybe so," answered Charley, "but it certainly could have been a lot worse!"

Feeling it was time to change the subject, Harry interrupted. "Yuh should've seen the nice buck that we saw on the way out. Anybody around town put any down yet?"

"Ol' Pete Leggo brought me a jar of venison last Friday evenin'. I tried 'r Saturday mornin' an' it tasted purty good. Haven't heard ov anybody else getting any."

"I'll have tuh take a stroll over tuh the marsh when we get back.

I'm workin' up a pretty good appetite for some muh self!"

"Where'd yah get the little lamp?" asked Charley, having noticed Mary holding it on her lap. "S'pose yuh stole it from a leprechaun!"

"I did not!" replied Mary. "I bought it from Murphy . . . and he dropped the price by ten cents." She smiled as she spoke.

"I guess he was glad tuh get rid ov it, for there ain't so many leprechauns around these parts anymore." Charley was having fun teasing his sister about her little lamp, but she was getting annoyed with him.

"Keep it up and there'll be one less Charley O'Reilly around these parts as well!" was Mary's quick reply.

"Anybody hear the weather report?" interrupted Harry, again trying to change the subject. "Hope it don't rain till we get back!"

"Be tough on the bullfrogs if it don't," offered Charley.

"Since when did you start caring about the bullfrogs?" questioned Mary.

"Ever since I heard that little song about 'em!" answered Charley, smiling.

"And what song was that?"

Charley's smile widened and then he began to sing.

Bull frog sitt'n on a lily pad gazin' at the sky,
Lily pad broke and he fell in, got water in his eye.
Well, it ain't gonna rain no more, no more,
It ain't gonna rain no more.
How in the heck can I warsh my neck
If it ain't gonna rain no more!

By the time he had finished the song, Harry was laughing.

"That's a good one, Charley, it sounds pretty good!"

"A good one, all right," said Mary. "Do you think you will ever grow up?"

She had turned her head sideways, looking straight at Charley.

"I've thought about it, but I don't have the time!" Charley was smiling, his head turned, looking out the side window.

"You'll be an old man one day, and still be acting like a child!"

"I figger if I keep it up till I'm in my second childhood, then I won't have tuh make any changes." Charley was still smiling and looking out the window as he spoke. He found it easy to get on his sister's nerves; and let's face it, he was way too old to be changing.

As the old red truck rattled on down the gravel road, the conversation continued on. Nothing too exciting, but it did help to pass the time.

4

Billy Arrives

By the time the truck had disappeared at the end of the laneway, the boys were already starting their work.

Mick was the oldest of the boys and well into his sixteenth year. He was mature in his ways, a natural leader, and a hefty fellow with broad shoulders. His blue jeans were a little tight, while his flannel shirt had some room to spare, giving him the shape of a football player.

He was now on his way to the well to get a pail of water.

Then there was Dan. He was two years younger than Mick, tall and lean, the nervous type. His pants and shirt hung loosely on his thin frame, showing that he had some filling out to do.

Dan was on his way to the barn, intending to finish up the chores that Paw had left for him.

With nothing better to do, Joey grabbed ol' Jake by the ears and wrestled him to the ground. The big furry mongrel was as kind-hearted as he was big, but he still gave Joey a good wrestle before going down. The growling and guttural sounds made by the dog were all stage play; this Joey knew all too well. Once on the ground, Joey wasn't long straddling the old dog and continuing the play fight. The vicious sounds, along with the snapping and showing of teeth, would make a stranger think the kid would be torn to pieces. But ol' Jake wouldn't hurt a flea, unless of course he was defending Joey. The boy knew this and was having a great time cuffing the dog's ears and pulling at his nose.

Right in the middle of the play fight, a hand reached down and caught Joey by the back of his shirt, pulling him off the dog.

"Leave that ol' dog alone, and come with me to the house. We have work to do!" The voice was stern and commanding.

From there, Mick made his way to the old log house, a pail of water in one hand and a fun-loving boy in the other.

Mick took control when Paw wasn't around, and this Joey was well aware of; it caused him to listen up and do what he was told.

"Help me with the bread dough!" ordered Mick, as he set the water pail on the washstand. Without any hesitation, Joey took his place behind the table, ready to start work. He was waiting for further instructions when Mick asked, "Did you warsh your hands?"

"Yep, I did," came the reply.

"When?"

"Before I ate breakfast."

"Yah, and since then you've been out there fightin' with that dirty ol' dog. Now get out from there and warsh your hands!" Joey knew from the sound of Mick's voice there would be no fooling around.

"Okay! Okay!" came the cry of submission, as he quickly dismounted the chair and headed for the washstand.

As soon as all the requirements were met, Joey was back behind the table, kneeling on his chair.

Satisfied that all was in order, Mick started slicing hunks of dough from the bread dish and handing them over to Joey. Joey took the dough and carefully shaped it, then placed it into the bread pans. The work in progress was going well until the screen door opened and Dan stepped in. Joey was holding a piece of dough in his right hand as he looked up and saw Dan. His eyes flashed as he cocked his arm and let 'r fly. There was a loud "smuck!" as the hunk of wet dough caught the unsuspecting Dan just above his left ear. His head snapped sideways and his cap went airborne, landing upside down in the wash dish. There it swam in circles until it filled and sank.

"What the —!" exclaimed Dan, not knowing what had hit him. After making contact with Dan's head, the hunk of dough landed on his left shoulder. Seeing the dough he reached up and grabbed it. Thinking that Mick had thrown it, he cocked and fired. Totally unaware of what had just happened, Mick looked up from the bread pan just in time to catch Dan's returned fire; it got him square in the face.

There was a loud "kersmuck!" followed by, "Hey . . . what the — !"

The reaction was without any hesitation, Mick fired the dough that was in his hand at Dan. And this is how the bread dough war got started. A free-for-all with every man looking out for himself, and no holds barred. The hunks of dough that had been neatly placed in the pans were now being pulled out and used as missiles. The pans went tumbling onto the floor as the house became a battlefield.

The smacking sound indicated the bread dough had found its target, and mixed in with it was the yelling and the laughter of the boys playing their war game. Ol' Jake was watching through the screen door and barking, wanting to come in and join the fun.

The screen door was designed to let as much air in as possible while keeping the flies out. And ol' Jake could have come right on through it if he'd really wanted to, but he knew better than to try, so he just kept on voicing his opinion from where he was.

Joey was teetering on the edge of his chair while frantically reaching for a hunk of dough that had landed on the table. Dan, not wanting to miss an opportunity, aimed and let fly. The dough ball caught Joey up the side of the head, peeling him off the chair and sending him headlong into the corner.

Seeing what had just happened, and realizing there was a possibility of someone being injured, Mick quickly raised his voice and called for a cease fire.

"Okay! Okay! Let's stop this nonsense before somebody gets hurt. And if Maw ever sees this mess, we will all be as dead as a doorknob by the time she's done with us!"

Mick, who had been caught up with the thrill of the moment, had forgotten that he was in charge of things. And he would be held responsible and accountable if Maw were to ever find out. Upon realizing his situation, he was almost ready to enter panic mode.

The place was an absolute disaster; the bread dough that had been so neatly placed in the pans was now all over the place. On the floor, on the cupboard, one piece was in the wash basin along with Dan's cap. Another was trying to send a message out by smoke signal from top of the old wood stove. And not one piece of the dough was in any condition to be made into bread.

When things had finally settled down, Dan said, "Okay, what do we do now? This stuff is all dirty, and we can't put it back in the pans for Maw to bake!"

Caught between a rock and a hard place, Mick was ready for some good advice and Joey immediately stepped up to the plate and came to his rescue.

"Give 'r to the pigs!" said Joey, still hyped and ready for action. "They'll eat anything!"

"Sounds good tuh me," agreed Dan, smiling as he looked at Joey; "that's exactly what we should do!"

"And do you think Maw won't notice that some is missing?" inquired Mick, knowing that he would be held responsible for whatever went wrong, and not totally persuaded that this plan would solve the problem.

"Tell her the yeast cakes were too old and the bread didn't rise very well." Again, Joey was right there on Mick's behalf. "I've heard her say stuff like that lots ov times!"

"Okay," said Mick. His smile was gone, and his face stern. When all was said and done, it was his neck that would be in the wringer if things went wrong.

"But we had better keep our story straight or we're all going to be in for big trouble if Maw ever figures out what really happened!"

"Yah," said Joey, with a smile and a little snicker, "I'd sure hate to have tuh watch you big fellows gettin' it!"

"Don't you worry none!" said Mick, his face turning red and his voice rising a little. "I'll see to it that you get your share — you started it!"

"Don't worry," replied Joey, sounding cool and confident, "Maw will be too taken up with goin' away to be worrying about some ol' missin' bread dough!"

Satisfied with Joey's advice and reasoning, they went to work at cleaning up the mess and putting the remaining dough into the pans. The pigs were satisfied with their portion and promised not to squeal.

Next, the separator needed cleaning. In the evening they ran clean water through it to remove any milk that may be still trapped inside, but every morning it had to be taken apart and carefully cleaned.

When the cream separator was in operation, it was Mick's job to turn the handle, while Dan kept the bowl filled and changed the pails. The cream went directly into the cream can, which was supplied by the creamery.

When the job was completed, the milk went back to the barn and was given to the calves to drink, with a small amount going to the pigs. Occasionally Maw would save some cream for cooking.

When their morning work was completed, they came into the house and sat down. They were relaxing in silence when the screen door opened and Billy walked in.

Mick looked up and said, "Well, how are yuh today!"

"Good," said Billy, speaking in his quiet and shy manner.

"Did Maw stop and ask yuh to come back?" asked Joey, a smile spreading across his face.

"Yep," came the reply, as Billy's head nodded up and down.

"See any bears on the way back?" asked Dan, teasing the boy.

"No!" came the quiet reply. "There ain't no bears 'round here!"

To reach Joey's house, Billy had to travel through an area where the road ran through a mature forest. If he had any fear of bears, the trip could be a bit of a concern for a young boy.

"Oh, there are some real big ones prowling around," said Mick, also teasing.

"Ain't scared of no bears!" said Billy with a grin.

He knew the boys were teasing him, so it was okay to talk big.

"When was the last time yuh seen one . . . up close and friendly?" asked Mick, daring the young boy.

"Never have, an' I don't want to, either," was the humble but honest answer.

"Do yuh know how to skin a bear without puttin' a hole in the hide?" Mick had stopped smiling and was trying to sound serious in his attempt to trick Billy.

"No," Billy's reply was slow and uncertain.

"First yuh get a stick and sharpen one end, bring it to a very fine point. Then you find a bear and start poking him with it." Mick was nodding his head trying to get Billy to agree.

"I don't think so!" said Billy, not wanting any part of this idea.

"Hey, no problem, yuh just keep on poking him till he gets good and ugly. Then he'll come at yuh with his mouth wide open. Yuh just push your sleeve up as far as yuh can, then step aside and run your arm right down his throat as far as it'll go. Reach out the little hole at the back end and grab his tail and pull. Yuh'll turn that ol' critter right inside out. When the job's done, give a good snap ov yuhr wrist and the hide'll peel right off. And not a hole in 'r anywhere. Then yuh give 'em a good swift kick in the butt and tell 'em to get out o' there and go grow another one. Works just as smooth as silk and yuh got a perfect hide. Just watch yuh don't scratch your arm on his teeth when yuh're goin' in."

Billy was listening to Mick with his mouth open and his eyeballs almost popping out of his head. "Yuh don't need tuh worry none about my arm, 'cause it ain't gonna happen in the first place. I ain't poking no bear with a stick!" Billy's mind was made up and it was rock solid. There was no way this ol' boy would ever be caught playing that kind of a trick with a bear.

The two boys were close to the same size, although Billy was almost a year younger. They both had brown hair and brown eyes, and their dress code was much the same. Ankle-high boots, jeans with patches, and belts that were a bit too long and curled back at the end. Their cotton shirts were short-sleeved, buttoned almost to the top, and tucked into their jeans. Their dispositions were a bit different, but close enough to be mistaken for brothers. They both had a tendency to be very quiet and were well-behaved when on their own, but when they were together, well, that was a different story. It was beyond one's ability to imagine what might happen next.

"Let's go outside," suggested Joey, wanting to get away from the older boys.

Billy nodded his head in agreement.

They both turned and moved toward the door.

As soon as they were outside, Joey asked, "What would you like to do?"

"Not sure," came the reply, as Billy's mind was searching for ideas. Then his face lit up and he suggested, "Why don't we go and torment the roosters!"

"What d' yuh mean?" asked Joey, not sure what Billy had in mind.

"You know," said Billy, "put the Bandy rooster in with the big rooster and let 'em fight it out."

"Not a good idea," Joey was shaking his head, "The last time we did that, the Bandy got a good lickin', and Paw was wondering what had happened to him."

After thinking about it for a minute, Billy said, "That's because the big rooster has a pretty good set of spurs. Why don't we just cut 'em off?"

"No way! Paw would see it and I'd really get into trouble!"

Billy was silent for a minute then he says, "If we were to wrap something soft around his spurs, then he wouldn't be able to hurt the Bandy, and I'll bet that old Bandy will really put 'm in his place."

"That might work," said Joey, his eyes shining as a smile slipped across his face.

"Sure it will!" encouraged Billy, always in a hurry to get the show on the road.

"Yah, but what can we use on his legs?" pondered Joey, speaking more to himself than to Billy.

"Does your paw have some old winter underwear?" asked Billy.

"Yah . . . he has some, but I don't think it's all that old."

"Don't matter, we could just cut a little strip off the bottom," said Billy. "It wouldn't hurt none — his socks go halfways up to his knees anyways."

"Yah," laughed Joey. "His one leg would be shorter than the other; I think he'd know!"

"No!" argued Billy. "Cut one strip off each leg then there wouldn't be any difference!"

"Might work," said Joey, as he thought about it, and his smile widened as he pictured Paw's underwear with the legs shortened.

"Let's give 'r a try," encouraged Billy with enthusiasm in his voice. "He won't find out till next winter anyways, and by then he'll never figure out what happened!"

"Okay!" said Joey. "If it works, then we could get a good fight goin' without either of 'em really getting hurt."

The boys quickly and quietly re-entered the house. Joey slipped over to the cupboard and took a pair of scissors from the drawer while Billy waited by the washstand. Then they both hurried up the stairs.

Mick, who was listening to the radio and watching the boys, called out, "What are you fellas up to?"

"Nothin'," answered Joey, trying to sound casual.

"Don't you two be gettin' into any kind ov trouble," warned Mick.

"Don't worry, we won't," came the reply, trying to assure Mick that everything was under control, not wanting him to become a hindrance to their plans.

After rummaging through some of the dresser drawers, Joey found a pair of his father's winter underwear. "How much should we cut off?" he asked, looking to Billy for advice.

"Oh, about a couple of inches, right about there on both legs," said Billy, marking off about three inches from the bottom.

In a minute the job was done. The boys had two pieces of soft cloth, and Paw's underwear had two short legs, which just happened to be a bit ragged where they had made the cut.

"We're gonna need some string tuh tie 'em to the rooster's legs!" said Billy.

"Maw keeps a ball of it in the cupboard, saves it when she opens the flour bags. I'll get a couple of pieces when I put the scissors back."

"That should do it!" Billy's plan was making progress. A big grin crossed his face and his eyes sparkled as he visualized the feathers flying.

The boys hurried down the stairs, cut some string, and put the scissors back where they had found them. After closing the drawer, they turned and hurried outside.

"You fellas are definitely up to something!" insisted Mick as they went out the door.

"Nothing," replied Joey over his shoulder, letting the screen door slam behind him. They left the front step on a dead run and headed for the old log barn.

After gaining the barn, they kept on going to the chicken coop.

"Where's the Bandy rooster?" panted Billy, running low on breath.

"He's around here someplace . . . he'll be with the hens, wherever they are!" answered Joey, sounding like he was having the same problem.

"I see 'm," cried Billy. "There by the barn door, but how will we ever catch him?"

Joey stopped for a minute. "We'll chase 'm into the horse stable. You go open the doors."

Billy hurried over and opened the two big stable doors.

"Okay . . . now let's fix the big fellow first!" Joey carefully opened the gate to the chicken coop, so as not to disturb the chickens.

"Give me a hand," he called to Billy, as the big rooster was staying just beyond his reach. "He's too fast for me to catch!"

The rooster ran and half-flew around the chicken coop trying to avoid the boys, and in doing so he stirred up dust, spare feathers, and all the hens. Working together, they soon had him cornered. Slowly they moved forward with their arms reaching out to grab him. They were close enough so they could almost touch him, but the rooster wanted no part of this. The only escape route left for him was to fly over their heads, and he took it.

Reaching up, Billy caught him by a leg, and down came the rooster with Billy landing on the ground beside him. He was holding on with his teeth clenched and his eyes closed, while he took a pretty good beating from the rooster's wings.

"Help me," he called out through the dust and clenched teeth. "This ol' boy's a fighter!"

Joey quickly grabbed the rooster by the neck, helping Billy to get control.

"I got him." yelled Joey, his arms wrapped around the rooster. "Now you tie the stuff on his legs!"

Billy quickly wrapped the underwear pieces around the rooster's legs and tied them in place.

"There yuh go!" cried Joey, as he released the rooster.

"Look 't the way he's walkin'," laughed Billy.

Feeling something different about his legs, the rooster was strutting around taking unusually high steps. He'd lift one leg and shake it, then the other, trying to dislodge the foreign material, but it was no use; it had been very well secured.

"You just hold on, ol' boy, till we get the Bandy over here. It won't take him long to put some ginger into your step," warned Billy, laughing as he talked.

Their attention now turned to the Bandies as Billy called out, "Okay, let's round 'em up!"

They lost no time in herding them into the horse stable. Joey closed the one door and stepped inside.

"Pull the other door closed, too; there's enough light coming in through the manure hole to see what we're doin'."

The manure hole was about two feet square with a small door on it. It was used for throwing the manure outside when the stable was being cleaned.

After closing the doors, it took a minute for their eyes to adjust to the dim light.

"You watch he doesn't fly out the manure hole," warned Joey, as he closed in on the little rooster. In the dim light the rooster was reluctant to fly, so Joey soon cornered him.

"Got 'm," cried Joey as he held the rooster in his arms. "Now open the door and let the hens out!"

The boys quickly made their way over to the chicken coop.

"Put 'em in and watch the fun!" he cried.

The big gray rooster spied the intruder and immediately reacted. Forgetting about the leg wraps, he made straight for the Bandy. Seeing the big guy coming at him, the Bandy tried to run, but the big rooster was way too fast. Before the Bandy could get away he was on him. He gave the Bandy a peck on the back that made him squawk. But the Bandy, being smaller and pretty fast himself, turned quickly to the side and ran in among some hens. The big rooster never halted, he stuck right with him, eager to take care of this intruder. The Bandy, realizing there was no escaping, turned to fight. The big rooster was still coming in full flight when the Bandy went up in the air, striking his legs with both wings, driving his spurs into the big fellow's breast. This stopped the big boy in his tracks, but the force of the collision sent the Bandy backwards and onto his tail feathers. He quickly got up, shook himself, and the confrontation continued.

"Look at 'em go at it!" cried Billy, his enthusiasm rising. "Come on, little fella, give it to him!"

It wasn't long till old Jake, realizing something was going on inside the chicken coop, wanted to get in on the action. He raced around the outside barking at the roosters; this caused the hens to fly around, keeping the dust and all the misplaced feathers stirred up. But even with the commotion caused by the dog, the roosters never lost track of each other. Each time the big rooster would strike, the Bandy would go for a tumble. But with the big guy's legs being bundled up, there was no damage. Humiliated but unhurt, the Bandy would get right back up and go at it again.

Joey's attention quickly withdrew from the action as a hand landed on his shoulder and Mick said in a stern voice, "So this is what you two are up to! If that Bandy rooster gets hurt, Paw will skin you alive!"

"He can't get hurt," came the quick reply. "We padded the big rooster's legs!"

"Well I'll be darned," said Mick with admiration. "You did, too. You two little rascals think of everything."

Right in the middle of the excitement, old Jake stopped running around the pen and started barking toward the house.

"Hold it!" yelled Joey with panic in his voice. "Maw and Paw are back. Help me get the Bandy rooster out of there!"

Both boys rushed to the gate, eager to get inside. Mick started to casually walk back to the house as if nothing was happening. He knew that if the boys got caught he'd be in trouble for not keeping an eye on them. So he wasn't about to draw any attention to what was going on.

The roosters were so taken up with each other they didn't even notice that the boys had re-entered. Billy grabbed the Bandy while Joey opened the gate. They threw him out then Joey went after the big rooster and caught him by the wing. He was flopping, squawking, and kicking up dust as he tried to get away. Billy joined in, and they quickly subdued him.

"Get the pads off him!" squeaked Joey, choking in the dust.

"I can't untie the strings," replied Billy, there was now panic in his voice as well.

"Use your teeth," cried Joey, "and be quick about it. We got to get outta here before Paw sees us!"

Following Joey's instructions, Billy grabbed the string with his teeth. Spitting and sputtering, he said, "I tell yuh I've tasted better!"

"Pay no attention," said Joey, stuffing Paw's underwear cuffs into his pants pockets. "Now let's get outta here!"

Hurrying through the gate, they quickly closed it behind them. Then, after dusting themselves off and catching their breath, they walked casually down to the house, strolling along as if they were at peace with the world and everything in it.

5

Uncle Charley Arrives

The boys were taking their time while strolling toward the house, giving the appearance that they didn't have a care in the world. The rooster problem had been taken care of, and, let's face it, Paw wouldn't discover that his underwear legs had been shortened till next winter. For now, everything was on the level.

Uncle Charley removed his packsack from the back of the truck and set it on the grass. Standing beside it, he watched the boys approach the house.

Charley was in his usual dress code: blue jeans that were well-worn but clean, and a large belt buckle with a silver steer's head mounted on it, a trophy from his trip out West; a faded plaid shirt with the sleeves rolled up to the elbows; a dark blue cap that had seen better days; and a pair of long-top work boots that were laced halfway, with the pant legs stuffed into the tops. From head to foot, he was the country boy of the time.

"Well, now," said Uncle Charley, "I'll bet you fellas are ready for a few days ov some miss-be-havin', along with a bit ov mischief!"

"We sure are," replied Joey with enthusiasm. "An' I hope you are, too!"

"I come well prepared!" came the quick reply. "And I brought muh mouth organ along with me, so we can have a little music!"

"Oh boy!" said Joey under his breath, "not again!"

Uncle Charley was pretty good with the mouth organ, but all he could play was "Oh Susanna" and "Turkey in the Straw," and he'd play them over and over again till everybody was sick and tired of hearing them.

Mary was on her way to the house with two brown paper bags in her arms and the little lamp in her hand.

"Where did yuh get the little lamp?" asked Joey.

"Stole it from a leprechaun!" said Uncle Charley, being quick to answer for her.

"Did yuh, Maw?" asked Joey, his face lit up with amazement.

"Of course not," was Maw's answer, disgust being evident in her voice. "I think one ov those little leprechauns tapped your Uncle Charley on the head, and he hasn't been the same since."

"Did you bring us a treat?" asked Joey, sounding hopeful as his attention moved from Uncle Charley to his mother.

"I did if you were good!"

"Maw, you know that we are always gooder than good when you leave us here!"

"Are you sure?" his mother asked.

"Yep, I'm sure, just ask Mick!"

"Okay . . . then come over here."

Maw set the bags down on the table, reached in and pulled out a small brown paper bag and handed it to Joey. He took it and shoved his hand inside the bag.

"What do you say?" asked his mother.

"Thanks!" came the reply.

Pulling his hand out, he popped a candy into his mouth.

"What are they?" asked Billy, eager to try one.

"Pepper nuts!" said Joey, rolling the candy around in his cheek.

"Pepper*mints*!" corrected his mother. "And give Billy some!"

Joey held the bag out to Billy, who was quick to reach in and grab one. The candy was white and hard, round on the sides with a flat top and bottom, and well blessed with a strong peppermint flavour. Billy's candy, like Joeys, went straight into his mouth without any hesitation.

"You'd think you boys had never seen a candy in your life, the way you go at them!"

Ignoring his mother's statement, Joey asked Billy, "Ever have these before?"

"Yah, lots of times. Paw always gets them for himself when he goes to town, but he gives me some. Murphy's store has 'em in a big cardboard box, sitt'n right there on the counter, just scoop 'em up and put 'em in a bag and you're good to go," said Billy.

"You gotta pay for them, don't yuh?" inquired Joey.

"Sure do!" laughed Billy. "Old Murphy don't give yuh nuthin' for free. Usually costs Paw about ten cents for what he gets."

"Now you boys wash your hands and get up to the table, your bologna sandwiches are ready and waiting."

Joe turned to Billy and asked, "Do yuh like bologna?"

"Yep," answered Billy. "Paw says its good ol' horsemeat!"

"Horsemeat!" cried Joey. "Is it, Maw?"

"No! It's made from bulls."

"You had me scared for a minute."

Billy was laughing, "Paw says you can run like a horse if you eat enough of it."

"You musn't have eaten very much, cuz you ain't that fast."

"Can out run you!"

"Yah, but that's only to the table," laughed Joey.

Maw had stirred the fire and was busy putting the bread pans into the oven.

"I thought there should be more dough than this," she said half to herself.

Joey winked at Billy and smiled, but neither boy said a word, just kept stuffing their sandwiches into their mouths.

"Those darned ol' yeast cakes that I got from Murphy was probably ten years old," she said as she closed the oven door and went on to something else.

Paw and Uncle Charley were just making their way through the door. Paw was laughing as Uncle Charley told him the latest town gossip.

"Serves him right, yuh know!" Paw was saying. "And it was good for him, he's had it comin' for a long time!"

"Hey, Maw!" Paw called out, "Charley has a pretty good story to tell yuh! You know ol' Tommy Clodhopper, always bumming around town look'n for handouts? Well, old Mrs. Taylor straightened him out but good."

"Yes, I know him," said Maw, looking up from where she was putting things away in the lower half of the cupboard.

"Well you tell her what happened," Paw said, nodding to Charley.

"Well . . ." said Uncle Charley, drawing it out a bit.

"Old Tommy'd been hangin' around Mrs. Taylor's — he'd get there just about suppertime, arrivin' about half an hour or so before it was time to eat. He'd just walk right in, sit down, and shoot the breeze. Mrs. Taylor'd be fryin' up some pork an boilin' some potatoes. Hardly had enough for herself, but she'd always ask ol' Tommy to have some, and he'd be just sitt'n there wait'n for the invite. He'd eat tuh the point where he could still chew but was havin' some difficulty in swallowin'. After him showin' up every day for 'bout a week or so, she was getting sick and tired of it. But she's not the kind to throw somebody out or not give 'm somethin' to eat, so she figgered out a way to get rid of him.

"One day he come stroll'n in and she handed him a handful o' peanuts. She told him there was more if he wanted them. So, ol' Tommy jammed them all into his mouth, figgerin' he'd be getting some more when these were gone. Well . . . when he was almost dun chew'n 'em, she said to him, 'Those peanuts came all the way from the United States ov America. My daughter and husband went down there on a holiday, and they like to shop around while they are there, look'n for new things. They always have better and newer things than we ever see up here. She happened tuh find some chocolate-covered peanuts, said she'd never seen the like of that before. Said they didn't taste too bad either, so she thought she'd bring me some. Well, anybody can see that my teeth are all but gone. So it's hard for me tuh chew the darn things anymore, so I just suck the chocolate off 'em!'

"She said that right about then ol' Tommy's gills turned a little green, he sorta slid off the chair 'n headed for the door. He hit the veranda railin' just in time for all 'ell to break loose. She said there was peanut butter an' chewed-up peanuts flying all over the front yard. When he was all done spittin' and gaggin', he headed for the road and never looked back. Said he hadn't been back for over a week, the last time I was talkin' to her. I guess she knew how to fix ol' Tommy's little red wagon," laughed Charley.

Maw and Paw were laughing so hard the tears were streaming down their cheeks.

"It's about time somebody fixed that old coot," said Maw, trying to hold back the laughter.

"Maybe he'll learn not to be so bold!"

"I doubt it," said Paw, "he'll just go an' bother somebody else; it's hard teachin' old dogs like him new tricks."

"Did she really suck the chocolate off the peanuts?" asked Maw.

"Naw," said Uncle Charley. "There was nothin' on them in the first place. She just made that up for tuh sick'n ol' Tommy."

Joey and Billy had both stopped eating, and they now had a strange look on their faces. They set down the last half of their sandwiches and pushed them away.

"Let's go do somethin' else!" said Joey, sounding a bit disgusted.

"Yah," agreed Billy as they both got up and headed for the door.

"Sorry if I spoiled your appetite," chuckled Uncle Charley. "Didn't notice that yuh were eatin'."

"That's all right," replied Joey. "Wasn't hungry anyways!"

Once they were outside, Billy said to Joey, "Can you imagine that happening to you?"

To which Joey replied, "I think I'd be sick for a week. That was a dirty trick to play even on that ol' fella."

"Yah," said Billy, "I don't think that I could ever do that to anybody; I'd probably get sick myself just thinkin' about it."

Maw came to the screen door and called after the boys. "Tell Mick and Dan to get in here and I'll make them some lunch. I bought some salmon for Dan. I know that's what he likes for a sandwich. Now tell them to hurry it up because we'll soon have to leave for Uncle Walter's."

"Okay!" came the reply as they hurried on to the barn.

Joey turned to Billy and said, "I hope they don't tell that story while Mick and Dan are eatin', 'cause Dan'll probably puke right there at the table if they do."

Mick and Dan were cleaning out the horse stable, a job that needed doing every day. Paw was particular about his horses and the stable where he kept them. There would be fresh hay in the manger and oats in the oat box for when the horses came in at night. The stable was cleaned out and fresh straw was spread on the floor so the horses would be clean if they were to lie down. Paw always said that if the horses were brought in every night and given a little oats for a treat, they would be a lot easier to catch when he needed them.

Their hay was fresh cut each day, and it was Dan's job to mow it. He was careful not to hit any stones with the scythe blade, because Paw would make him turn the grindstone while he re-sharpened it, and that was one job that Dan did not like to do.

He always carried a whetstone in his hip pocket, and used it every few minutes to keep a good edge on the blade when he mowed the hay.

Paw kept three horses: a gray mare to handle the buggy in the summer and the cutter in the winter; and two workhorses to handle the heavier farm work. The gray mare's name was Nell, and the team of blacks were named Topsy and Turvey.

The old pickup was the newest addition to the family, but Paw said the horses were still the best deal because they didn't use any gas. But then, the old truck was handy to go to town and such.

Joey informed Mick and Dan that lunch was ready and they had better get a move on because Maw was anxious to get going. Mick asked Joey if Maw had said anything about the bread.

"Just that she had expected more than she got, and then she blamed old Murphy for selling her yeast cakes that were ten years old." Joey couldn't help but chuckle as he told it, for it was pretty much as he had predicted.

"Just like I told yuh," laughed Joey. "She's more interested in getting on out o' here than she is in that old bread dough!"

Mick and Dan hurried on down to the house, as they didn't want to keep Maw waiting, while the boys wandered aimlessly looking for something on which they could spend their time.

It was mid-afternoon by the time Maw got the dishes done, the house tidied up, and all the packing done that she thought they might need. Now it was time to say goodbye to the boys and Uncle Charley. They all got a hug, starting with Uncle Charley, and on down to Joey and Billy. Meanwhile, Paw stood waiting by the open truck door, whistling a tune while Maw did her ritual. They all got told to be careful, to behave, and the younger boys to be obedient to Mick and Uncle Charley. The part about Uncle Charley was just wasted breath, but they usually showed him respect out of kindness.

Again, Maw had changed her clothes and her hair style. Her hair was in a bun at the back of her head with a big black hat sitting on the top; it was held in place with a good-sized hatpin.

Paw had changed as well. He now wore a pair of dark blue dress pants that had seen better days, and a white shirt that displayed a noticeable shade of yellow, a by-product that comes with age. His suspenders were frayed around the adjustment area, and he was wearing a green necktie, tied in a half-Windsor knot, which was determined to turn sideways.

He had traded in his work boots for an old pair of brown shoes that needed a bit of polish and a very good brushing. A few extras had been placed in a cardboard suitcase, along with his shaving gear.

They were both dressed and ready for the road. As Maw made her way around the pickup, she again reminded them to be good and to be careful.

"Aw Maw, you know that we are gooder than good when you're gone!" replied Joey.

"And don't be sittin' up all night listening tuh the radio; those batteries cost money, yuh know!" These were Paw's instructions as he closed the truck door.

"Don't worry, we won't," answered Mick.

"The last battery cost a dollar and fifty cents, and they don't seem tuh last very long these days."

"I'll keep an eye out," assured Uncle Charley.

They all waved goodbye as the old truck rattled on down the lane. Each time Paw placed his foot on the brake, the cloth that was tied over the tail light showed red. A telltale sign that the old truck was held together by a lot of makeshift mechanics.

"It'll be a miracle if that old rattletrap makes it down there and back. More black smoke rollin' out ov her than most freight trains," mumbled Charley, more to himself than anybody else.

As much as he tried, Joey couldn't hold back the feeling of being left behind as he watched the back end of the old truck roll out the laneway. It flowed through his middle like cold water. How he wished he was sitting in the front seat watching the world roll by. He felt tears welling up, but he didn't dare let it show. He was a big boy, and Billy was here with him, for which he was glad. He had ol' Jake and Billy to help pass the time till they got back, and anyway, three days wasn't really all that long.

"He's worried about a dollar and fifty cents for a radio battery!" complained Dan, "and he'll spend ten dollars on gas goin' down there and back. We work darn hard here, 'n we can't even listen tuh the radio?"

Dan's feelings were slipping out through his lips. He didn't have bad feelings about being left behind, but he felt his self-worth was on the line.

"Yes, we can, just not all night." Mick was trying to console Dan, as he could see he was getting upset about it.

"Yah, well Paw likes tuh listen to the Happy Gang at one o' clock, after the news is over. 'Knock, knock, who's there? It's the Happy Gang! Well come ooon in.'" Dan's mocking was evident.

"And Maw listens to *The Pepper Young Family* most every day. We know more about them than our own family. They live in a town called Elmwood, his father is Sam, his wife is Linda, his kid is Buttons, and his best friend is Nick. And if we listen to a bit ov country music, we're wastin' the battery? I don't get it!"

It was obvious that Dan was upset about the radio restrictions and Uncle Charley wasn't about to let it spoil their time together.

"Now, now," said Uncle Charley, "it ain't like that at all. He just wants yuh tuh get tuh bed 'n get some rest so yuh'll grow a bit taller!"

"Yah, well, I'm tall enough now!" grumbled Dan as he turned away.

"What do they listen to?" asked Billy.

"Mostly WWVA Wheeling West Virginia, and that's only when they can get it," answered Joey. "But they don't listen all night."

"I listen to Bill Bessy every Saturday morning; he calls his show *The Wired Woodshed*," said Billy. "Good ol' Country and Western music. An' sometimes I listen to *The Lone Ranger* on Tuesday evening if I can remember. Him and ol' Tonto sure clean up on those outlaws. I just wish I had some of those silver bullets that he uses."

"Do you really think that he uses silver for to make bullets?" asked Joey, sounding a bit doubtful. "Paw says silver isn't soft enough to use for bullets."

"I don't know for sure, but the fellow on the radio says that he does!"

"Well . . . maybe," agreed Joey, "I guess the fellow on the radio should know."

Mick found his way into the house and stretched out on the chesterfield, while Dan sauntered off toward the barn. There was always something there that would help him to pass the time.

Uncle Charley directed his attention to the boys. "Speakin' ov music, I guess it's about time we had some."

Reaching into his pants pocket, he pulled out his mouth organ, wiped it on his pant leg, and raised it to his mouth.

"Now, let's see," he said, speaking to Joey, "you can play the juice harp, can't yuh?"

"Nope," replied Joey, "I gave 'r up 'cause it pinched my tongue every time I tried it."

"Now . . . I never figgered you for a quitter. You were doin' good on "Turkey in the Straw," and we sounded pretty darn good playin' it together."

"Nope," replied Joey, his mind was made up, "I had enough of it, and I got sick ov the way it vibrates against my teeth!"

"Well then," said Uncle Charley, "I guess I'll have tuh give 'r a go all by muhself!"

Again he wiped his musical instrument across his pant leg and put it to his mouth. As he exhaled into it, there comes out an almost perfect rendition of "Turkey in the Straw." And now the show was on the road, with Uncle Charlie's fingers working the mouth organ, and his right foot stomping the ground.

Billy stood in awe, his eyes fastened on uncle Charley's hands as his fingers rose and fell with the notes.

"Are there words to go along with the tune?" asked Billy, his fingers twitching to the music.

"Not sure," said Joey. "All I know is what I heard Paw sing."

"What's that?" asked Billy, eager to know.

"Well . . . he sings, 'Turkey in the hay, turkey in the straw, turkey has his ass up, hee haw haw!'

"But I think he just made it up."

"Sounds good tuh me," laughed Billy. "I wish there was more to it."

When Uncle Charley had worn out "turkey in the hay," he turned to "Oh Susanna" and gave it a go. Joey was bored with it all as he had heard it time and time again, but Billy was quite intrigued with Uncle Charley's skill with the mouth organ, and it held his interest for a while. But he, too, got tired of it and started to move away. Uncle Charley realized he was losing his audience; so he put away his musical instrument and cleared his throat.

"Well, boys," he said, "how would yuh like tuh hear a real good story?"

Being in front of the house, Uncle Charley moved closer to it and sat down on the grass. Once he was settled, he leaned back against the wall. He was a big man and it wasn't all that easy for him to get down to ground level. But with a few grunts and groans he managed to do it, the bubble in his middle giving him most of the trouble. Once he found a comfortable position, he asked the boys, "Did I ever tell you fellas about the time I went West?" Uncle Charley was looking to find a point of interest with the boys.

"Don't remember," said Joey, not sounding very interested in the storytelling.

"Not me," replied Billy with real interest. "I'd sure like tuh hear it!"

"Well, let me tell yuh a bit about the trip. I was quite a bit younger then, able to move around a lot better, too."

He adjusted his position against the wall, making himself a little more comfortable. Then he beckoned to the boys to sit down in front of him. Joey turned to Billy, his eyes asking the question, "Do you really want to do this?" to which Billy nodded yes. "I like good stories," said Billy, "especially about cowboys!"

Both boys dropped to the ground in front of Uncle Charley and crossed their legs. Joey plucked a piece of grass and slowly pulled it through his fingers as he waited for the story to begin. Billy sat cross-legged with his elbows on his knees and his head in his hands; he, too, was eager to get on with the story.

"Now this ain't exactly 'bout cowboys," said Uncle Charley, hesitating a second, then stating, "well ... I guess it *could* have a little somethin' to do with them, I suppose." He wanted to be sure to hold Billy's attention.

Uncle Charley's voice and manner of speaking changed when he told stories to the boys. He dearly loved holding their attention and watching their eyes bulge out as he stretched the truth ... but it was just a little ... and only when necessary. When talking to adults, he was more his normal self, mostly quiet, and sometimes almost shy.

"About fifteen years ago," began Uncle Charley, "me and a few other fellas jumped a freight train that was head'n west. We were all lookin' for work and there wasn't much of anything do'n around here. But we heard there was work in the West, so we thought we'd give 'r a try. So we tried the freight train. It wasn't much of a ride, just old wooden boxcars, but it was free transportation. The old cattle cars had a pretty good space between the boards; this was to let air in tuh keep the cows cool, but it also let the water in when it rained. And let me tell yuh it got plenty cold at night, 'specially go'n up past the lakehead. One fella thought about makin' a fire, and I asked him if he was out ov his head. I said this thing that we're ridin' in is made out o' wood, an' if she goes, we 'r definitely goin' tuh be going right along with it!"

"Did he do it?" asked Billy.

"No ... I guess he realized it wouldn't work, so he settled down in a corner. Pulled the collar of his coat up as high as he could get it, then sat there until he shivered so hard that the vibrating warmed him up.

"Now let me tell yuh . . . those prairies were something else. So flat that yuh could see for miles in any direction. A feller could sit on his back porch and watch his dog leave home for three days a runnin'!"

"Why would your dog want tuh leave home?" asked Billy, honest curiosity showing in his face.

"Well . . . . . . sometimes they just do things like that for no good reason, just like some people do."

"Yah, I guess that was what you were doin', wasn't it?" replied Billy.

"Yah, yuh got that right . . . I sure was, wasn't I! Leavin' home on a train goin' West."

Uncle Charley paused for a moment to collect his thoughts, then he got back to his story.

"We worked on quite a few farms out there, cuttin' and stookin' wheat and oats. This went on for days. Then the old thrashin' mill would run for weeks as we drew the stuff to it. Our old hands were blistered and calloused like yuh wouldn't believe. Yuh know, the farms out there are big, not like these little rabbit runways that we have back here. Their property would run for miles in all directions.

"One old rancher wanted to brag about the size of his ranch. So he told us he had to ride his horse for four days just to get across his property. One of our boys spoke up and said that he had had a horse like that one time, too, but he shot it."

Billy's expression changed with the story, but he said nothing.

"Yuh likely won't believe what I tell yuh about the weather they have; it ain't nothing like around here. They have winds that they call Chinooks, or somethin' like that. It will be forty degrees below one minute, and two minutes later it will be forty degrees above. Doggone weather changing like that's about enough to give a man the death o' cold."

Charley paused for a minute, looking up at the sky as if collecting his thoughts.

"I remember one day an old rancher and I went to town in his horse and cutter. There must a be 'n about two feet ov snow on the ground when we left for town. We got there and did some shoppin' for about half an hour, then he stopped and looked at the sky. He said, 'grab your stuff and let's get movin' — there's one o' them Chinooks a-rollin' in!' Well, we jumped in tuh the cutter and he poured the whip to that ol' horse all the way home. She was runnin' on about two feet ov snow, but it was a-meltin' so fast that the bare ground was appearin' about ten feet behind the cutter. That's just how fast it was meltin.' All the way home it was like that. Yuh couldn't let that horse stop for a minute or yuh'd a be 'n slide 'n that old cutter on bare ground. That ol' horse ov his seemed tuh know that, too, for she never let up. She was wringin' with sweat, but she kept right on a hoofen 'er. It was a good job the road was straight and flat or we'd a never kept ahead of the bare ground. Sure glad we don't have that kind ov weather 'round here, 'cause a horse couldn't run like that on these hills."

Uncle Charley paused to catch his breath and Billy took the opportunity to get some answers to this mysterious weather.

"You mean it could be winter one minute and summer the next?" asked Billy, his face lit up with wonder at Uncle Charley's story.

"Yah, somethin' like that," said Uncle Charley; "somethin' like that."

"Oh boy!" said Billy, "I don't think I'd like it there. You wouldn't know what tuh wear!"

Uncle Charley was quick with his response. "That's why them fellas wear those long coats. They put 'em on when it's cold and peel 'em off when it gets hot!"

Uncle Charley had the boys' undivided attention and he was glowing with pride, so he carried on.

"Another time I went to town with this other rancher. He'd just bought himself a brand-new car, and it looked like he was kinda proud ov it.

"It was in the wintertime as well, and I was wearin' them old black gum rubber boots. They'd give yuh cold feet in the summertime, and this was the middle ov winter, and me with no socks. So I asked him if his car had a heater in it, because my feet was getting cold. I think he sort o' took offence to me askin' if it had a heater, 'cause he turned 'r up full blast, and it definitely was capable of doin' its job, 'cause in about two minutes he'd melted them old gum rubber boots right to muh feet. Let me tell yuh I wasn't long in askin' him tuh turn 'r back a little. I had one heck ov a time tryin' tuh get them ol' rubbers off my feet that night."

By this time Billy was sitting there with tears running down his cheeks. "Tell us some more about the West," he begged. "These stories are pretty good!"

Uncle Charley was smiling, as things were going his way.

"Yuh know, those folks out there were somethin' else. I met this Irish fella one day, his name was O'Leary. He had this ol' nag ov a horse, guess somebody must have seen him comin' a mile away, 'cause it was done like a dinner long before he ever got his hands on it. He asked me if I'd lend him forty dollars 'cause he needed tuh buy another horse, said his was sick 'r somethin' 'cause it could hardly walk anymore. I told him if I had forty dollars, I'd be ridin' a horse ov muh own. Anyways, I see him in town a couple o' weeks later, an' he was ridin' a pretty good-lookin' mare. I asked him where he got the money tuh buy such a fine lookin' animal. He said he got it from sellin' the other one. Now I wouldn't o' given him five dollars for the old one, so I said, how in the world did yuh make such a deal?

"He said he raffled off the old one, 'cause he knew it was about tuh die. And he said it did, just a day before the draw. So I asked him what happened, didn't the people get upset about the horse dyin'? He said the only one that complained was the winner, and he gave him back his money an' kept the rest for himself. He said the winner really wasn't very happy about it, but what could he do, the horse was dead. He didn't lose anything, 'cause he got his money back. I guess this ol' boy was a bit ov a shyster, but he certainly turned a pretty darn good buck on that deal. I tell yuh, lettin' them Irish fellas in tuh the country will be the ruination of it," said Uncle Charley, tongue in cheek.

"Ain't you Irish?" questioned Billy, "isn't your name O'Reilly?"

"Oh, I just borrowed that name from a neighbour. I think my real name is Williams, 'r somethin' like that. They said my daddy came from the Himalayas. From there they sent him to Australia. You know that's where they used tuh send all the bad fellas. But he was so bad they wouldn't keep him there, either, so they sent him on tuh Canada. They say that they'll let anybody come and stay here!"

"What was so bad about your paw?" asked Billy, taking it all in.

"Oh, he was just a lazy fella!"

"You said he came from the Himalayas; then you're not Irish?"

"Well... yuh see, he was so darn lazy that they said he must be one ov them Him-a-lay-en people, 'cause every time they went lookin' for him, they'd be sure tuh find him-a-lay-'n somewhere!"

"Uncle Charley, you are nuts," laughed Billy. "You are really nuts! And I see what yuh mean about the Irish ruinin' our country. We should throw them all out!"

To Uncle Charley that was a compliment, so he just widened his smile and nodded his approval.

"What else can you tell us about the West?" inquired Billy, eager to hear some more stories.

"Well..." chuckled Uncle Charley, quite happy with his audience, "let me tell yuh about a hunt'n trip I went on. Some fellas that I knew wanted me tuh go with them, up into the mountains tuh hunt them big horn sheep."

He paused from his story and asked, "You fellas ever see one?" Both boys shook their heads no.

"Well.....let me tell yuh, their horns grow in a kind ov a circle. Startin' at the side of their head, they grow forwards, then upwards, and then backwards, and then down and back tuh the front again. And then they come to a pretty good point at the end."

Charley traced the lines through the air with his hands, hoping the boys would understand.

"Anyways, we went up the mountain, 'bout a good day's ride. We made camp that night, and the next day we went lookin' for them big horn sheep.

"Now those fellas never told me much about the sheep, so I'm thinkin' they'd be just like the reg'lar old sheep that we have back here. Well, let me tell yuh, I was wrong!

"The rest ov the way up was too steep for the horses, so we had tuh go on foot. And we spread out to increase our chance ov findin' them. After climbin' for about an hour or so, I spied this big ol' ram. An' he had one extra-large set ov horns on him. He was standin' out on one ov those rocky ledges . . . yuh know the kind. If yuh were tuh fall off, it would take two days before anyone would hear the crash. It looked a little bit too dangerous for me tuh trail out there. So I tried tuh figger out how I'd get him off there if I shot him.

"Let me tell yuh, I really wanted to get this old boy. 'Cause he was one big ol' ram, and them boys out there like to brag about what they get. So I thought I might like tuh do a little braggin' muh self.

"Now, there was absolutely no way that I was goin' tuh go out there tuh get him. So I thought maybe if I stone pegged him he'd move to a better place. So I picked up a rock about the size o' my fist and I flung it at 'm. It caught him just on top of his left shoulder as he was standin' there facin' me. The instant that it hit him, he reared up on his hind feet, pawed the air, and slammed his front ones down hard. Then he looks right at me and snorted. I figger'd that I had definitely gotten his undivided attention. So I thought that I'd give him another one. This time I got him in the ribs, and he did the same thing. 'Cept this time he gave two snorts and looked straight at me.

"I'm thinkin', what in the world is it gonna take to get this old boy tuh move? So I give 'im another one, only this time I clocked 'm right between the eyes.

"Let me tell yuh, that got things movin' . . . boy did he unwind. He went up in the air with all four feet. Landed on his hind legs, and pawed the air with his front ones, and then he snorted three times. I figger'd he was just about tuh lose his temper, and then it happened. He jumped up in the air again and lands with his four legs all spread apart. This time there was fire in his eyes, let me tell yuh they were a blazin', and the hot steam was rollin' out each ov his nostrils, just like one ov them ol' freight trains.

"Then I saw somthin' that made muh hair stand straight up . . . his ol' horns started tuh unwind. I tell yuh they unwound till they were straightened right out, and pointing right at me.

"Reminded me ov the poles the knights used tuh shove each other off their horses with. Only this old boy had two ov 'em.

"As soon as they got straightened out, he started a-comin' across the top o' them rocks . . . and let me tell yuh the sparks were a-flyin' off his hooves every time they hit a rock. And man could he move . . . just like greased lightnin'.

"Well . . . I'm a-gonna tell yuh, I pitched that old rifle and took to muh heels. Down over the steep side ov that ol' mountain I went . . . and let me tell yuh I was movin'. I went head over heels . . . ass over apple cart . . . end over end . . . sideways . . . endways, sometimes on my hands and knees. I didn't care how I went just as long as I was puttin' some distance between me and that old billy goat.

"Got caught on somethin' and tore the ass out o' muh pants. I was all skinned up and lookin' a mess by the time I reached level ground, but that old ram was nowhere to be seen. I'd left him a long ways behind me in a cloud o' dust. When I reached muh horse, I saddled up and rode the dickens out o' him all the way back to the ranch. Packed muh stuff, an' rode for town. I caught the next train out and headed for home. Took a while to git back here, but here I am, and I ain't a-goin' back there, and that's a for sure. I guess my rifle is still up on the mountain with that ol' billy goat, and it can stay there as far as I'm concerned. If he can figger out how tuh use the thing, then he can have it, an' he's more than welcome to it. 'Cause I sure ain't goin' back out there tuh argue with him over who owns it! Let me tell yuh, boys, don't you ever mess around with them big horned sheep, no sirree!"

By this time both the boys were bent over laughing. Billy looked up at Uncle Charley and said, "you got to be kidding, his horns never really straightened out . . . did they?"

"Oh boy, they sure did. I'd swear to that one on my deathbed!"

replied Uncle Charley with a twinkle in his eye.

Charley was in his glory, but it was time to quit and get on with somethin' else.

"Well," said Uncle Charley, "I guess it's about time to end the storytellin' and get some supper on the stove."

"Ahhh," grunted Uncle Charley as he struggled to get up. "I ain't as young as I used to be, but I guess I ain't as old as I'm gonna be, either!

"Reminds me of a story old Jack told about a fella that was lost. Came to his door lookin' to find his way tuh Bark Lake. Jack gave him the directions of how to get there, and the stranger thanked him and said, 'Looks like you know these parts pretty well. Guess you've lived here all your life.'

"Old Jack looked him square in the face, and said, 'No! not yet.'

"The stranger laughed and said, 'I guess you're right or else yuh wouldn't be standin' here talking to me, and thanks again for the directions.' He said the stranger made his way back tuh his car laughin' and shakin' his head."

Bull's Eye through a Knothole

Uncle Charley opened the screen door and stepped inside. Once inside, he drew back and let out a high-pitched yell, "Heyyyaaaah!" and then continued with, "It's daylight in the swamp!"

Mick, who was sound asleep on the couch, immediately came upright to a sitting position. The look of fight or flight was stamped all over his face. He just wasn't sure which one it would be.

"Wha . . . what?" he said, his eyes blinking as he tried to focus on his surroundings.

Uncle Charley continued, "What in the world are yuh do 'n stretched out there? Life is way too short to be a wastin' good daylight!"

Then he added with a big grin, "Didn't scare yuh, did I?"

"Not at all!" Mick replied; meanwhile, his heart was doing ninety, as he tried to rub the sleep from his eyes. "I think I only lost about three years' growth!"

"That's good, 'cause yuh didn't need it anyways. Yuh 'r plenty big enough now.

"Why don't yuh go get some potatoes and peel them while I light a fire in this old cookstove, and I'll see if I can get some water boilin'."

Charley looked at the two boys and said, "And why don't you two fellas run up to the henhouse and see if the hens have laid any fresh eggs . . . and if yuh see Dan, tell him supper'll be ready in a little while. That should give him time to stop whatever he's doin' and get them long legs ov his down here in time to eat."

The boys ran up to the henhouse and, seeing the horse-stable doors open, they called out to Dan. He was in there tinkering with something or other and said he'd be down in a minute or two.

On entering the henhouse, Joey spied the wooden eggs his paw had made to put under the clucking hen. The idea was to get her to sit on those so she wouldn't bother the laying hens.

Paw had done a good job in carving the eggs, and he painted them white to fool the clucking hen. In fact, at a glance, they looked like real ones.

Joey's eyes lit up and he said, "Hey, Billy, put the eggs in your pockets so Uncle Charley won't see them, and I'll give him the wooden ones, and let's see if we can fool him."

Billy did as requested and then the boys hurried back to the house, hoping to have some fun with Uncle Charley. Joey handed the wooden eggs to Uncle Charley and he took them without a word.

"Well, would yuh look at that!" he said; "them darn hens knew we were in a hurry for supper and if they didn't go and lay us some hard-boiled eggs. I'm gonna give each one of you boys one for supper, don't have to do a darn thing with them except to put 'em on yuh 'r plate."

Billy gave Joey a look of despair, then whispered, "This ain't workin', an' I ain't eatin' no wooden egg. I think I better give him the real ones."

Uncle Charley chuckled and said, "Did you boys think that I was born yesterday? I'd know them was wooden eggs a mile away, so why don't yuh just give me the real ones so we can get some supper goin'." Billy, who was now blushing, reached into his pocket and produced the real ones and handed them over to Uncle Charley.

"Now, that's better," said Uncle Charley with a smile. "Tell me, what do yuh think would have happened if that old dog would have decided to jump up on yuh with them eggs in yuh 'r pockets?"

Billy paled a little at the thought. "Didn't think about that, did yuh? Just tryin' tuh have some fun with ol' Uncle Charley. Well . . . that's all right, a fella needs to have a little fun now and then. I'll bet in the next three days yuh'll have enough fun tuh keep yuh rememberin' for a lifetime."

Uncle Charley wasn't known to be a prophet, but the remembering of the next three days . . . well, on that statement he would be dead-on.

Dan stepped in through the door and asked, "Well, what have we got for supper that I needed to be here in such a hurry?"

"Tea, toast, an' toenails with bedbug soup!" came Uncle Charley's quick reply.

Dan stopped dead in his tracks. "What did you say?"

"I said, Tea . . . toast . . . an' toenails . . . along with some good ol' bedbug soup." Uncle Charley repeated it with a bit of a grin.

Dan turned on his heels and said with disgust, "I'm go 'n back to the horse stable before I puke!"

"It's a lot more fillin' than north wind and deer tracks," replied Uncle Charley with an even bigger grin.

"Could be," said Dan, "but I think I'll do quite well without it."

"Git back here an' sit down!" commanded Uncle Charley, who was now chuckling. "We've got fried eggs, boiled potatoes with milk gravy. Now does that sound better? I'll soak some beans tonight an' bake 'em tomorrow; should be good by suppertime."

"Yah . . . sounds a bit better," said Dan, "but I think yuh just spoiled my appetite."

"Got a weak stomach?" inquired Uncle Charley.

"Nope," said Dan, "I can pitch 'r just as far as anybody else can!"

"Aahhh," said Billy as he puckered up his face, "This is get 'n worse by the minute. I don't think I'm gonna want to eat either!"

"Pay no attention," said Joey, "it won't bother you if yuh don't think about it!"

After they all had eaten their fill, Dan pushed back from the table.

"Okay, Mick, I guess it's time tuh go milk the cows and do the rest of the chores."

This meant they would be feeding the chickens, the pigs, the calves, and the cats, and putting the horses in the stable for the night.

"Sounds good tuh me," said Uncle Charley. "I'll do the dishes and clean up while you two boys go and get some firewood for the morning. And be careful with the axe that yuh don't cut yuh'r feet off."

"Don't you worry," said Joey, "we've dun it before." His voice was cool and casual as if he were a pro.

"Chop the hardwood up nice 'n fine so it starts good an easy and doesn't last long. This time o' the year, the sun makes things hot enough without havin' a fire burnin' all day."

Uncle Charley busied himself putting things away, then he took the milk out to the milk house for the night. Upon returning, he placed all the dirty dishes on one corner of the table. Setting the dishpan down beside them, he filled it with hot water from the big kettle that was always on the stove. He put some soap in the dishpan and swished it around with the dishcloth, then wrung it out and wiped the far side of the table where the clean dishes would go.

The boys were busy cutting wood; Dan and Mick were doing the chores; Uncle Charley was busy cleaning up the house. Everyone was busy doing their job as the day drew to a close. It all added up to another one of those fine country evenings.

Billy was working on the kindling, while Joey was busy with the hardwood. About halfway through their task, Joey leaned on his axe handle and looked over at Billy.

"Boy . . . let me tell yuh, Billy, you're just like lightning with that axe!"

"I am?" replied Billy, smiling as if he'd just received a compliment.

"Yep . . . yuh never seem tuh hit the same place twice!" said Joey, trying not to smile.

"Thanks, and I don't see you doin' any better!" Billy's voice was now showing disappointment.

"You're welcome . . . just thought I'd let yuh know," replied Joey, tongue in cheek, trying to pretend that it was just a casual remark.

"Yah, well, if you don't start being more careful yuh'll have six toes before we're done!" Billy's reply was an attempt to get even, sort of a Johnny come lately that lacked the punch that Joey had delivered, so he just shook his head and went back to work.

"There yuh go," said Joey as the boys each placed an armful of wood into the old woodbox.

"I do thank yuh, boys," said Uncle Charley as he opened the screen door and threw out the dishwater. After wiping the pan dry, he hung it on a nail behind the door and spread the dishcloth over the top of it to dry.

"Another job done for t' day," said Uncle Charley with a sigh; he then turned and said, "Think I'll light the lamp; it's gettin' dark in here!"

He lifted the glass chimney, struck a match, and laid it on top of the wick. The flame quickly rose, giving off a stream of black smoke. Putting the chimney back in place, he adjusted the wick and set the lamp in the centre of the table. The glow from the lamp gave the windows a mirror reflection as the night sky slipped into semi-darkness.

"There now, I can see tuh soak the beans."

Mick and Dan came in with four pails of milk. They made their way to the back room, where they would run it through the separator.

Meanwhile, Uncle Charley took the old bean kettle from behind the stove and brought it to the table. From there he made his way to the pantry, opened the door, and rummaged about in the dark. Eventually he came out with a half-empty bag of beans that had a string tied around one end. This was to keep the beans from spilling out and other things from getting in. He untied the string and took hold of the front and back of the bag, then poured about three inches of beans into the old cast-iron pot.

"There, that should about do it!" he said to himself.

He retied the bag and put it back in the pantry. On his way back, he took the bean kettle over to the water pail and dipped enough water to cover the beans. Then he placed the pot on the reservoir to soak for the night.

"There, by tomorrow they should be ready for cookin'!" Uncle Charley, satisfied with his accomplishment, was now planning to relax for the evening.

With the separating completed, Dan ran a pail of clean water through the separator to rinse out any remaining milk. Then the skim milk was taken back to the barn to feed the calves and pigs.

Returning to the well, they rinsed the pails and turned them upside-down to dry.

Ol' Jake entered with Dan and then went over and sat beside the boys. In a few minutes Mick joined them, also planning to relax for the rest of the evening.

Outside, the crickets and night creatures were starting up their usual choir. The evening had quickly and quietly slipped away, and the darkness of night was settling in. The world was now seeking its time of rest. The evening breeze had subsided, and the air was perfectly still. Not a leaf was moving; it was time to settle down and relax.

The boys were sitting on the couch and not saying a word, just relaxing. Although their day had been busy, they weren't ready to cash in just yet.

Dan sat on the bench behind the table, while Mick and Uncle Charley pulled up chairs at the ends. Jake moved away from the boys, went under the table, and lay down at Dan's feet. For a moment everything was silent; then Dan asked Uncle Charley how Toby was doing.

Toby's home was situated at the edge of town, and not very far from Uncle Charley. He was a twenty-five-year-old who still needed his parents to watch over him. And try as he would, it seemed he could never get all his ducks to line up; there were always a few that were wandering. His eyeglasses looked like they were made from the bottom of a coke bottle, and it was hard to tell when Toby looked at you if he was squinting or grinning. Everybody around town knew Toby, and he was well liked in spite of his difficulties.

"Yah... he's doin' okay," answered Uncle Charley, a softness coming to his voice, "but it seems poor old Toby is either coming from it or goin' to it.

"Joe Long took him down to Eganville a few weeks back. It was just for the drive an' tuh give Toby somethin' t' do. Well, it turned out that Joe went into the hotel for a pint or two and this big redheaded fella that he knew joins him. After a while the redheaded fella gets to realizing that ol' Toby is a bit different, so he asks Toby if he likes riddles, and Toby says, 'Yah, I sure do!'

"So he says to Toby, 'My mother had a baby and it wasn't my brother, an' it wasn't my sister, so who was it?'

"Toby looks at him for a minute with a kind of a blank stare, shrugs his shoulders, and says, 'I dun know, who was it?'

"The redheaded fella starts to laughin' and says, 'It was me, Toby, it's me!'

"Toby starts in tuh laughin' along with him, thinking it was somethin' funny. Anyways, later on they make their way back t' town, an' Joe is still a bit thirsty so he goes in tuh the hotel and Toby follows him in. He finds some fellas that he knew so he sits down with them an' gets t' talkin' and laughin'. Toby ain't sayin' nothin' for a while, just sittin' quiet. Then he gets the idea to join in and see if he could get a little somethin' go'n for himself.

"So he speaks up an' says, 'You fellas like t' hear a good riddle?'

"Well . . . of course they all stop talkin' and give him the floor. They tell him tuh go ahead an' tell his riddle.

"Ol' Toby perks right up, gets a big smile on his face, and says, 'My mother had a baby, and it wasn't my brother and it wasn't my sister, so who was it?'

"They all wait for a minute, then say, 'We don't know, Toby, who was it?'

"Thinking he knew somethin' that they didn't, ol' Toby gets this silly grin on his face — it was a lot like a horse when he's eatin' bull thistles — and he says, 'What's wrong with you fellas? Everybody knows it's a big redheaded fella down in Eganville!'

"Well . . . they all started in tuh the laughin', and this made Toby's day; he thought that he done somethin' really clever.

"After things settled down a bit, Raymond, wearing a big grin, said to him, 'I'll bet your father doesn't know the answer to your riddle.'

"Harold had stopped laughin', but was grinnin' to the point that his eyes were squintin', and said with a chuckle, 'Why don't yuh go on home and ask him?'

"Gerard spoke up, tryin' to control his laughter, and with tears strollin' down his cheeks, said, 'And make darn sure your mother's there when yuh do!'

"Well, now . . . Toby, thinking that he had everyone's approval, got up and strolled toward the door as proud as a peacock. Edgar, who was still shaking and wiping tears from his eyes, said, 'Ohhh, ohh, oh, how can any man be so foolish!'"

"Did he go home and ask his father?" inquired Billy, who'd been sitting there taking in every word.

"Well . . . " said Uncle Charley, "old Jim, who lives across the road from them, says he heard some kind of a ruckus late that afternoon. So he goes t' the door t' see what was happenin'. He said he saw Toby a hoofinner down the road, and every few steps he was glancin' back over his shoulder. His mother was standin' on the front porch with a corn broom in her hands, and not lookin' any too happy. He said Toby went over to Walters and stayed there for 'bout a week. I guess he stirred up a real hornet's nest with his riddle."

Just as Uncle Charley finished his story, ol' Jake got into the sneezing and snorting. He was carrying on like he had some urgent business to attend to somewhere's else, and from the sound of his toenails, he wasn't able to get to his feet nearly as fast as he would like to.

Mick looked down and said, "What's the prob . . . ooooh . . . lordee . . . lordee . . . pheew . . . . Dan, did some critter crawl up your back end and die in there?"

Uncle Charley put his hand over his face and said, "Oh, my gawd, I can't breathe! Pheeew."

Ol' Jake made it to the screen door and stood there sneezing and snorting. His nose was pressed against the screen, drawing in as much fresh air as he possibly could. By this time the not-so-fragrant odour reached the boys on the couch.

"Oooh," said Billy, "I think I'm gonna be sick!"

"Then get outside," said Joey, urgency ringing in his voice, "cause I ain't cleanin' up no mess!"

Mick slid his chair back from the table, as did Uncle Charley.

"You must a fallen asleep behind some stone fence and a groundhog crawled up in there and wasn't able to find his way back out!" said Mick, still blowing air out through his nose as if that would somehow help get rid of the unpleasant odour.

Dan's face was getting redder by the second. He was trying hard not to smile but he was losing ground. The carrying on was more than he could handle. When he couldn't hold it any longer, he started to laugh and said, "No, you dummy! It must be the sauerkraut and sausage that I had at Joe's last night. I took the piece ov angle iron over to him, like Paw told me to, an' he said his wife had supper ready and wanted me tuh stay, so I stayed."

"She must ov made the sausage from some leftover wolf kill that she found in the back forty, because let me tell yuh, what you just passed has a fragrance that no skunk could match! Pheww." said Mick, "You even blistered the paint on the wall behind yuh!"

Dan turned and looked at the wall. "You donkey, those bubbles have been there for the last forty years!"

"I don't think so." Mick wasn't smiling, trying very hard to sound serious.

"I know so! So forget it! I ain't that stupid!" Dan's smile was fading, but he was still red from blushing.

"It's a darn good job that both doors were open 'r yuh mighta took out a winda," warned Uncle Charley. "Bet that poor ol' dog'll walk right up tuh a skunk now an' never even know the difference. I'm sure yuh must have burnt the smeller right out ov him!"

"Good job the fire wasn't on," said Mick, "or we might have had an explosion."

"Will that stuff explode?" asked Billy, trying to sound serious.

"Yuh're dealin' with natural gas," said Uncle Charley, "an' natural gas will definitely explode. And there ain't no gas that meets the qualifications for be'n natural any more than what Dan just passed.

"Now you fellas may not want to believe this, but there was a fella over at the loggin' camp that bent over one day an' let one rip. At the same time, another fella behind him struck a match. There was a big explosion, an' that bent-over fella took off like a flame-shootin' rocket. Almost drove his head right through a white pine tree!"

"I don't think I believe that!" said Billy, trying to get in on the fun, "or Paw would ov blown our house apart a long time ago, 'cause he's even worst than Dan!"

"I wouldn't strike a match at a time like that," cautioned Mick, going along with Billy, "or you just might be the cause ov one big ol' disaster."

Joey poked Billy with his elbow and asked, "Are yuh gonna be all right?"

To which Billy nodded and said, "Yes."

Joey followed up with, "Want tuh go upstairs and look at my comic books?"

Joey had a half-dozen old worn-out comic books that someone had given him. They may have been old to somebody else, but they were new to Billy, so up the stairs they went, two at a time. Joey lit the coal oil lamp that was on his dresser, then pulled out the drawer that held the comics. They scooped them up and climbed into bed, content to stay there and enjoy themselves till sleep time.

As the boys made their way up the stairs, Mick and Dan brought out the checker board. They were ready to settle down to some serious checker playing.

Uncle Charley went into the pantry and came out with the old baby cradle. He set it on the floor beside the stove, then took a pillow from the couch and placed it in the cradle box. After making things as comfortable as possible, he got down and got his back on the cradle. This isn't easy for a man the size of Uncle Charley, but with some grunting and groaning he succeeded. The headboard supported the back of his head, while the pillow supported his upper back and shoulders. His lower back and hips extended out past the end of the cradle. After some wiggling and squirming, Charley found his comfort zone and settled down.

His hand slipped into his pocket and pulled out his mouth organ. Wiping it on his pant leg, he put it to his lips and proceeded to entertain himself with "Oh Susanna."

All seemed to be peace and contentment, but don't hold your breath.

Meanwhile, the boys had worked their way through one of Joey's comic books. While they were turning the pages, Billy had been doing some wiggling and squirming. Joey, becoming aware of this, asked, "Somethin' wrong?"

"Yah," replied Billy, "I need to pee, but I don't want to go outside in the dark!"

"Don't have to," said Joey; "there's a pot under the bed. Pee in it; that's what I do!"

"Don't you be lookin'," said Billy, a bit self-conscious about what was going to take place.

"At what?" laughed Joey.

"Never mind," said Billy, as he crawled over him, making his way off the bed.

Billy looked under the bed and found the pot. He pulled it out and proceeded to wring his mitt. When the task was completed, he gently shoved the pot back under the bed and tried to regain his sleeping position. As he climbed over Joey, Joey gave him a friendly push with his elbow, causing Billy to lose his balance, and also his footing. His foot slipped off the bed and shot downward. Before it reached the floor, his big toe caught the edge of the chamber pot, and turned it on its side. All the golden liquid rushed out and hurried over to a knothole that was about a foot away... and gravity did the rest.

As we re-enter the scene below, Mick and Dan are at the table puzzling over the next move in the checker game. Uncle Charley is gently rocking from side to side to the tune of "Oh Susanna."

At the sound of the chamber pot falling over, Uncle Charley removed the mouth organ from his lips and started to speak. But before he could complete the sentence, the golden liquid dropped down through the knothole and hit him square in the face.

"What was th'... pheww... pheww... phew," spat Uncle Charley. "What in the world was that?"

"Piss-pot!" said Dan without lifting his head or losing his concentration.

"Piss-pot?" echoed Uncle Charley, still lying on his back, and not fully aware of what had just hit him. A very brief pause and then, "Piss-pot!" he roared.

Now fully aware of what had just hit him in the face, he sprang to his feet like the release of a young willow. The cradle was still clinging to his back as he came upright, but with a violent shrug of his shoulders it went crashing onto the floor. At the same time, his mouth organ went sliding across the room and into a corner.

While wiping his face with his sleeve, Charley headed for the wash basin on a dead run. Upon reaching it, he drove his face into the water, splashing water with both hands. Spitting and sputtering, he opened the door and threw the dirty water outside, then he quickly refilled the basin. Again, he drove his face into the water and gave it another good splashing.

Grabbing the towel from where it hung on the wall, he started drying his face. When he was about half done, he stopped and declared, "What 'n the world should I expect next?"

Mick and Dan just smiled and said nothing. They both knew that if they laughed, they'd get into trouble with Uncle Charley, and if they were to speak there was no way they could hold it back, so they both kept their eyes on the checkerboard and their mouths closed.

As Uncle Charley finished drying himself, two little faces peeked around the corner of the staircase. They were both showing signs of fear and uncertainty, wondering what was going to happen to them.

"Are you okay?" Joey's voice was soft and low as he addressed Uncle Charley.

"AM I OKAY?" thundered Uncle Charley. "Would you be okay if somebody dumped a piss-pot in yuhr face?"

"Sorry, it was an accident," came Joey's soft reply. "Billy was trying to get intuh bed and his foot caught the edge of the pee pot and upended it."

He didn't bother to tell him about Billy being pushed.

"Didn't mean to," came Billy's soft voice, as he sought forgiveness.

"Oh . . . all right," replied Uncle Charley, his voice a bit lower. "I guess things like that can happen at the best o' times, and if that's all that happens, I'll most likely live t' see the mornin'. Now you two fellas get back tuh bed and be more careful about what yuh're doin'!"

Uncle Charley may have been willing to forgive, but he sure wasn't smiling as he wiped the back of his hand across his mouth. His actions clearly indicated that he wasn't convinced things were as clean as he would have liked them to be.

The boys turned and lost no time in going back up the stairs. Joey gained the bed from the side while Billy went up and over the end. Once under the covers, Billy, still visibly shaken, said to Joey, "Boy, that was close, thought he was gonna kill us. He sure is loud when he gets mad!"

"Don't worry," said Joey, "he wouldn't hurt yuh — just likes to make a lot o' noise when he gets his temper up."

"Sure coulda fooled me," insisted Billy, still not sounding convinced that he was safe. "I thought we were dead!"

"Paw can get pretty loud when he gets mad. You shoulda heard him the time he stuck his arm into the boilin' water. Maw had drained the potato water into the wash dish just before he came in, and it was boilin' hot. He was all dirty and was goin' tuh wash before supper, so he laid his arm in 'r, right up tuh the elbow. I tell yuh he didn't leave it in there very long," said Joey, chuckling as he spoke. "Faster'n greased lightning, it was in and out. Then yuh should ov seen him go. He did a little dance around in a circle, and he was usin' some pretty bad words, and let me tell yuh they were comin' out good an' loud.

"He took a kick at the wash dish and sent it climbin' up the wall, water flyin' all over the place. I think it reached the ceilin' before it tumbled back down tuh the floor. It was doin' that wobble, wobble, around on the floor when he jumped on 'r with both feet and flattened 'r out like a pancake. Scared Maw half tuh death. She took off up the stairs and stayed in the bedroom till he quietened down."

"Did she hide under the bed?" asked Billy.

"No, that wouldn't do much good. Once you're under the bed, there's noplace else yuh can go, so you're stuck there. I tried it once and it didn't work out too well."

"Why ... what happened?" asked Billy. Now that he wasn't so scared, he wanted to hear about Joey's misfortune.

"Maw was up at the barn gathering the eggs, and I was in the house playin' with my toys. It was in the winter, and I was inside most o' the time. So, I thought I'd take the dirt from Maw's flowerpots and use it to make roads on the floor. I tell yuh when she came in and saw it, she got mad and grabbed the fly swatter. She was talking pretty loud and I knew that I was gonna get it, so I got scared and run upstairs an' slid under the bed. She told me tuh come on out and take my medicine, and I said there was no way that was gonna happen. She said I would if I knew what was good for me. I said no way, I ain't comin' out. She said, okay, and went down and got the broom. Let me tell yah, when yuh get the bald-headed end o' that ol' broom handle in the ribs a couple o' times, you ain't long in changin' your mind!"

By this time Billy was laughing his heart out, but Joey didn't see the funny side of it and he said so.

"It wasn't funny!"

"It sure is when you tell it. And what was the medicine she was gonna give you?"

"The fly swatter on my bare ass!"

"Why did she call it medicine?"

"'Cause she felt that if yuh got a good enough dose, it would cure you from doing it a second time."

"Did it?" asked Billy, tears strolling down his cheeks.

"It sure did. I never tried *that* again," said Joey, sounding like he wanted to end the subject on medicine.

"Let's go t' sleep. We can look at the comics some other time."

Joey placed the comics on the dresser, and they both snuggled in for the night.

He didn't want to admit it, but a little fear had crept up his back as well, and he certainly did not want to get Uncle Charley's temper up twice in one night.

7

Billy Gets Introduced to Ol' Zack

Uncle Charley turned to Mick and asked, "Did yuh see where my mouth organ went?"

"I think it's over there," said Dan, pointing to the corner of the room.

The coal oil lamp didn't give a lot of light, but it was enough to show the shiny side of the mouth organ, giving away its location.

Uncle Charley walked over and picked it up while mumbling to himself, "Now, who'd wanna put the like o' that to their mouth, piss all over it?"

His lips curled up in disgust as he spoke. He walked over to the table to get a better look. The mouth organ had dried off and so had the floor; it was the pillow and Uncle Charley that had received most of the liquid.

"You could wash it," offered Mick.

"With what?" asked Uncle Charley in disgust.

"Hot water and Javex?"

"'Twould probably ruin it for good." Uncle Charley's voice showed his disappointment as he thought perhaps his favourite musical instrument was ruined.

"You could try a little turpentine," offered Dan, trying to be helpful.

"Turpentine?" replied Uncle Charley, his voice rising a little. "Who in the world would wanna get the like ov that in their mouth?"

Dan shrugged his shoulders and let it go.

"You probably could use some water with a little Javex," said Mick; "wipe the outside with a rag. Split a match and then place a little bit of cotton batten, which Maw keeps from the pill bottles, in the crack. Push it in and out of those little holes a few times, and that should clean it."

"Might work," agreed Uncle Charley. "Let's give 'r a try." Hope had now returned to his voice.

While Mick and Uncle Charley carried out their painful task of cleaning the mouth organ, Dan folded his arms on the table and then laid his head on them. In a few minutes he was sound asleep.

When Uncle Charley was satisfied that his mouth organ was clean, he put it in his pocket and said to Mick, "That should hold 'r for now, I'll try 'r in the mornin' after she's had time t' dry. And if it's all the same t' you, I think I'll head for bed."

"You bet," said Mick. "See yuh in the mornin'."

Uncle Charley headed for the stairs while Mick was putting things away for the night. When he was finished, he looked over at Dan with disgust. Trying to wake him up after he'd fallen asleep was like trying to raise the dead.

Then he got an idea. He went over to the cupboard and got a nice long piece of string. He ran softly up the stairs and dropped one end of the string down through a crack in the floor; the other end he tied to the bedpost. Quietly he hurried back down and tied the other end to a piece of Dan's hair. Placing the lamp on the stove, he blew it out. The room was now filled with darkness. Mick quietly and carefully made his way up the stairs and into bed. Once under the covers, he reached over and pulled on the string. This aroused Dan enough to realize someone was pulling his hair. Swinging his arms around him, he said, "Go away and leave me alone!"

Mick waited a minute then gave a few more pulls on the string. Dan was now aware that his hair was being pulled, but he couldn't feel anyone close enough to be doing it. So he opened his eyes to see what was going on. The room was completely dark, and there was no one there, so who in the world was pulling his hair? The stories that he had heard about old Zack, the fellow that had lived there years ago, and was still roaming around the place at night, suddenly became a reality. A blood-curdling yell escaped Dan's lips.

"MICK ... MICK! Help me! Old Zack has me by the hair o' the head. Help me, Mick!" Dan was no longer asleep at the table — he was on his feet and trying to make his way around it. As he worked his way toward the stairs, he was determined to break free from old Zack's grasp. Chairs went crashing as he pushed his way through them.

Ol' Jake, who was sleeping by the stove, scrambled to his feet and started barking. Not too sure at what, but let's face it — something must be wrong.

Dan yelled, "Sic'm Jake, sic'm!" as he pushed through the darkness.

When he reached the end of the string, it felt like someone was trying to hold him by the hair, but there was no stopping him now.

"Mick ... he has me by the hair ov the head. Help me!" Again he yelled for help. By this time, his voice was high and pleading. He was pushing forward with all of his might, and the string couldn't hold on any longer. It slipped from his hair, and he was finally free from old Zack's grasp.

He went up the stairs on his hands and knees, and he didn't waste any time in reaching the top. Once there, the lamp on Joey's dresser lit the room.

Jake stopped at the bottom of the stairs, but continued barking, not really sure at what, but it did add to the confusion.

By this time both boys were sitting up in bed, scared out of their wits, but they weren't sure of what. They had wakened to the sound of Dan screaming and the dog barking, but they had no idea what was going on.

Mick had pulled the covers over his head; the whole bed was shaking but it wasn't from fear. He was laughing so hard the tears were streaming down his cheeks, but he didn't dare let Dan catch him at it.

Charley heard the screaming and he also had pulled the covers over his head. It wasn't because he was laughing, but because he believed the rumors of old Zack prowling around at night were true, and Charley had no time for ghosts. With the pillow and covers over his head, his feet were sticking out at the bottom. But that didn't matter to Charley, for he couldn't see with his feet, and he did not want to make visual contact with old Zack should he ever venture up the stairs.

Having gained the stairs, Dan beelined it for his bed, pulled back the covers, and slid in beside Mick, with all his clothes still on him. Pulling the covers up to his chin, he watched the top of the stairs, expecting to see old Zack following him.

Joey also was watching the stairs. Billy, scared half to death but not sure of what, whispered to Joey, "What happened?"

"I think old Zack almost got Dan."

"What!" exclaimed Billy. "Who is old Zack?"

Fear was now evident in Billy's voice.

"Some old feller that lived here a long time ago," said Joey in a whisper.

"So what's he doing here now?"

"Just prowlin' around."

"D' yuh think he'd hurt somebody?" Billy's voice was quivering.

"Don't know if he can."

"What d' yuh mean, you don't know if he can?"

"Well . . . he's a ghost, and I don't think they can hurt people, they just scare yuh t' death."

Billy turned deathly pale, and quietly uttered, "I think I wanna go home."

"Too late now, nobody around here will be going anyplace tonight."

"Ohh," said Billy and slid down under the covers till just his eyes were peeping out. He also was watching the top of the stairs as if he expected to see someone enter the room.

"Please don't put the lamp out," pleaded Billy.

"Don't worry, I'm not that stupid."

"Can a ghost get yah under the covers?"

"Don't think so," whispered Joey.

"Then let's pull the covers over our heads."

"I ain't, we might smother."

"Yah, yuh're right," said Billy, "then *we'd* be ghosts."

"Brrrr!" said Joey, "don't talk like that, okay?"

"Do yuh think he'll hurt Jake?" asked Billy, concern evident in his voice.

"Don't think they can hurt animals, and animals don't seem tuh be afraid of ghosts."

"Jake stopped barkin'; are yuh sure he's okay?"

"Yah, he's okay or he'd be kie-yiein'." whispered Joey, trying to make himself believe that everything was all right.

"I ain't closin' my eyes no more tonight," declared Billy, while vibrating from head to foot.

"Don't think he'll come up here with the light on," suggested Joey.

"Yuh sure?"

"Yah, I'm sure," Joey's voice wasn't all that convincing, but he was hoping that he would give Billy some peace of mind.

Billy's knees were knocking as he lay there not knowing what to expect next.

"Don't think there'll be any more goin' on here tonight," offered Joey. "Try an' go tuh sleep, if yuh can."

Billy was looking around the room at the shadows, searching out every detail. Looking up at the roof, he saw the ends of the rusty shingle nails that were sticking through the boards. He recalled the way they had looked in the winter when he had stayed over. There would be white frost on the tips of the nails on a cold winter's night. He remembered how cold his nose had felt, and how warm it was under the blankets. How the wind would blow and the windows would rattle with each gust. How they had to break the ice on the water pail in the morning so they could get a drink. If any water was left in the wash basin, it would be frozen solid, and they'd have to place it on the stove so it could thaw enough to be thrown out.

With his thoughts moving away from the ghosts, Billy's eyelids slowly closed, and he drifted off to sleep.

Meanwhile, in Uncle Charley's room, a low voice could be heard from under the covers. "Why in the world did I ever come here in the first place? I knew that old boy was still hangin' around. Be no sleepin' done in this bed tonight, and that's for sure!"

Uncle Charley's siblings had spent hours scaring him half to death when he was a child. They told him stories of ghosts and the boogeyman, and played mean tricks on him. As much as he had tried to shake it in the passing years, it was no use. The roots went too deep. Just to talk about spooks would send shivers up his spine.

Meanwhile, Dan was far from sleeping; he was so scared that he was physically shaking. Mick, in his effort to hold back the laughter let out a couple of snorts. It was enough to let Dan know that Mick was enjoying his near disaster. Dan's temper began to rise until it matched his fears; then he drove his elbow into Mick's back.

"You're laughin'? I was almost killed by that old fella and you're laughing?" Mick couldn't contain it any longer; he was laughing so hard he could hardly talk.

"There was nobody down there — it's just your imagination!"

"Just my imagination, was it?" said Dan, his voice rising along with his emotions. "That old bugger had me by the hair ov the head and was givin' 'r a purty darn good pullin'. But you don't care if he'd a killed me, just lay up here and laugh with the light on! Sure didn't see yuh runnin' down the stairs in the dark to help me!"

Mick was still shaking with laughter. "There ain't nobody down there," he insisted in a low voice.

"Laugh, you half-baked idiot, it wasn't your hair he was pullin'!" Dan's fear was subsiding as his temper rose.

If Dan were to beat him half to death, Mick couldn't stop laughing. "Believe me, Dan, there was nobody down there," pleaded Mick with tears streaming down his face.

"Mick, if this was one of your tricks, you'll not see the light ov day!" declared Dan with feeling.

"Go to sleep, we'll talk about it in the morning," said Mick, trying to hold back the laughter.

Dan slid down under the covers, half convinced that somehow this was one of Mick's tricks. But how could he have pulled his hair if he was upstairs in bed? Anyways, he'd find that out tomorrow. Now, if he could just settle down and get some sleep before morning arrived. But that would take a miracle, for every part of his body was vibrating, including his jawbone.

8

Applesauce

The morning sun was well above the treeline before there was any sign of movement in the house. Everyone was clinging to the bedsheets. Either they were trying to get back some of the sleep they had lost the night before or they didn't want to be the first to go downstairs and face old Zack. Mick was the only one who knew what had really happened, and the rest were in no hurry to go down and check it out.

It was Mick's job, when Paw wasn't around, to be in charge. Having decided it was time to get up and get the day started, he propped his head up on his elbow and looked across at Dan.

"I see that you're still with us, Dan me boy," he said with a grin.

Dan rolled over and gave him a stern look. "Was that some of your doin'?" His voice demanded an answer.

Mick, with a big grin on his face, placed his finger to his lips indicating silence. Then he pointed downstairs.

Dan nodded, understanding that whatever it was, he didn't want the others to hear. Dan threw back the covers and sat on the edge of the bed. He was still dressed in the clothes that he was wearing the night before.

Mick, trying not to laugh as he remembered last night's events, crawled out behind him. He pulled on his pants and buttoned his shirt, then said to the boys, "Okay young fellas, it's time to rise 'n shine."

Billy, who was barely sticking his head out from the covers, asked, "Is it safe t' get up?"

Mick answered with a chuckle, "Yah, I think all is safe and peaceful on the home front this morning."

"How come Uncle Charley isn't up yet?" asked Joey.

"Why don't you go ask him?" replied Mick, glancing over his shoulder as he descended the stairs, chuckling as he went.

After last night's event, Uncle Charley would not be the first one up, and you could bet on that. This Mick knew only too well. Although it wasn't his intention to scare him, the fact that he did gave Mick some new ideas for the coming night.

Dan followed Mick down the stairs and outside. Jake was waiting at the door, wanting out to see the new day and to sniff out the scent of any visitors that may have stopped by during the night.

Mick was smiling, for there was no way that he could keep a straight face. A short distance from the house he stopped and turned around. He was ready to tell Dan what had really happened the night before.

"I dropped a string down through a crack in the ceiling and tied it in your hair while you were sleeping at the table. I never thought that you would blame old Zack for it."

Dan's fists were clenched white as he glared at Mick.

Mick raised both his hands up to his chest with the palms open and outward.

"I'm sorry, Dan," he said, trying not to laugh. "I didn't know that you were scared of the dark."

"I'm not scared of the dark," declared Dan, his face turning scarlet. "What would you think if you woke up in the dark and someone was pullin' your hair, but you couldn't feel anyone around you? If a person was pullin' your hair they would have to be standin' close to yuh, now wouldn't they? With all them darned ol' stories Paw and Uncle Charley tell about old Zack, what was I supposed to think?"

"I'm sorry ... I'm sorry," declared Mick, unable to hold it any longer, as he broke into a fit of laughter. "But I never thought of it that way. I didn't realize you took those old Zack stories seriously."

"I didn't!" declared Dan, "I just didn't have time to think."

"OKAY, OKAY," said Mick, trying to see it from Dan's point of view. "I'm sorry, and I promise not to do it again," wiping tears from his cheeks as he spoke.

"You bet you won't!" Dan turned to go back into the house, relieved that he now knew what had really happened, but totally disgusted with Mick for putting him through such a scary ordeal.

"Hold on . . . wait a minute," said Mick. "I didn't think of old Zack when I pulled your hair, but I believe we scared Uncle Charley half to death with your carrying on. I think he still believes old Zack was the problem."

"And you scared the young lads half to death as well. I don't think they slept at all last night!"

"We'll have to tell them the truth, but let's string Uncle Charley along. It was his stories about old Zack that scared you in the first place, wasn't it?"

"Yah . . . I guess it was," replied Dan, lightening up a little. "A little of his own medicine won't hurt him none either. What d' yah plan to do?"

Mick folded his arms and leaned a little forward as he explained what he had planned.

"We'll put the boys in the spare room tonight, and you can sleep in Joey's bed. We'll tie some tin cans together, tie a string on each end, and run it up through the ceiling to our beds. You can pull them across the floor to one side of the room, and I'll pull them back. That should keep Uncle Charley's hair standin' up for most of the night."

Dan's face lit up with a grin. He liked the idea of not being the only one that would be made a fool of.

"Sounds good to me. A little hair from the dog that bit yuh will also cure yuh, is what Paw always says." Dan nodded his approval as he thought about it.

"You'll have tuh tell the boys," Dan said over his shoulder as he turned to re-enter the house, "or yuh'll scare the livin' daylights out of them again. And tell them to keep it to themselves."

As Mick was closing the screen door, he could hear Joey and Billy descending the stairs. They both stopped at the bottom and looked around the corner as if they expected to see old Zack standing there.

Mick, sensing the boys were a bit on edge, asked them to step outside with him for a minute.

"Can you wait till I get my boots on?" asked Billy, "'cause I'm goin' home right now!" His voice rang with the determination that clearly stated there would be no changing his mind.

Billy had enjoyed about as much as he could stand, and the only solution was to be up and gone before it got dark again.

"Can't you wait for breakfast?" asked Dan.

"Nope," said Billy, "I ain't hangin' around here any longer."

Mick started to chuckle, "Yuh afraid of old Zack?"

"Don't know," said Billy, as he laced up his boots, "but last night somethin' scared me half to death, and I ain't waitin' around to lose the other half."

Mick chuckled quietly while Billy did his boots up, then he held the door open for the boys to exit.

"Before you go runnin' home," Mick said to Billy, "I have somethin' to tell yuh. The ruckus you heard last night was caused by me tying a string in Dan's hair. He was sleeping at the table, so I blew the light out, then went upstairs and pulled on the string. When he opened his eyes and saw it was dark, he tried to feel around to see who was pullin' his hair. When he couldn't find anybody, he remembered the stories of old Zack and thought it must be him and scared himself silly."

By this time Joey was shaking his head and laughing, "Mick, you are an idiot, a sunburnt idiot. You scared Dan and the both of us out of about seven years' growth."

"That's okay, 'cause he's tall enough anyways, and you fellas still have lots of time tuh make it up," laughed Mick.

"You not only scared the livin' daylights out ov Billy and me, but I think Uncle Charley is still too scared to get out of bed."

Billy was standing there with a forced smile, still not sure if he could trust Mick's story of what had happened last night. Things like this never happened at home, and right now he had the gut feeling that was exactly where he should be.

Mick looked at Billy, "You don't have to go home, there's nothin' here that's gonna hurt yuh." Mick's voice was reassuring as he reached over and ruffled Billy's hair.

"We were just havin' fun, and now that we got Uncle Charley on edge, we're gonna play some tricks on him tonight."

Mick's efforts had won out. Billy was ready to believe his story and get in on the fun, and it always felt better when the shoe was on the other foot.

"What are yuh gonna do tonight?" asked Billy, his face showing a real smile.

Mick explained to the boys what he had in mind and told them not to be afraid, and not to dare tell Uncle Charley.

"I won't," said Billy, "and now that I know what you're up to, I won't be afraid."

So the mischievous troop headed back to the house, their hearts set on nonsense and anxious to get on with it.

Realizing the boys were up and things seemed to be on the safe side, Charley decided it was time for him to roll out as well. The situation Charley found himself in, was that he not only told the scary stories, but he believed them to be true, and this made him the perfect target for the boys and their nonsense.

Charley entered the downstairs room with a "Good morning, fellas," and went straight to the wash basin and washed his hands and face. Taking the towel, he dried himself, and said nothing about last night's events. He did not want to hear about it or discuss it with anyone.

Dan had started the fire, and now he and Mick were heading out to do the morning chores. This left Uncle Charley to set the table and get breakfast ready. The boys were sitting on the couch discussing their plans for the day. All seemed normal, but Uncle Charley had the gut feeling there was a lot more going on than met the eye. Things were way too normal after last night's commotion, but he wasn't going to be the one to bring it up or talk about it. He believed it was best to let sleeping dogs lie.

With breakfast over, and the dishes cleared away, Uncle Charley was feeling more at ease.

Speaking to the boys, he said, "Why don't you two fellas take a basket an go fetch me some apples so I kin make some applesauce for dessert?"

"You can make applesauce?" questioned Billy, his face beaming.

"You bet I kin. I live by myself so I have t' do my own cookin'. A man ain't completely helpless just 'cause there ain't a woman around. I may not be able tuh cook like Grandma did, but I kin still cook. An' I kin cook most anything yuh 'd want, except for kidney pie!"

"Don't think I'd care for it anyways," said Billy, sounding a little disgusted with the idea.

"Speakin' ov Grandma, let me tell yuh a poem that my mother used to tell me about Grandma. She said,

> I love muh grandma's cookies and I love her apple pie.
> And I love the way she scolds me with
>   that twinkle in her eye.
> I love the way she hugs me when she holds me on her knee.
> And I love those little secrets that she tells tuh only me.
>
> I love tuh go tuh Grandma's house
>   when skies are dull and gray,
> 'cause the love that comes from Grandma's
>   heart drives all the clouds away.
> I really love my grandma, she's the best in all the land.
> And I love the name they gave her, 'cause
>   my grandma's really GRAND."

"That's a nice poem," said Billy, with a big smile on his face. "Grandmas are really nice people!"

"Now, you fellas go get some apples, and while yuh're gone I'm a gonna have a shave."

Uncle Charley walked over to the stove, picked up the kettle, and poured hot water into the wash basin. After placing the kettle back on the stove, he put the washcloth in the hot water. Then he fastened one end of his razor strop to a nail in the wall, and took his straight razor, unfolded it, and sharpened it on the razor strop. After running it up and down a few times he set the razor down and took the washcloth out of the hot water. Wringing it out, he placed the hot cloth over his face and held it there for as long as he could stand it. He believed the heat would soften the whiskers and make it easier to shave. Putting the cloth down, he picked up the shaving brush, dipped it in the water, and then swirled it around inside his shaving mug. Once he obtained a foaming lather, he brushed it on his face. Putting the brush down, he picked up his razor, tested the edge with his thumb, and then proceeded to remove both the lather and the whiskers, leaving his face smooth and clean.

Upon finding an old basket, the boys were gone in a flash to get the apples, and in a few minutes they were back and all out of breath. By then Charley was clean-shaven and ready to go to work.

"Here yuh go!" they said to Uncle Charley as they handed him the basket.

"Well, thank yuh." Charley took the basket and ran his hand over the apples. Picking one up, he looked at it and said, "Well, fellas, what in the world do yuh expect me t' make with these things?"

The boys looked up at him, wondering what was wrong.

"Applesauce!" said Joey. "Just like yuh said."

"Well . . . let me tell yuh, that ain't a-gonna happen, 'cause these apples are harder than a hammer-headed woodpecker's bill."

"Where did yuh get them?" inquired Mick.

"From the tree behind the barn," replied Joey.

"Those are winter apples!" declared Mick. "They're no good till the frost hits 'em in the fall. Not only are they hard as a rock, but sour as rhubarb this time of the year. Go to the tree at the end of the cow pasture and get him some of those white apples; they'll make good sauce. And give these tuh the pigs, maybe they'll eat 'em."

"Doubt it," said Uncle Charley, "unless yuh put the sugar to 'em, 'cause the way they are right now, they'd be sour enough tuh make a pig squeal!"

Again the boys were off, wanting to get on with the making of the applesauce.

The cow pasture had poles across the gap in the fence where they were about to enter. Joey tossed the basket over the poles and he and Billy slid under. About twenty yards out into the pasture, Joey stopped dead in his tracks.

"What's wrong?" asked Billy.

"I forgot about that ol' bull — see him standin' there under the tree . . . beside the cows?

"Paw says we're not to trust him now that he's getting older; he might go for yuh."

With that, the two boys turned and headed back for the gap on a dead run. They couldn't have travelled any faster had the bull been hard on their heels. When they reached the gap, Joey threw the basket over the poles as they both dropped and slid under them, raising a cloud of dust as they went. On the other side, they dusted themselves off, and Billy said, "I guess that was a close call."

"A close call?" said Joey. "That old bull didn't even move!"

"Oh yah? If you'd o' forgotten till we were halfway across the pasture and he'd decided to chase us, we'd o' be 'n done like a dinner!"

"Okay . . . I guess you're right," agreed Joey. "Now we'll have t' walk all the way around."

"And when we do get there, I bet there'll be a bear up the apple tree," added Billy. "Our luck hasn't been very good today."

"If there is one, you just show him your bear, and he'll hightail it outa there," said Joey with a grin.

"My bear?' questioned Billy. "What's my bear?"

"Drop your pants and show him your bare ass," laughed Joey.

"And you called Mick a sunburnt idiot; you 're worse than he'll ever be," laughed Billy.

No longer in a hurry, the boys were taking their time, laughing and talking, stopping to pick some berries here and there, slowly making their way around the field. Upon reaching the back of the pasture, Joey pointed out the apple tree.

"There you go, lots ov apples on 'r, too. This shouldn't take long."

Joey climbed up on a big rock at the edge of the tree and pulled down a branch loaded with apples. Billy picked what he could reach from the bottom of the branch, and Joey picked from the top. He held the branch with one hand, and handed the apples down to Billy with the other. In no time the basket was full and the boys were merrily on their way, laughing, talking, and joking, fully enjoying the wonderful summer morning.

In a little while they were back with the second basket of apples. "That's more like it," said Uncle Charley. "Now I can get down t' business and get the show on the road. All I need is some sugar and a little cinnamon and we're good t' go."

Charley found the things he needed and proceeded with making the applesauce.

Billy and Joey were leaning on the table, watching him as he peeled the apples.

Uncle Charley took note of what they were doing, and he figured there were better ways in which they could be spending their time.

"Now why don't you two fellas go on over to the potato patch, instead o' standin' there gaze'n at me, and help Mick pick some o' them bugs. There's a couple o' old tin cans there on the winda sill that yuh can use!"

"Don't really care much for them bugs," said Joey, the lack of enthusiasm showing in his voice.

"Yuh'll care about havin' some potatoes come wintertime, and I'll sure bet a dollar on that."

"Okay, Billy, let's go pick some bugs," said Joey, halfheartedly, but yielding to Uncle Charley's method of persuasion.

They took the cans from off the windowsill and started for the door.

"Now don't forget t' put some coal oil in the bottom ov the cans."

"Why?" asked Joey.

"'Cause the bugs 'll crawl back out if yuh don't. And a good dose of coal oil'll help tuh turn their runners up. Then when yuh're dun, yuh can touch a match to it; that'll finish 'em off."

With their instructions complete, they headed for the potato patch; not really enthused about it, but it did need doing.

Mick stood up and watched the lackadaisical approach of the two boys, but glad to see them coming to help.

"Start at the far side," instructed Mick, "I've got the first five rows done on this side."

"Many bugs?" asked Joey.

"Enough to keep you two busy for a week!"

"I ain't staying that long!" declared Billy, not wanting any part of the job in the first place.

"Aw, come on," said Joey, "isn't this fun?"

"'Bout as much as a toothache."

The boys started where they were told, one on each side of the row, and with them picking from both sides, there was little chance of a bug escaping.

"Pick 'm as clean as you can, but don't worry if you miss a few," said Mick. "I'm gonna give 'em a good dose ov DDT after we're done pickin'. That should take care of any that we miss, and kill any eggs that they've laid."

At the end of the potato patch stood the old horse-drawn cultivator. It was used to kill the weeds and hill the potatoes. This method covered the potatoes with dirt so the sunlight wouldn't reach them. If it did, the skin would turn green and the potatoes would have a bitter taste.

It seemed like no time till the boys had finished the first row and started on the second. They were moving right along when the welcome sound of Uncle Charley's voice fell on their ears.

"Dinner's ready, come and get it or I'll throw it out!" Then he added, "Don't forget to burn the bugs!"

"How come he wants 'em burnt? I thought he made soup out o' them," said Billy.

"No," laughed Joey, "it was bedbugs that he made the soup out ov."

"Ohh yah . . . I forgot."

After torching the potato bugs and making sure there were no escapees, they made their way back to the house.

With their hands washed and their place found at the table, Uncle Charley filled their bowls with fresh, homemade potato soup. "There's fried eggs and bologna with pork and beans waitin' for yuh when the soup is done. And there is applesauce for dessert. Fellas, yuh got enough good chuck there tuh make a king smile."

After they were done eating, Billy spoke up, "Uncle Charley, the applesauce was really good."

"Well, thank yuh," said Uncle Charley. "Don't forget you fellas helped in the makin' of it."

"Yah, and if that ol' bull would have got us, there wouldn't be any," said Billy.

"You guys weren't foolin' around with that old bull, were yuh?" questioned Mick in a very stern voice. "When I put the salt lick out the other day, he stood there watchin' me, bawlin' an pawin' sand. I wouldn't trust him for a minute!"

"See, I told yuh we were lucky," said Billy, looking at Joey.

"What do yuh mean, you were lucky?" questioned Mick, his eyes hard and fast on Joey.

"We started to cross the cow pasture and I remembered that Paw said not to trust that old bull."

"Yah," said Billy, "we weren't long in hightailin' 'r out o' there!"

"The way things had be 'n goin' for us, Billy figured there would probably be a bear up the apple tree when we got there. So I told him that if there was, he'd just have t' show 'm his bear and the bear'd run."

"His bear?" questioned Uncle Charley, as if he was missing something. "What 'n the world is his bear?"

"My bare ass!" offered Billy.

"Oohhh, my goodness," laughed Uncle Charley. "Where in the world did yuh get that idea from?"

At this point, Dan was turning blue from choking. Laughing and swallowing tea at the same time wasn't a good idea.

Mick was chuckling as he spoke. "Now Uncle Charley, do yuh really have to ask?"

"Joey told me!" came the eager reply.

"And where did you get it from?" asked Uncle Charley, still chuckling as he was talking.

"I dunno," replied Joey. "Just something I'd heard somebody say."

"Well," said Uncle Charley, "that reminds me ov a story ol' man Murphy told me 'bout a Yankee that stopped at his store. This here Yank thought he'd come up tuh Canada tuh hunt moose. Well, he gets in with the Hix gang and goes across Bark Lake. One sunny afternoon, when they were done early and things were quiet, he decides tuh go for a walk. And away he went, all by himself, and if he didn't come across this big ol' moose. And he had one big set o' horns on him, so he just couldn't resist. Never thinking as to how late in the day it was, and how far from camp he was, he up and, "bang," down goes the moose.

"Well, he gets all excited 'bout everything and starts to do the guttin', an' that's a big job for just one man. Anyways, he goes at it with pretty good enthusiasm. It takes him quite awhile, and when he gets the job done, he realizes just how late in the day it was. So he starts tuh thinking as to what he's gonna do. It would soon be dark and he wouldn't be able tuh find his way back tuh camp. He had no matches, so he couldn't start a fire, and after the sun goes down it gets cold enough t' freeze the balls off a brass monkey. And he wasn't dressed warm enough tuh stand the cold all night without some protection."

"Whoa, Uncle Charley, whoa!" cried Billy. "What in the world is a brass monkey?"

"Well," said Uncle Charley, "bein' you fellas have never be 'n tuh sea, maybe I kin help yuh understand. What they call a brass monkey, is some kinda dish-shaped piece o' brass that is fastened tuh the deck ov a ship. It's placed beside the cannons, and the cannonballs are stacked on the piece o' brass. When it gets really cold, the brass shrinks, an' the balls roll off. That is when they say it's cold enough tuh freeze the balls off a brass monkey."

"Okay," said Billy, "I think I get it, but why call it a monkey?"

"Darned if I know," said Uncle Charley, "but it was probably a smarter man than me that named it, so what do yuh say if we just leave it at that!"

"I want tuh hear the rest ov the story," said Dan. "What happened tuh the yank?"

"Now where was I?" asked Uncle Charley.

"He had just gutted the moose and realized he had tuh spend the night there," said Dan, "and he was getting cold."

"Yah ... that's right.

"So he gets tuh thinking, that ol' moose carcass is still warm, and the cavity is big enough for him to curl up in. So he gets inside ov that ol' moose and goes tuh sleep. Well . . . in the mornin' he tries tuh stretch, and he can't. He can't even move. Why that ol' moose had froze as hard as a rock durin' the night, an' he couldn't even so much as wiggle inside the thing. He tried tuh twist an' turn, but it was no use. That ol' moose had been nice an' warm when he crawled in, but after freezing all night it was as cold as ice. An' he knew that if he didn't get out pretty soon he'd freeze t' death, 'cause he was already startin' to take chills.

"The boys would be out lookin' for him, but with no snow on the ground it'd be pretty hard to track him. It wouldn't do any good tuh try 'n yell from inside the moose, and he couldn't reach his gun to fire a shot to guide them to him. He was done like a dinner an' he knew it. It was all over but for the prayin'."

"How did he get out?" interrupted Billy. He couldn't believe what he was hearing. This man was going to die inside the moose.

"Well . . . ," said Uncle Charley, "they say that before a man dies his whole life flashes before his eyes. And he remembered votin' for the Democrats; and when he thought about what he had done, he felt so small that he slid right out that little hole in the back end o' that ol' moose. Now let me tell yuh . . . he sure did!"

Both Mick and Dan let out a sigh of relief and began to laugh as they realized Uncle Charley was just telling a tall tale.

"You sure had us taken in on that one, and right to the end. It was a pretty good story, and believable as well, especially when you said he was with the Hix gang," laughed Dan.

Billy turned to Joey, "Could he really do that?"

"Do what?"

"Slip out through . . . that . . . little hole?" asked Billy in amazement.

"I guess he could, if Uncle Charley said so."

"Wow, that's pretty darn small."

"You bet," said Joey with a smile, realizing he had Billy believing it could actually happen.

9

Two Little Buddies

"Time tuh clean up," said Uncle Charley as he started removing things from the table.

Joey tugged on Billy's sleeve and pointed to the door. Once outside, he whispered, "Come on, let's get out of here before they give us somethin' to do."

"What do yuh want to do?"

"Not sure," said Joey, "but how about if we go and see if we can find some blackberries."

"Okay!" agreed Billy, and off they went, just as fast as their legs could take them, up past the barn and down the lane to the fields. Old Jake was running along beside them, his tongue hanging out the side of his mouth. Once they were a good ways from the house, they stopped to catch their breath.

"Where do we find the berries?" asked Billy, bending forward to catch his breath.

"Down there, by the edge of the bush," pointed Joey. "They grow a lot better if they're in some shade."

"Okay," said Billy, "but what if there's a bear down there?"

Joey laughed, "You know what to do."

"Don't think so," replied Billy. "Can't run with my pants down."

The two boys took off for the berry patch, running and laughing. Old Jake ran on ahead of them, stopping and looking back to make sure they were still coming.

The boys stopped to catch their breath and continue their conversation.

"Ain't no bears 'round here," said Joey. "Paw would shoot 'em if he found them hangin' around. He don't trust them if they're stickin' too close to the buildings; he says they're up to no good. Probably lookin' tuh take a calf, or a small pig, 'r somethin'."

"Don't really care to be around the real ones," said Billy; "don't mind a teddy bear."

"You still sleep with a teddy bear?" Joey asked, as a smile lit up his face.

"No!" Billy said with disgust. "And I never did either!"

"Okay, okay . . . now don't get mad, I was just checkin'," said Joey in his usual teasing manner.

"Ever get scared by a bear?" asked Billy.

"No, but Mick sure did!" came the reply, followed by a smile.

"What happened?"

"He was fixin' some fence last fall . . . behind the ol' cow pasture. Anyways, he was leaning against an oak tree, havin' a bit ov a rest. Oak nuts an stuff was fall 'n down, an' he figured it was squirrels up there lookin' for nuts, so he hauled off an hit the tree with the side of the axe tuh see if he could scare 'em. He'd no more 'n hit the tree when down drops a big black bear right beside him. He throws the axe an' heads for the house as hard as he could go. When he reached the house, he was all skinned up from trippin' and fallin'. His shirt was ripped and he was covered in mud."

"What'd the bear do?" asked Billy, having stopped dead in his tracks and his eyes wide with amazement.

"Don't know, he never stopped tuh look back. He just high-balled 'r for the house as hard as he could go."

Joey was smiling as he told the story. It was fun telling about it, as long as he wasn't the one doing the running.

"I don't blame him, 'cause that's what I would do. That's if I wasn't too scared tuh run," offered Billy.

"Paw went back with the rifle tuh get the axe, an' said there was no sign ov the bear. Guess he took off in the other direction, probably more scared than Mick was."

"Yah," said Billy, "That reminds me of somethin' that happened to Paw. He was up on the mountain huntin' cows one evening. He had Tom and Peter with him. Old Bingo was runnin' all over the place, just lookin' for trouble. When all ov a sudden he starts to tie-iee. Paw said he could hear him comin' down through the bush just a rippin' on 'r, squealin' and barkin'. He figured the dog musta run into a bear, and sure enough the ol' bear was right on his heels. Ol' Bingo run around behind Paw and stopped. Then he sat down and growled at the bear. Guess he figured Paw would protect him. Paw said the ol' bear stopped about ten feet in front ov him, with his hackles all standin' up, and Paw didn't even have a gun with him. Tom and Peter were about eight and ten years old at that time. Tom got so scared that he fainted, but Peter said he wasn't that stupid. He never seen a bear that close before so he wanted to get a good look at 'm.

"Paw said the ol' bear looked at him for a minute or so, then slowly backed away and headed on back to wherever she had come from. He figured she must ov had cubs and just wanted tuh chase the dog away. I tell yuh, Paw always took a gun with him when he went tuh the bush after that.

"He said if he would ov had a gun that day he'd a shot old Bingo right there on the spot. He said that ol' bear scared him half tuh death, comin' at him like that.

"Okay, where do we find the berries?" asked Billy, as they continued their journey to the edge of the bush.

"Over along those trees, where it's kinda shady; they grow better there," said Joey, as he pointed with his finger to some low bushes under a stand of white birch.

The boys, having great expectations, hurried on over to the spot.

"Yah, you're right," agreed Billy, "there's lots ov 'em here and they're big and juicy."

After eating a handful, Joey said to Billy, "Do yuh know what the elderberry said to the younger berry?"

"No, what did he say?"

"I'll kick yuhr raspberry till it's black an' blueberry."

This caused Billy to start laughing again. "Berries can't talk, you corkscrewed dummy!"

"But they can pick yuhr seat!"

"That's only if yuh sit on 'em."

"Do yuh know why they're called 'wait a minute bushes'?" asked Joey.

"No, why?"

"Because they're so friendly, that when you walk through them, they grab ahold of yuh and say, 'wait a minute.'"

Billy chuckled, "They don't say nothin', they just hang on tuh yuh while your tryin' tuh get untangled."

"Did you know yuh can pick yuhr finger, an' yuh can pick yuhr nose, but yuh can't pick yuhr relatives?"

"Darn good job, or yuh'd have no place tuh go," said Billy, laughing out loud.

"Guess I'd have tuh come and live with you."

"That's what you think; there ain't no corkscrewed dummy coming to live with me," was Billy's reply, while still laughing.

The berries were big and juicy and hanging from the canes in abundance.

After the boys had their fill, they sauntered on over to the laneway, slowly making their way back to the barn. Just as they were about to top the little hill that would put them in view of the house, Joey said, "Let's stop here for a rest, 'cause if Mick sees us, he'll put us to doin' somethin'."

Joey plopped himself down beside the stone fence. The cows had done a good job of keeping the grass short as they travelled the laneway to the bush and back.

"Watch out for fresh cow plasters," warned Joey, as Billy went to sit down.

"Ever step in one with your bare feet?" Billy asked.

"Nope, I always wear my boots. I don't like walking around outside in my bare feet just for that very reason."

"I did once," said Billy, "and it feels awful squishin' up between your toes."

"Did yuh lick it off?"

"No, you idiot," was Billy's response as he started laughing. "But I did wash it off in the water trough, and Paw gave me the dickens for doin' it. He said the horses didn't want to drink the water after that, so I had to go and clean out the trough."

"Yah... they're a pretty clean animal, not likely they'll drink any bad water. Paw says that if a horse will drink the water, it won't harm anybody else either."

The boys were lying on their backs, hands behind their heads, with their caps shading their eyes. They were both chewing on a straw of Timothy hay while gazing up at the sky. They were a picture of peace and contentment with the wildflowers growing all around them. Much like ol' Tom Sawyer and Huckleberry Finn, except these fellows didn't have a river raft to lie on.

They were quiet for a few minutes, then Joey broke the silence, "Ever notice the clouds?"

"Sure, I see 'em every day," came the casual reply.

"That's not what I meant!" replied Joey in disgust.

"Then what did yuh mean?"

"Well... sometimes it's like yuh see faces and things in them.

"See that one over there?" Joey pointed with his finger. "A man's face, with a long nose; reminds me ov ol' Dan Ratacatakuskie."

"Yah, it does, too," laughed Billy, "but now it's movin' and it's changin' as it moves. Kinda weird, isn't it?"

"Yah, sometimes I sit and watch 'm for hours and get tuh see all kinds of things."

"That's if Mick doesn't ketch yuh at it!" laughed Billy.

"That's for sure, he'd put me tuh doin' somthin'."

"D' yuh think God makes all those things we see in the clouds?" asked Billy as he gazed up at the sky.

"I don't know, maybe He does... I bet you don't know God's name?" questioned Joey in a more serious tone.

"What d' yuh mean, do I know His name?" asked Billy, expecting some kind of nonsense.

"Everybody has a name. Do yuh know God's name?" Joey was obviously eager to show off his knowledge about God.

"Didn't know He had a name; all I ever heard Him called was God."

"No, He has a name just like everybody else," insisted Joey.

"He does?" questioned Billy, his eyes wide with amazement. "Then what's His name?"

"His name is Andy," said Joey as casual as if everyone in the world should know it.

"Andy!" exclaimed Billy, staring at Joey. "Who in the world said it was Andy?"

"That's what Uncle Charley said His name is."

"How would he know that?"

"He said that when he was out West, they used t' go to a place called The Mission House. Times were hard, so when they went to town, they'd go there to eat. The meals were free but yuh had t' listen to 'm preach and sing. They preached about being born again, and having tuh get saved if yuh wanted to go tuh heaven, and stuff like that, and they sang about God being Andy."

"Never heard the like o' that before — what did they sing?"

"He said the song was, 'Andy walks with me, Andy talks with me, Andy tells me I am His own.'"

Billy, who was looking at Joey in a very serious manner, now burst out laughing. His arms went across his stomach, then his knees pulled up to meet them, as he laughed his heart out. With tears rolling down his cheeks, Billy looked up at Joey and said, "You idiot, it's 'AND HE' . . . it ain't Andy!"

"It's what?" asked Joey, feeling a little embarrassed.

"It's, 'AND . . . HE . . . walks with me,' not Andy walks with me." Billy could hardly get the words out he was laughing so hard. While wiping the tears from his face, Billy said, "Uncle Charley is just pullin' your leg. There ain't no God named Andy!"

"Are you sure?" asked Joey, looking a little embarrassed while forcing a grin.

"Yah, I'm sure. Maw sings that song all the time, and I hear it on the radio. It's 'and . . . He' walks with me, not Andy walks with me."

Billy rolled over on his back wiping the tears from his eyes with the back of his hand.

"Some people sure don't know nothin'," laughed Billy, trying hard to gain control.

"Well, it sounded good at the time," added Joey, trying to justify his mistake. He rolled over on his back with his hands behind his head, looking up at the sky like nothing had happened.

By this time, old Jake had had enough of the sitting around. So he got up and walked over and gave Joey a big lick up the side of the face. It was the perfect target, as Joey had his hands behind his head, leaving his face unprotected.

"Get outa here, you ol' dummy," was Joey's response to the sloppy kiss as he pushed the old dog away and wiped his face with his shirt.

Billy couldn't miss the golden opportunity: He chuckled and said, "Ever notice them ol' dogs usually lick their back end before they give it to yuh in the face?"

"Uuuugh, you would have t' say that, now, wouldn't yuh!" said Joey as he gave his face another wipe.

"Yah," laughed Billy, "Paw says ol' Rover 'll lick his back end for half an hour an then travel for the next twenty minutes look'n for somebody tuh lick in the face!"

"I said, get outa here!" Joey gave ol' Jake a swat up the side of the head as he closed in for seconds.

"Now get, or I'll wire your stupid ol' mouth shut!" Joey's voice echoed his disgust as ol' Jake backed away.

"Don't be cruel," laughed Billy, "he loves yuh."

"Yah . . . well, I love him too, but he ain't goin' around lickin' my face, that's for sure," said Joey, as he wiped his face for the third time.

Ol' Jake walked over by the fence and lay down, looking rejected and disgusted with the boys for not getting up and moving on.

"Did yuhr Paw really say he licks his back end, or did he say somethin' else?" asked Joey with a smile on his face.

"Well," laughed Billy, "he usually says he's lickin' his arse, but that's only if Maw ain't around. If he said that in the house she'd tell him tuh go tuh the horse stable if he wants tuh talk like that."

"That's what my Maw says, too, and Paw says that's okay 'cause the horses don't mind."

"Good thing the horses can't talk or they'd be usin' that kind ov language as well."

"Paw said he had a horse that could talk."

"No way!" said Billy, in disbelief.

"Yah, he really could," said Joey, nodding his head up and down, trying to look serious.

"What'd he say?"

"Paw would ask 'm if he'd like some oats, an that ol' horse would lift up his tail and say, 'pheuuw.'"

"You jackass . . . that's breakin' wind, not talkin'," laughed Billy, tears streaming down his face.

"Got yuh on that one," laughed Joey.

"I wonder where they got those words in the first place. Yuh know, 'arse' an' 'wee-haw,' an' stuff like that. Paw always says wee-haw if he jams his fingers, or somethin' scares him."

"Maybe our grandparents taught 'em that kinda stuff."

"Never heard my grandpaw say anything like that," said Joey. "He was always nice. Gave me candies when we went to see him, and he liked to tell stories about things he did when he was younger. I liked tuh listen to him 'cause they were always about bears an' huntin' and stuff like that. He used tuh trap an' paddle a canoe, camp out in the bush for a week at a time. Said they would spear whitefish down at the river in the fall, an' get bags full. It always seemed like they had a lot ov fun doin' those things. Said sometimes when they got mixed up with the bears it got a bit scary, but that didn't happen very often. I never got tuh see much ov him, an' he went an' died about two years ago."

"What'd he die from," asked Billy, "old age?"

"Paw said he thinks it was Grandma's cookin'."

"Your grandma's cookin'?" questioned Billy in disbelief.

"Yah, she'd fry pork so hard the dog couldn't chew it, and then expected him to eat it, an' he had hardly any teeth left." Joey's voice was low and sympathetic.

"That is pretty tough," said Billy, taking it seriously. "And that's probably what killed him."

They paused for a minute, then Billy spoke. "I don't remember my grandparents; they were all dead before I was old enough tuh get tuh know them. I've no idea what kind ov language they used. Paw might ov picked it up from them."

"What'd they die from?" asked Joey.

"I don't know, but I don't think it was from somebody's cookin'!"

After thinking for a minute, Joey asked Billy, "Do you know where 'shit' comes from?"

Billy, who seemed to always be ready for a good laugh, broke out laughing like he was about to burst at the seams.

"You flat-headed dummy, everybody knows where that stuff comes from!"

"No! I didn't mean that, I mean the *word* 'shit,'" said Joey, in defence of what he had said.

"I have no idea," declared Billy, "but I bet you think that you do."

"Yah, I do, Uncle Charley told me."

"This should be good," declared Billy. "I hope it's better than that Andy story."

"No, this one is really true."

"Okay, then tell me."

"It means, 'store high in transit.'"

"Whats that supposed tuh mean?" asked Billy, as he rolled over on his stomach, propping himself up on his elbows while pulling a blade of grass through his fingers.

"Well, you take the first letter from each word and you have S-H-I-T."

"Yah, but where in the world did yuh get the, 'store high in transit' from?"

"Well, Uncle Charley said that they used to bag horse manure and sell it for fertilizer, and if they sent it on a ship they marked it, 'store high in transit,' so it wouldn't get wet. You know that if it gets wet when it's packed tight it will start to heat, just like the manure pile in the spring. You know, when yuh 'r forkin' it into the manure spreader, and yuh get half way down the pile, your feet start tuh get hot from standin' on it.

"There was always water in the bottom ov them ol' wooden ships so yuh had tuh store the horse manure high so it wouldn't get wet and start a fire."

"So, what if it did, there was always lots ov water around tuh put it out."

"Wouldn't help much after yuh burnt a hole in the boat."

"Okay . . . if that's all it means, then it isn't really a bad word."

"I guess not."

"Then why do I keep getting my ears cuffed for saying it?"

"'Cause not everybody knows what it means, so now yuh can tell 'em."

"Don't think it'll help much; Maw'll just think I made it up and she'll give it to me anyways."

Joey looked up at the sky for a minute or two, then he said, "A couple of years ago, Mick an Dan figger'd they were old enough tuh start swearin'. I heard them talkin' about it every morning before they went downstairs for breakfast. Mick was goin' tuh say something with 'hell' in it, and Dan was gonna say something with 'damn.'

"They talked about it for a while, then one morning they worked up enough courage tuh give 'r a try. I got up and followed them down tuh see what was gonna happen.

"Maw asked Mick what he wanted for breakfast, and he said, 'Oh, what the hell, I think I'll have some cornflakes.' Maw stopped dead in her tracks, then her face got red. She grabbed him by the hair o' the head an' pulled him off the chair, smacked his ass with the other hand all the way tuh the stairs. Then she shouted at him from the foot ov the stairs, 'Now, I'll have none of that kind of language around here!'

"Then she turned tuh Dan an' said, 'Okay, young man, what would you like for breakfast?' He looked like he was scared half tuh death, his bottom lip was quivering, an' he sorta got all mixed-up an' said, 'It damn well won't be cornflakes, that's for sure.'

"He got pretty much the same treatment as Mick. I haven't heard either one of them try it since."

Billy was laughing his heart out, "You are all a bunch o' half-baked idiots. I bet there's not another bunch like you fellas anywhere else in the world."

"You sure seem tuh like hangin' around with us," spoke up Joey in his own defence.

"That's 'cause yuh make me laugh with all your nonsense."

After Billy stopped laughing, he asked Joey, "Did you ever get a good lickin'?"

"Yah, once when I was just a little kid, about five years old."

"What in the world did yuh do tuh get it?"

"I wanted some chicken an' dumplin's."

"What's wrong with that?"

"Nothin', till yuh kill the pet hen!"

"You killed your pet hen?" exclaimed Billy in disbelief.

"Well, . . . sort ov.

"It was in the wintertime, an' Paw had a bunch ov wood piled outside. It was just in blocks and it needed splittin'. The ol' splittin' axe was there, and when Maw said, 'No, we aren't gonna kill any hens,' I said, then I'd do it myself, and went out to get the axe. Maw sent Dan out tuh drive it into a block ov wood so I couldn't get it.

"Soon as Dan went back in the house I got a stick and hit the axe handle up and down till it worked its way loose. Then I put it on the bobsleigh and headed for the barn.

"I couldn't ketch the hens 'cause they could run faster than me. So when I came to the old pet hen, I grabbed her. She was so old she couldn't run — so she'd just squat down and let yuh pick her up. So I picked her up and headed for the bobsleigh.

I wasn't big enough to hold the axe with one hand and the hen with the other, and I had tuh get her neck over somethin' so I could chop her head off. And every time I put her down she'd walk away. So, I got this idea. I lifted the rack on the sleigh and stuffed her under it. I put her neck over the bunk and then I let the rack back down. Her head was stuck so she couldn't pull it back out and her neck was between the boards ov the rack. Now I could use both hands tuh lift the axe and chop her head off. Seemed like a good idea at the time, so I let her have it. The old axe was so dull it wouldn't have cut hot butter; it just bruised her neck and made 'r squawk. The ol' rooster heard the racket and came runnin' at me. So, I dropped the axe and headed for the house with that ol' rooster right tight on my heels. I never stopped till I got in the house, an' Maw asked what I was runnin' from. I said, nothin'. Then

Mick come in with the hen. He was in the cow stable and heard her squawkin' and come to see what was wrong. He realized what had happened and he finished her off. I got chicken and dumplins for dinner that day, but I had to eat 'm standin' up."

"Why was that?" asked Billy.

"'Cause my ass was too sore tuh sit down!"

"I guess yuh got a pretty good tune 'n, did yuh?"

"It was one that I'll remember for a long time!" laughed Joey.

Again the boys got quiet as if they had run out of things to say. Joey reached over and hugged ol' Jake, who was looking kind of lonely and rejected. Billy had picked a daisy and was slowly pulling off one petal at a time and tossing it in the air, watching it float away in the breeze.

"She loves me, she loves me not," said Joey.

"Dummy," said Billy in disgust.

"You tryin' tuh find out if Shelly loves yuh?" teased Joey.

"Shelly! Are you nuts? She's uglier than a brush fence!"

"So, Paw says beauty is only skin deep."

"Yah, well you go right ahead an' skin her an' I bet she'll still be ugly!"

"Awh, come on, you like her," insisted Joey.

"I like her 'cause she's nice, not because she's pretty!" was Billy's defence.

"What's the difference?"

"You gone totally blind, dumb, and stupid?" asked Billy in disgust.

"Yuh know that I'm not as stupid as I look," said Joey, backing off a little because Billy was getting fed up with his teasing.

"Thank God for that!" came the quick reply.

"I'm just teasin'." said Joey with a grin.

"Well yuh can quit anytime. And what about you an' Mary?" now Billy was making his comeback.

"Me an' Mary? I tell yuh, if yuh ever tried to kiss that gal, I bet she'd tear the lips right off yuh. I never seen a person with such a wicked set a teeth as hers. I'll bet that girl could eat an apple right through a picket fence!"

Billy was laughing as he responded, "You are nuts, you are absolutely nuts."

"Well, does she not have one wicked set ov teeth in her mouth?"

"Yah, she sure does. They're shaped a lot like the cowcatcher on the front end ov a freight train. Maw says they must have gotten that shape from her suckin' 'r thumb!"

"I don't care what she was suckin', she sure ain't kissin' me," laughed Joey. "If yuh ever got your teeth tangled up with hers it'd take a dentist a week tuh break yuh loose!"

After the boys stopped laughing at their nonsense and realized they had run out of conversation, it was time to go.

"Well, I guess we should go back tuh the house before they come lookin' for us."

"Yah, and then we'll find out what Mick's got planned."

10

Target Practice

Slowly the boys got to their feet and started making their way back to the house. Ol' Jake was happy to be on the move again; he'd run on ahead, stop, and look back to make sure the boys were still coming. As they approached the house, Mick was drawing a pail of water from the well.

"Where have you fellas been all this time?" he asked as he poured the water from the dipping pail into the one he would be taking into the house.

"Oh . . . just lookin' for some berries," offered Joey, casual and unconcerned.

"More like staying away from work," added Mick, tongue-in-cheek.

"We can't be working all the time, yuh know!" said Joey in defence.

"Yah, but while you're relaxin', who's goin' t' do the work?"

"You older fellas — that's what you're here for, isn't it?" Joey was smiling as he said it. He knew Mick only gave him work if he saw that he was just hanging around or if something needed doing.

"Must be nice to be the youngest brother!" offered Mick, still teasing.

"You bet it is, specially if yuh need your back scratched, 'r somethin' like that done."

"Git outa here before I throw a pail ov water on yuh," warned Mick, teasing, with affection in his voice.

"Okay, but remember you told us tuh go."

After going a few steps, Joey turned around and, in his usual pleading voice, he asked, "Can we use your twenty-two? I want to see if Billy can hit anything with it."

"Yah... but yuh better be careful that you don't shoot somebody!"

"Don't worry, I don't want them t' hang me!" Joey replied, knowing what Mick's next line would be, and saying it before he did.

"Don't you worry about that; Paw will have the job done before anyone ever gets near you!"

This Joey knew all too well, and it made him extra careful while handling a gun.

"The shells are in the cupboard in the orange cream jug. Six should be enough." Mick spoke over his shoulder to the boys, as they held the door open for him. He didn't want his little brother to grow up to be lazy, so he made sure that he always had some work to do. But he also knew that he had to have a little fun time with his buddy, especially while Maw and Paw were away.

Uncle Charley had given Mick a single-shot trappers .22 when he was about Joey's age. In Paw's opinion, this gun was just the right size for a young fella to be toting around. Mick and Dan were now using the 30-30, which was considered a man's gun, but they still liked using the .22 for small game and target shooting.

Mick would skin squirrels in the wintertime, then trade the fur at Murphy's store for ammunition. This guaranteed there would always be lots of .22 shells around the house.

Joey went over to the cupboard and counted out six shells, then went into the room where the guns were kept and took the .22 from off the wall.

Now it was time to go out and have some fun with Billy.

Joey took pride in the fact that he was trusted with a gun. He had been taught the importance of knowing how to safely handle one, and the consequence of carelessness. If he was ever caught misusing a gun, he would have trouble sitting down for the next week, plus lose the privilege of handling one.

He would always remember Paw showing him the power of a gun. He had taken a gallon paint can, filled it with water, then put the lid on good and tight. He then placed it at the base of a fence post and shot it with a rifle. The lid lifted to about fifteen feet in the air, and there was a hole in the front of the can about the size of your finger; but the back of the can was blown apart like there had been a stick of dynamite in it. He then looked at Joey and said, "A person is mostly made up of liquid. Once you pull the trigger, it's too late tuh say I'm sorry." This was one demonstration that he would never forget.

Joey walked over and placed a soup can on one of the old cedar posts that supported the dipping pole at the well. After walking back about thirty-five feet, he stopped and put a bullet in the gun. He then handed the gun to Billy with the breech open.

"Okay, when you're ready, shove the bolt ahead an' you're good t' go."

Billy moved one foot in front of the other, while keeping them spread apart. With his balance set, he closed the breech. Slowly the gun reached its level and stopped; then Billy pulled the trigger.

"Craack!" The report of the gun discharging echoed through the trees as the tin can went airborne.

"Got it!" said Billy, quite proud of himself.

"Okay, let's see where yuh hit it."

Billy laid the gun down and they hurried over to where the can lay on the ground.

"Yuh almost missed it; the hole is just at the top and to the side."

"Yah, but I'm not used to your gun, wait till I try it again."

"My turn," said Joey, as he placed the can back on the post. Returning, he picked up the gun. With Billy standing behind him and a little to the side, he pulled back the bolt, ejecting the empty shell. He then placed a live round into the chamber and closed the bolt. He took his stand and slowly brought the gun up to its level and squeezed the trigger.

"Craack!" Again the report echoed through the trees as the can went flying from the post.

"Okay," said Joey, as he laid the gun on the ground. "Let's see where I hit," sounding confident as he rushed over to the can.

"Look 't that, almost dead center o' that ol' tomato!"

"Put 'r back up there, and I bet I can do better this time," said Billy, his voice ringing with confidence.

As the boys rushed back to the gun, Uncle Charley was standing beside it with his hands on his hips.

"What in the world do you fellas think yuh're doin'?"

"Target shooting," answered Joey.

"Where's your target?" asked Uncle Charley, as if he hadn't seen it.

"Right there," said Joey, pointing to the can.

"That ain't no target," insisted Uncle Charley with a little contempt in his voice.

"'Tis so," insisted Joey. "That's our target."

"Put the gun down and I'll show yuh a target."

They left the gun and followed Uncle Charley to the old cedar post. He reached into his pocket and removed a small box of wooden matches. Opening the box, he removed a match and placed it horizontally into a crack in the old dry post.

"Now *that's* a target!" he said with a big grin.

"You got t' be kidding!" exclaimed Joey. "I can hardly see it."

"Bring your gun a little closer so yuh can see it better, and try from there."

Joey got the gun and brought it a little closer.

"Nobody can hit that match even from here!" said Joey, sounding a bit discouraged from just thinking about it.

Uncle Charley held out his hand, "Can I have the gun?" His voice was confident and steady as he asked for the gun.

Joey handed him the gun, and he pulled back the bolt, ejecting the empty shell.

"Now, can I have a bullet?"

Joey handed him a bullet, which he placed in the chamber; then he closed the breech.

Kneeling down on one knee, he used the other knee to put his elbow on. He took a slow and careful aim, then he gently pulled the trigger.

"Craack!" Again the sound echoed through the nearby trees.
"Okay, go and take a look."

The boys ran over to the post and examined it for a bullet hole.

"Wow!" exclaimed Billy. "Right under the match. That's darn good shootin'!"

"Well . . . " said Uncle Charley, "yuh practise on that match till yuh kin hit it or come mighty close, and there won't be very much that yuh'll miss when you 'r huntin'.

"Now listen up. When yuh aim the gun, float the match head on the top ov the front bead or yuh won't be able t' see it.

"Now go ahead an' have some fun. And don't be discouraged if yuh miss a few times. It'll take a whole lot ov practice before yuh get it right. But once you get the hang ov it, you won't miss much, and that'll make yuh feel good about have 'n put in the effort."

He handed the gun to Joey and turned to go.

"Can we have a couple o' those matches?" asked Billy, excitement rising in his voice.

"Why, sure yuh kin." Uncle Charley reached into his pocket and pulled out the matchbox.

"Here yuh go." He handed Billy a couple of matches, then returned the box to his pocket. "Now, don't bring 'em back the way I give 'em to yuh . . . okay?"

"Then how do yah want 'em back?" asked Billy, his eyes squinting as he looked up at Uncle Charley.

"How do yuh think they should look after a bullet hits 'em?"

"I don't think we're gonna be that good for a while, but that don't mean we 're not gonna try."

"All yuh have t' do is try," said Uncle Charley, his voice calm and encouraging. "An' if you 're missin', stop an' figure out why. Yuh'll get the hang of it sooner or later. Show the same determination the old Roman did when he said, 'I'll find a way or I'll make one.'"

"Okay, thanks," said Billy, anxious to get on with it.

Uncle Charley turned and walked back to the house as the boys ran over to the post to set up their targets.

"Let's stand 'm up on the top of the post," suggested Billy. "We'll never hit them the way he did it."

"Okay," agreed Joey. He also wanted to get things going, plus make it as easy as possible.

"I think we'll need a few more shells," suggested Billy. "There's only three left."

"Right . . . let's go and ask Mick if we can have some more." With that, the boys turned and ran for the house.

They were hardly through the door before Joey was asking Mick if he could have a few more shells to use on the match targets.

"How many will yuh need?"

"Lots," said Joey. "We're tryin' to hit some wooden matches that Uncle Charley gave us for targets, an' that ain't goin' tuh be easy."

"Okay, I'll give you a box," replied Mick, "but save a few for another day."

"Thanks!" said Joey as he hurried over to the cupboard and picked up a box.

Back at the shooting range, the boys set out to do business. Billy took the first three shots. Three times the crack of the .22 discharging could be heard.

"Never touched one of 'em," said Billy, the enthusiasm slipping from his voice.

"Let's see what I can do." Joey's voice held a little more confidence.

Three more times the gun cracked, but the results were the same.

"I'm not so sure we can do this!" exclaimed Joey. "Maybe Uncle Charley is just kiddin' us."

"But we saw him do it; let's try another three bullets and see what happens."

"You take the first three shots," offered Joey.

Billy took aim and fired; the results stayed the same. He then handed the gun to Joey, and his luck wasn't any better.

Uncle Charley had been watching the outcome, and, seeing their frustration, he stepped forward with a piece of cardboard in his hand.

"Put this behind the match so yuh can see where you're hittin'." Uncle Charley walked over to the post and placed the cardboard in a crack just behind the matches. "Okay, try that and see how close you 're comin' tuh the target."

Joey handed Billy the gun, and he took careful aim and fired. As the report of the rifle echoed through the trees, Uncle Charley went forward to take a look.

"Well, would yuh take a look at that! That bullet was as close tuh the target as damn is tuh swearin'. Yuh just missed 'r by a hair, but without the cardboard behind the match, yuh 'd never have known that. Keep workin' on it and yuh'll get 'r before long. Remember, practice paves the way tuh perfection."

Half a box later, there was still no improvement, just close calls. Their frustration was rising, as their patience was running low.

Joey looked at Billy. "Had enough? I don't think we're gonna make it today."

"Don't want tuh quit yet, we gotta get at least one!"

Joey handed Billy the gun. He took it, his face set and determined.

Kneeling down, he paused for a moment. Taking a few deep breaths, he then took careful aim. Resting his elbow on his knee, he mimicked Uncle Charley. The gun came up to a level and stopped. The crack of the .22 broke the stillness, followed by a cry of victory from Billy as the top of one match disappeared.

"Yesss, I got one! I finally got one! See, we can do it, just hold your breath and squeeze slowly."

Billy handed the gun to Joey; he took it and loaded a shell. He then dropped to one knee and placed his elbow on the other knee. Again, the gun reached a level, stopped, and fired. The match remained intact.

"Take one more shot," pleaded Billy. "Keep the front bead right on the match and squeeze slowly so yuh don't pull the gun to the side. Pull easy and hold your breath. Paw says yuh shouldn't know when the gun is gonna go off when yuh 're target shootin'. Just keep your eye on the sights and the target, and gently squeeze the trigger."

Joey followed Billy's advice to the letter. The gun cracked, and the top half of the last match disappeared.

"Yuh did it! I knew yuh could do it!" shouted Billy, more excited than if he had done it himself.

"Now let's go an' get what's left ov the matches and give 'em to Uncle Charley."

The boys ran to the house, and, while Joey put the gun back, Billy took what was left of the matches and handed them to Uncle Charley, looking as proud as a peacock.

"Uh-huh, well I'll be jiggered! Who dun it?"

"We both did," answered Billy. "Not bad, eh?" He was looking for Uncle Charley's approval, and he didn't have to wait long.

"That is purty darn good for beginners; see, I told yuh if yuh stuck with it yuh could do it.

"Yuh don't quit 'cause you didn't get it right on the first try. Remember, if somebody else can do it, so kin you. Yessirree, you did all right for a couple ov young fellas. Keep it up and yuh'll be one fine pair ov shooters one day!"

11

A Buggy Ride

Supper was ready, and they all sat down at the table. There was a hunk of pork with baked beans, boiled potatoes with milk gravy, bologna, and lots of Maw's homemade bread, and more applesauce for dessert.

Once everyone had eaten their fill, Uncle Charley started gathering up the dishes.

"I think I'll go down t' Hilliard's and play some cards for the evening," he said.

"Can we come?" questioned Joey, eager to be going somewhere.

"No . . . I think yuh two mischief-makers should stay put!" Uncle Charley's answer was slow and thoughtful.

"You'll probably be late comin' home, and it'll be pretty dark comin' through the bush. With old Zack on the prowl, it probably wouldn't hurt to have somebody with yuh." Joey's response to the "no" from Uncle Charley was both quick and pointed.

Uncle Charley stopped and thought for a minute.

"Well . . . okay, if yuh want to come so bad, but yuh better behave!" Uncle Charley knew what Joey was getting at. If he had to face ol' Zack, he'd rather not be alone.

"No problem, we're always good, ain't we Billy?"

"You bet we are," Billy replied with a big grin, having noticed how well Joey had handled the situation.

"While I do the dishes an' clean up the place, yuh two fellas can bring in some wood for the morning. And Dan . . . would yuh hitch up the horse an' buggy for us? I don't feel like walkin' there and back."

"You bet," said Dan, as he headed for the stable. It wasn't just that he was willing to carry out Uncle Charley's wishes; there was nothing Dan liked better than to be working with the horses.

By the time the dishes were done and the wood was brought in, Dan had the horse and buggy at the door. All the brass on the halter and harness was sparkling in the evening sun, and the horse had been brushed till her hair was smooth and shiny. The buggy would need a coat of paint and a few minor repairs if it was to match the horse and harness. But it was in good mechanical condition. It took them where they wanted to go, and that was all they required of it.

Charley took the lines from Dan and mounted the buggy. He sat in the middle of the seat with a boy on either side of him. There wasn't a lot of room left for them, but they didn't care; they were going somewhere, and for the moment that was all that mattered.

Charley flipped the lines and clicked his tongue and they were on their way. Nell bowed her neck and immediately went into a trot, leaving little puffs of dust rising from her hooves and little streams of it rising from the back of the buggy wheels. Nell was a fine mare; she could pick her pace and hold it all day if it was required of her, and in no time at all the trio were down the lane and out onto the road.

Other than Charley's whistling of "Oh Susanna," the only sound was the rattling of the buggy and the clicking of Nell's hooves.

After they were well into the woods, Charley pulled back on the lines and said, "Whoa, Nellie Bell, whoa!"

The horse stopped, and Charley handed the lines to Joey.

"Hold 'r steady while I step down and ring muh mitt." He walked to the back of the buggy and relieved himself. Returning to his seat, he took the lines and encouraged the horse to move on. A smile crossed his face and he said, "That stop reminded me ov a little rhyme I learned as a kid."

"What was it?" asked Joey, looking up at Uncle Charley with a smile and a look that indicated he was expecting something good.

"It was a cutie, and it told the truth!" Uncle Charley moistened his lips, and then he spoke.

"When I was just a wee wee tot,
I had a wee wee pot,
An' my momma made me wee wee
If I wanted to or not."

Uncle Charley said the lines with a straight face; the only sign of a smile was the twitching at the corners of his mouth.

Both boys started to giggle.

"What woulda happened if you didn't wee wee?" giggled Billy.

"Well, that reminds me ov another little ditty!

"When I was just a little boy about so high,
My momma took a stick an' she made me cry.
Now I'm a big boy and Momma can't do it,
So Poppa takes the boots and he goes right to it."

This got Billy to giggling even harder.

"You musta had the same paw as Joey."

"No sirree! Mine was twice as bad, an' he sure did have a good pair o' boots, an' he didn't mind usin' 'em, either. If yuh check my back end, yuh'll still see bruises there from when I was a kid."

"They must o' be 'n good ones 'cause that's a pretty long time ago," laughed Billy, as he warmed up to Uncle Charley.

"They were, an' yuh can bet yuhr dollar bottom on that one."

"My bottom is worth more than just a dollar," exclaimed Billy, still laughing. Then, with a giggle, he said to Uncle Charley, "Did you hear the poem that Joey wrote for school?"

"No, I didn't, so why don't yuh tell me 'bout it?"

"The teacher asked him to write somethin' about a pistol. This is what he wrote:

"My paw an Uncle Charley bought a
    keg ov homemade brew;
They drank an' drank till way past ten
An' then they pist'l two."

"And what did the teacher say tuh that?" laughed Uncle Charley, his tummy shaking.

"She wouldn't let him read it in class; said it wasn't very nice."

"An' who helped yuh write it?" Uncle Charley asked Joey.

"Mick."

"I sorta thought so." Uncle Charley shifted himself on the seat, straightened his back a bit, and said, "Well, when I went tuh school, we learned poetry, too."

"Tell us some of it," pleaded Billy, turning his head and looking up at Uncle Charley.

"Well . . . let me see now.

"Jack 'n Jill went up the hill tuh get some homemade liquor.
Jack fell down an' broke his crown, an' Jill was even sicker."

"Never heard that one before," laughed Billy. "Know any more?"

Uncle Charley moistened his lips again and carried on.

"Last night the moon an' stars were lit,
As Paw went out t' stroll a bit.
When Paw come back, Maw had a fit;
The stars were gone, and he was lit."

"Any more?" questioned Billy, grinning from ear to ear.

"Well, maybe I can dig up one more.

"I went t' see muh girl last night,
Some pleasure I was seekin',
I missed her lips and I kissed her nose,
An' the doggone thing was leakin'."

"Ugh, that one's messy. Are you sure you learned those at school?" asked Billy, laughing and talking at the same time.

"Well . . . maybe it was on the way *home* from school that I learned 'em, but it was somewhere back in those days.

"Speakin' ov noses," said Uncle Charley, "I once heard a fella sing a song about his wife. A part ov it went like this.

"I'd buy yuh anything yuh want,
I'd give yuh everything I got,
If my nose was runnin' money —
But *it's not*."

"Oh, Uncle Charley," laughed Billy, "that sounds awful!"

After the giggling stopped, Billy asked Uncle Charley, "Can you sing?"

"Well, I guess I could, but you boys'd most likely get out o' the buggy an' start walkin'."

"I don't think so," said Joey.

"Try it and we'll tell yuh if it's bad," encouraged Billy.

"Well . . . I guess I could try; it usually makes the horse go faster. You see, they try to run away from the noise."

Again the boys giggled at Uncle Charley's humour, and Uncle Charley began singing.

"I had a dog and his name was Fido.
He was such an intelligent pup.
He'd walk all around the floor on his hind legs
If yuh held the front ones up."

By this time, Billy was in tears. "I have a dog that can do that too. Give us another one. You sound pretty darn good, and we won't be walkin' if you sing more."

"Well . . . let me see, now. How about ol' Paddy . . . somethin' or other?

"He travelled around like a wanderin' Jew,
He hadn't a sound tooth in his head, only two.

He had a gray mare with a hump on her back,
'An there wasn't a hair on her that wasn't coal black.
He had an ol' pig with a curl in 'r tail,
That he milked twice a day, an' he'd get half a pail.

He had him a musket that was beat-up and old,
But it played a big part in the stories he told.
When he pulled on the trigger, it shot flame and smoke,
And hit his ol' shoulder one heck ov a poke."

By now, Billy was in tears again. "That's impossible. How can she be a gray mare if she's all black?"

"Well . . . I guess it's somethin' like the words ov 'Oh Susanna,'" said Uncle Charley. He cleared his throat and started to sing again.

"It rained so hard the day I left; the weather it was dry.
The sun's so hot I froze tuh death; Susanna don't yuh cry.
Oh Susanna, don't yuh cry for me;
I'm goin' tuh Alabama with my banjo on my knee."

"Do you know any songs that are a little longer than that?" inquired Billy, wanting to hear more of Uncle Charley's singing.

"Yah . . . a few. There was one about an ol' fella that lived up this way. Let's see if I can remember it."

Again, Uncle Charley moistened his lips and concentrated on the road ahead.

"In the north end of Hastings, way up near the Park,
Where the nights are long and unusually dark,
Stories and legends abound 'way up there,
And one's 'bout a feller by the name of Will Tare.

A bushman by trade that sure liked t' boast
An' when telling a story, he'd sidle up close.
With a smirk on his face an' a gleam in his eye
You'd know beyond doubt Will was telling a lie.

He'd tell of his musket and the balls that it spent;
And then he'd inform yuh of the barrel bein' bent.
He'd tell it so straight-faced, so nice if yuh please,
This trusty old musket, it shot around trees.

He shot over a hill in pursuit ov a deer
When some blood-curdling yells fell on his ear.
His victim was screaming; it cursed and it swore.
He knew without looking he had just shot Ben Tore.

Will took to his heels with the greatest ov ease;
And the wind he created tore bark from the trees.
His young son said, 'Papa, what brought yuh so fast?'
'I'm being chased by a fella that I shot in the ass.'

Will hung his old gun on a peg in the wall
And he said, 'I've quit huntin' till maybe next fall.'
If yuh think that this story may not be all true,
Well the next one, young feller, could be about you."

"That's better," said Billy. "I liked your singin'. Can yah sing us another one like that?"

"Well . . . if 'n this ol' mare will stop tryin' to get away from the noise, I should have time for one more."

Uncle Charley pondered for a moment and then started again.

"This one's about the folks that opened up this neck ov thuh woods and got our country goin'.

"In the Madawaska Valley, not so many years ago,
There were men that took on nature, fought
   the wind, the cold, the snow.
It was hard to make a livin' in this land o' rock an' hill,
But their hearts were full o' courage, and
   their memories linger still.

They would leave their homes and families
   in the cold ol' wintertime.
They would cross the lakes and rivers
   just to fall the lofty pine.
They would take along their axes and
   their trusty crosscut saw,

Lots o' beans, an' bread, an' bacon, an'
   ov course their mackinaw.

In their camp along the lakeshore,
   carin' not for winter's chill,
They could hear the cold wind sighin'
   as it swept the lake an' hill,
Hear the wolf up on the mountain with
   its hauntin', ghostly wail,
As he filled the night with sadness, like a long an' lonely trail.

Yuh could hear their axes ringin' in the early rays o' dawn,
Hear the zingin', zangin' crosscut as it sang a logger's song.
Yes, their lives were filled with danger as
   they sought their work to do,
Watchin' out for snappin' spring poles
   that could break a jaw in two.

Barber chairs, and widowmakers, that
   went flyin' through the air,
Ridin' runs on slippery sandhills, down
   the mountain, steep and glare.
In the spring when—

Whoa, Nelly Bell, easy there!"

Uncle Charley's song was interrupted as Henry's dogs came running out to the road. They came barking like they were going to eat someone, causing Nell to shy sideways. Uncle Charley leaned over and snapped the buggy whip at the lead dog. The snap of the whip turned him around and he joined the others at the back of the buggy. This ended the chase, and all three dogs went back to the driveway where two more were waiting. They felt victorious in sending the buggy on down the road. They could now quietly return to the house and wait for the next passerby.

Uncle Charley was now wearing a frown, and his voice was a little more serious as he spoke.

"Those darn dogs, makes yuh wonder what a man wants with so many ov 'em. Drive your buggy intuh the yard, an there's a dog cockin' his leg at each wheel an' half a dozen more standin' in line, waitin' their turn."

"Why don't somebody shoot half ov them?" asked Billy, disgust rising in his voice as he agreed with Uncle Charley.

"I don't think I'd wanna be the boy t' do that," replied Charley, a warning had slipped in and changed the tone of his voice.

"Why? What would happen?" asked Billy, sounding a bit doubtful of his first statement.

"Well ... ol' Henry is the kind that mostly minds his own business, and he sure don't like somebody else tryin' to mind it for him. There ain't no law that says yuh can't have a dozen dogs; it's just that they 'r such a darn nuisance when yuh go there."

"What do you think he'd do if somebody shot one?" asked Billy, sounding as if he might be just a little intimidated after Uncle Charley's warning.

"Well ... I don't know, but I also wouldn't want t' be the one t' find out. He ain't the kind of a man that yuh want mad at yuh."

Uncle Charley paused for a moment, looking for the right words, then he continued talking.

"Yuh see, ol' Buckeye, the fella who owns the hotel in town, he told me one time that he hired two good men for bouncers. He said that some o' the lumberjacks were comin' in an' get 'n drunk an' tearin' the place apart, so he needed somebody to keep the peace. He said he picked two hefty fellas that looked capable o' doin' the job, an' they were doin' a pretty good job ov it, too.

"Well ... by an' by, Henry comes in an' sits down with some fellas that he knew. After a few pints he gets a bit loud, just havin' fun, not doin' any damage or bother 'n anybody. But these two bouncers thought it was their job to throw Henry out for bein' noisy.

"Ol' Buckeye said that he saw them talking it over an' headin' over to Henry's table. Said he tried tuh get their attention and tell them tuh leave him alone, but they weren't lookin' at him, so he thought he'd watch an' see what was about tuh happen.

"Tuh his surprise, the boys walked over and each one took

Henry by an arm, and Ol' Henry never said a word. Just got up an' walked calm an peaceful tuh the door. At the door, the one fella held Henry with one hand an' opened the door with the other.

"As soon as the door swung open, Henry broke loose ov the hold on his arm, grabbed the fella by the back o' the shirt, an' give him a boot in the behind that sent him headlong down the steps into the snow. He then turned and grabbed the other fella by the shirt an' the ass o' the pants an' sent him down the steps on top o' the first fella. Closed the door an' went back tuh drinkin' his beer.

"In a few minutes, the two fellas come in an' dusted the snow off, then went over an' sat down in the corner an' said no more. When Henry left, he tipped his hat to the bouncers an' said, 'Now, you gentlemen better not be makin' a habit ov goin' outside in the snow without your coats on, yuh might just catch your death o' cold.' They just nodded back at Henry and said nothing."

"I guess he showed them who the boss was," said Billy, hosting a beaming smile and rising to the occasion. "They shoulda left him alone if he was only havin' fun."

"Well, I guess they thought they could have some fun in throwin' him out; they were lucky Henry was in a good mood, or it coulda gotten a bit ugly." Charley's voice got serious as he thought of what could have happened.

"What do yuh mean . . . it coulda got ugly?" asked Billy; he was now eager to learn more about Henry.

"Well, ol' Henry is a pretty easygoin' fella, likes tuh have fun, an' is good tuh most everybody. But don't get 'm riled or he'll turn your ol' runners up in one 'ell ov a hurry."

"What do yuh mean, he'll turn your runners up?" Billy wasn't used to Uncle Charley's lingo, as he was referring to a sleigh being turned upside down, runners up. So Uncle Charley explained it to Billy, just that way.

"Well, let me tell yuh . . . a bunch o' fellas got tuhgether over at Henderson's garage a while back. They were talking about the war an' how many good men were killed or wounded on the battlefield. Henry said that his uncle went through the whole thing, front lines an' all, an' was lucky, 'cause he never even got a scratch on him.

Ol' Paddy O'Leary was standin' just back ov Henry, an' he said, 'Most likely he laid down an' hid when the fightin' started.' Henry heard him and, turning around, he said to Paddy, 'What was that yuh said?' Henry's voice had turned ice cold, as to give Paddy a stern warning. Paddy, with sort ov a sheepish grin, repeated the statement. 'I said he musta laid down an' hid when the fightin' started, that's why he never got hurt.'

"Henry's face went red an' he said tuh Paddy, 'You lyin', no good, useless, yellow-bellied son-ov-a-perch!'

"Ol' Paddy's eyes bulged out as he clenched his teeth an' made for Henry. Henry grabbed him by the front ov his shirt, swung him around, an' slammed him hard against the wall. I don't think Henry really intended tuh hurt ol' Paddy, but Paddy swung his right arm around with a fist full ov knuckles an' tried tuh hit Henry up the side o' the head.

Well . . . Henry saw it comin' from half a mile away; he lifted his left shoulder an' dropped his head a bit. The blow glanced off his shoulder and might o' touched the top ov his head; it was a harmless effort. But it got things goin'.

"Henry held Paddy by the front ov his shirt with his left hand, an' I saw his right elbow come back 'bout three times. By the third time, Paddy was screamin' for Henry tuh stop. Henry let 'm go, an' he just slid down the wall an' sat on the floor with his knees up and his hands down by his side. On the floor between his feet was what looked like a couple ov chicklets, but it wasn't. They were just a few ov Paddy's teeth that he wouldn't be needin' any more. There was a gash over Paddy's left eye, his nose was bleedin', an' there was a split on his lip. From that day on, ol' Paddy whistled a different tune."

"How come he whistled a different tune?" asked Billy, his curiosity getting the better of him.

"'Cause most ov his front teeth were missin,'" chuckled Uncle Charley.

"Wow!" declared Billy, greatly impressed with the image Uncle Charley was painting of Henry.

"Like I said, Henry's a good man; just don't get 'm riled."

"Could you beat Henry?" Billy asked Uncle Charley, his voice filled with excitement.

Uncle Charley stiffened a bit with the question, his face reddened, and his voice raised a little.

"Just you hold on there, boy, you ain't gonna get no rivalry goin' 'tween Henry an' me!" Uncle Charley's voice was sharp and rang with a warning. "Like I said, Henry's a good man, an' let's just leave it at that! You just remember, a man ain't a coward 'cause he doesn't like tuh fight. He's a coward when he won't stand up and fight for what's right. A good man don't go 'round braggin' 'bout hurtin' people, or putting others down. He does what he has tuh, an' he leaves it at that.

"A good man will walk around it if he can, an' let it go. If he can't, then he does whatever needs doin'. He ain't much ov a man that thinks it's fun to go around hurtin' people. Those kind ov fellas go looking for the weak and helpless, somebody they figure they can beat. But when they meet a real man, they ain't long in turnin' tail. Henry isn't like that, he's a good man, an' he don't go around lookin' for trouble; an' we ain't gonna start any."

"Sorry ... I didn't want you tuh fight Henry ... " Billy's voice was now on the timid side again, with a ring of regret in it.

Then Uncle Charley picked it up again. "I know yuh didn't, yuh just got carried away with the moment. But that's a good way tuh spoil a friendship, by putting somebody else down, thinking you're better than them. Think about what you're sayin' 'bout somebody else before yuh say it, 'cause word always gets back tuh the ones yuh put down, an' then there's trouble. Good friends are hard tuh find an' easy tuh lose, so take good care ov the ones that yuh have, 'cause yuh never know when you 'r gonna need one."

Things got quiet for a moment as Uncle Charley settled down. Then he carried on with his stories.

"Now let me tell yuh what ol' Murphy told me 'bout Henry's Uncle Jack. He was a strappin' good fella that backed away from nobody.

"He said one day Jack got off the train, an' the boys were havin' a ball game over behind the water tower. Somebody saw him an asked him tuh come an' help them out. Said the other team had a real good pitcher, an' they were havin' trouble hittin' the ball. Well, Jack said that he wasn't in the mood for runnin' that day but he'd like to try out the pitcher. So they all agreed t' let him bat.

"The first pitch went whizzen on by him, an' he never even turned a hair. The second went on by him, an' he just stood there lookin', so the other team started t' get at him. When the third pitch came in, he swung the bat, ker-smuck. They said the ball went out over the field an' so far out into Butchers swamp that they still haven't found it. Jack dropped the bat an' said, 'I don't see nothing special about that fella,' nodding to the pitcher. Murphy said ol' Jack was a terribly strong fellow, terribly strong!"

By this time, they were gliding along by the lake, leaving a faint trail of dust floating in the evening air, and Nell was still keeping her pace.

The sun had set, but it was still showing pink on a few of the scattered clouds. The lake was as smooth as glass, and along the shore a mirror image of the trees had been painted on the surface. The loons were calling across the bay, showing their appreciation for a beautiful evening. The frogs were warming up for the night's singsong. It sounded like the whole choir was practising, from the bass to the tenor. The dragonflies were skimming over the water looking for some early evening mosquitoes, while the bass were surfacing, picking off some unfortunate water bugs. It seemed the whole world was at peace as the horse and buggy, with its three occupants, went rolling on down the road.

When they had passed the lake, Billy asked Uncle Charley if he knew any more songs.

"Well . . . I remember a poem a fella used to recite in the lumber camp. I always thought it was kind ov an interesting one to tell just before bedtime. Let's see if I can remember it all.

"I'm snuggled in bed and the room sure is dark;
'Way off in the distance I hear a dog bark.
A star through the winda is just a faraway spark,
In a deep, dark, adventurous heaven.

Now this is so peaceful, contentment at last;
Sweet fresh air's replacin' the gas that I passed.
Now to fall asleep quickly, for the night goes so fast,
And the next thing I know t'will be morning.

All of a sudden the night's filled with dread;
Some darn thing is crawlin' up the foot ov the bed.
The pilla an' covers fly over my head,
And oh, how I wish it was mornin'.

It slowly advances o' 'r the tips of my toes;
I can't move a muscle, it seems that I'm froze.
A bear couldn't scare me as far as that goes,
But this thing, I'll bet, isn't fooling.

It's walkin' my leg an it's up t' my knees;
I'm no longer breathin', it's more like a wheeze.
Oh what I'd give t' hear somebody sneeze,
And know that some help was arriving.

It's ridin' my hip like the crest ov a wave;
I'm doin' my darndest t' try an' be brave.
God gave me one life, and that's all that He gave,
And I'll bet ten to one I shall lose it.

Over my rib-cage it does slowly advance;
By now there are spots on the seat o' my pants.
I'd sure love t' see it, but I won't take the chance
Ov' stickin' my head from the covers.

It's up on my shoulder and I'm shaking with fear;
It's quiet and deadly, and It's after my ear.
I'm screaming my loudest, but not a word can I hear;
I guess this is it, it's all over.

My body's prepared for a surge of great pain;
Will it bite off my ear and go after my brain?
The tears are now streaming from my eyes like rain,
But don't ever think that I'm crying.

In the midst of it all, I'm feeling soft fur;
The sound that I hear is a lot like a purr.
If the darn thing's a cat, I will kill it for sure,
For I've died the worst death nine times over.

I stand in the room with my feet wide apart;
And I can't hear a thing for the beat o' my heart.
There's a hole in the winda, where the cat, like a dart,
Sailed over my head an' crashed through it.

Now I'm back in tuh bed, but it isn't much use:
My skin is all puckered like the hide on a goose.
'Tween me an' them cats, there will n'er be a truce,
As long as there's one ov us livin'."

By the end of the poem, the boys were in tears and laughing their hearts out.

Billy wiped his face with the back of his arm and looked up at Uncle Charley.

"Have you ever been that scared?"

"Well . . . maybe not that scared, but I had the little hairs on the back o' my neck stand up one time."

"When was that?" asked Billy, in disbelief.

"Well . . . I was visitin' ol' Tom Bennett one evening. He lives across the river. An' we were sittin' on his veranda havin' a nice chat when I heard his big pitcher leave the wall and fall on tuh the floor. Yuh could hear the glass fly'n all over the place. I said, what in the world was that? He said, nothin'. I said, it sounded like your pitcher fell from off the wall. He said, no, it's still there. Then I heard the screen door slam shut on the other side of the kitchen.

"I said, somebody just come in the house. An' he said, nobody's there. I said, I just heard somebody slam the screen door. He said, go 'n look for yourself, nobody's there. So I did. The pitcher o' the ol' black horse was still on the wall, an' there was nobody else in the house. The little hairs on the back o' my neck all stood up at the same time, an' it felt like half a dozen o' them ten-legged spiders, with the cold feet, were walkin' up muh back.

"I closed the door an' walked right on a past where he was sittin', an' said, I think it's time for me tuh be go 'n home.

"He said, have a good night, an' I said, the same tuh you, an' I kept right on a-leggin' 'r. I headed for home, and let me tell yuh, I didn't waste any time in get 'n there. I haven't been back since, and I ain't a gonna be a goin' back, either."

"Brrrr," said Billy, "I don't blame yuh, I don't think I'd want t' go there either. The place must be haunted by ghosts."

"Yuh bet it is, and wherever those fellers are, that's one place I don't want to be."

With that, the conversation ended, and no one was about to mention ol' Zack or the night before. The boys knew the truth, but they weren't about to say anything, and Uncle Charley wasn't about to bring it up.

"Gee, Nelly Bell, Gee!" Uncle Charley pulled on the right line, turning Nell's head into the laneway leading up to Hilliard's house. It was made of logs and sat on the shore of the lake. Behind it was a summer kitchen, a woodshed, a drive shed, and a log barn. It was a peaceful place with a wonderful view.

On the other side of the line fence lived the Hatfields. They were nice folks, but they had a couple of teenage boys who were always up to their ears in mischief.

Nell and the buggy splashed through the shallow creek and on up the gentle slope that led to the house. The centre of the laneway had grass growing on it; only in the wheel tracks was there bare ground.

"Whoa, Nelly Bell, whoa." Uncle Charley pulled back on the lines, stopping the buggy in front of the house, where Hilliard was waiting.

"I seen yuh comin' up the lane with Harry's horse and buggy

an' I thought it was him. What brings you down here this fine evening?"

"Oh, just thought we might have a game o' cards t' pass the time."

"Sounds good t' me, step down an' go on in. Festus is inside; he'll be glad t' see yuh. I'll take the horse an' buggy over t' the drive shed and tie 'm in."

Uncle Charley stepped down from the buggy, handed the lines to Hilliard, and then walked to the house.

12

A Bottle of Turpentine

Hilliard walked beside the buggy as he drove the horse to the drive shed. The boys kept their place on the seat, not saying a word. He stopped the buggy in front of the shed. There he unhitched the horse, hooked the lines over the hame, and walked Nell to the manger. Tied the halter shank in place, then went over to the corner and picked up a pitchfork. Gathered some hay and placed it in the manger for Nell. Turning to leave, he stopped and spoke to the boys, who were standing there watching him.

"How was your drive down with Charley?" asked Hilliard, trying to make conversation.

"Pretty good," said Billy. "He sang some songs an' told some stories 'bout ghosts an' stuff. Sounds like he's scared tuh death o' those creepy things."

"Well . . . " said Hilliard, "if he is, that's about all ol' Charley's scared ov!"

"What d'yuh mean?" asked Billy, looking up into Hilliard's face.

Hilliard took a long draw on his pipe, then took it from his mouth and blew a smoke ring. He watched it rise and disappear, looking upwards, as if he were going 'way back in time.

"Well . . . " said Hilliard, who was a pretty good storyteller, and just wondering where to begin.

"You young fellas don't know the ol' Charley that I knew in our younger days. He has slowed down a lot. Gotten more mellow as time passes. Not that he ever was a bad fellow, but he used t' drink a bit. Never seen the man drunk, but he liked t' get out with the boys and have a few pints and a few laughs.

"Let me tell you boys what happened in the hotel one night. Might help yuh get a better understandin' of this man we call Charley."

As with most young boys and a good storyteller, Hilliard had Billy and Joey's undivided attention.

"Yuh see, after the war there was a lot o' mixed emotions and opinions about what happened, didn't happen, or shoulda happened. And your Uncle Charley," he pointed at Joey with his pipe, "was sittin' at a table in the hotel with me and a few other fellas that he knew. We'd all had a few pints an' was discussin' some ov the things about the war."

Hilliard took a couple more puffs on his pipe and slowly let the smoke out; he was looking up at the roof as if he could see through it and back in time.

"Ol' Charley's voice was getting a bit high an' loud, so most o' the fellas around us could hear what he was sayin'. He had his own opinions 'bout some o' these things and was makin' it pretty plain as to what they were."

Hilliard took a couple more puffs on his pipe and watched the smoke disappear, timing his pauses like a good storyteller.

"Well . . . yuh see, the fellas at the next table had some different views and opinions about what Charley was saying, an' they decided they were gonna let ol' Charley know what they were.

"Well . . . ol' Charley is a lot like a mule in this way. When he makes up his mind about somethin', there ain't nobody on God's green earth that's ever gonna change it. But this one big fella at the next table decided that he would take a shot at it.

"Now . . . by an' by, things got pretty hot an' loud between the two o' them. An' this ol' boy asked Charley if he'd like him to come on over an' shut him up. Well, let me tell yuh . . . this ol' boy didn't know your Uncle Charley very well, but he sure was well on his way t' findin' him out.

"Charley told him that he could come on over any time he thought that he was man enough t' do it, an' he could bring his whole table with him if he liked. An' the best part of it was, Charley wasn't foolin'.

"Anyways . . . this big fella had a pretty good temper, an' it looked like he had lost it with Charley. He grabbed his bottle o' beer an' fired it against the wall, glass and beer flyin' all over the place. He stood up an' kicked his chair over backwards, an' came at Charley.

"Charley just sat there as calm as you please; he had carefully placed one foot on either side ov his chair. And just as the big fella got within strike 'n distance, ol' Charley's legs straightened. As he came up, he sort o' swivelled at the waist, and a big right hand full o' hard knuckles caught the big fella square on the side o' the jaw, just below the left ear. Pretty much like takin' it from a sledgehammer. That ol' fella never even had time t' make a fist before he hit the floor. He stopped dead in his tracks, just like he run into an invisible wall. His head flew backwards and a little to one side as his eyes sorta rolled up into his head. Then he went over sideways, hit the floor, and lay there; didn't even whimper. Out stone cold."

Hilliard took a few more puffs and watched the smoke disappear, then smiled as he watched Billy's mouth and eyes open as wide as he could get them. The boys were not missing a word or making a sound. They were spellbound with Hilliard's story and waiting breathlessly to see what happened next.

"Well, now . . . as Charley had invited, they all stood up an came at him. He just stepped back a bit, kicked his chair out ov the way, stepped away from the fella on the floor, placed his back t' wards the wall, and waited for them to come.

"The first fella to arrive had his hands up in front ov his face, like he was ol' Jersey Joe or somebody like that. He was doin' a little dance as he came forward; his eyes were just lookin' over the top ov his fists. Charley clenched his teeth but never moved, just let him come. Then that big right hand full o' hard knuckles came right up between the fella's elbows an' caught him squarely on the point ov his chin. The fella never even had time t' lower his hands. His head flew back like he'd been kicked by a mule. He went over backwards just like an ol' pine tree fallin'; hit the floor an' laid there.

"The other three came in low and tackled him, one on each side an' one on the front. I guess they thought if they could get him down and all three go at him they could get the job done. But that wasn't about to happen.

"Charley cupped his hands, pulled his arms back, an slapped the fella in front ov him on both ears at the same time. Now that fella dropped pretty much like when yuh take the clothespins off a dress that's hanging on the line. He just went limp and dropped down in a pile at Charley's feet. Then he started rollin' across the floor holdin' his ears and squealin' for all ov his might.

"Then Charley pushed himself backwards an' the fella on his right side was caught between Charley an' the wall. I guess things were a bit tight back there, so he stuck his head out past Charley's shoulder. Charley pulled his right arm forward and drove it back, ketchin' that poor ol' fella on the butt ov his left ear with the elbow. Now that fella's head hit the wall with one heck ov a thud, an' he slid on down 'r like wet paint; never made a sound."

Hilliard's pipe had gone out, so he just held it in his hand.

"Charley had his left arm around the other fella's neck, so he pulled him around to the front ov him. He grabbed him by the front ov the shirt an then brought his right hand around, wide open, an' smacked him up the side ov the head like he was gonna tear it off. His hand hit and then went right on past, an' when he brought it back, the back ov his hand caught him on the other side o' the head. When Charley let go ov his shirt, that ol' boy dropped t' his knees, fell over backwards, an' went straight t' sleep without even sayin' a prayer.

"The whole thing happened in less than half the time it took me tuh tell you about it. At that time in his life, let me tell yuh, that man could move. He made greased lightnin' look slow, and he was stronger than a mule!

"Charley then stepped over the fellas on the floor an' said, 'Good men died tuh give me the right tuh speak my mind, an there ain't nobody that's gonna stop me from doin' it. Is there anybody else in here that thinks they might like t' try?'

"The place went so quiet you could hear a pin drop. After a minute, Charley said, 'Okay, then let's get back t' what we come here for.' He sat down an' carried on his conversation pretty much where he left off, and there were no more contradictions that night."

"WOW!" exclaimed Billy, discovering a brand-new hero. "Did he *really* do that?"

"He sure did. I was right there at his table an' saw it all first hand. He didn't always have the bubble in his middle, and he wasn't always the way that you boys have got t' know him. He was long, lean, an' harder than a rock, but as quick as a cat. He was way too stubborn to ever back down from anybody, an' when they figured that out, they usually let it be. He never bragged, boasted, or bother'd anybody that didn't need bother 'n. He's the kindest man I've ever known — he'd give yuh the shirt right off his back and never mention it again. But, he has his own way about him and that's the way it is. It's best that yuh get t' like it, cause yuh ain't gonna change it, and yuh can bet your life on that."

Both boys were standing there looking up at Hilliard and not saying a word, hoping to hear more. But Hilliard had had enough storytelling for one night and wanted to get inside and play cards with Charley.

"Well, boys, no more stories tonight, so maybe we should go on in an see what the rest are doin'."

The boys fell in step with Hilliard as he made his way back to the house. There was a plank platform in front of the door, with a step leading up to it. The screen door was a full screen from top to bottom with a small piece of wood crossing the middle; it was to give the door some stability. A spring latch held the door in its closed position.

The main door was open, letting the evening air flow in and out again through the window facing the lake. The log building was a storey and a half, with a summer kitchen made of boards added onto the south end. The logs had grayed with time, as had the lumber, making the statement that hard times had been here along with the rest of the country. Paint was hard to come by.

The house was situated on a gentle slope, about forty yards from the shore, with a magnificent view of the lake.

Hilliard stepped aside and held the door open for the boys to enter. Inside, the coal-oil lamp was sitting in the middle of the table, giving a warm glow to the room as darkness was closing in on the outside. Festus was seated at the far end of the table, with Uncle Charley sitting across from Gertrude.

"Yuh've been holdin' up the game," said Charley, as he shuffled the cards in an impatient manner. "Suppose yuh been out there telling stories t' the boys an' waste 'n good time."

"Not likely," replied Hilliard with a grin. "There ain't nobody around here that's worth talking about."

He winked at the boys and they both grinned and said nothing.

"Why don't yuh come over here an' sit down. The evening's slippin' away." Charley was trying to sound impatient.

"Not a problem," replied Hilliard, as he pulled a chair up to the end of the table. He looked across at Festus and asked, "Yuh ready t' skin 'em?"

"Yar darn right I am; just itchin t' git at 'r."

Festus was in his mid-forties, short, slim, and a bit on the scruffy side. He looked as if he hadn't shaved for a week or more, and most of his teeth were missing, which didn't do much for his appearance. But he was kind and good-natured, and a lot of fun to have around. He lived in a two-room house across the bay from Hilliard, with his wife, whom he had nicknamed ol' Buckskin.

"Okay," said Hilliard, as he settled in. "Shuffle an' hand 'm out, and no stackin' the deck."

Charley handed the cards to Gertrude and said, "Ladies first."

"There'll be no need for that, now will there?" Charley asked Gertrude, nodding to her at the same time.

"We'll make short work o' these two ol' coots," she replied with a grin.

Gertrude was Hilliard's seventeen-year-old daughter, slight of build and medium height. She was kindhearted and friendly, with a warm, sweet smile that would win you in a heartbeat. As well, she was a very good euchre player.

"We've got the cat in the bag. This should be pretty much like take 'n candy from kids. Now, that's as long as you do your part, Charley!" she teased.

"Don't yuh worry none 'bout me, little lady. Tonight we're gonna see who the boss is when it comes t' play'n cards."

"Maw and I have been playin' these two ol' coots and beatin' the pants off 'em, so this should be easy."

"Yah," said Festus, "that's 'cause we be 'n takin' it easy on duh ladies an' let 'n dem win. Now dat yuh got thet ol' Charley boy playin' with yuh, it won't be so easy, 'cause we won't just let yuh win, yuh'll hav tuh earn it."

"Now Festus, you know that lying is a sin. So you can expect the devil tuh fix you but good for a lie like that. You probably won't win at all, and that will just serve you right, so there!"

Gertrude's smile and cheerful voice told Festus that she was just having fun with him, and the truth of it was, he was thoroughly enjoying every bit of it.

The boys were leaning on the washstand and watching what was going on at the table. They were always extra quiet and shy when in someone else's house, and this was no exception. Hilliard's wife was sitting on the couch at the far end of the room, quietly doing some mending. She beckoned for the boys to come over and sit beside her, but they shook their heads no. Instead they moved over and leaned on the cupboard behind Gertrude, watching the card players.

The cards were dealt and the jack of diamonds turned up. They all passed. Then Gertrude picked it up and said, "I'll go it alone with diamonds."

"Do yuh need my best card?" asked Charley.

"No ... I'm good," assured Gertrude, smiling confidently. She dropped the ace on the table and both players played a small diamond. Picking up the cards she said, "Bingo!"

She then placed the Queen on the table. Hilliard put down a small diamond and Festus played slush. She then laid down her hand, both bowers along with the ten of diamonds.

"Yuh got it," said Charley, "'cause I got the king."

She clapped her hands and said, "Bingo! Now that was easy."

They gathered the cards and dropped them in front of Hilliard to deal.

"Cheatin' ag'in," said Festus as he grinned at Charley. "Set 'n up duh girl. Don't worry, duh night's still young."

Festus reached into his pants pocket and pulled out his crooked pipe, pinched some tobacco from the package in his shirt pocket, and jammed it into the bowl. He placed the pipe in his mouth, and once again his hand went into his pocket. He brought out a small box of matches, removed a match and struck it on the side of the packet. The tip of the match burst into flames; he then placed it on the top of his pipe and puffed. With each puff the flame of the match drew down into the tobacco and smoke began to rise. After a couple of puffs, he removed the pipe from his mouth and exhaled the smoke. It drifted over and formed a blue halo around the top of the lamp.

"Now, how in the world did yuh crack your pipe?" asked Charley.

"Ah-ha, durn near blew muh head off," said Festus with a big grin, showing all his missing teeth. "Run out o' tubakee, so I scraped the remain'ns out o' muh shirt pocket. Stuff fell out o' duh package, an' I jammed 'r intu duh ol' pipe an lit 'r up. Puffed for a minute 'r two an den "ker-bang-go!" went duh ol' pipe. Stuff blew down muh troat thit come out tru duh stem; darn near choked me tuh death. Couldn' get muh breath. Stuff from duh bowl flew up inta muh eyes an' darn near burned muh eyebrows off."

"Now what kind o' tubakee was that?" asked Charley with a chuckle.

"'T wurnt duh tubakee, 't was a durned ol' .22 bullet thet was in wit it w'en I jammed 'r intu duh pipe! Coulda blowed muh durn head off."

By this time everyone in the room was laughing, including Festus.

"Well, yuh better be careful what yuhr settin' on fire from now on," laughed Charley.

"Don'tchuh wurry nun, big feller, 'cause yuhr dayz a-cumin'," laughed Festus. "The laughin' usely makes duh rounds."

"How did the .22 shell get in yuhr pocket in the first place?"

"Was hunten partridge, an' I got tree or four. Was walkin' home w'en a half-a-ton truck pullz up b'side me. A feller says, w'at yuh got der? I sez some birds; I'm gonna make some soup wen I git 'ome. He sez yuh can't be shootin' dem birds outa seazon. I sez don't matter, I'm jus gonna make some soup. He sez does so matter, yuh kin go tuh jail f'r dat. Sez I don't wonna go der. He sez den yuh better give me dem birds. So I giv' 'em tuh him."

"Did he say thank yuh?" asked Uncle Charley, still chuckling.

"No, jist said, don't be do'n dat no more till duh seazun's open."

"I says, when's dat?"

"He sayz in a munt 'r so."

"Did he pinch yuh?" asked Charley.

"No."

"Did he take yuhr gun?"

"No, dist da birds. Guess he wanted tuh make some soup too."

"Well . . ." said Hilliard, "are we gonna play cards or shoot birds all night?"

"Okay," said Charley to Hilliard, "shuffle 'em up."

The boys were tired of standing, so they sat down on the floor with their legs crossed.

"Guess we should ov stayed at home," said Joey. "Nothing t' do here."

"Yah, we could ov read your comics," offered Billy. "Only got one done before I upended the pee-pot on Uncle Charley."

"That was a pretty good shot yuh made," snickered Joey. "Got 'm square in the face."

"Couldn't do that again if I tried," replied Billy, holding his hands over his face, trying to smother the laughter.

"I don't think it's a good idea tuh try it again," said Joey with a chuckle.

"Yah, I thought he was gonna kill us; his voice can sure get loud when he's mad. An' after what Hilliard said, I bet your teeth would rattle for a week if he ever give yah a good shake 'n."

"More like your head would fly off," offered Joey. "I never heard him tell any stories about him fightin'; it was always about somebody else doin' it."

"Paw always said that a good man never brags," offered Billy.

"Yah, and from what he said on the way down, good men don't go 'round hurtin' people for no reason, and if they do have tuh deal with somebody, they don't talk about it."

"I think he's a pretty good man!" stated Billy.

"Yah, and he might be my uncle, but I'm still learning things about him."

Their conversation was interrupted by Festus as he voiced his complaints.

"Binga, Binga, Binga. Every time yah win it's Binga," said Festus.

"If you don't like it, then why don't you try doing a little winning, and then I won't be saying it so much," offered Gertrude.

"If 'n yuh'd stop dat darn ol' cheatin', a fella could do a bit o' winnin'."

"Poor loser, Festus, poor loser!" teased Gertrude.

"Jus' wait a minute till I gits ready an yuh'll see."

"Yah, sure, we'll be waitin' all night till you get ready. Okay, Charley, let's get at it an' see how many more 'Bingos' I can get before we're done."

While waiting for the cards to be dealt, Charley looked at Hilliard and asked, "Where the boys t'night?"

"Oh, probably over at Hatfield's with their lads. Bunch o' mischief-makers when they're all together. Hard t' say what they'll be intuh, each generation gets a little worse than the last.

"Old Tom, their grandfather, was sittin' on a chair enjoying the sun, and most likely half asleep. The youngest one, little Albert, came by with a rhubarb stalk in his hand and said I wonder what I should do with this? He looked at ol' Tom, then gave it to 'm right across the face. His ol' pipe went flyin', an' he started intu the roarin'. I could hear him over here. He was a-callin' that young fellow everything he could lay his tongue to. I guess Hatfield caught him an' was givin' him a pretty good flailin', 'cause the old fellow was a-yellin', 'Pour it to 'm, pour it to 'm! If he was mine I'd kill 'im!'"

Uncle Charley was laughing, "Do yuh think it did any good?"

"No, not at all. The next day, he tried to set fire to the old fella's beard. He got another good shellackin' for that, too. And a couple o' days later I saw him with a bandage on one hand. So I asked him what had happened. He said he put a tomcat in a burlap sack, and then tried to put another one in with him, wanting tuh see if they'd fight. Well, I guess when the second one saw the other cat already in the bag, he decided that joinin' him wasn't such a good idea. So he put the teeth tuh Albert's hand till he turned him loose, then he moved on, lookin' for a safer place tuh hang out."

Uncle Charley was laughing and shaking his head, "Do yuh think they'll ever change?"

"Not too likely. Sure as ol' thunderin' an' lightnin', by the time they're grown up they'll be the worst bunch o' hellions that ever lived.

"Bill Mathews said that old Tom made the comment, that if he'd known the grandkids would be so much fun, he'd ov had them first. But somehow, I got the feelin' that maybe ol' Bill was doin' a bit ov lie'n."

By now Hilliard had all the cards handed out, and turned up the ace of spades.

Everybody passed, so Hilliard picked it up.

"Now what did I tell yuh," said Gertrude, "cheatin' again! Dealin' from the bottom ov the deck. These two would do anything to win! But don't worry, we've got the cat in the bag."

"Just don't try tuh put two ov 'm in it!" warned Hilliard.

Tired of sitting, Billy leaned backwards and almost fell into the bottom part of the cupboard.

"Look out," said Joey as he grabbed him by the arm.

The cupboards had no doors, just a piece of cloth hung down to cover the opening. When Billy had leaned back he pushed through it.

"Be careful or yuh'll bust somethin' in there an' we'll be in trouble again!"

"Wonder what's in there?" whispered Billy, as he pulled the piece of cloth to one side and took a peek.

"What d'yuh see?" asked Joey, in a whisper.

"Pots an' pans an' stuff. Can't see much — it's too dark."

Then Billy reached in and pulled out a bottle.

"What's that?" whispered Joey.

"Don't know. It's too dark t' read what's written on it."
"Pull the cork an' smell it."
Billy pulled the cork out and put the bottle to his nose.
"Turpentine!"
"Turpentine?" repeated Joey, "that's good stuff!"
"For what?"
"Well, ol' Bob's tomcat used t' hang around and fight with ours. So, one day Mick caught him an' put some o' that stuff under his tail. Man... yuh should o' seen that ol' cat go! When he crossed that ol' field he was travellin' like greased lightning. I tell yuh he coulda passed a motorsicle doin' ninety, and he's never come back."

Billy was snickering. "That's funny."

Billy leaned over toward Joey and whispered, "Next time, tell Mick tuh put the two tomcats in a bag instead ov using turpentine — sounds like more fun."

"I don't think so. Paw would kill him if he ever caught him doin' somethin' like that."

Just then Gertrude slid forward on her chair and played her card. When finished, she slid back again, just like she'd been doing all evening. Joey pointed this out to Billy who looked at him with a frown, not understanding what he meant.

At the back of the chair was a hollowed-out portion, designed to fit one's backside. When Gertrude slid ahead, this space was vacant and it would hold at least a half cup of liquid. Joey indicated that Billy should put some turpentine in the open space when she slid forward. Billy's eyes opened wide as he shook his head, "no."

"Yah... go ahead," whispered Joey. "See if she's as fast as the tomcat."

"I don't think so," whispered Billy. "She might kill me."

"Shouldn't hurt much; didn't kill the cat."

Billy hesitated, not sure of what he was getting into.

"No way, I'll get into trouble if I do."

"Don't be chicken. Give 'r a shot," persuaded Joey.

"You do it," said Billy, offering Joey the bottle.

"No, you have the bottle; you do it," insisted Joey, wanting no part of it.

"I don't think it's a good idea," suggested Billy. "A cat is different — he'll run, but she'll scream!"

"The cat didn't scream," laughed Joey, "so why would she?"

"If he was travellin' as fast as you said he was, he wouldn't have time for screamin'!" replied Billy with a big grin.

"Oh, don't be such a chicken! Even the bandy rooster has more courage than you.

"Give 'r a shot and see what happens!" coaxed Joey.

Caught between knowing better and the dare to do it, Billy paused, then he pulled the cork and poured. After a few glug, glug, glug's from the bottle, he put the cork back in and quickly placed the bottle back in the cupboard where he had found it. He then sat with his arms folded waiting for the results; it didn't take long.

Gertrude shoved back into the chair, then sat straight up as she felt something wet. There was a brief pause, much like when the fire reaches the dynamite; there's that split second before the explosion.

She screamed and came up off the chair, throwing her cards into the air as she rose. Her chair went over backwards on top of the boys, and her thighs caught the edge of the table on her way up, lifting her side of the table and sending the coal-oil lamp sliding toward Charley. He caught the lamp, but the chimney kept on going and landed in a thousand pieces. What Charley was now holding was more like a torch; the flame of the lamp was out of control. It was flipping up and down, giving off a lot of smoke but not much light.

Gertrude danced in small circles around the floor with her knees coming up to her waist, her hands in her hair, yelling, "Fire, fire, I'm on fire!" She then made a beeline for the door; her momentum was such that when she put her elbow out to push the door open, it punched a hole in the screen, and she went right on through it, with nothing but slivers flying from the cross member. Without slowing down any, she made a left turn around the corner of the house and headed for the lake.

Festus said, "What 'appened to 'r? Did ol' Binga bite 'r?" His face showed total amazement at what he had just seen.

"Don't know," said Uncle Charley, "but somethin' sure as ol' 'ell did."

By this time Gertrude was splashing around in the water yelling, "Fire, fire, I'm on fire."

Hilliard jumped up and headed for the door. "I didn't see any fire or smoke; what could be wrong with that girl?"

His wife dropped her mending and hurried out after him. The boys looked at each other with eyes that were bulging out of their heads, their faces were now as white as snow, and the grin that was there a few minutes earlier had quickly disappeared.

Joey nodded to Billy and said, "I think we'd better be gettin' out o' here, while the getting's still good!"

They started out on their hands and knees, then scrambled to their feet as they headed for the door.

They also didn't take the time to open the door, but went out through the hole that Gertrude had made in it. Behind them they could hear Uncle Charley speak. "Now what 'n the world did you fellas do t' that little girl?"

Outside, they could hear Gertrude splashing around in the water, yelling, "Iee, Iee, Iee, it's burnin', it's burnin'!"

Hilliard was asking, "What's burning? What's wrong?"

"I don't know what's wrong, but my ass is burnin'."

As Uncle Charley came out through the door, he said, "Okay, boys, let's get outa here before yuh get yuhrselves killed. I don't know what yuh did, but I'm sure there'll be 'ell tuh pay for this one!"

It would be another hour before the moon came up, but there was enough starlight to let them see where they were going. Charley made his way toward the drive shed with the boys trotting along on his heels. He took the lantern from the buggy, pushed the lever, and raised the glass. Striking a match, he touched it to the wick. "Kerpoof!" The lantern exploded into flames; he pitched it out into the green grass so as not to set the buggy on fire.

"Now who in this wide world o' mortal wisdom would put gas in a coal-oil lantern? Now *there's* a feller that I'd like t' give a slap up the side o' the head with a flat rock!"

The flames from the lantern were going four feet into the air, giving enough light for Charley to see into the drive shed.

"Easy Nelly Bell, easy." Her nostrils were flared and her eyes were flashing as she turned sideways, watching the fire. Charley reached over to untie the halter shank and got another surprise.

"Now what 'n ol' 'ell is goin' on here?" Charley's hands kept slipping on the rope as he tried to untie it.

"Axle grease! Who 'n their right mind would put axle grease all over a man's halter shank?"

Charley used hay from the manger to try and remove the grease from his hands. It took the excess, but they were far from being clean.

Next, he put his hand into his pocket and pulled out his pocket knife, but try as he would, he couldn't get the blade to open. His fingers kept slipping off just as it would start to move. Frustrated, he clamped it in his teeth and pulled; this time it opened all the way. He spit a few times, then cut the rope.

"Shame t' waste a good piece ov rope, but what's a fella tuh do? Time could be more precious right now than this ol' rope will ever be!"

Backing the horse toward the buggy, he said to the boys, "Yuh fellas hold the shavs up while I back ol' Nelly Bell into place."

When everything was in place, he pulled the lines through the ring on the hame and mounted the buggy.

"Well, would yuh take a look at that? Them dirty little beggars got the wheels all cockeyed." Charley's emotions were running high. They had taken a back wheel and interchanged it with a front one. The two big wheels were kitty-cornered to the small wheels; this would make for a most interesting ride home.

"I see what the boys were doing while we were play'n cards. I'd sure like t' get muh hands on 'em, but that won't happen right now. I'd better get you two fellers outa here while yuh're still in one piece."

Charley mounted the buggy with a boy on either side of him and clicked his tongue and said, "Okay, Nellie Bell, take 'r home."

As they were passing the house, Hilliard came around the corner.

"Whoa, did yuh find the problem?" asked Charley, all in the same breath.

"No, but her mother is with her in the water. Says her backend is burnin'; don't know what would cause that t' happen all of a sudden."

"Hope it ain't ketchin'," said Charley. "Best be goin', I think I've had enough excitement for one night."

"Yah, me too. Come again," said Hilliard, "and we'll finish the game."

"You bet!

"That's my coal oil lantern burnin' over there in the grass. Them hool-i-guns filled 'r with gas. It should burn out in a few minutes!"

Charley snapped the lines and they moved off into the darkness.

13

The Return of Ol' Zack

The dipsy-doodle motion had the boys holding tight to the handles at the end of the seat. Driving into semi-darkness was scary enough, but the thought of being thrown from the buggy was even worse.

Uncle Charley held a line in each hand with his feet braced to the sway of the buggy. It wasn't the most comfortable way to ride home, but he dared not wait to put the wheels back in order; for if they found out what it was the boys had done to the girl, there would, as the saying goes, most likely be "hell to pay." And without the lantern, there would be no stopping along the way to correct the matter. So, it was ride it out, and pray that no one got seasick before reaching their destination.

They travelled on in silence for a minute or two, then Charley spoke.

"I reckon this is about the worst contraption that I've ever ridden in. Those darn yo-hockers ruined the lantern, so now we can't fix the wheels. I guess we'll just have tuh put up with it. It looks like yuhr paw will have t' get himself another lantern. I doubt if the old one owes him anything; I'm sure he's had it since Adam was a child.

"Now go easy, Nellie Bell, for if this thing should ever decide tuh take a sashay it could throw a fella right out intuh the ditch."

When crossing the creek, the small front wheel hit the ground first. Then it switched to the small back wheel, giving the buggy a dip to the front right, then to the back left.

"I've never rode in anything like this before, and I sincerely hope and pray that I never will again. I think it's gonna be a long ride home, fellas!"

They wobbled along in silence for awhile, then Uncle Charley spoke.

"Okay . . . now what in ol' 'ell did you fellas do tuh that little girl, t' put her in such a state?" There was a moment of dead silence as if nothing had been said.

"Did yuh hear what I said?" Uncle Charley's voice was stern and demanding.

"Turpentine." Billy's voice was weak and low with a bit of a shake to it.

"Waddayuh mean . . . Turpentine?" thundered Uncle Charley.

There was a bit of a pause, then the voice came low and trembling."I . . . I . . . put it on her chair."

"What in this wide world ov wonders would ever possess yuh t' do that?"

"We . . . we found a bottle of it in the cupboard . . . a-and Joey said Mick put some under a tomcat's tail to make him go home, and he went like greased lightning."

"So yuh thought yuh'd try some on the girl tuh see how it'd work on her, did yah?"

"Well . . . sort ov . . . something like that." The voice was timid and low.

"Well . . . now let me tell you fellas somethin'. There is one wide world ov difference between that little gal's back end an' that ol' tomcat's ass. But I guess you fellas wouldn't know much 'bout that, now, would yuh . . . "

Again there was silence, which Uncle Charley broke after a moment or two. "Turpentine . . . they'd smell that as soon as they got back into the house. Guess I just got you fellas out o' there 'n time. Ol' Hilliard woulda skinned the both ov yuh!"

Again they rode in silence. There was just the sound of the horse's feet on the road, the jingle of the harness, and the buggy wheels grating in the gravel.

"I know yuh fellas didn't mean no harm," Uncle Charley's voice was soft but serious, "but yuh gotta think about what yuh're do'n' t' other people. What yuh did tuh that wee gal wasn't funny. Yuh gotta stop an' think about what yuh're do'n before yuh do it. If that ol' tomcat took off like greased lightnin', then there must o' been a darn good reason for him tuh be scratchin' gravel like that. Bad enough t' do something like that to a nuisance cat, let alone a person, and a sweet little girl like that tuh boot!"

"Are we gonna get into some kind o' trouble?" asked Billy, sounding like he'd been pretty well shaken up by what had happened.

"Well, yuh'll probably get away with it this time, but yuh best remember. The Man above is pretty good at keepin' records, an' yuh'll have t' answer tuh Him someday when yuh get up there."

"Yuh mean God?" asked Joey.

"Yep, that's who I mean," replied Uncle Charley, slow and serious.

"And His name ain't Andy," offered Billy, still on the serious side.

"Waddayuh mean it ain't Andy?" chuckled Uncle Charley.

"You told Joey God's name was Andy. Well it ain't. It's 'AND HE' walks with me, 'AND HE' talks with me. 'T ain't Andy!"

Uncle Charley was now having a soft chuckle and Billy's voice was a little more at ease.

"Well . . . I guess I got me a little mixed up with their singin', but it sounded somethin' like that."

"I think you were just pullin' his leg."

"Well . . . whatever His name is, He keeps a pretty good eye on things that 'r goin' on down here, an' you boys had better get a good understandin' o' that or you're gonna get into real trouble with Him one day."

"How do you know that?" asked Billy, sounding a little surprised, but serious.

"'Cause I read muh Bible most every day before I go t' bed."

"You got a Bible?" asked Billy. Surprise was evident in his voice.

"Sure do! It belonged tuh my grandmaw, an' she give it t' muh mother, an' she give it tuh me. Sorta ragged at the edges, but it still reads good."

Again there was a moment's silence.

"Do you think we'll go tuh hell for what we did tonight?" asked Billy, his voice betraying his concern.

"Maybe . . . or maybe not . . . dupendin'."

"On what?"

"Whether yuh say you're sorry 'r not. He says if yuh ask Him, He'll forgive yuh when yuh do wrong."

Again there was silence.

"The preacher said one time when he was preachin' at the old school, that if we didn't repent and ask God tuh forgive us, we were all gonna go straight t' hell."

"Uh hu, it says something like that."

"He said if we asked God to forgive us, and really meant it, He'd save us from hell!"

"Yep, that's what it says! God sent His Son into the world tuh die on the cross. His life was perfect so he didn't have tuh die, but he took the place ov the ol' sinner . . . people just like you and me. And if we ask Him tuh forgive us and save us, He will, and we won't have tuh go tuh hell, 'cause he died in our place tuh pay for the cost ov our sin. I had a debt I couldn't pay, an' He paid a debt He didn't owe!"

Billy said, "I remember when the preacher was at the old school talking about hell. I closed my eyes to try an' hide from his preachin'. But when I closed them, all I saw was the ol' devil lookin' at me. I tell yuh, I didn't keep 'em closed very long. He used tuh scare me half tuh death with his preachin' ov hell.

"But Paw said he was telling the truth and that I should be listenin' to him. Paw is always talkin' about the Man above; I guess he means Jesus." Billy stopped talking and again they rode on in silence, as if there were some serious thinking going on.

After a minute or two, Billy spoke to Uncle Charley, his voice soft and serious.

"Maw says the Bible tells us not tuh fight, but sometimes you do . . . how come?"

Uncle Charley remained silent for a minute as if he were collecting his thoughts, looking for the right words.

"Well... I sorta see it this way. God doesn't want us tuh go around hurtin' other people just because we don't like them, or just because we can. He wants us to be good tuh others, but sometimes they won't let yuh. So what 'r yuh gonna do? God says it's better tuh give than tuh receive, and I can't think ov a better time to apply it than when a fella is come 'n at yuh with a hand full ov hard knuckles, an' he fully intends to give'm to yuh.

"Yuh see, if a fella was tuh come into yuhr house and wanted tuh hurt yuhr maw, do yuh think your paw should just stand there an' let him? Or do yuh think he should do something about it?"

Billy's reply was fast and certain. "I think Paw should knock his head off!"

"So there yuh go, and so do I. That's why God made the men tuh be the head ov the home an made us mostly stronger than the woman, so 's we could protect 'em. God also says that if a man goes out and kills another man, that man should pay with his life 'cause man was made in God's image, an' we're not supposed tuh kill somebody just 'cause we're mad at 'm. Now, if a person kills somebody, I don't think they're gonna walk into a police station and say, okay, here I am, hang me. They will have tuh go an' get him an make him come in, and probably use some force in doin' so. So there yuh go, I do believe there are times when it's much better tuh give than receive and that's one ov 'em. At least that's how I see it."

After a minute of riding on in silence, Billy looked up at Uncle Charley and asked, "How come yuh never got married?"

"Why d' yuh ask that?"

"Well... yuh seem like a nice enough person to be married tuh somebody."

Again there was silence as Uncle Charley collected his thoughts.

"Well... I almost did get married once, but I changed my mind."

"How come?" asked Billy, his voice soft and sympathetic.

"Well... it's sort ov a long story."

"That's okay... we'll listen," replied Billy, eager to hear the reason.

"Well.... yuh see, there was me an' this Sally Ann girl. We went tuh school together. Sort o' were good friends most o' the time.

Had little scraps now an' then, but we always made up again. I'd tease her an she'd chase me, an I'd let 'r catch me, so's I could get tuh hug her. Then as we got older she grew into a pretty nice young lady. Good look'n, good manners, an' a pretty darn good cook tuh boot. We spent a lot ov time together, went for walks, went fish'n, went tuh the dances. It seemed that when we weren't busy with somethin' else, we were always together. This went on until she was eighteen or so, an' we talked about gettin' married an' such. But I started tuh notice that no matter what she did, her mother was either involved, or was telling her how tuh do it."

Again Uncle Charley paused, as if someone were pulling the strings connected to his emotions. "This wasn't too bad, a mother an' daughter be'n sorta close, but when she started to do'n the same with me, it was just a little too much o' mother. An' I told her so, an' she didn't like it, so I told 'r straight out, I'd sure like tuh marry you, but I ain't about tuh marry yuhr mother."

"Can you do that?" asked Billy, sounding surprised.

"Do what?"

"Marry somebody's mother?"

Charley chuckled. "I didn't mean it just that way. I meant it would be *like* I was married to her mother 'cause she'd be underfoot all the time, try'n tuh tell me what I could an' couldn't do."

"Oh, I think I see — she'd be a darn ol' nuisance."

"Uh-huh, I think yuh got it."

"Reminds me ov a fella I once knew. He asked me if I knew the mean'n o' mixed emotions. I said I thought I did, but for him tuh go ahead an tell me his version ov it. Well . . . he said it's like when yuhr mother-in-law goes over the cliff with your best horse an' new buggy."

"I don't get it," said Billy.

"You don't want tuh lose your horse and buggy, but . . . ." Joey was trying to explain.

"But, yuh're glad tuh get rid ov the ol' lady," interrupted Billy.

"I think yuh got it, uh-huh . . . I think yuh do," said Uncle Charley, hosting a big smile and nodding his head in agreement.

"So, what happened tuh Sally Ann?" asked Billy, trying to keep the conversation going.

"Well... you know, we got tuh fight'n over her mother, an' couldn't agree, so one night I said goodbye and meant it. I walked away and I never went back."

"What did she do?" asked Billy, sounding a bit disappointed with the way the story was going.

"Well... I guess she got over it, an' ended up marrying some feller from Pembroke. He was smart enough tuh take 'r away from her mother, an' I guess things went well for a while. Then her father died, an' her mother went tuh live with them. A couple o' years later, he moved out an' got a place ov his own."

"Guess he didn't want to be married to her mother either," offered Billy, with a bit of a grin.

"I guess not," chuckled Uncle Charley. "I guess not."

Again they rode on in silence, their feet braced for when the buggy tipped. Then again Uncle Charley spoke.

"Yuh know, marriage ain't all bad; some have it pretty good. Some people are just meant for each other, an' they seem tuh make it all worthwhile.

"Sissy was tell'n me that she was meet'n ol' Kelly every morning on her way tuh Murphy's store. She'd be'n workin' at the store. So one morning she asked him where he was go'n so early every morning, an' he said down tuh the Home tuh have breakfast with his wife. So, she asked him how his wife was do'n, an' he said not too badly. Her memory was pretty well gone; hadn't known who he was for the last three years. An' Sissy said, she doesn't know who yuh are, but yuh still go an' have breakfast with her every morning? He smiled and said, 'Sissy, she may not remember who I am, but I still know who she is, an' I'll keep on a-go'n till she's just a pitcher in a frame!' Now that's the real thing, that's what marriage is all about!"

They wobbled on down the road for awhile in silence, letting things sink in, and then Charley spoke again.

"That also reminds me ov another story about a fella that lived here in town some time ago. It seemed him an' his wife never had a fight, always seemed tuh get along no matter what. So, ol' Jim Daniels said that when he was thinking 'bout get'n married, he went over tuh talk tuh this ol' fella. Asked him what his secret was.

The ol' fella said that he wasn't sure what it was, but they'd only had one fight an' that was on their wedding day.

"He said the fella down at the livery stable had always be'n a pretty good friend ov his, and he offered him a horse an' buggy tuh go for a ride on their wed'n day, no charge. All seemed fair, but this ol' fella was always up tuh some kind of devilment.

"Well, when the wedding day come, there was the horse an' buggy sit'n outside the church. Worst ol' nag yuh ever saw; should have been done away with years before. Anyways, he helped his bride up into the seat an' laid his rifle in the back of the buggy. Always carried that ol' rifle no matter where he went; yuh'd think it was his brother, or somethin' like that.

"Anyways, this ol' nag staggered along till they got tuh the railroad tracks. There she stopped. No way would she go forward. She was one balky ol' sun-ov-a-gun. So the fella had tuh get down and lead the horse across the railroad tracks. On the other side, he put his finger on the horse's nose an' said tuh the horse, that's once. He then got into the buggy an' drove on.

"A little while later, they came tuh a crick running across the road. Again the balky ol' mare stop'd and refused to go across the crick. So, the fella got down an' took off his boots, rolled up his pant legs an' led the horse across the crick. On the other side, he put his boots back on an' laid his finger on the ol' mare's nose an said, horse, that's twice, an' got back in the buggy.

"Next, they come tuh that ol' wooden bridge, an' no way would that ol' mare cross the bridge. So . . . he gits down again an' goes tuh the front ov that ol' horse an' lays his finger on 'r nose an' says, horse, this is the third time. He then goes tuh the back ov the buggy an' gets his rifle, jacks a shell into 'r, sticks the barrel in the horse's ear, an' pulls the trigger. 'Bang!' Down goes the ol' mare.

"Well, the old mare had hardly hit the ground till his bride stood up an started tuh scream an holler. She called him every name she could think ov. Said she'd ov never married him had she known he was so cruel. He said that when she run out o' names that she knew, she must ov made some up, 'cause she was sayin' words that he had never heard before.

"Said he didn't know what tuh do or say, she was talking faster than he could listen. So when she finally paused tuh ketch her breath, he put his finger on the end ov 'r nose an said, woman, that's once. He said she immediately stopped the yell'n an' such. She got down from the buggy, put her arm in his, and walked back tuh town as nice as yuh please ... Yep, her on one arm an' that ol' rifle in the crook ov the other, walk'n right along. Said she never said another angry word tuh him to the day that she died.

"Now, that one was just the opposite ov the first one. The first one got along because they loved each other, the second one because she was scared tuh death ov that ol' rifle."

"Did she ever get tuh number two?" asked Billy.

"No ... I don't think so, I guess she was smart enough tuh realize that if she got tuh two, she could accidentally slip into three, an' that would be the end of it."

"Don't think I'd wanna live like that," said Billy, "thinking somebody might shoot yuh if yuh made a mistake or someth'n."

"Yah, me neither," replied Uncle Charley, tongue-in-cheek.

"Do yuh think that he would really shoot her?" asked Billy, not sure what to make of it.

"No, I don't think so ... maybe an old horse, but not a person. Though, some folks live like that, scared tuh death ov the other person; it just ain't right."

"How do yuh know if you 'r marrying the right person?" asked Billy.

"Well ... you know, I guess it ain't easy figger'n it out, but yuh need tuh take yuhr time and get tuh know the other person. Yuh can't love somebody that yuh don't like."

"What do yuh mean?" asked Billy, looking up at Uncle Charley, puzzled by what he had said.

"Well, some folks think that when a boy meets a girl, an' they take that sly glance at each other, an' they get this all-over fuzzy feel'n, that it's love. Well, it ain't no such a thing. Yuh got tuh get tuh know the person first, then figger out if yuh like 'em. Yuh know, yuh like be'n around them, do'n things with them, be'n where they are. An' if yuh like 'em enough, yuh'll get tuh love 'em. An' if yuh love somebody then yuh make the decision tuh stand by 'em through thick or thin. And yuh'll have tuh decide tuh work at it, 'cause yuh won't always feel like love'n 'em if they do something that yuh don't like. But yuh got tuh do it anyways, 'cause yuh said yuh would. And the more yuh do things for the other person, the more yuh'll get tuh like 'em.

"Yuh know, if an ol' stray dog comes by an' he's gaunt and hungry, look'n the worst for wear, an' yuh feed 'm an' look after 'm for a while, pretty soon yuh'll get tuh lik'n that ol' dog and feel that you own him. Well... it's a lot like that with people. If yuh do things for 'em, yuh'll get tuh like 'em. It's called go'n the second mile."

"What does that mean?" asked Billy.

"Well... in Bible times, the Roman soldiers could make the Jews carry their packs for one mile. Jesus told them tuh carry it for two. The first mile they had to carry it, and they hated the Romans for that reason. But the second mile was because they *chose* tuh do it, and this made the difference. If yuh *choose* to be good tuh someone, it's awful hard tuh hate 'm at the same time."

"I think I see what yuh mean," nodded Billy.

Feeling that he had answered the question, Uncle Charley carried on. "If yuh marry 'em yuh got tuh be good to 'em. Treat 'em better than yuh treat yuhr self. If yuh think yuh'd like tuh marry a gal, ask your self if yuh think yuh'd take a bullet for her. Step in front ov her if somebody was gonna shoot at her. If yuh say no, then leave 'r alone and move on, 'cause she ain't for you. The only worthwhile reason for stepping in front ov a bullet is 'cause you just don't want tuh face tomorrow without her, and it's not that yuh want tuh be some kind of a hero. Sort ov selfish, but you'd rather go first than live without her.

"Yuh need tuh be like that ol' fella go'n for breakfast. Yuh got tuh be willing tuh keep on till she's just a pitcher in a frame.

"It's sorta like fight'n in reverse — yuh do thu best yuh can tuh out-give the other person, an' outdo 'em in kindness. At least that's how I see it."

"Do yuh think you could like Sally Ann's mother?" asked Billy.

"Yah, sure, not a problem. Just as long as she learned tuh keep her nose outa other people's business."

Again there was a pause where no one spoke. Then Billy broke the silence; his voice was soft and kind. "Yuh know, I think you're about the smartest and kindest person I've ever met."

"Yuh do? Well, thanks, but I think there's a few that would give yuh some opposition on that one. Take it easy, Nelly Bell, or yuh'll throw us out o' this ol' buggy! Good job the horse knows where she's go'n, 'cause I can't see a darn thing ten feet past the end ov her nose. I do know that we're going past the lake, 'cause them ol' bullfrogs are still go'n at it.

"They just can't seem tuh make up their mind about anything. The little ones say, its knee deep, knee deep. The medium-size ones say, go round, go round, and the big ol' fella says, yuh'll drown, yuh'll drown. Total confusion!"

For the rest of the trip, they rode in silence. The boys were tired but they dared not close their eyes in case they fell asleep and got pitched out of the buggy. They kept a good hold on the handle at the edge of the seat, and their feet braced on the floor as the buggy pitched back and forth; they were not taking any chances.

Nell turned down the laneway leading home without any instructions.

"Kinda glad this trip is over; any more o' this wobbling an' I'd be sick as a dog."

In a few minutes, they could see the lamplight coming through the window. It gave a feeling of warmth and comfort as it shone through the darkness. The moon was just starting to brighten the eastern sky, and in about twenty minutes it would be above the treetops.

They drove up to the door, and Dan came out to meet them.

"Would yuh take the horse an' buggy an' put 'm away for me?" asked Uncle Charley. "You know where everything goes."

"No problem."

"Yuh'll need a lantern, 'cause the one we had is still in Hilliard's barnyard. Last I seen ov it, 'twas burning like a torch. Hatfield's young lads musta filled 'r with naphtha gas.

"Yuh'll need a new halter shank as well; I had tuh cut the other one. They loaded 'r down with axle grease; 'twas as slippery as a greased monkey, an' I couldn't untie it. Just in case yuh're wonder'n, they changed the buggy wheels around as well."

"You drove home with the wheels like that? Why didn't yuh change them back the way they should be?"

"Yuh don't want tuh know, but I'm sure the boys will tell yuh!"

"This doesn't sound good," said Dan, casting a glance at the boys, who were standing quietly with their heads down.

"It's worse than it sounds, but that's another story. By the way, that's axle grease that's all over Nell."

"Yah, I noticed. She looks more like a dapple gray; thought yuh traded horses while yuh were away. That's gonna take some cleaning, and I better get it done before Paw gets home."

"Do the best yuh can. I'm gonna try an' clean myself up an get tuh bed. Didn't get much sleep last night."

What Uncle Charley didn't know was that it would be even worse tonight.

After applying some gas, hot soapy water, and a good supply of elbow grease, Charley felt he was clean. Then he tried cleaning his clothes. When he was satisfied that he had done the best he could, he headed for the stairs.

"Goodnight, sleep tight, an' don't let the bedbugs bite; I'll see yuh in the morning." With this, Charley headed for bed and a good night's rest.

After Charley had gained the stairs, Mick turned to the boys and said, "Okay, what exactly did you two fellas do to get Uncle Charley upset?"

Billy looked at Joey and kind of shrugged his shoulders. Joey looked at Mick, and a slight smile passed his lips.

"Turpentine!" said Joey.

"Turpentine?" questioned Mick.

"Yah, Billy put some on Gertrude's chair."

"You did what?" Mick released a bit of a chuckle as he looked at Billy.

Billy blushed and dropped his eyes. "She was slidin' to the front of her chair to play her card, an' then she'd slide back again. I found a bottle ov turpentine in the cupboard, an' Joey said you put some on the tomcat's ass an' he took off like greased lightning, so we thought we'd put some on her chair tuh see what she'd do."

"You're jokin'?" said Mick, smiling, but realizing this was for real.

"No . . . Billy poured half a bottle on the chair, an' when she slid back into it, you should ov seen her go," said Joey, raising his hand to his face, trying not to laugh. "Just about upset the table, did a little dance, screamed, then went straight through the ol' screen door without even opening 'r. Ran down and into the lake just a scream'n. But she was no match for that ol' tomcat; he was cover'n ground a lot faster than she ever could!"

"That's why Uncle Charley was in a hurry tuh get us outa there before Hilliard found out what had happened an' killed the both ov us," said Billy. His eyes were wide open as if the realization and fear of what had just happened had finally gotten to him.

"You might use that stuff on nuisance cats an' dogs tuh get rid ov them, but not on a person. Man, that must ov stung," said Mick, sucking air in through his teeth.

"I think it did," said Joey, "'cause she wasn't wast'n any time in get'n tuh the lake."

"Uncle Charley said that was 'cause her rear end was a lot different than that ol' tomcat's ass," offered Billy, "but he didn't think that we would understand that. And we didn't; never even thought of anything like that."

"It sure is different," commented Mick. "Poor girl. You guys are something else; just one thing after another."

"We didn't know," offered Billy in his defence. "We were just try'n tuh have some fun."

"Yah, at someone else's expense. Paw finds out he'll probably skin the both of you and roll yuh in salt, and that's just for a starter."

"Think we should go to bed," said Billy, sounding a little worried.

"Yah, let's go," agreed Joey. His smile also had vanished.

"And don't forget tuh sleep in the spare room," reminded Mick.

"Yah, this should be fun," said Joey over his shoulder as they headed for the stairs.

The boys were asleep in the spare room when Mick and Dan came to bed, and, as planned, they slept on the opposite sides of the loft. After all was quiet and everyone was settled in bed, the noise started. Dan pulled the cans across the floor to his side, and Mick pulled them back. If Uncle Charley had been sleeping, he wasn't any longer.

"What'n ol' 'ell is going on now? Ol' Zack must be at 'r again; too bad he can't rest in peace an' let everybody else do the same. Keep'n folks awake half the night, he needs tuh be ashamed ov himself."

Uncle Charley wasn't talking loud, mostly to himself, but loud enough for the rest to hear him. After a while the noise stopped, and everyone faded off to asleep.

Later on in the night, Uncle Charley got a call from Mother Nature. His getting up roused Mick, and just before Charley reached the top of the stairs, Mick pulled on the string and the cans rattled. Charley stopped dead in his tracks.

"Don't think I'm gonna be goin' down there tonight," he muttered to himself, and made his way back to the bedroom.

The problem was that nature's call kept getting louder, so he got up, closed the door, and went to the chamber pot at the bottom of the bed. With the room being on the dark side, he didn't want to miss the pot, so he decided it would be easier if he sat on it rather than kneel down and aim. Lifting his nightshirt, he gently sat down. As he settled himself on the pot, he realized the rim didn't feel right . . . sort of squishy. He tried to stand up again, but the pot came up with him.

"Now what in ol' 'ell is going on here?" he muttered to himself.

Holding his shirttail in one hand, he tried to pull the pot away with the other. When it finally let go, he touched the rim of the pot to see what the problem was. Smelling his finger, he uttered right out loud, "Molasses! Who in this big old wonderful world ov wonders would put molasses on a piss-pot? — I think I just might have a pretty good idea!"

He was now in a real predicament. It wasn't enough to have a ring of molasses around his butt, but now he had it on his fingers as well. With his clean hand, he reached around behind himself, trying to hold his nightshirt away from his body, so as not to get molasses on it. He couldn't touch his spout with the hand that had molasses on his fingers without contaminating it. So now the problem was: How could he aim to make sure he would hit the pot? He dared not lay it on the rim because it would stick to the pot and then he'd have another problem.

"What in the world trailed me here in the first place? I should have known better. Now look at the mess I'm in. Well, ol' fella, looks like yuh're gonna get a taste ov molasses, 'cause I can't let 'r fly all over the floor, an' it's too dark for me tuh see what I'm doing."

There was the thundering sound of water being poured into a pot, then all was silent again.

"Looks like we're in need ov some water tuh clean up this mess. I guess it's tuh 'ell with ol' Zack, I have tuh get downstairs, like it or not."

Uncle Charley pushed open the door and walked out, making his way to the top of the stairs. He was walking bent forward with his arm held behind his back, holding his nightshirt out, trying to keep his shirttail away from the molasses.

Just as he reached the top of the stairs, Dan pulled the string, and the cans rattled. Uncle Charley stopped and waited, undecided as to what he should do.

"Well that settles it. I ain't go'n down there tonight!"

The noise wakened Billy, who took a look out the bedroom door, and then gave Joey the elbow.

"Joey, wake up, there's a great big rooster at the top ov the stairs!"

Uncle Charley was bent forward, holding his shirttail out the back end; he sure did look the part.

"What?" said Joey, still half asleep.

"There's a big rooster at the top ov the stairs!" repeated Billy, his voice getting a bit anxious.

Joey rubbed his eyes and took a look.

"You idiot, that ain't no rooster, its Uncle Charley!"

"Sure does look like one tuh me."

"Yah, it does," chuckled Joey, "wonder what's ail'n him?"

Uncle Charley hurried back to the bedroom and closed the door. He walked over to the bed, then stopped. He thought for a minute then turned back to the door.

"I gotta get some water, an' that's all there is to it."

He reached for the doorknob.

"Gonna get molasses on the knob, but it can't be helped."

He opened the door, then quietly made his way to the stairs. He hesitated at the top and listened for a minute; all was deathly quiet. He slowly went down one step at a time. After three steps, Mick pulled the string and the tin cans rattled. He spun on the stairs and made haste to regain the floor. Travelling somewhere between a slow trot and a fast walk, he headed for the bedroom and closed the door. Then climbed into bed.

"It's gonna be one 'ell-uv-a mess by morning, but I guess that's how it has tuh be, 'cause I sure ain't gonna go down there with that ol' fella play'n hockey with a bunch o' tin cans!"

Mick and Dan both had their pillows over their heads and were doing their best not to laugh out loud, but the whole bed was shaking as they tried to keep control.

"Awh — awh — now everything is sticky, won't be much sleep'n again tonight, but this is the end ov 'r. Go'n home tomorrow come 'ell or high water, an' that is final!"

As the early light of morning touched the eastern sky, Uncle Charley slipped out of bed and quietly made his way to the stairs. His nightshirt was stuck to his butt, and his pants and shirt were held securely under his arm. After descending the stairs, he looked around for a place to undress and wash himself. He spied the backroom where the box stove was and he decided on doing it there. He could warm the water on the stove by burning the junk that Mary had left in it.

Placing his pants and shirt on the table, he took a couple of matches and went over to the stove. He opened the door, struck a match, and started the fire. Making sure the fire was going well, he closed the door and adjusted the damper, then turned to leave the room.

Uncle Charley's getting up and starting the fire woke Mick and Dan. As they listened to the noise from the stove, Dan sat up in bed. "Is he making a fire in the old box stove?"

"I think he is," said Mick.

"Lordie, lordie," replied Dan, as he scrambled to get out of bed, and on the other side of the loft, Mick was doing the same.

"He doesn't know about the dynamite caps!" yelled Mick, as his feet hit the floor.

"Kerbangangang!" the whole house shook as the fire caused the dynamite caps to explode.

Billy woke up screaming. Again he was scared half to death, but he didn't know why. The upstairs window glass was still rattling when Joey's feet hit the floor.

Mick looked at Dan. "Too late," he said, "he's already found 'em." Neck in neck they went down the stairs, three steps at a time, and when they reached the bottom, they could not believe their eyes. Opened-up stovepipes were lying all over the floor. The air was filled with ashes and soot, along with bits of paper that were still burning. All that was left of the ol' box stove was the four legs and the base. Uncle Charley was standing at the end of the table in his stuck-up nightshirt, with both hands over his ears. His hair was standing up, and the north side of him, from head to foot, was covered with ashes and soot. He was far worse than ol' Santa Claus could ever have been, even under the worst of conditions.

His eyes were the size of saucers and he was looking at them like he couldn't understand what had just happened. Mick and Dan slowly walked over to him.

"Are you okay?" they asked.

"What'd yuh say? Can't hear a darn thing. There's a whole lot o' ring'n going on in there!" As he spoke, he pointed to his ears.

"Are yuh hurt?" asked Dan, raising his voice a bit.

"What's wrong with muh shirt?" answered Uncle Charley, "is there a hole in 'r?"

"I think he's gone deef," said Dan, turning a little pale.

"What in ol' 'ell happened tuh thu stove... was she full o' denimite?"

"No... just caps."

"What'd yuh say?"

"Paw hid some dynamite caps in the stove," said Mick, raising his voice.

"Caps?"

"Yah," said Mick, nodding his head up and down.

"Looks like it was a pretty good place tuh keep 'm. I couldn't o' thought ov a better way tuh blow the ole stove all tuh slivers, even if I tried! I think the front end ov 'r went straight out through the winda, 'cause there's just a big hole in the wall where the winda used tuh be."

Uncle Charley just shook his head in disgust.

"I think you fellas have one 'ell-ov-a mess tuh clean up. I'm going tuh the milk house tuh clean up an' dress muh self. Surely tuh 'ell it won't fly tuh pieces before I'm done!"

Uncle Charley was not in a good mood and the tone of his voice made that very clear.

With his clothes under one arm, he picked up a facecloth and towel and went out the door. Just then two little faces peered around the corner of the staircase.

"What in the world happened?" asked Joey, as he looked around at the mess. "What made the stove blow up?"

"You don't want tuh know," replied Mick, his voice showing that he was totally disgusted.

"I asked yuh, didn't I?"

"Go back tuh bed!" replied Mick, not wanting to discuss it. His voice was sharp as if his temper was getting close to the surface.

"Wouldn't be much use in doin' that. Nobody could go back tuh sleep after that kind ov a racket. Billy's still shak'n from head tuh foot!"

"Will the house fall down?" asked Billy, his voice flat and serious.

"No! Now would you two get outa here!" Mick was getting impatient as he looked at the mess.

"Go easy," said Joey. "I think Billy has already wet himself."

"I did not!" replied Billy, his voice raising. Then a smile touched the corners of his mouth, "But let me tell yuh, I came pretty darn close to it — scared me half to death again!"

"Want me to put a fire in the cookstove so we can make some breakfast?" asked Joey, trying to find favour with Mick.

"Yah . . . no! The smoke'll come out the tee pipe where the other pipe is missing. I'll have to plug it with something first."

"Why don't yuh pick up the stovepipes and put 'em outside the back door," suggested Dan. "Place stinks like soot and ashes as it is. Maw sure ain't gonna be happy when she gets home!"

From the tone of Dan's voice, it was obvious that he fully understood that if Maw wasn't happy, no one else was going to be either.

"Well, let's see what we can do 'bout cleaning it up," suggested Mick. "I'll have tuh put some cardboard over the winda for now; it'll keep the rain out."

"What do yuh want me to do with these tin cans?" asked Joey. "Yuh know, if yuh hadn't been torment'n Uncle Charley, yuh wouldn't be in this mess. Serves yuh right, yuh know. Maybe next time yuh'll know better than tuh be bother'n him."

Joey sounded sympathetic toward Uncle Charley and a bit disgusted with Mick and Dan. But, no one thought that having fun with Uncle Charley would turn out like this.

"Take 'm out behind the house, an' don't be drag'n them. Make too much noise an' Uncle Charley'll figger out what we were doin' last night."

"Yuh don't need to worry about that. I don't think he's hearin' all that well this morning," offered Joey.

Mick wasn't in a good mood and the tone of his voice made it obvious. He had started out to have some fun with Uncle Charley, but it backfired on him, and there was no one to blame but himself. Now he had this mess to clean up before Maw and Paw came home. But his main concern was that Uncle Charley's hearing would be okay.

After the stovepipes were placed outside, and the place was cleaned up to the best of their ability, Joey asked, "Where's Uncle Charley? He should be cleaned up by now!"

"He's sitting on the well-box, look'n at the trees. Every so often he gives his head a shake. I think his ears are still ring'n," offered Billy.

"I hope he ain't gone deef," said Dan. "That was a pretty big bang, an' he was standing right there beside it."

"He'll be all right... he's a tough ol' bird." Mick was trying to ease the situation.

"Yuh got the hole in the pipe fixed?" asked Joey.

"Yah, I wired a tin pie plate over it."

"Now can I make a fire?"

"Yah, go ahead. An' get 'r going as fast as yuh can. Uncle Charley could probably use a cup ov coffee 'bout now!"

With the fire going and the table set, Mick called out to Uncle Charley. "Would yuh like a coffee?"

"What?" Uncle Charley looked at the house but he wasn't sure what was said.

"Would yuh like a coffee?" Mick called a little louder.

"Yah... okay!"

"I'll bring it out to yuh while breakfast's cook'n!"

Mick brought him a cup while he waited on the well-box, his nightshirt rolled up beside him.

"What in ol' 'ell happened in there? Was it really denimite caps?"

While trying to keep from smiling, Mick said, "Paw hid some caps in the ashes so Joey wouldn't find 'em. I never thought yuh'd be making a fire in the ol' stove or I'd ov told yuh."

"Who in their right mind would put denimite caps in a stove tuh hide 'em?" Charley wasn't happy and he didn't mind letting it be known. "Muh ears 'r ringin' pretty much like one ov them big ol' church bells. Can't hear much on muh left ear, probably go deef in it."

"You'll be okay in a day or two," said Mick, trying to ease the situation. "We got the mess cleaned up. Come on in an' have some breakfast."

Uncle Charley got up and followed Mick to the house. He kept digging in his left ear with his little finger, as if there were something in there doing the ringing and he was determined to get it out.

Breakfast was on the table, and Uncle Charley sat down and ate without saying a word. When he was finished, he went upstairs and packed his packsack. As he left the bedroom, he turned and looked back. "Sure is one 'ell ov a mess, but it ain't my fault!"

As he entered the downstairs room, everyone was quiet. They were just looking at him, saying nothing.

"Well, fellas, I definitely enjoyed my stay, but I've enjoyed about as much ov this as I can stand. So I'm hitting the road. I'm afraid my luck could come to an end at any minute, so I'm go'n while the going is still good.

"Anyways, your folks will be home pretty soon, so I'll be moving on tuh higher ground. And if I don't... I'm pretty sure that I'll only be needin' one more white shirt!"

"Why's that?" asked Billy.

"'Cause it'll be the one that I'll be wear'n for muh goin away party."

"Where is he goin'?" asked Billy, as he turned and looked at Joey.

"Six feet under!" was Joey's response, and he wasn't smiling.

"What?"

"He thinks if he stays any longer something is gonna kill him."

"Oh!" Said Billy, being not too sure where this conversation was heading.

"If yuh'll wait, Paw'll drive yuh home; it's a lot better than walking," offered Mick.

"Thanks, but no thanks. God only knows what'll happen next, and whatever it is, I do not want tuh be around when it does. And walk'n ain't no sin!"

"Are yuh okay?" asked Mick.

"Yep, I'm in pretty good shape, an' darn lucky tuh still be alive!"

The tone of Uncle Charley's voice clearly indicated that he was fed up and was moving on.

"Okay, but take it easy an' be careful," said Mick, his heart on the down side. He didn't like to see Uncle Charley leaving like this. It had not been his intention for things to happen as they had, but sometimes things just happen the way they happen, and there is not a thing you can do about it. It all started out as fun, but in the end it almost killed Uncle Charley.

"I'll try, but it don't seem tuh make a lot ov difference one way or the other. Things just happen as they will."

Uncle Charley opened the door and stepped outside; the others followed close behind him. He entered the laneway, and the boys watched him depart.

He was walking at a pretty good pace, with no looking back. He looked a lot like a man who wanted to be someplace else, and he wasn't about to be wasting any time in getting there.

"Do yuh think we were too hard on him?" asked Dan, sounding a little on the downside.

"What do yuh mean?" responded Mick, trying to sound casual about the whole thing.

"Well . . . yuh know, we scared him pretty darn good."

"I guess we didn't help any by getting in trouble down at Hilliards," said Billy, regret showing in his voice.

"I think the ol' stove blow'n up was the real problem," added Joey, trying to find something else to blame.

"Well, whatever it is, I'm sure he'll get over it," said Mick, sounding a little down but trying to raise the situation to a higher level.

"I hope he ain't mad at us," said Billy, "'cause I think he's a pretty nice fella, an' he wouldn't hurt anybody, even when he gets mad."

The whole group looked like they could use a little cheering up as they watched Uncle Charley disappear at the end of the lane. Ol' Jake nudged at Joey's hand trying to get his attention, as if to say, "It's okay, you still have me."

"Okay, let's get this place in order. Maw and Paw will soon be home, an' you know what will happen if things are a mess." Mick was giving the orders, and the rest were ready to respond. They wanted things as close to normal as possible before the folks got home.

It may have been a rough exit, but give it some time, and Uncle Charley would be back the next time they needed him; so all was not lost.

14

Maw Comes Home

I am anxious to get back home and see how things are going with the boys, an' it will be so nice to sleep in my own bed again. I enjoyed seeing the folks, but, when all is said and done, there's no place like home."

"I hope they had a good time on their own. Joey didn't want to be left behind, but I'm sure he was okay once we were gone. He'll be happy having Billy to play with; they get along well and they are both pretty good boys."

Mary had been away for the better part of three days, away from the boys and from her day-to-day activities. They say the grass always looks greener on the other side of the fence, and it was a nice change, but only for a day or two. By then she was ready to get back to her own little world where she was in control. She worried about the boys and if they were taking good care of her things. She didn't have very much, but what she had was precious to her.

"Oh, everything will be all right; the boys are old enough to take care ov things, an' Charley'll keep 'em in line." Harry was trying to build up Mary's confidence.

"I hope he didn't drive them crazy with his ol' mouth organ; the boys get tired of listening to the same old stuff over and over again . . . " Mary's voice trailed off as if she was picturing it in her mind.

"Well, we had a pretty good time, and it was good tuh see the folks again. And we did all right with what we got as well. I got a pretty good suit, two more white shirts, a couple ov neckties, another pair ov shoes, and a couple o' pairs ov pants. And what all did you get?"

"I got two dresses, two skirts, three blouses, two petticoats, two pair of shoes, and another purse. So we didn't do too badly. I won't have to go to the Good Will place in Combermere for a while now."

"If we were to figure out the cost ov buyin' the stuff, it would be more than the cost ov our trip. Plus we got a visit, and a trip to the restaurant which we didn't have tuh pay for. So we did okay, except for the gas an' oil. It must o' be'n a quart ov oil for every gallon ov gas. Those ol' rings gotta be in real bad shape. But it got us there and it looks like it'll get us home; it ain't far now."

"Who's that walking up ahead?" asked Mary, seeing a figure coming down the road.

"Looks a lot like Charley."

"Wonder why he's way out here?"

"Hard to say . . . guess we"ll find out in a minute." Harry rolled down the window and stopped beside Charley.

"Where yuh goin?"

"Home!" came the reply, flat and cold.

"Why yuh walkin'? Yuh know I'd give yuh a ride, and it's a pretty long way."

"It's a matter ov a choice between a long walk an' a short life!" was Charley's reply, and he wasn't smiling when he said it.

"Oh lord, what happened?" cried Mary, putting her hand over her mouth.

"Nuthin' much . . . it's a long story!"

"We'll wait — Charley, please tell me," begged Mary, with panic in her voice.

"Well . . . things was go'n pretty good till the boys went upstairs and upset the piss-pot. She came down through a knothole an got me square in the face. I was cradling by the stove at the time. Then ol' Zack got Dan by the hair o' the head an' scared 'm half tuh death, along with everybody else."

"He did what?" exclaimed Harry.

"Oh, my lord!" exclaimed Mary, placing her hands on the sides of her face.

"Dan fell asleep at the table while Mick an' me were cleanin' muh mouth organ. When we were done, I went up tuh bed, an' Mick blew the light out an' left Dan there sleepin'. Wasn't long till Dan was screamin' for help 'cause somebody was pullin' his hair. Reached out but couldn't find anybody, so he headed for the stairs just a screamin' for Mick tuh help him. He had 'm by the hair ov the head till he reached the stairs, an' I can tell yuh, he wasn't long climbing 'em. Sounded like it was jump for jump all the way up, but he made it. Jumped right intu bed with his clothes still on."

Mary's face tightened and a look of disgust slipped across it.

"That can't be right, Charley, you're just making it up!" exclaimed Mary.

"Yuh think so? Well let me tell yuh, last night ol' Zack an' the divil played hockey most o' the night with a bunch o' tin cans. An' I wasn't about tuh go down an' see who was doin' the winnin'." Charley's face was stern and serious.

Harry put his head forward on the steering wheel and started to laugh.

"Ol' Zack is just talk — there ain't no such a thing. The boys were playing tricks with yuh."

"Maybe so, but 't was very convincing, and I never heard Dan scream so loud in my life."

Charley wasn't giving an inch; he was convinced that it had happened and that was that.

He paused for a minute like he was collecting his thoughts, then he said,

"Used your chamber pot 'cause I wasn't go'n down there with the hockey game go'n on, an' somebody'd ringed 'r with molasses. Now that made a pretty good mess. couldn't go downstairs so I had tuh sleep in your bed with that sticky ol' mess on me. I probably ruined muh nightshirt, and it made a pretty good mess ov the bed tuh boot!"

Uncle Charley didn't think it was funny and his voice conveyed his feelings.

"Went down this morning an' tried tuh clean muhself up. Made a fire in the box stove tuh warm up some water, an' blew 'r all tuh 'ell. Some ring-tailed idiot put denimite caps in 'r an never said nothin' about it."

His voice was gradually rising as disgust and contempt slipped into the conversation.

"The front half ov the ol' box stove flew right out through the winda, and she went through 'r slicker 'n snot on a doorknob. Fire flew all over the place. Set me deef on muh left ear, an' she's be'n a-ring'n like a church bell ever since.

"I guess the explosion had a pretty good force, 'cause the ol' stovepipes undid like a zipper all the way tuh the chimney. Then down they come an' rolled around on the floor like a bunch o' injured ducks. Couldn't see nothin', 'cause the room was full ov smoke an' soot."

By this time, Mary had her hand over her mouth and her eyes were open as wide as they could go. "Oh my God," she said, "you've destroyed the place!"

"She may be in a bit ov uh mess, but it ain't my fault. Yuh can blame the fella that put the caps in the stove. Coulda killed somebody."

Charley wasn't happy and he was letting them know it.

"Mick closed up the winda with a cardboard box tuh keep the birds out."

Mary was almost in tears.

"I can't even go someplace for a couple of days without you fellows tearing the house down," declared Mary. "And I thought you would take care of things while I was gone, being my brother and all!"

Charley bent down and looked across at Mary; it was obvious that he wasn't taking the blame. "Yuh know what thought did?"

"What?"

"He stuck a feather in the ground and thought he'd grow a hen!"

"Oh, you and your Irish nonsense!" Mary sounded like she was truly disgusted and about one step away from crying.

"Can't be that bad," said Harry, trying to ease things up a little. "I guess we'll have tuh go an' take a look."

Charley paused then carried on. "The boys were cleanin' up the mess, so I went out tuh the milk house tuh be private while I was wash'n up, an that ol' spring water was cold enough tuh give yuh the cold shakes in July. Sat on the well-box for a half an hour in the sun just tuh warm up again. An' just try an' get that ol' molasses off your arse with ice-cold water; it'll slide all over the place but she won't let go."

"Who in the world would put molasses on the pot?" declared Mary.

"Probably was ol' Zack!" offered Uncle Charley, tongue-in-cheek.

"There ain't no such a thing as ol' Zack," was Mary's comeback, and getting just a bit touchy. "I suppose it was those young lads trying to get me into a mess, and I suppose my bed's a mess as well!"

Mary had wanted to come home and have a rest after her travels and now all she could picture was a big mess to clean up.

Charley's voice changed, and he was trying to find even ground.

"A bit ov a mess, but so's my nightshirt," offered Charley. "But I'll bet if cold water can get 'r off my ass, hot water will get 'r off the bedsheets a lot easier."

Then his voice changed back to a more serious tone.

"Hilliard'll probably want tuh talk tuh yuh next time yuh're down there."

"What about?" asked Harry, sounding a little anxious.

"Went down there tuh play some cards an' tuh visit. Took the two young lads with me, and that was a mistake. They were foolin' around an' put some turpentine on the young lady's chair. She darn near upended the table an' set fire tuh the place tryin' to get outa there. Then she went right out through the old screen door without even opening 'r, an' on down tuh the lake. Waded right in tuh the waist yell'n, fire, fire, muh arse is on fire!"

"Where in the world would they get the idea to do the like of that?" demanded Mary.

"Well . . . I think it started with Mick putting turpentine on some ol' tomcat's ass tuh try 'n get rid ov him. They said that between the cat an' the girl, the cat was way the fastest."

Harry was just shaking his head, but Mary was getting upset.

"That was a cruel thing to do to anybody, let alone a girl!"

"I told 'em that after it happened, but I think I was just a bit too late. I believe it scared the daylights out ov 'em, but that didn't help the girl any. I guess it's just another lesson for the learnin'.

"I tried tuh get the boys outa there before Hilliard found out what happened and killed the both ov 'm.

"Then somebody filled the ol' coal-oil lantern with naphtha gas. Darn near blew muh head off when I lit 'r. Had tuh fling it out into the grass so as not tuh burn the place down. Now yuh'll need tuh buy a new lantern. Tried tuh untie the ol' gray mare but the halter-shank was greased from one end tuh the other with axle grease. Harder tuh hang onto than a greased piglet. Was no use in try'n to untie it, so I cut 'r in two. So yuh'll need a new halter-shank. When I was finished hookin' the mare tuh the buggy, she'd pretty well turned into a dapple gray with muh handprints all over 'r."

"Yuh got axle grease on muh mare?" Now Paw sounded a bit upset.

"Couldn't help it, I was in one 'ell ov a hurry tuh get outa there."

"Has she still got grease all over her?"

"I think Dan got 'r cleaned up.

"An' when I finally got in the buggy, all the wheels were turned around. One big one on the front an' a small one on the back. Couldn't wait tuh change 'm, so I drove 'r home like that. Reminded me ov one ov those carnival rides."

"Sounds like yuh had a pretty hard time with the boys!"

"It wasn't all bad, it's just that I've enjoyed about as much as I can stand for now, and I ain't go'n back. I'm a-headin' on home."

"It's a pretty long walk — wait an' I'll give yuh a ride."

"They say a man has only so much luck in one lifetime, an' I figger mine must be comin' pretty darn close tuh an end, so I'm willin' tuh take the long walk over a rough endin'.

"Now do yuh remember what I said when yuh picked me up? Every time I go in there, some kind ov a disaster is bound tuh happen! You said what could possibly happen in such a short time. Well that was only for three days; thank God it wasn't for four!

"You folks just go on home an' straighten things out, an' all the best o' luck tuh yuh, for I think that you're a-gonna need 'r."

Charley took his hand off the truck door, turned, and headed on down the road. He'd be back the next time they needed him, but for now he was definitely moving on.

Paw put the truck in gear and headed for whatever was left of his home. Half an hour ago, Maw couldn't wait to get there for some peace and rest; now she couldn't wait to get there to see what was left of the place after three days with Uncle Charley and the boys.

As they entered the laneway, she could see the cardboard over the window and the pile of stovepipes outside the back door.

"The outside sure looks a mess; I can hardly wait to see what the inside is like. Why in the world would you put those dynamite caps in the stove in the first place? Have you lost your mind? The kids could have been killed and the house burnt down."

"I thought it would be a good place tuh hide them from Joey; he'd never think tuh look in there for them."

"You bet he wouldn't, nor would anybody else, till it's too late.

"And you know what thought did ... oh, never mind that nonsense."

"And to think of those two boys putting turpentine on that poor girl's chair makes me want to smack the both of them! What in the world would ever possess them to do a thing like that?"

"They were just doing what they thought would be funny. Mick did it to the ol' tomcat an' they all laughed; they never thought of the harm it would do to a person. Probably scared the livin' daylights out ov the both ov them when they saw what happened to the girl."

"That's just the problem, you older fellows do these dumb things and never think that the kids are watching you. Then they try it and get into trouble or hurt somebody. You all need to smarten up!"

Maw's voice indicated that temper was close to the surface, and Paw was not going to rock the boat. He just nodded and kept driving, doing his best to dodge the rocks and mudholes.

As they approached the house, the boys were standing outside waiting for them. Joey and Billy were standing a little behind and to the side of Mick and Dan, obviously not interested in holding the front line.

The truck stopped in front of the house, and Maw spoke to the boys through the window; it just wouldn't keep till she got out. "Well, what kind of a mess have we got here?" The tone of her voice indicated that she was very unhappy, and not the same person that had left just three days ago.

"It's all cleaned up!" said Dan, trying to sound calm and casual.

"It had better be!" said Maw with feeling. She wasn't in the same butterfly mood like when she left and it didn't take the boys long to figure that out.

"The winda is gone but I covered it up with cardboard. 'Twill have to do till we can get some glass," offered Mick.

"All that's left ov the ol' box stove is the bottom and the legs," said Dan. "The rest ov'r all flew to pieces."

"How's muh mare?" asked Paw as he stepped around the front of the truck.

"She's all cleaned up," said Dan. "Got all the grease off her, an' she's out in the pasture with the rest ov 'm."

"Now, what's this I hear 'bout ol' Zack be'n on the prowl?" asked Paw, not really sure if he should be serious or not.

"Not really," laughed Mick. "I ran a string down through the ceiling and tied it in Dan's hair while he was asleep at the table. I blew the light out and went upstairs and started to pull. He woke up and thought it was ol' Zack doing the pull'n and he started to scream. Scared himself and everybody else half tuh death.

"This got Uncle Charley thinking that ol' Zack was on the prowl. So we tied some cans on a string and pulled them around the floor last night. Scared Uncle so bad that he wouldn't go downstairs tuh take a leak."

"Yah, and who put the molasses on the chamber pot?" asked Maw in disgust.

"Must o' bin ol' Zack!" offered Mick, with tongue in cheek.

"Ol' Zack my foot!" declared Maw. "One of you fellows did it, and now I've got a mess to clean up. I should horsewhip the lot of you!"

Maw's temper was getting hot, and the boys knew it, but it was too late to do anything about that. They'd have to suffer the consequences, if there were any.

Joey and Billy kept the background position, looking at the ground and not saying a word. There was no asking for a treat this time, and there'd be no drawing any attention to themselves if they could help it. They just stood quietly waiting for their turn to come, and come it did.

"And exactly what happened at Hilliards?" asked Paw, his voice holding the middle of the road.

Both boys kept looking at the ground and saying nothing.

"I think they were testing the travelling speed between the girl and the tomcat," offered Mick with a slight smile, trying to take the pressure off the boys.

"You boys should be ashamed of yourselves," declared Maw. "That was an awful thing to do to that poor girl! But I don't blame you boys; it's you older fellows that teach them those kinds of things, and I'd like to skin the lot of you!"

"They should keep the turpentine someplace else; it shouldn't be sittin' right there for the kids tuh find!" said Paw, offering some defence for the boys.

"Yah, they should keep it in the box stove, and you could be sure that they'd never find it there!" was Maw's comeback.

"Well, it's over now, not much we can do about it," said Paw, trying to move on with the situation.

"And what did yuh do to Charley that got him on the move?" asked Paw.

"I think ol' Zack had him on edge, but the stove blowin' up finished it off. He said he thought his luck was running out, and he was move'n on before it come to an end."

"Superstition... yah, just stupid superstition, too bad," said Paw, as he reached into the back of the truck and retrieved the suitcase and a couple of bags. "Well, let's go inside and see what's left ov the place."

Once inside the door, Maw declared, "Good! All I can smell is that dirty ol' soot; I'll bet it'll take at least a month for the smell to go away. You fellows may think it's funny, but it's me that has to stay in the house all day and smell it. Boy, I'd like to wring the necks of the lot of you!" Maw's temper was on the rise and she didn't mind letting them know it. This situation took away all the joy of her visit, and things were now worse than when she left. And if Maw wasn't happy, nobody else was going to be, either, and that was a for sure.

Billy looked at Joey and said, "I think it's time for me tuh leave; this could be a lot worse than ol' Zack be'n on the prowl."

"Lots ov time," replied Joey. "Yuh don't have tuh leave just yet; stay a little longer."

"Don't think so, the day is getting late and who knows, maybe ol' Zack is on the prowl, an' I don't want tuh meet him in the bush when it's getting dark."

"Don't worry about ol' Zack — he's just a story they tell," said Joey, trying hard to persuade Billy to stay. "Yuh can stay all night if yuh want to, and we can do somethin' tomorrow."

Billy wasn't going to be persuaded to stay any longer, and it wasn't ol' Zack that worried him. If Maw lost it and started into wringing necks, he didn't want his to be on the list. And the way she was talking, it could happen at any minute, so the best thing he could do was to be like Uncle Charley and be moving on.

Joey wasn't only thinking about playing. He knew that when Maw got around to dealing with him, if Billy was there, Maw would most likely go a lot easier on him. But it looked like it was no use. He'd have to face the music on his own, and if there was any singing to be done, he'd be doing it alone.

"No, I'm goin' now, and we'll play again some other time."

"Okay, but watch out for the bears!"

"I will, and don't worry none, 'cause thanks tuh you, at least now I know how tuh scare them!" Billy headed on down the lane doing a fox trot. He had been scared half to death twice in the last three days and he wasn't about to wait for it to happen a third time.

15

A Ride with Eddie

Charley had reached the top of Burley's Hill, tired and disgusted, but determined to keep going. Puffs of dust were rising with each weary step, and sweat was running down his face. His chest was gently rising and falling with each breath. It was a long, steep hill, with the sun shining on his back.

The ground levelled out ahead of him, and he could see a shade tree by the side of the road. It was time to catch his breath and rest a bit. With any luck he'd be home in an hour or two, and he'd be glad to be there. Something to eat, a hot bath, and a good night's rest and he'd be his old self again.

He took a couple more deep breaths and used his handkerchief to wipe the sweat from his face. He had just put the handkerchief back in his pocket when he heard the sound of a vehicle coming up the hill. He turned to see Eddie's old green pickup coming over the crest; it rolled up beside him and stopped. Eddie leaned forward and called to him through the window, "Charley, what in the world are yuh do'n 'way out here?"

"Walkin'!" The reply was short and simple.

"I can see that," chuckled Eddie, "but where are yuh goin'?"

"Home!"

"Would yuh like a ride?"

"Yah . . . yuh darn right I would." Charley stepped forward and reached for the door handle.

"Hold on a minute, I have tuh untie the rope. It keeps the door from swinging open when I hit a bump."

Eddie had a small piece of rope tied from the door handle to the base of the shift lever.

"Tie'n 'er down keeps it from swingin' open and hittin' somethin'," Eddie said while undoing the rope. "There yuh go, she'll open now!"

Charley tossed his packsack in the back, opened the door, and climbed in. This would be a lot easier than walking and a lot faster as well. He settled himself back on the seat, and put his arm out the window. This way he could hold the door shut should it decide to open.

Eddie was a man in his mid-thirties. He was of medium build with sandy-coloured hair. His hair had a natural wave, and a few strands of it were always hanging down over his left eye. He had a straight nose and a square chin that gave him a rugged look. But his smile was easy and his bluish-green eyes always had a twinkle in them. He liked to laugh, and Charley gave him plenty of reasons for doing it, so picking up Charley was always a pleasure.

While looking straight ahead, Charley inquired, "What took yuh so long?" He was trying to sound serious.

"What?" replied Eddie, not understanding the question.

"I said, what took yuh so long tuh get here?" repeated Charley, a smile touching his lips.

"What do yuh mean, what took me so long?" Eddie still hadn't caught on.

"Why weren't yuh here when I was at the *bottom* ov the hill? 'Twas a long, hard climb getting tuh the top ov 'r, and a ride would have made it a lot easier!" Charley's smile was broadening.

"I would have be'n here about then if yuh'd o' phoned me." Eddie smiled. He was catching on to what Charley was getting at.

"I couldn't — I didn't have a tin can, and the string I had wasn't quite long enough. Thought about smoke signals, but 'twas a bit windy." Charley was just teasing Eddie with his nonsense, so Eddie just smiled and changed the subject.

"Hope yuh don't mind the mess. Have most ov my tools there on the floor."

Charley could see that he wasn't joking. He saw an axe, a cant hook, a good length of chain, a hammer, and some empty pop bottles, along with an empty beer bottle or two. It definitely was a mess.

Eddie popped the clutch, pressed the gas pedal, and they were on their way. As Charley looked at the floor, he could see the road passing underneath the truck. There was a hole about the size of a silver dollar where the firewall and the floor met. The road rats had been busy, as they had with all the other vehicles from the area. Things were tough, and the folks had to make do with what they had.

The truck was no longer a bright green; the oxidation from the sun had dulled the paint and left it with a grey mist sitting on the surface. The rust on the fenders showed signs of exposure to the weather. The box on the back had a few holes in it, but Eddie, like most folks, didn't have the money to fix or replace it.

The box had a chair tied in each corner behind the cab. This is where the overflow went when the cab was full. Eddie never left anyone walking as long as he had a ride. The rest of the box was filled with cardboard boxes, cans, and bottles, along with whatever else got thrown in. The front tires were bald, but the back ones had a little tread left on them. The spare was covered with junk, and it was bald. There was one windshield wiper on the driver's side; the other had been taken off. To replace it cost money, and there was no need for the passengers to be watching the road anyways. There was a spiderweb pattern on the top right of the windshield, the results of a stone chip. There was no hole as yet, so everything was okay.

Charley had turned his head and was digging in his left ear with his little finger.

"Somethin' wrong with your ear?" asked Eddie in a serious tone.

"Yah, I got this ringin' in 'r."

"What got it tuh ringin'?"

"Stove blew up!" answered Charley, disgust being evident in his voice.

"Whose stove?" asked Eddie, amazed at what Charley had just said.

"Harry's!"

"What in the world were yuh burnin' ... gas?" Eddie's curiosity was on the rise.

"No ... just denimite caps," answered Charley, as if it was the most common thing in the world.

"Denimite caps? Why would yuh be burnin' *them*?" Eddie was finding it hard to believe what he had just heard.

"Didn't know they were there!" Charley was sounding like he would rather avoid the questions as he turned his head and looked out the window.

"Then who put them in the stove?" Eddie wasn't about to give up at this point.

"Harry," came the flat answer.

"Why in the world would he do that?" At this point Eddie wasn't sure if Charley was pulling his leg or telling the truth.

"Wanted tuh hide them someplace where the young lad wouldn't find 'em."

"Uh-huh, and I guess you found 'em instead." At this point Eddie was starting to grin, realizing Charley was on the dead level.

"That's for sure, went tuh start a fire an' blew the old stove all tuh 'ell! The front end ov'r flew out through the winda. Just left a big ol' hole in the wall where the winda used tuh be."

"And where were you when all this happened?" Charley now had Eddie's undivided attention.

"Stand'n right beside 'r." Charley's face had now lost some of its seriousness, and it was looking like he could break into a grin at any moment. He was starting to see the funny side of it. After all, he did survive the ordeal, and this was the second time he was telling the story.

"I guess that's why your ear is ringin'," Eddie said with a bit of a chuckle.

"Most likely is." Charley was looking out the side window as if he'd like to leave well enough alone, but Eddie wasn't about to stop now.

"I tell yuh, you fellas are a bit different than most," offered Eddie, chuckling as he spoke. "Hide'n denimite caps in a stove? Never heard the like ov that before." With this, his chuckle turned into a hearty laugh.

"An' yuh probably won't ever hear ov it happenin' again, either," replied Charley. "I don't think anybody else in this world could ever be that stupid!" Disgust had again entered Charley's voice.

"Ol' Harry *is* a bit different," laughed Eddie, then carried on with a story of his own. "The ol' blacksmith in town told me he got kicked in the head by a horse one time. And it left him with a ring'n in his head. And even though everythin' else healed up, the ring'n never went away. So he went tuh the doctor tuh see if he could do somethin' about it. The ol' doctor said not tuh worry about it, that given some time it probably would just come and go."

"Did it?" asked Charley, showing an interest in the answer.

"Did it what?" asked Eddie, looking over at Charley.

"Come an' go?"

"Oh, for sure, it come an' went all right . . . came every morning and it went all night!"

"Just what I thought; I guess mine'll be pretty much the same," offered Charley, not getting any hope from Eddie's story.

"Yuh can always go an' see the doctor an' see what he has to say," encouraged Eddie.

"Yah, give him two dollars tuh find out what I already know!" Charley is now sounding a little impatient with Eddie.

"What's that?" inquired Eddie.

"That my ears are ring'n!" came the reply, flat and cold.

Eddie was having a pretty good chuckle about the whole thing, but Charley was still holding to the serious side.

"How long were yuh at Harry's?" asked Eddie, trying to keep the story going.

"About three days longer than I should have been!" Charley wasn't about to offer any more information than necessary.

"Why, what happened?" Sensing Charley's withdrawal from the story, Eddie was stoking the fire, eager to hear the rest.

"Yuh don't really want tuh know!"

"Can't be *that* bad," said Eddie with a chuckle. "Go ahead an' tell me."

Charley paused for a moment and then he gave in. "Well . . . the first night ol' Zackariah come back for a visit; don't know why he can't stay put an' mind his own business. He started pullin' Dan's hair downstairs in the dark an' scared him half tuh death, along with everybody else." Charley was now speaking through clenched teeth.

"You're jokin'!" Again, Eddie isn't sure of where this is going.

"Like 'ell I am. Never slept for two nights." Again Charley is uptight and dead serious.

"What happened the second night?" Eddie is still fishing.

"It sounded like the devil, an' ol' Zack was playin' hockey with a bunch o' tin cans most ov the night!" Charley was looking at Eddie, speaking as a matter of fact.

"No way, it must ov be'n the boys!" Eddie didn't sound as if he was about to swallow this one without chewing on it for a while.

"They were all upstairs in bed."

"I've heard ghost stories, but nothing like that." Eddie is now getting serious as well.

"Well, that's another one for your list," said Charley. After a brief pause, he continued. "I stopped over tuh see ol' Tom Bennett one Sunday afternoon, an' we were sit'n on the front veranda talking when I heard the big pitcher fall off the wall, an' I could hear the glass flyin' all over the place. I said, your pitcher fell down. He said, no it didn't, it's still there on the wall. Then I heard the screen door open and slam shut at the back. I said, yuh got company. He said, ain't nobody there, and paid no attention, just kept on rock'n. Then he said, go an' look for yourself. So I did, an' nothin' had happened.

"That's when them ten-legged spiders with the cold feet started to climb up muh back and all the little hairs on the back ov muh neck all stood up tuh greet 'm. That was just about enough for me. I said goodbye tuh ol' Tom an' headed for home an' I haven't been back since, nor do I have any desire tuh go back." Charley's voice was cold and deadly, like nobody needed to try changing his mind on this situation. The matter was settled.

There was a pause in the conversation, then Eddie spoke.

"Yah, I've heard that some strange things have happened over there. Goin' back tuh when Tom's wife was still alive, Pauline said that she worked for them one summer. Said that one night she woke up and heard the old churn dash just a-goin' at it. Thought Tom's wife was up an' churn'n butter. Thinking that she musta slept in, she got up an' dressed an' headed for the stairs. But everything down there was pitch black, not a light on. She stopped at the top ov the stairs for a minute an' then she heard somebody draggin' a chain across the floor and doin' some moanin' as they went. She said she turned an' run to Tom's room an' jumped into bed between him an his wife, an' stayed there till mornin' come.

"Another time, ol' Bill was telling me he cut hay over there; had the two young lads with him. Nobody was livin' on the place, so they decided tuh stay in the ol' house at night.

"Well . . . the young lads got tuh teasin' each other about ghosts, an' they both said they weren't one bit afraid ov 'em. So when they all got in bed an' the light was blown out, Bob said tuh Dick, are yuh afraid of 'em now? Dick said he wasn't one bit afraid. Just about then, it sounded like somebody took a rip across the kitchen floor an' slammed intuh the old cookstove. Hit 'r so hard the lids an' stovepipes all rattled. Bob said, are yuh afraid now? Dick said, not one bit, sounded like the ol' fool hit the stove so hard that he must ov killed himself. Dick was have'n a pretty good laugh about it till it sounded like somebody started put'n the hard knuckles tuh the wall just above his head. The covers flew over Dick's head an' he never made another sound till the light ov day.

"Now I don't think Ol' Billy would stretch the truth about a thing like that!"

The smile had disappeared from Eddie's face when he and Charley started into the ghost stories. He was now looking very serious as he stared out the windshield, watching the road ahead.

Things got quiet for a moment or two, then Charley carried on.

"Well . . . I know what happened at Bennett's 'cause I was there. An' ol' Zack was sure raisin' a ruckus the other night, but Harry says nothing happened; he just doesn't want tuh let on 'case he scares the kids."

"Well, yuh can't blame him for that," offered Eddie. "Trouble is, that in the over-all, yuh can't really tell when a fella is telling the truth or if it's just his imagination."

Eddie caught his breath and carried on, for he wasn't about to stop there if the story hadn't ended.

"Anyways . . . what else happened back there?"

"Well, I tell yuh everything was goin' pretty good the first night. I was on the floor with my back in the cradle, playing muh mouth organ an' mind'n my own business, when the young lads went upstairs and upended the piss-pot. She come down through a knothole an' got me square in the face. Couldn't o' aimed it any better if they'da run'r through a funnel." Charley had left the seriousness behind and was now showing a smile.

Eddie began to laugh, "How did it taste?"

"Don't know. The mouth organ was in my mouth when it hit, and I didn't bother tuh lick muh lips." By this time Charley was grinning as he realized that Eddie was enjoying the story.

"Is there any more?" inquired Eddie, hoping there was.

"Yah, it was that night when Dan fell asleep at the table while we were clean'n my mouth organ. Mick left 'm asleep an' blew out the light. We were all upstairs in bed when Dan starts in tuh the scream'n an' yellin' that ol' Zack had him by the hair o' the head. Made every hair on my head stand straight up.

"I tell yuh, Mick didn't even budge. So when Dan finally got loose, he headed for the stairs an' it sounded like it was jump for jump between him an' ol' Zack all the way up. When he got tuh the top, he bee-lined 'r straight for the bed and jumped in 'r with clothes and all.

"Next morning, nobody said a word; it was just like nothin' happened."

"I guess they were too scared tuh talk about it," offered Eddie.

"Most likely, an' I wasn't about tuh bring 'r up."

Eddie was driving with one hand and wiping tears from his eyes with the other. This was good stuff and he wanted more.

"What else happened?"

"Well, the next night I thought I'd go down tuh Hilliards an' play some cards. Took the buggy an' the gray mare. Made the mistake ov take'n the two young lads with me, as I was about tuh find out.

"Festus was there with a cracked pipe, so I asked him what happened tuh the pipe. He said he filled 'r with loose tobaca from his shirt pocket an' he jammed a .22 shell in along with it. He lit 'r up an' took a couple o' good puffs an' she went kerbanggo."

By this time, Charley was chuckling as he talked.

"Said the stuff in the stem flew down his throat an' darn near choked 'm tuh death, while the ashes from the bowl flew up intu his eyes. I think his teeth are still viberatin' from it; at least whatever teeth he's got left.

"And that ain't the best ov it, either. While we were play'n cards, the two young lads found a bottle o' turpentine in the cupboard. Mick had put a little under some tomcat's tail and they said that it felt so good that the ol' tomcat took off an' tore sods all the way across the field. Said he cuda passed a motorsicle doin' ninety. So they thought they'd try 'r on Hilliard's daughter. She was sit'n at the table playin' cards an' mind'n her own business, till they poured some on the seat ov her chair just tuh see what would happen. Well, when it soaked up through her dress an got intu her pride an' joy, she came up out o' there with a why won't yah, cards flyin' up in the air an' all over the place. Darn near upset the table on top o' me. The ol' lamp came slide'n across the table an' was headin' for the floor when I grabbed it. The chimley flew off an' landed on the floor; it smashed intu a thousand pieces. She knocked her chair over backwards, did a little dance, squealed a couple o' times, an' headed for the door. She went straight through the ol' screen door without even opening it, and there was nothing but slivers flyin'. Never stopped till she was halfway across the bay, jump'n up an down, shoutin' fire, fire, my arse is on fire. I heard the young lads sayin' later, that even though she was travellin' at a pretty good pace, that ol' tomcat was still the fastest."

By this time Eddie had pulled off the road, his head was on the steering wheel, and he was laughing so hard he couldn't drive. Wiping the tears from his eyes, he looked over at Charley and said, "If a fella searched the whole world over, he'd never find a bunch o' hillbillies that could match you fellas. No sirree, never in a lifetime!"

Eddie put the truck in neutral and let out the clutch, intending to sit out the story. There was no use in trying to drive till this encounter had ended. He couldn't see for tears blurring his vision and he didn't want to chance running into anyone who might be coming toward him.

Charley was also in a better mood; Eddie's reaction to the story made him feel a lot better about his discomfort and near-tragedies.

"I figger'd I'd better get the young lads out o' there before Hilliard found out what had happened an' killed the both ov 'em. So we headed for the door. Before I got near it, both young lads passed me and went on out through the hole the girl left in it. I think reality had set in and they realized the fun was over and trouble would be definitely following.

"Outside wasn't black dark, but dark enough in the drive shed that I needed a light. So I struck a match an' lit the ol' coal oil lantern. Well let me tell yuh, that bunch o' Hatfield hooligans that live on the other side o' the stone fence had beat me to it. They'd poured out the coal oil an' filled 'r with naphtha gas. The minute I put a match to 'r, she blew flames about ten feet intu the air. I had tuh throw 'r out intu the grass so as not tuh burn down the drive shed. Now, the oldest fella is the one that I'd love tuh slap up the side o' the head with a flat rock, but I don't think it would do 'm any good. He's gone too far down the gully for even that tuh be ov any help.

"I could see well enough from the lantern burnin' outside in the grass tuh undo the halter shank. An' that was another mess; they'd axle-greased 'r from one end tuh the other. Tryin' tuh untie that was 'bout the same as tryin' tuh grasp a slippery teat on a kickin' cow. So I pulled out muh pocket knife tuh cut the rope, but my hands were so well greased by then that I had tuh use muh teeth tuh open it, an let me tell yuh the flavour ov axle grease ain't quite the same as vinela puddin'."

At this point, Eddie snorted, "I'll take your word for it, 'cause I've never tasted axle grease and I really don't have any desire to!"

Charley continued on with a chuckle; he was well satisfied with the way the story was going.

"I cut the rope an' backed ol' Nellie Bell out, an' hooked 'r up tuh the buggy. By the time I was done, she had turned from a gray into a dapple gray; there were handprints all over her.

"Anyways, we got intu the buggy an' started off, an' the dirty little beggars had switched the wheels around—one back wheel tuh the front an' one front wheel tuh the back. She was a rocken and rollen ride all the way home; never was so close tuh bein' seasick in my life."

By this time Eddie's face was red from laughing, and the tears were dripping from the end of his chin.

"Only you, Charley, only you could get intu so much trouble in such a short time, and without even tryin'. You take the cake hands down, Charley, you sure do!"

Charley was now starting to see the funny side, for he was chuckling as he talked. His trials were now behind him, and it was time to loosen up.

Charley continued speaking with a chuckle in his voice. "Hilliard said that old man Hatfield was sittin' on a chair sunnin' himself when the youngest lad went by with a rhubarb stalk in his hand. He said, now what shall I do with this? Just like lightnin' he turned and give it to the old fella right across the face. Hilliard said yuh could hear the ol' fella roarin' for half a mile. Hatfield caught the young lad and was pourin' the leather tuh 'm, and the old fella was yell'n at him, *Pour it to 'm, pour it to 'm, if 'n he was mine I'd kill 'm!* Then the very next day he set fire tuh the old fella's beard; never learned a darn thing from the first licken, and the second one didn't do much better.

"Hilliard said he saw him, little Albert, a few days later with a bandage wrapped around his hand, so he asked him what had happened. He said he tried tuh put two tomcats into a bag to see if they'd fight, an' the second one bit 'm. I guess when he saw what was already in the bag, he had other ideas ov how he wanted tuh spend the day. Yuh just never know what in ol' 'ell he's gonna try next. Hilliard often threatened that he was gonna kick his little arse but I don't think he ever did."

Eddie still wasn't driving, just laughing and listening.

"What else happened tuh yuh at Harry's?" asked Eddie, trying to hold back the tears.

"Well, 'twas like I said, we got home an' I cleaned some o' the grease off muhself an' went tuh bed. Was just about asleep when ol' Zack an' the divil got intu some kind ov a hockey game with a bunch o' tin cans. They were makin' one 'ell ov a racket downstairs, so I figured there'd be no sleepin' done again that night. Anyways, after awhile they quietened down an' I fell asleep. Woke up halfway through the night an' needed tuh wring muh mitt, so I started down the stairs tuh go outside. Got down about two steps, an' the game started up again; sounded like tin cans were flyin all over the place. So I said not tonight, an' went back tuh bed.

"Now, that didn't work too well, either, 'cause after a while it was either piss or bust, so I thought I'd try the chamber pot. 'Twas too dark tuh see where I was aimin 'r, so I thought I'd try sittin' on it. Another mistake — somebody had ringed'r with blackstrap molasses. I tried tuh get up but I couldn't get rid of the pot; it was stuck right tight tuh muh ol' arse end. Got muh right hand covered with molasses try'n tuh get the pot loose!"

Eddie cried, "Stop! Stop! ... Wait till I can stop laughin' 'cause I can't hear a word yuhr sayin', an' I don't want tuh miss a single thing!"

Charley paused with a big grin on his face; he was starting to enjoy Eddie's reaction to his story.

After a minute of trying to get his composure back, Eddie said, "Okay, carry on, but take it easy an' stop if I tell yuh."

"Well ... I had tuh try an' keep my nightshirt from getting messed up, so I used muh clean hand tuh hold it up in the air. The other hand was all molasses from tryin' tuh get the pot from off my back-end. Muh whole arse end was ringed with the stuff. Had tuh kneel down an' piss in the dark, so I had tuh hold muh hammer handle with the hand that had the molasses on it. Made a pretty good mess ov it as well; couldn't keep it from stickin' tuh my leg after that.

"Thought I'd try an' go downstairs an' wash muhself before I got back intu bed, 'cause I was one 'ell ov a mess, and tuh 'ell with ol' Zack; I was goin' anyways. I got tuh about the same spot on the stairs as the first time, and all 'ell broke loose again. I figgered it ain't worth the risk, so I turned back an' headed for bed just the way I was. I made a mess ov the bed, but what else could I do?

"Scared poor Billy half tuh death; he woke up an' saw me bent over with muh hand hold'n muh nightshirt out behind me an he thought there was some kind ov a big rooster runnin' around the house."

Eddie broke in again, "Only you, Charley, only you could this happen tuh ... please carry on."

"Well, when daylight come, I figgerd ol' Zack an' the boys were gone back tuh wherever they come from. So I'd slip on downstairs an' warsh muhself before the rest got up. Thought I'd go in the room with the box stove an' start a fire, heat some water, an' get cleaned up. I could close the door an' get the job done without the rest ov 'em gazin' at me. There was a bunch o' junk in the stove, ol' broken-up baskets an' stuff, so I set fire to 'r. Closed the draft an' was headin' out tuh get some water when the caps got hot, an' away she went. Kerbango! All I could see was ashes, soot, smoke, an' fire. I thought for a minute I'd died an' gone tuh 'ell, but I could hear what sounded like church bells ring'n, so I knew that I hadn't made it down there yet, an' they've been at it ever since."

"Charley, you don't need tuh worry about goin' down there, the devil would be too worried about yuh wreckin' the place!"

Charley just smiled and carried on.

"Yuh shoulda seen them ol' stovepipes go. When the force ov the explosion hit them, they undid like a zipper from the stove, clean tuh the chimley. Then they flew all over the place. They hit the floor and rolled all around like a bunch ov injured ducks. I tell yuh, the young lads weren't long in gettin' downstairs. They tried tuh talk tuh me, but it was no use; all I could hear was bells ringin'.

"I went out tuh the milk house tuh try an' get away from them and clean myself up. Well, let me tell yuh, if you've never tried tuh warsh blackstrap molasses off your bare arse with ice-cold water, yuh should certainly give 'r a try sometime. The cold water just thickens 'r and then she sticks just like glue. It'd slide all over the place, but it wouldn't let go. By the time I got 'r all cleaned off, I was take'n cold chills; darn near froze tuh death. I sat on the well-box for a half hour tryin' tuh warm up. Mick brought me out some coffee, then we went in an' had breakfast. They had the place cleaned up some by that time. But yuh could still smell the soot and ashes. I went upstairs, packed my packsack, an' left for home.

"I come darn close tuh be'n killed, an' I figger'd the Good Lord only gives a man so much luck per day. And I felt that I'd used up most o' mine, so it was time tuh be move'n on.

"I met Harry an' Mary out on the road. They were on their way back, an' I told 'm what had happened. Mary got upset about it; Harry wanted tuh laugh but I think he was a little afraid tuh while Mary was there. They went on back tuh look things over, an' I headed for home. It was tough goin', but I made 'r tuh the top ov the hill where yuh picked me up, an' that's pretty much the end ov the story."

Charley seemed to be more at ease now, and he was even smiling as he looked over at Eddie.

"Well, it's a good one," said Eddie. "I never heard the like ov that before and I most likely won't ever hear the like ov it again. I guess that should give yuh something tuh talk about when yuh get back tuh town. Yuh should be able to entertain folks for a day 'r two with that one!"

Eddie just kept on shaking his head as he used his shirt sleeve to dry the tears from off his cheeks,

Things had settled down and Charley was content to change the subject.

"How is ol' Peter Ratacatakuskie do'n?" asked Charley. "Haven't heard tell o' him in a while."

Eddie snorted as he pulled the old pickup truck back onto the road. He went through the gears and got her back up to speed, then he spoke.

"It's funny that yuh should ask; his wife went down tuh Pembroke tuh visit with her sister for a week. So, on the Friday night, ol' Tom

Barkley asked Peter over for supper. Guess his wife felt sorry for Peter have'n tuh cook for himself all week. Shortly after supper who drops in but ol' Shorty with a couple a bottles ov wine. He poured a few glasses intu Peter, then he started teasing him. He told him his wife didn't go tuh Pembroke tuh see her sister, she went down there tuh see ol' Jake Smally. Said maybe she wouldn't come home on Sunday if they'd been foolin' around all week.

"Ol' Peter looked Shorty straight in the face. His eyes were a bit glassy by this time, and it sounded like one side ov his tongue was thicker than the other. Anyways, he said, wouldn't surprise me one little bit if she didn't come back at all. Think I'll go on home'n have me a couple o' glasses ov Javex an' go tuh bed. Don't care if she never comes back, if'n that's what she went for.

"I guess ol' Peter got tuh his feet an' headed for the door. He was two steps ahead an' one back, an' three sideways. Ol' Shorty got scared in case he would go home an' drink Javex, an it'd be his fault for teasin' him. So he told Peter he couldn't let him go outside, 'cause the bears out there were thicker than fuzz on a pup. They'd have him eat before he ever got tuh the road. So he talked him intu stayin' an' drinkin' some more wine. After pourin' the second bottle into him, ol' Peter passed out on the chesterfield. So they put a blanket over him an' left him there for the night. Ol' Shorty slept in the armchair so he could keep an eye on 'm, just in case he did go home and drink Javex.

"Shorty said his neck an' back were sore for about two days from tryin' tuh sleep in that ol' armchair. Served him right for teasin' the ol' fella.

"When Peter woke up in the morning, he said he had a terrible thirst and his head was aching, so Shorty gave him some water and a couple ov aspirin. Then he tried to convince him that he was only teasin' about his wife foolin' around with ol' Jake Smally. Peter said, oh no, it could happen, that's how I got 'r in the first place. She was supposed tuh marry Jim Dunn, but Mrs. Blair got her tuh work for her for the summer, an' I was help'n Mr. Blair with the hay. I talked 'r intu goin' fishin' with me every night for a week, an' we got tuh foolin' around an' she decided tuh marry me instead o'

Jim. So yuh see, it could certainly happen a second time!

"Ol' Shorty said, that was when she was young an' foolish, but she's older an' a lot wiser now. Peter said, she may be a lot older but I have my doubts about the wiser."

"Did he try the Javex when he got home?"

"I don't think so, I saw him over at Murphy's store last week, an' he still looked pretty healthy. Said his wife come home that Sunday on the evening train, so I guess everything is okay. I think he saved the Javex for doin the warshin'."

"Darn warshboard roads!" exclaimed Eddie, his teeth chattering as the pickup came around the corner and doglegged to the left. "Somebody musta stole the grader, 'cause they haven't used 'r in months."

"Maybe ol' Ted Dunnigan's horses ain't up tuh pull it," offered Charley. "Seems sorta strange that he's the only one gets the job ov pullin' the grader." Charley's voice was a bit sarcastic as he made the statement.

"Rumour has it that while Ted's grade'n the road, the road boss is over at his house cleaning out the horse stable, or talking tuh his wife, or something like that. But then, that's only speculation I suppose." Eddie was being careful not to talk too loud, as the saying goes.

"Well . . . yuh know," said Charley, "where there's smoke, there's usually fire." Charley was holding onto the conversation, as he felt Eddie was trying to turn off to something else.

"Well," said Eddie, "nobody's ever caught 'm at anything, so we better not talk too loud." It was obvious that Eddie believed that caution was the best road to take.

"That don't mean a thing," said Charley, his voice becoming quite stern. "When's the last time yuh saw a fox catch a rabbit, an' that happens 'most every day!"

"I guess yuhr right," chuckled Eddie, looking to drop the subject. Things got quiet for a moment or so, then Charley smiled and spoke.

"I hear ol' goose-skin-off or what ever in ol' 'ell his name is, is gonna sue the municipality."

"It's Goshkinov," laughed Eddie, trying to help Charley out with the pronunciation. "An' what's he gonna sue for?" Eddie was glad to change the subject and get away from the road boss's affairs.

"Well... he's a bit short 'n the legs an' he says that the warshboard is so deep on Buckeye's hill that it keeps tearin' the skin off his knees."

Charley was back to his old self and smiling as he joked with Eddie.

"I know it's bad," laughed Eddie, "but I think this time yuhr stretching 'r a little bit further than necessary."

"Maybe so," chuckled Charley, "but I think he should sue 'm anyways."

Eddie pulled over to the left side of the road as he passed a horse and buggy, leaving them in a cloud of dust.

"There goes ol' Williams an' the wife," said Charley, looking out the back window, "headin' for town tuh get the month's supply ov groceries. I wondur what would happen if somebody changed his buggy wheels around?" Devilment was evident in his voice as he spoke. It sounded like he was entertaining the idea.

"Why don't yuh give 'r a try while he's in the store," taunted Eddie, taking him up on the idea.

"Don't think so. If 'n he ever caught a fella at 'r, he'd shoot yuh for sure. That ol' buggy's his pride 'n joy, and I don't think he'll ever buy a car for as long as he lives. He'll be sure tuh wear the ol' buggy out first. Then on the other hand, I don't think he wants tuh part with the money, either." Charley had everyone in the area figured out and he didn't hesitate to say so.

"You could give him enough tuh buy a car, now couldn't yuh?" offered Eddie with a grin.

"Don't think so," replied Charley; "have hardly enough for muhself. I'd a-had tuh get a finance loan from the bank tuh buy me a new mouth organ if 'n I couldn't have got the piss washed out of the old one!"

Again Eddie snorted. "Now, Charley, I hear there's a lot ov lumps in yuhr ol' mattress." Eddie was teasing.

"That's for sure, but they're all mouse nests. I'll soon be lookin' for a straw tick and a rope bed tuh sleep on." Charley wasn't giving an inch and his comebacks were good.

As they drove past the Mitchell farm, Charley commented, "I wonder how the Mitchells are makin' out? I guess ol' Jack Sullivan hasn't been over helpin' him in a while."

"Why's that?" asked Eddie.

"Ol' Jack was in the hotel a few weeks back, have'n a couple ov beers with us, and somebody asked him if he believed in flyin' saucers. He said he certainly did, he'd seen lots ov 'em. So, they asked where he saw them. He said it was over at George Mitchell's place. Now they wanted tuh know when he saw them.

"He said, oh, just a couple ov days ago. He was over there helpin' George with the hay and they went intuh the house for dinner. His wife had been churnin' butter with that old spin churn. Ol' Jack figger'd she must ov stopped and took a sample over to the sink for some reason or other. Anyways, she'd left the trap door unlatched, but ol' George didn't know that. So he thought he'd give 'r a spin on the way past. He give 'r a pretty good burl, an' the door flew open. It left a strip ov sour cream up the wall, across the ceilin', down the other wall, and back across the floor before he could get 'r stopped."

"He said the ol' lady had a pile ov dishes sit 'n on the counter. I guess she was gonna set the table for dinner. But before George could bring the ol' churn to a halt, the saucers were already flyin'. He figger'd there must've be'n at least three ov 'em in the air at any given time.

"Ol' Jack said that when he saw what was takin' place, he headed for the door and outside. He figger'd when the ol' lady ran out o' saucers, she must ov put the broom to 'm, 'cause he come out dance'n through the door, hold'n onto his elbow and said, 'Oh, my gawd, she is one dirty woman. I think she broke my funny bone!'

"Ol' Jack said the way George was dancin', it didn't look like there was anything funny about it!"

"Oh, lordie, you 'r something else, Charley, you are something else! You must be the greatest storyteller of all time.

"Where do yuh want me tuh let yuh off?" On the one hand,

Eddie was willing to take Charley wherever he wanted to go, but on the other hand, he hated to give up the entertainment.

"Murphy's store would be all right; I need tuh pick up a few things before I go home."

"This thing doesn't stop very fast; I've only got the front wheel brakes on 'r. They slow 'r down and then I pull the emergency brake tuh snub the back wheels. That usually stops 'r."

Eddie pulled up in front of the store and stopped.

Charley said, "Thank yuh, Eddie." Then he opened the door and climbed out. He was thankful for the ride. Not only did it save a lot of walking, but the laughing and talking had made him feel better. He was his old self again.

Charley retrieved his pack from the back of the pickup, and then said to Eddie, "Don't forget tuh tie up the door — wouldn't want tuh see yuh hurt somebody if she flies open. I held 'r this far; from now on yuhr on yuhr own. Thanks for the ride — sure as ol' 'ell beats walkin'."

"No problem," said Eddie. "I'm glad I picked yuh up; best darn story I've heard in a long time. Take care, Charley, and stop by sometime!"

16

Storytelling

Charley was making his way up the steps as Eddie popped the clutch, turning a little gravel as he pulled back onto the street.

Charley looked up at the old sign hanging above the door. It needed some repairs and fresh paint, but as long as the folks were buying his goods, ol' Murphy wasn't about to spend the money. The sign read, MURPHY'S GENERAL STORE, and general it was. He had everything from soup to nuts in it. Boots and clothing, hunting and fishing supplies, groceries and farm supplies, hardware and firearms — you name it, and he had it. If he didn't, he'd try and get it for you. He was there to make money, and it seemed that he was doing quite well.

Gaining the steps, Charley crossed the plank platform and entered the store. The normal crowd was inside. Some were walking the aisle looking for things; others were standing at the counter waiting to pay for what they had picked up. A few were hanging around the water pail and checking out the latest gossip.

Every so often someone would take the dipper, fill it, and have a drink, then pour the remaining water back into the pail. They didn't want to waste the water, because someone would have to go to the well for more.

Moving forward, Charley noticed that Murphy, a small and frail man with a bald head, was talking to Mrs. Randal. The difference in size was amusing. Murphy was roughly five foot seven, a hundred and thirty pounds, while Mrs Randal was five foot ten, and about two hundred and twenty-five pounds. A real Mutt and Jeff combination.

Murphy was in front of Mrs. Randal, looking up at her and trying to make a sale.

"Why don't yuh buy some apples? See those good lookin' ones in the barrel over there; they just come in this morning. A fella from Belleville brought 'm in. Fresh picked, soft an' delicious, darn good eatin' apples and good for bakin' as well!"

Mrs. Randal walked over to the barrel and picked one up, wiped it on her dress, and took a bite. She chewed on it for a second or two then spit it out on the floor. She looked Murphy right in the eye and said, "Just what I thought, you darned ol' liar. Soft and delicious are they?" her voice rising a little. "They're harder than the hubs ov hell, and twice as sour. Yuh'd need the blacksmith tuh sharpen your teeth before you could ever think ov chewin' on one ov them apples!"

She tossed the apple back into the barrel, and walked on with her grocery list as if nothing had ever taken place.

Adam, who was standing by the water pail, said to Charley with a bit of a chuckle, "Now what did yuh think ov that?"

"Well," said Charley, "that ol' gal ain't short on words, and she says what ever in ol' 'ell comes tuh her mind. She does pretty much what ever she likes, and if yuh ever cross her, yuh know yuh'r gonna get a pretty good blisterin', and that's a for sure!"

Adam smiled and said, "Russel told me a few weeks back that he was in the store an' watched her bend over tuh pick up somethin' from the floor. He said her skirt pulled up a bit and he could hardly believe his eyes. "Five Roses Flour" was written right across her back end. He said it was the nicest pair ov flour bag bloomers that he had ever seen!"

By this time the tears were rolling down his cheeks. "I guess times are pretty tough all over the place!"

Both fellows were having a good laugh, but making very sure they were well out of the hearing range of Mrs. Randal.

After Adam got himself settled down, he said, "Russel told him that last fall Danny got ol' Tommy to help him kill a beef. They kept Tommy overnight and was gonna take him home the next afternoon. Anyways, Mrs Randal cooked the cow's tongue for dinner, and when they come in, she told them they were going tuh have some fresh tongue that she had just cooked up. Ol' Tommy turned up his nose and said that he didn't think he could eat somethin' that came out of an animal's mouth. She didn't miss a beat, she said, now don't you worry none, Tommy, I'll fry yuh up a couple ov eggs and you know darn well where they come from.

"She certainly says what ever she thinks, and after sayin' that, ol' Tommy wasn't too sure if he even wanted the eggs. Said his appetite had be'n failin' him!

"She seems tuh be right in the middle of things no matter where she goes. About a month ago, she was in here doin' her shoppin', and Johnson came in. He'd been over at the hotel for a couple ov hours an' was about three sheets tuh the wind. He seen her and walked right over to where she was standin', and the funny thing is, that the two ov them always seem tuh get along pretty good. He's always talkin' foolish and she seems tuh have some pretty good laughs at him. Anyways, this time he's purty well loaded, and he walks right up to her and says, do you know what the bear said to the bees? She laughs an' says no, what? He reaches out and pinches the front ov her dress an says, 'Boo-Bees!'

"Well... she never hesitated for a moment. The laughin' stopped, and she drew back her right arm and give him one ov the nicest open-handers up the side ov the head, that I've ever seen. His ol' hat went flyin' through the air like it was jet-propelled, and he took about two steps sideways an' landed on his knees. He just stayed there for a minute lookin' off intuh the distance. I'm pretty sure he wasn't seeing a darn thing that he was lookin' at. I think he was just about the width of a hair from having his lights go out. I'll tell yuh, if he didn't hear bells ringin', then somebody must have removed the dingles.

"She stood there for a minute lookin' as if she might give 'm another one. Then she turned and said over her shoulder, 'Next time yuh talk tuh me, make sure you're not half drunk, or yuh'll be sure tuh get another one that's just as good, or a little better than what yuh just got!'

"She strolled away and did her shoppin' just as if nothing had ever happened. Well . . . as for Johnson, he walked on over to the counter on his knees, pulled himself up and leaned over it, shakin' his head. He looked up at ol' Murphy, who was laughin' his head off, and said, 'I think something just happened . . . but I'm not sure what!'

"Ol' Murphy, who could hardly talk for laughin', bent over an looked Johnson straight in the face an' said, 'Another one like that and you'd a be'n out for the count. 'Twas the best right hand'r that I've seen in a long time.'

"Still chuckling, he said, 'How'r yuh feelin'?'

"Johnson looked up at ol' Murphy and said, 'I never felt better. I'm just about as fine as frog's hair!'

"Ol' Jake's young lad picked up Johnson's hat and gave it back to him. He put it on his head and turned to ol' Murphy an' said, 'Well . . . if there ain't nothing too excitin' goin' on here, I might as well go back tuh the hotel.' He turned to leave but he could hardly find the door. I wasn't sure if it was the drinkin' that put him in that state, or if it was the swat he got up the side ov the head."

By this time Charley was laughing so hard his bubble was shaking.

"I sure would have liked tuh have be'n here tuh have seen it . . . and that's a for sure!"

As Charley regained his composure, his attention was drawn to the door and the person who had just entered the building.

"Would yuh look at that! The last time I saw ol' Blainie I thought one more white shirt would do 'm. But he's back on his feet and looks as healthy as a horse. But I think he's lost a few pounds."

"He certainly did," said Adam. "Russel told him it looked like he'd lost at least twenty pounds, but Blainie insisted that he hadn't lost an ounce. So Russell told him if yuh didn't lose it then somebody must have stole it, because it's definitely missin'."

"Anyways, it's good tuh see him up and about," remarked Charley.

"It sure is," said Adam, "but speakin' ov medical problems, Tommy told me ol' Buster was havin' problems with his backside. He probably got it from sit'n on those ol' cold logs while he was drivin' the team for Prince. And I don't think I ever saw him use a dry ass; probably couldn't be bothered putting the straw in a bag. So . . . anyways he went tuh see the new doctor . . . that young fella who just come to town. He told the doc that he had a problem with his asshole. The doc looked up at him with a frown and said, "rectum!" Buster said, 'Oh, for sure, doc. I don't think it will ever be the same again!' The doc shook his head and smiled. He let Buster describe the problem and then he said, 'It sounds like yuh got hemorrhoids.' Ol' Buster had no idea what that was, so he asked the doc what in the world he was talkin' about. He said he never heard ov anything called a name like that before.

"The doc started tuh laugh and said, 'I guess you would have had a better understanding if they'd called them ass-tur-oids.'

"Anyways, he tried to explain to ol' Buster what they were, but it didn't do any good. So he said tuh go on over tuh the drugstore and the fella there would give him somethin' to help him out.

"So ol' Buster went on over an tried tuh explain what the problem was tuh the fella at the drugstore. He said the doc called it a something or other which he didn't understand and he used another word which he had never heard of either. It sounded like ass-tur . . . something or other. The fella started tuh laugh an asked him if it was an asteroid, and Buster said, yah, that it sounded somethin' like that. So the fella asked him if the doc called it a hemorrhoid, and buster said, yah, that sounds somethin' like what he said it was. Then ol' Buster got real serious and said, 'Why in the world don't yuh just call it an asshole like everybody else does?'

"The druggist laughed and said, 'It's known as a rectum!'

"Ol' Buster had already been down that road with the doc, and he said, 'Yah, but that's after it's be'n all bent outa shape; before that it's an asshole!'

"After the druggist stopped laughin', he said, 'It don't matter — I think I can give you somethin' for your problem.'

"But ol' Buster still wasn't finished with him. He said, 'So why don't yuh just call it an asshole so every body can understand what yuhr talking about, instead ov all those fancy words that nobody ever heard tell ov?'

"'My mother used tuh put diapers on my ass, she powdered my ass, my daddy used tuh kick my ass, the teacher made me sit on my ass. Everybody knows where your ass is, and if there's a hole in 'r, then it must be an asshole. Huh! Would'n yuh think?'

"To prove his point, he turned to Mrs. Randal, who just happened tuh be standin' behind him, waiting her turn. He said to her, 'If somebody was tuh talk tuh you about an asshole, yuh'd know what they was talking about, wouldn't yuh?'

"She looked ol' Buster straight in the face an' said, 'I most certainly would, Buster . . . I married one!'

"He said the ol' druggist almost split a gut laughin'. I guess bein' new tuh town, he'd never heard such hilly-billy carryin' on before in his life. But she just stood there straight-faced as if it was the most normal thing in the world for her tuh say. Even ol' Buster had a little chuckle, nodded his head, and said to the druggist, see what I mean? And the ol' druggist while wiping the tears from his face said, I sure do Buster, I sure do!"

After Charley stopped laughing, he said, "If this modern age doesn't slow down we'll all have tuh learn a new vocabulary, 'cause the old one will be outdated."

"Oh, oh, oh," said Adam, "you sure got that right. I went tuh see the new doctor a few weeks back, and when he started tuh use some ov those new medical terms, he totally lost me. I didn't have a clue as to what he was talking about. So I had to tell him to slow down and explain himself, because I had no idea what he was sayin'."

"Did he do it?"

"Yah, he sure did. I told him that the people around here weren't too well educated; in fact some of them still couldn't read or write, so it was best that he learn to talk at our level so we could understand what he's tellin' us!"

"What'd he say tuh that?"

"Said he never thought too much about it, but he understood what I was sayin', and he made a point of asking me if I understood what he meant. From then on we got along just fine.

"But then he wrote somethin' on a piece ov paper, and told me tuh give it to the guy at the drugstore an' he'd give me the medicine. On the way over, I tried tuh read what he wrote, but it was absolutely no use. It looked just like a hen had stuck her feet in an inkwell and walked all over the paper. But I gave it to the guy anyways and he looked at it an' went an' got what I needed, so I guess he could understand it. Looks like we not only will need tuh learn a lot ov new words, but we'll have tuh learn tuh read and write all over again if that's the way its gonna be!"

Charley just shook his head in disgust. "This so-called modernization is completely gone tuh the dogs. Yuh'd think that they would know tuh leave well enough alone! But no, they have tuh keep meddlin' till the next thing yuh know everybody will have a telephone. What in the world is wrong with writin' a letter or walkin' over tuh the neighbours' if yuh want tuh talk tuh somebody. And they say that if yuh have a telephone, yuh have tuh pay a bill every month or they'll come and take it on yuh. Folks in town have the hydro bill tuh pay, yuh got the tax bill tuh pay, don't people think that we have enough bills now? The next thing yuh know yuh'll have tuh work all week just tuh pay all them darned ol' bills, an yuh'll have nuthin' for yuhrself. How in the world can a fella ever save a nickel when yuhr darn lucky tuh find a job that will pay yuh two dollars a day?"

Ol' Buckshaw had built some kind ov a shack on the edge o' town, an' said he thought he'd put fire insurance on it in case it burnt down.

"There's another bill for yuh tuh pay!"

"Yah," said Adam, "but if it burns down, yuh'll get some money tuh build another one."

"That's all well and good," said Charley, "and if it don't burn down, yuh paid all that money for nothen. The only way yuh'll ever get 'r back is tuh stick a match to 'r and let 'r go! I'm very glad I'm the age that I am, 'cause I won't have tuh put up with all this nonsense of everythin' changin' much longer."

Charley had turned from a jolly old soul to a downright old sour complainer, and in just a few minutes. Adam, realizing the conversation was headed downhill, decided it was time to pull up stakes.

"Well, Charley, it was good talking to yuh, but I think it's time tuh go home and do the chores. Don't seem long till the ol' sun is gone down these days. Well, you take good care ov yuhrself and we'll talk again."

"You bet," answered Charley, "and keep a smile on your face and a dollar in yuhr pocket, 'cause sooner or later yuhr sure tuh meet somebody that can use one or the other, and in some cases maybe both!"

"You too!" said Adam, as he made his way to the door, smiling as he went.

Charley stood there for a minute or two, rubbing his chin as if in deep thought. Then he took the list from his shirt pocket and started to pick up a few items that he needed at home.

With his mission accomplished, he took what he had collected and placed it on the counter. Murphy looked up at him, nodded and smiled, then said, "Well, Charley, where in the world have you been? I haven't seen you around town for a few days."

"Where I've be'n is exactly none ov your business," said Charley with a grin, "but I'll more than likely have tuh tell yuh anyways."

"Now Charley, unless you've been foolin' around with the women, what would be wrong with you telling me?" said Murphy with an even bigger grin.

"A lot ov things have happened in the last few days that you don't want tuh know about!" said Charley, pretending to be serious.

"Now Charley, you know you can tell me anything and I will listen and keep my mouth shut as well," replied Murphy, trying to keep a straight face.

"Liar, I wouldn't be out ov the store till you'd be a-telling everybody everything that yuh know and a lot ov stuff that yuh don't know." Charley spoke as if he meant it, while trying not to smile.

"Now Charley, did I ever tell you anything that wasn't true?" Murphy was trying to sound as if he were offended.

"The Pembroke newspaper couldn't print it all." Charley had to turn his head away so Murphy couldn't see the smile that was sneaking in.

"Now, Charley, don't be like that or I'll have to charge you extra."

"Not tuh worry none, 'cause yuh will anyways!"

"Now Charley, why can't you tell me about your latest adventure?"

"'Cause I ain't got the time tuhday, so we'll have tuh make an appointment for another time."

"Charley, Charley, you're starting to sound just like that new doctor; we have to make an appointment just to talk to you. Getting on the uppity side, are we?"

"If 'n yuh have tuh know that bad, I was at Harry's an all 'ell broke loose and it lasted for three days. Now I just want tuh go home, have somethin' tuh eat and go tuh bed. I haven't hardly slept for the last two nights and right now I'm a bit on the tired side!"

"Oh my goodness, you have me so curious that I won't be able to sleep tonight wondering what happened!"

"Good! I told yuh it was none of your business, and if yuh'da listened tuh me in the first place yuh wouldn't be all twisted up now. So why don't yuh go on over tuh Buckeye's an' get a bottle ov moonshine. Let it keep yuh company if yuh can't sleep. And work on it till yuh can answer your own questions; by then yuh should be able tuh lay down and sleep like a baby."

Murphy finished tying the string around the paper bag and shoved it across the counter to Charley.

"Charley, Charley, you'll never change. May God love you the way you are for you always make me smile!"

"If yuh don't quit your gabbin' an make out muh bill, yuh sure won't be a-smilin' when I go out the door without payin' yuh!"

"Don't you worry, I know where you live."

"Come out there botherin' me an' I'll sic the dog on yuh."

"Charley, my boy, you don't have a dog!"

"That's all right, I'll borrow a half dozen from ol' Henry. He must have a few extras that he can spare! It'll be either that or face the ol' shotgun!"

"Okay, okay, that will be two dollars and fifteen cents!"

"See, I knew you'd charge extra!"

Charley placed a two dollar bill, a nickel, and a dime on the counter, picked up his bag of groceries, and headed for the door.

"Now get rested up and come back tomorrow and finish your story!" Murphy called after Charley.

Charley never halted, just spoke over his shoulder as he continued to the door. "If'n yuh don't stop sneekin' in Cooney's back door while he's up workin' in the bush, I'll give the whole town somethin' tuh talk about." As he stepped through the door, he said to himself, "I guess that should hold 'm for a minute or two."

Charley knew that ol' Murphy wouldn't cheat on his wife if you held a gun to his head. He was just trying to teach him to mind his own business.

While the rest of the people in the store burst out laughing, Murphy just smiled and shook his head. "You just can't beat that fellow no matter how you try!"

17

Wild Bill

Fifteen minutes from the time Charley left Murphy's store, he was standing in front of his house. It was a two-room building with a bedroom at one end and a kitchen and living room at the other.

The board and batten siding was showing its age; it had turned a barnboard grey from being exposed to the weather.

Charley used paint only on the inside of the house; to paint the outside cost too much. The cedar shingles were showing their age as well, and some were missing. The old stovepipe had a lean to the southeast, as the prevailing winds from the northwest had taken their toll. The windows could use some cleaning, and the old door was weather-beaten, but this was home to Charley . . . a place where he could go in and close the door and leave the world outside.

Putting his hand in his pocket, Charley pulled out the key to the door, unlocked it, and stepped inside. He closed the door and set his packsack under the window.

It was getting dark on the inside, but Charley knew every inch of his house like the back of his hand. Going over to the table, he picked up a matchbox, removed a match, and struck it on the side of the box. As it burst into flames, he removed the glass chimney from the lamp and lit the wick. He then replaced the chimney, illuminating the room.

Charley opened the back door and stepped outside. The evening stars were shining in the eastern sky as he made his way to the old shed where he kept his odds and ends. He opened the door, and just inside was his old copper tub. He brought it into the house and set it beside the door.

He took the pail from the washstand and poured most of it into the tub. Taking another pail from underneath the stand, he went out to the well.

The old wooden pump looked the worse for wear but it was still in good working condition. Charley lifted the pump handle and poured the remaining water from the pail down the centre of the pump. Holding the handle with his right hand, he held the pail beneath the spout with his left. He pumped the handle till it regained its prime and the water came gushing out of the spout and into the pail.

He filled both pails, then brought them in and poured the water into the tub. Then he returned to the well for two more. One he placed on the washstand, the other he poured into two large pots that were on the stove.

It was bath time. He would start the fire, have something to eat, take a bath, and then go straight to bed. How he had missed his bed, but tonight he would have all the comfort and rest that his old bed could possibly give him. With the covers pulled up to his chin, he would drift off into a deep and peaceful sleep, forgetting all the recent happenings. Now that ol' Zack was in the past, he could regain the sleep that he had lost the last two nights.

With the the fire being well established, he removed the small lid from the centre of the large one and placed the kettle over the hole. In a few minutes, the kettle should be boiling and the tea water ready.

He went over to the cupboard and picked up the bologna and the bread. He sliced two pieces of bread and one thick slice of bologna on the cutting board. Then he returned both items to where he had found them.

Once the bread was buttered, he placed the slice of bologna on it, covered the bologna with mustard and a large slice of onion. Not sparing the salt and pepper, he placed the other slice of bread on top. He cut the sandwich in two and set it on a plate. With a few pickles and a cup of black tea, he'd be ready for supper.

Walking over to the cupboard, he picked up a bottle of pickles, removed the top, and placed them on the table. Reaching over to the cutlery box, he picked out a fork and put it beside his plate.

From the cupboard he chose a cup and set it down on the counter. Picking up the container that held the tea, he screwed off the lid and, reaching into the can, took a pinch of tea and put it in the teapot. Replacing the top, he put the can back where it came from. Next, he took the kettle from the stove and poured the boiling water into the teapot. After pushing the kettle to the back of the stove, he replaced the small lid and went to the table and sat down.

Now he was ready to have his supper, and by the time he was done eating, the water should be hot enough for him to have his bath.

Charley was hungry, and rightly so. He had had nothing to eat since breakfast; the walk had been long and tiring, and now it was time to eat and relax.

Before starting to eat, he bowed his head and silently gave thanks for the food.

With supper over, Charley placed his plate and utensils in the dishpan. With his hand he brushed the bread crumbs from the table onto the floor to be swept up later. He then checked the water on the stove and found it hot enough for his bath.

Charley poured the hot water into the tub, got a towel from the washstand, and put it over the back of a chair. He then picked up a bar of soap and placed it on the chair by the towel. Last of all, he hooked the latch on the door and closed the curtains on the window. After taking off his boots, he undressed himself and sat down in the tub.

"Ooh, this feels good!" slipped from his lips along with a sigh.

His back was upright at one end off the tub, and his feet were at the other end, with his knees sticking up in the middle. It wasn't the most comfortable bathtub, but what the heck, it was a whole lot better than nothing. He sat there soaking up all the comfort that was available to him under the circumstances. It had been a rough day, but he was home at last and all was well.

As he glanced around the room, there were only a few items that made up his furnishings. His eyes stopped on the oval picture of his mother hanging on the wall by the window.

"Well, Maw, a lot of things have happened since yuh left this ol' world; won't be long till I'll be there with yuh. Then I'll tell yuh all the stories. That's if yuhr still interested in the goings-on down here. I just had one 'ell ov a time at Harry's. The ol' black lad tried tuh do me in, but he didn't quite make it. I guess yuh were prayin' for me.

Let me tell yuh, things are gettin' pretty bad, not like when you were here. This modernization is goin' tuh ruin everything. Soon yuh'll have tuh have a licence tuh put up an outhouse. Anyways, I'm have'n a bath, then go'n tuh bed. Miss yuh, Maw!"

Charley picked up the soap and looked down at himself. "Well, ol' buddy, I'm a-gonna finish the job that I started this morning. I'm gonna get the rest ov the molasses off yuh, maybe then yuh won't feel so stuck-up!"

Charley soaped himself down and then rinsed the soap off; he sat there with his feet out over the end of the tub. The rest of his body was up to his chest in the water. He was sitting there relaxing and soaking up the warmth when a knock came at the door.

"Charley!" ... You in bed?"

"No!"

"Then why duh yuh have the door locked?"

"If it's any ov yuhr business, I'm have'n a bath!"

"Oh ... yah, I have one of those at the changing ov each season, whether I need it or not."

"Uh-huh, that's what I figgered the last time I was downwind ov yuh. Now ... what in ol' 'ell would yuh want at this time o' the night?"

"Let me in an' I'll tell yuh!"

"Well ... yuh 'll have tuh wait till I get myself out ov this tub, dried off, and dressed. It'll take a minute ... and don't be peekin' through the winda!"

"Yah ... at what? Ain't nuthin' in there worth lookin' at!"

In a minute or two Charley was dried, dressed, and at the door. He unhooked the latch and opened it.

"Well . . . if it isn't ol' Wild Bill!" Charley sounded surprised, as if he hadn't known who it was, "and what 'r yuh plannin' tuh do with the rifle?"

"Well, Charley, there'll be a full moon in about half an hour, an' I thought that maybe you and me could go down tuh the marsh and get us a buck!"

"Yuh didn't give any thought tuh the blackflies and mosquitoes being down there as well, did yuh?"

"Yes I did, but there's a bit ov a breeze since the sun went down, and it's a bit cooler as well. If yuh want, yuh could rub a little Minards liniment around your neck and ears. That should help tuh keep 'm away."

"Uh-huh," Charley looked at him, shaking his head, "it probably would, but what makes yuh think that a deer can't smell? The stink ov that stuff would be tuh the other side ov Renfrew County within the half ov an hour. And the smell of that stuff would choke a deer right tuh death if he was within half a mile ov yuh. How far do yuh think that gun ov yours can shoot?"

"Now, Charley, you've be'n known tuh stretch things a little, but this is a bit too much. The stuff's a bit smelly, but 'tain't that bad."

"I know . . . it's a 'ell ov a lot worse!" declared Charley with a smile.

"Come on, Charley, get yuhr boots on an' let's walk over an' see if there are any deer there tonight."

"Well . . . maybe, but yuh better leave the liniment at home if yuh want tuh see any!"

Charley hadn't forgotten about his lack of sleep, but he wasn't about to trade a chance to go hunting for a night in a soft bed.

"Yah, sure, Charley, we'll leave it at home. Now where's your gun?"

"Up on the wall where it belongs!" Charley said, pointing to the spot above the door where the gun hung on two nails.

Charley pulled on his boots and laced them up, then went over to the sideboard, pulled out a drawer, and picked up a handful of bullets and put them in his pocket. He walked over to the table and turned the lamp down, then went to the door, reached up, and took down his rifle.

"Looks like a .30-30!" said Bill.

"Yep . . . a .30-30 Winchester; they're a pretty good deer gun."

"How well does it shoot?"

"It'll clip the head off a partridge without any problem."

"Can't ask for much better than that! But Charley, you were always a good shot, that's why I come for you tonight. Just in case we meet a bear!"

"If that happens, he's all yours, 'cause all that I'm goin' for is venison. You can shoot the son-ov-a-gun, but I don't want nothing tuh do with him."

"The fellows south of the border seem tuh like 'm!"

"And they can have 'm . . . I hear they'll eat anything. Imagine eatin' a squirrel! You'd sure need tuh be on the hungry side tuh tackle somethin' like that!"

Charley stepped outside and closed the door behind him. Standing together, they looked like a midget and a giant. Charley stood about six feet and Bill was five foot six.

"You know the way from here, don't yuh?" Bill asked.

"Yep . . . I've be'n there a few times, and mostly in the dark."

The rising moon was brightening the eastern sky as Charley and Bill made their way to the road. In a few minutes, the moon would be up and it would be bright enough to cast a shadow.

It was a beautiful evening. The crickets were chirping, the insects were offering their songs, while down the road a whipperwill was calling.

They made their way to the road and turned left, travelling southeast. They walked along, each holding his gun in the crook of his arm, saying nothing, quickly moving on toward their goal.

Charley had felt exhausted when he arrived home, but after having his supper and a bath and being out in the fresh air again, he felt like he was recharged and ready to go. Hunting had always been in his blood; as he got older, it had diminished a little, but not enough to say no to the chance of a late-night hunt. There was the challenge and also the excitement of the unknown. Anything could happen out there in the dark, and the storytelling after it was over was by far the best part of it.

They walked on in silence for about half an hour; the only sound came from their boots as they walked on the gravel.

There is something about carrying a gun that puts one in a hunting mood, and with it comes the desire to be quiet. Also, Charley did not want to talk about the events of the past three days. That would be for another time and place. The ringing was almost gone in his left ear, and he was willing to let the memories of it slip away as well.

The moon was up, and there was no problem in seeing where they were going. On their left was Bailey's place, and there was still a light showing in the window, which meant Bill was probably up listening to the radio. His guidelines and restrictions were, most likely, a little different than Dan's.

They walked on for a ways, then Charley spoke.

"I think the trail should be up there somewhere on the left." His voice was low as he peered into the shadows ahead of him.

"There should be a big rock on the bank just before the trail ... there, I see it." Charley pointed to it with his left hand.

"Yah, I see it," said Bill. "It's still dark under the trees. Now can yuh see where the trail starts?"

"I think so, it should be right there ... beside that big spruce." Charley's eyes weren't what they used to be, but they were still good enough to see the trail in the moonlight.

Leaving the road, they climbed the bank and started on their way. Under the trees, the light was limited, but the well-worn path made it easy to follow. For years, people had used this path when they went fishing at Oblong Lake, and even a few used it, as these two were doing, moonlighting for deer.

The lay of the land started on high ground and then it slowly dropped eastward. About halfway to the lake it started to rise again; the south side of the rise sloped off gently until it almost reached the marsh. Then about thirty-five yards from the marsh the descent was rapid.

The marsh was located at the south end of the lake, where the creek ran out. This was where the deer came at night to drink and to get away from the flies.

The land on both sides of the lake rose to a great height. On the east side it was like a mountain; the west side, where they were coming in from, wasn't quite so high.

About twenty yards from the edge of the treeline, and just about where the land dropped off to the marsh, there was a large boulder, which they would climb up on and wait for the deer. Once on top, it was good shooting down to the marsh.

"The Indians say that when you walk in the dark, you must see with your feet!" Charley said quietly over his shoulder to Bill, who was walking very close behind him and stumbling every now and then.

"That's easy tuh say if yuh'r wearin' moccasins — they're like havin' socks on your feet; yuh can feel everythin', even a pebble. But these leather-soled boots don't work quite the same... they cause yuh tuh stumble when yuh can't see where yuh'r puttin 'em."

They'd been on the trail for about twenty minutes, and moving quietly. At the start, they had travelled mostly through a hardwood bush, which let in a lot of light, but as the land dropped, more balsam and spruce appeared, and the trail grew darker. This was, most likely, the area where Wild Bill was afraid of running into a bear. Without a light, it would be hard to see well enough to shoot him. So, their desire was that if there were any bears in the area, they would stay clear of them.

The only sounds came from the crickets and the flying insects; occasionally the evening breeze would gently rustle the leaves. The breeze had cooled off a bit, but it was just about the right temperature for lying in wait for the deer.

They were about halfway to their destination when an owl, perched in a pine tree about twenty yards to their left, broke the silence. "Whooo-whooouh!"

In the stillness of the night, the sound was loud and eerie. Then the owl left its perch and, as it flew, it let out a haunting screech, causing those tiny little spiders with the ten cold feet to start up

Charley's back, and all the little hairs on the back of his neck to stand up and greet them.

"Brrrrh... those darn idiots can scare a fella half tuh death," said Charley, with a slight tremble in his voice.

It was all that he needed to remind him of ol' Zack. A cold shudder ran through him and all of a sudden he felt a chill. Something had changed in the night air; it was eerie, and this feeling could not be explained. Now Charley was wishing he was at home in bed, instead of being out in the dark looking for deer.

"I think my heart stopped beatin' for a good minute," said Bill. "Never heard one so close and sound so horrible." Bill wasn't sounding like he was any too brave, either.

Charley physically shook himself, trying to shake off the fear and dread of the night.

Bill was good company, but not one to give you courage if things got scary. It sounded like his teeth had already started to chatter.

Charley stood still, listening to the night sounds. The silence was almost deafening, all he could hear were the insects and the gentle breeze in the leaves. But he had a feeling that something was wrong... very wrong.

Then from across the lake and on the top of the mountain, came the sound that no one wants to hear when he is out in the bush at night without a light: the eerie sound of the timber wolf making his lonesome wail.

"Ooo... oh, lord!" was all that Bill could say as he froze in his tracks. Before he could draw enough breath to say another word, another wolf sang out just south of the marsh and straight out in front of them. In the silence of the night it was hard to tell just how far away the second one was.

"This... this doesn't s-sound too good," stuttered Bill.

Charley said nothing, for he knew that Bill was scared to death of wolves. He also needed to calm himself down before he commented.

Charley pointed to the pine tree where the owl had been. "Let's go over there and listen for a while." An uncertainty had come over him, go on or go home? He'd take a minute to decide.

The tree stood alone on the top of a rocky rise in the land. All that was around it were juniper and some scrub maple and birch. You could see for thirty yards in all directions; with the moon up it was a safe place to be.

"G-good idea," said Bill. We can c-climb the t-tree if we need to!"

Charley said nothing; he was just listening. Then he heard what he was hoping he wouldn't hear. A third wolf howled west of them; this one settled the matter. Bill looked at Charley and said, "Th-that one is between us and th-the road!"

There was no way Bill was ever going to go back in the dark, not if there was any sign of a wolf being anywhere near. This Charley knew all too well, and at this point he wasn't all that sure if he wanted to go, either. He had heard of only a few times when the wolves had ever bothered anyone, but it gave him an uneasy feeling to know they were close by, and in the dark, he could not judge just how close, for you couldn't see them. He would feel better if he had a light of some kind, but the thought had never crossed his mind.

As they approached the tree, Charley could see that the limbs were quite close to the ground. They were large, as was the tree, and it would be easy to climb up and sit in it if necessary.

On arriving, Charley stood listening for more sounds that would indicate the positioning of the wolves. He didn't have to wait long. Down where the creek ran into the marsh, came another wail. Most likely the one from the top of the mountain was moving this way. It hadn't ended its howl till three or four more joined in from the same area. Charley calculated there must be at least six or seven of them in the pack, and that may be enough to give them the courage to be dangerous.

"D-did yuh h-hear th-that?" asked Bill. His whole body was shaking.

"Yah . . . I did," answered Charley, his voice low and serious.

"I . . . I . . . think w-we should make a f-fire!" declared Bill; there was an urgency in his voice.

"Well . . . then we will need to gather enough wood to last for a while, if we're gonna make one, 'cause once we do, yuh won't be able to see beyond the fire line. The glow of the fire will darken everything else."

"I-I'm gonna fire one shot, just t-to scare 'em away, in case there are any c-close by."

Charley had thought of the same thing, but didn't want to say it and take away Bill's confidence in him.

"Go ahead, but just one!" Charley tried to sound calm and steady.

Bill levered the rifle, placing a round in the chamber, then raised it to his shoulder.

"KERBANG!"

The report of the rifle left the ears of both men ringing, as it echoed across the landscape like a clap of thunder.

"That should put the fear into any that might be close by," offered Charley. "Now let's gather some wood."

Charley leaned his rifle against the tree, while Bill kept his in the crook of his arm as he went about collecting firewood. There was a couple of small birch trees close by, so Charley went to them and peeled off whatever loose bark he could find. With both hands full, he made his way back to the base of the pine tree. He placed the bark on the ground, and then gathered some small twigs. These he arranged on top of the bark. Bill was back with a small dry maple that had died and fallen down; he dropped it by the dead pine limbs.

"There's another one just over there," Charley pointed with his finger. "Maybe yuh could go and get that one, too, and with the limbs that are under the tree we should be good for a while. Duh yuh have any matches? I didn't think tuh bring mine, left 'm on the table."

"Good thing I smoke a pipe now and then, or we'd be in a good mess with no matches!"

"Uh-huh . . . yuh could rub a couple ov sticks together tuh get 'r goin'," chuckled Charley. He could tell Bill had calmed down a bit, for his stuttering had stopped, and now a little humour might help to get him back to normal.

"Yah, well . . . I don't think so . . . we'd be here all night rubbin' sticks!"

Bill handed Charley his box of matches. He removed one and struck it on the side of the box. The match flared and he placed it beneath the bark. In a second, the bark had ignited, sending the flame up through the dry twigs.

"There, I think we got 'r goin'," said Charley, also sounding a bit more relaxed. He broke off some of the dry branches from the maple and placed them on the fire. In a few minutes, the fire was doing well. Charley took some of the pine limbs and criss-crossed them over the fire.

"That should do for a while. When the limbs burn in two, we can shove what's left ov them into the fire; saves cut'n wood."

Charley stood facing the fire, enjoying the heat while trying to avoid the smoke, which was constantly moving with the breeze.

Bill stood like a sentry with his back to the fire. He was looking out into the darkness, carefully watching the shadows. Without turning around or taking his eyes off the junipers, he spoke to Charley.

"I . . . I suppose a-a wolf would go for a fella's throat, if he were to attack."

"I doubt it . . . he's more of a leg biter," answered Charley with a grin.

"O-oh, really? That's a lot better!"

"Uh-huh, and why is that?"

"Well . . . it — it would give a fella a chance." Bill was sounding like he was very much relieved by Charley's answer, but not certain what his next move should be.

"Uh-huh . . . and tuh do what?"

"Well . . . well, yuh could do *somethin'!*"

"Uh-huh . . . and like what?" Charley was determined to draw an answer from Bill.

"Yuh could . . . yuh could . . . pull his ears . . . or somethin' like that . . . !"

"Uh-huh . . . I think that pullin' his ears would be way your best bet." Charley was almost chuckling.

"Well, Charley, why is that?"

"'Cause, if yuh pulled hard enough, he'd have tuh squeal. And tuh squeal properly, he'd hafta let go. When he lets go, then yuh can kick his little arse and put 'm goin." Charley was enjoying the conversation and having a hard time not to burst out laughing. He was having fun with Bill's nonsense.

"Charley, I think that you are pullin' my leg."

"I'm nowhere near your leg, but I think pullin' his ears is way the best idea!"

"Yuh really think so? What would you do?"

"I'd definitely go for the ears!" said Charley, laughing quietly.

Charley's smile was from ear to ear, and he was pleased that Bill was looking the other way and couldn't catch him at it.

"Hmmm, you really think so?"

Bill was rubbing his chin, staring off into the darkness, not really sure if there was some truth in what Charley had told him, or if he was just leading him on.

When the first wolf had howled, Charley was looking toward the sound and noticed a cloud bank was moving in from the southeast. He figured it would cover the moon in about an hour, and that would mean the darkness of night would prevail. He was confident they had enough wood to keep the fire going all night, and that would give them some heat and light.

"See anything?" Charley spoke with a little sarcasm in his voice as Bill was still peering out into the night.

"N . . . no, haven't seen anything yet!"

Charley knew that if there were any wolves close by when the gun went off, they would certainly have scattered. But, this being a hunting area, the sound of a gun could also mean that someone had killed a deer. The guts would be left behind and this would be supper for the wolves. So, in about an hour or so, they most likely would be back to check it out. Just about the time the cloud bank would cover the moon. Charley said nothing to Bill, for Bill was nervous enough, but he would certainly keep it in mind.

"Any idea what time it might be?" Charley asked.

"Well . . . . it was about nine thirty when we left your place . . . maybe ten thirty . . . eleven at the most."

This sounded about right, and that would mean maybe another

five or six hours before daylight, and another night with no sleep. That would be three in a row, and just like always, he wondered what in the blue blisterin' blazes brought him here in the first place. If it wasn't for that little sawed-off runt standing with his back to the fire, he'd a-be'n home in bed.

Being totally disgusted with the way things were going, he said to himself, "Maybe someday, Charley, maybe someday yuh'll smarten up and learn tuh stay at home where you belong, and then yuh won't be gettin' your self intu these messes. But no, Charley, yuhr too darn stupid to consider the possibilities and say no. Maybe someday, Lord, if yuh get me through this one, I'll learn. But somehow I sorta doubt it."

Time was passing in silence. Bill was too scared to talk, so he just listened to the night sounds, and Charley was so fed up with himself that he didn't feel like talking to anyone.

The pine limbs burnt in two, and Charley picked them up and shoved the burnt ends into the fire. There was enough fuel on the fire to last another hour. Charley watched the sparks as they floated upwards and disappeared; he could see the cloud bank had slowly moved up to the moon and was ready to cover it. To the north, the big dipper was tilted enough to be spilling out water. A sure enough sign of rain.

"I guess it's gonna get a bit darker in a few minutes," said Charley.

"W-why's that?" asked Bill, turning around to look at Charley.

"'Cause the clouds are going to cover the moon!"

Bill quickly stepped away from the fire to see past the tree.

"Yuh got that right! ... And they look pretty heavy. I think it might rain. T..that 'll be sure tuh put t.. the fire out." Bill was turning pale again with the thoughts of being in the dark with wolves hanging around, and these were not the kind of thoughts that he cherished.

"I-I ... think I'll climb the tree before i-it happens!"

"Oh ... yuh got a half of an hour at least before the clouds reach here."

"W-well ... well, there's no reason not tuh get a head start, now is there, Charley?"

"I guess not. Here ... let me hold your rifle!"

Bill handed Charley his rifle and got up on the first branch, which was about three feet from the ground. From there, he pulled himself up and onto the next limb, which was about three feet higher and about two feet to the right. There, he was stuck; the next limb was again about three feet higher and about three feet to the right. It was just too far for Bill to try and reach.

"Charley, I'm stuck. I can't reach that far, I might fall!"

Bills voice was desperate, he was now five or six feet from the ground but that wasn't good enough. He wanted to be higher, a wolf could jump that high and Bill wasn't about to take any chances.

"Here ... step on my shoulder." Charley stepped into the opening between the two limbs.

"Are yuh sure?"

"Yah ... it's okay."

Bill gently stepped on Charley's shoulder and pulled himself up. He straddled the limb, which was about a foot across, and placed his back to the tree.

"Thanks, Charley. I'm a bit short for tree climbing."

"Yah ... but yuh'r only short on one end," said Charley with a grin.

"What was that yuh said?"

"Nothin!"

"All I heard was, one end!"

"I said yuh'r a bit short, but only on one end!"

"Only on one end? ... Which end is that?"

"The one that couldn't reach the limb!"

"I guess yuh'r right, but there ain't much I kin do about that."

Charley reached for Bill's rifle while shaking his head. This was ol' Joseph Murphy's brother; how on earth could one be so smart and the other one be just plain stupid. But then who was he to talk; Bill was smart enough tuh get him out here in the middle of the night, when he really should have been home in bed.

Charley took Bill's rifle and handed it up to him.

"Here's your gun ... now be careful what yuh'r shooten at — yuh ain't alone, yuh know."

"Thanks... not tuh worry!"

"I will so!" said Charley in a low voice.

"What did yuh say?"

"I said it's getting dark; the moon's gone."

"I guess I just got up here in time!"

"That's for sure! 'Cause the wolves should be arrivin' at any minute!"

No sooner had the words left Charley's lip's than a wolf let out a mournful howl just a little to the south of them.

"Ch... Charley, yuh had b-better get your little ass up here before it rains and the fire g-goes out!"

"Its gonna be hard sittin' on those limbs all night..."

Another wolf let out a howl about two hundred yards southwest of them.

"It's a-a lot b-better than bein' t-torn tuh pieces b-by them d-darn ol' wolves!"

On this Charley could not disagree, but he felt safe with the fire going and a rifle by his side.

"I think I'm gonna put some more wood on the fire first."

Charley gathered up a few more pine limbs, along with some other pieces of wood that were on the ground, and placed them on the fire. With the moon gone they could see only as far as the firelight shone.

He would be sitting up above the fire, so he didn't want to pile it too high. It could get mighty hot up there before it went out.

With the job done to the best of his ability, Charley stepped up on the first limb, reached across and pulled himself up onto the next one. This was where he was going to spend the rest of the night, about six or seven feet from the ground, and about the same distance from Wild Bill. The limb wouldn't be too bad to sit on; it was at least sixteen inches across, but his legs hung down on both sides. It wouldn't take a lot of effort from a wolf to nail his legs and pull him down out of the tree. He didn't like that idea too well, and wondered what he could do about it. He looked up into the tree.

On his right there was another limb about two feet higher and about a foot over. It wasn't as big as the one he was sitting on, but if he sat on that one he could use the one he now sat on for a foot rest. This seemed like a better idea.

Pulling himself up, Charley adjusted to his new seat and it worked like a charm. He could now lean against the tree and lay the rifle across his knees. It wouldn't be comfortable for long, but for now it was just fine.

Up here he could smell the scent of the pine and hear the sighing of the breeze through the needles. The sound was relaxing and peaceful, and at any other time he could have enjoyed sitting there and listening. But this wasn't any other time.

"What was that yuh were doin'?"asked Bill, with no other reason than to break the silence.

"Try'n tuh keep my feet from becoming wolf bait!"

"Oh yah, lettin' those long legs ov yours hang down could get yuh intu a lot of trouble. Even at that, yuh still ain't very high from off the ground."

"Thanks for tellin' me; I'd ov never thought of it myself." Charley sounded more than just a bit sarcastic with his remark.

"Now, Charley, I didn't mean no harm. I sincerely hope that you make it through the night without any problems!"

"That'll make two of us." Charley didn't sound very happy, and he wasn't. He was fed up with himself for coming here tonight instead of staying home and going to bed; but the lure of the hunt had gotten the better of him, and now he was about to pay for it.

After the passing of a few minutes, Bill said, "You know, Charley, I think I've been hearing thunder off in the distance."

"Yuh sure have. There's a storm comin' in from the west, and it's gonna meet with the cloud bank that covered the moon, and that meeting should take place right about here!"

"Charley, I don't think I like this situation," said Bill, sounding a little uneasy.

"Uh-huh, and just what are yuh plannin' tuh do about it? Call a taxi?

"I couldn't ov dreamt up a situation like this in a lifetime. Wolves sittin' down below, we're sittin' in a white pine tree on top ov a rocky hill, and one ol' snappin' thunderstorm rollin' in. The only one that could possibly gain in this situation would be the wolves. If yuh should get hit by lightnin', yuh'll most likely come down already cooked . . . supper served . . . hot and steamin'!"

"Now, Charley, only you could come up with somethin' like that!"

"It wasn't too difficult, because it definitely could happen!" said Charley, not trying to be funny, just facing reality.

Again there was silence, as they considered the seriousness of the situation that they were in. Then Bill complained about the fire, which was sending an excessive amount of sparks, smoke, and heat up and around his perch.

"Sure is getting hot up here; how much wood did yuh put on the fire?"

"Not half enough." Externally, Charley was sounding just a bit annoyed, while inwardly, he was wishing that he could roast the ol' buzzard.

"Enjoy it while it lasts, 'cause it won't be for long!"

"Ch . . . Charley, I think I saw some movement out there, j..just past those junipers."

Charley had seen it as well, but not being sure if it was just the flickering of the firelight, he hadn't said anything.

"If yuh think yuh see somethin' out there, go ahead and take a peck at it; just don't knock yuhrself out of the tree when the gun kicks."

"Yah . . . I'll be careful."

"Yuh better be, 'cause I sure as ol' 'ell ain't about tuh carry yuh out ov here!"

About ten minutes passed and all was silent; the fire was going strong and the light was still reaching the junipers. Again, something caught Charley's attention by the junipers; he was sure he saw something moving out there.

"KERBANG!" The crack of the rifle on the still night air almost made Charley lose his position. And unbeknownst to Bill, it brought back some of the ringing to Charley's ear.

"What in ol' 'ell are yuh shootin' at? . . . couldn't yuh give a fella some kind o' warning? . . . I purty near fell out o' the tree!"

"Sorry... I'm s-sure I saw one sneakin' around out there, b-but I guess I missed." Bill sounded a little disappointed with his shooting, but then again, he was nervous and had the shakes.

He was higher and farther around the tree than Charley, so his view of the area was a little better. If he missed, at least the noise would scare them off for a while.

The rain was about to start at any minute, and a good downpour would be sure to put the fire out. The wind was picking up and sending showers of sparks and smoke up to where Bill was sitting. It produced a lot of coughing and choking, but no more complaints.

The thunder and lightning was getting close, and with each flash, the thunder followed almost immediately, indicating the storm was at hand..

Charley's courage was also fading. He thought that if he talked to Bill for awhile, it might help to calm them when the rain came and the fire went out. The way the wind was picking up, they would most likely be chilled to the bone before this was over. Their seats weren't the best in the house, but there was no use complaining, for things weren't going to get any better, and there certainly was the possibility of their getting a whole lot worse.

"How did you ever get the name ov Wild Bill?" asked Charley, trying to sound as if he was interested.

"Oh... you can thank ol' Shorty for that one... I was at the hotel one night, drinkin' with Gerard, Walter, and Harold. I thought I could drink along with them fellows, but by the time they left, I didn't know who I was or how I had gotten there. Well... I guess I thought I was superman, because I stumped out everybody that was in the hotel that night. Nobody took me serious, just laughed it off, so I was told, except this one fellow from Madawaska. They said he was about my size and wanted tuh try me out, so we went at it. Wasn't much of a fight... and it didn't last very long. Only one punch was thrown, and that ended it."

"Yuh stoned 'm, did yah?" asked Charley with some enthusiasm.

"No, Charley... no, it didn't work out like that at all; he put my lights out with the one punch. I never even seen it comin', but the next day when I woke up I had one terrible headache and a very sore jaw. It was then that Shorty started callin' me Wild Bill. The name has stuck with those that know about it, but that was the last time I ever tried tuh out-drink those fellows."

As Wild Bill finished his story, Charley could hear the rain coming through the trees. It sounded a lot like a freight train, and to make matters worse, the air that was coming in front of the storm had cooled down considerably.

"Charley . . . do yuh think lightning has ever hit this tree?" Bill's voice sounded hopeful that maybe it hadn't.

"Now, how do yuh think all those dead limbs that I was pickin' up below the tree got there? This tree ain't that old that they'd be fallin' off it."

"Oh, lordie, Charley, yuh'r scare'n me half tuh death!" Bill sounded like he was about to start stuttering again.

"And the other half may not be long in coming! But on the other hand, there ain't nothing like goin' out on a good hot bolt ov lightning!" Charley still had his sense of humour but there was also reality in what he said.

As Charley finished speaking, the rain arrived, driven hard by the wind and stinging any bare skin that it hit. Along with it came a bolt of lightning that struck close by; the instant clap of thunder made both men jump.

"Wee Haw!" declared Charley. "That was much too close for comfort!"

"What did yuh say?" called Bill, raising his voice against the wind.

The driving rain made it impossible to hear what was being said, so Charley decided not to answer. In a couple of minutes, the fire was out, and both men were drenched and chilled to the bone.

Charley bent forward till his knees were against his chest. He wrapped his arms around them and leaned hard against the tree. He was thinking that it couldn't be any more than one o'clock in the morning and four more hours of this would be unbearable.

If it wasn't for that sawed-off runt up in the other side of the tree he would be at home, and in a nice warm and dry bed. Oh, how dearly he wished he could blow him right out of the tree and let the wolves have him, the useless outfit!

He also knew that wasn't a very nice thought to be thinking, so he said under his breath, "Lord forgive me, and would you give me more sense than to trail around with the like of that. Amen."

The lightning and thunder flashed and crashed around the old pine tree for the better part of an hour. It seemed the whole area was constantly lit up by the lightning flashes, and the force of the thunder shocks almost shook them out of the tree. Both men were convinced that they'd never see the light of day again. Charley remembered what he had said while looking at his mother's picture and made amends.

"Maw," he said under his breath, "I said I'll see yuh in a little while; well . . . I think that the way things are goin', it could possibly happen at any second!"

As the rain started, so did it stop, but the water kept on dripping from the foliage and running down the trees. It was dripping down the neck of Charley's shirt, sending shivers up his spine.

The lightning flashes moved off to the east, and the sound of the thunder faded to just a rumble. There wasn't a dry thread on either man, and the cool night air had gotten to both of them.

"How 'r the match's doin' . . . any chance of lightin' a fire to dry off?" asked Charley, sounding a bit hopeful.

"Not a chance — everything is soakin' wet . . . maybe with the exception of some woodpecker hole somewhere on the east side ov a tree."

"That ain't gonna be much help tuh us. I think I'll catch a death of cold before morning comes!"

"Me too, I'm nearly paralyzed, and taking chills. And Charley, can yuh pray for us?"

"And exactly what duh yuh think I've be'n doin' for the last hour? Let me tell yuh, when the lightnin' was dancing all around us, I expected the upper-taker tuh call my name at any second! "

"Well, don't stop now; we're not home yet!"

"And if I have my wish, you'll never get there, either," Charley said under his breath; then he added, "Lord, I think it best that yuh forgive me for that one as well!"

"Charley, your prayin's got us this far, so please don't stop now!"

"I didn't intend to!"

There was silence for a while, then Bill asked Charley, "Are yuh still prayin'?" His voice sounded as if he was very concerned.

"Yah!"

"Can yuh speak louder? With all this water drippin', I can't hear yuh."

"I didn't intend for yuh tuh hear me!"

"Well . . . I'd sort ov like to. 'Twould make me feel better."

"Why don't yuh pray for yuhr self?"

"Don't think God would listen tuh me!"

"I guess He's a lot smarter than me," said Charley under his breath. And then said, "And why not?"

"Well . . . I haven't be'n tuh church in years, haven't prayed since I was a kid, don't think He'd even know who I am."

"Oh, but that's what *you* think. He knows who yuh are, all right. He knows yuh so well that even the hairs ov your head are numbered. At least that's what the Good Book says!"

"If that's what the Good Book says, then it must be true. But I'm sure He must hate me; I've never done anything good or worthwhile in my whole life!"

"Well . . . it says that He keeps a record ov all we say, do, and think!"

"Then my goose is cooked for sure, because His ol' book must be full and overflowin' on my account."

"Don't matter. He'll still forgive yuh if yuh ask Him tuh."

"All I have tuh do is ask Him? I don't have tuh pay nothing or do nothing?"

"Nope, not a thing!"

"How come?"

"'Cause His Son paid it all when He died on the cross." Charley's voice carried some emotion as he spoke.

"And tell me now . . . how does that work?"

"Well . . . " Charley was thinking, trying to get the right words so he could make it simple. "God gave us the Ten Commandments and said if yuh keep 'em all, yuh can come to heaven and live with me. But nobody could do that, and He said that if yuh break one commandment we will die and go tuh hell. Then He said that all have sinned and come short ov the glory ov God. So then, nobody is good enough tuh get tuh heaven. On that account, God sent His only Son to come and live with us. Remember Christmas, that's what it's all about. God's Son being born in a manger. He lived a perfect life; never once did He break any commandments, so He didn't have tuh die, but He did anyways. He took my place and your place when He died. He paid our sin debt.

"The Good Book says, the blood of Jesus Christ, God's Son, cleanseth from all sin! So . . . now our sin debt is paid by Him, and all we have tuh do is ask God tuh forgive us, and own up to the fact that we are all sinners, and then He will save us from goin' tuh hell. And that's all there is to it."

"I find that hard tuh believe."

"What?"

"That God would let His Son die for me!"

"Well . . . that's what the Good Book says, and yuh can read it for yuhr self."

"I don't have a Bible!"

"Then go tuh the church and ask them, and they'll give yuh one!"

"Are yuh sure they will . . . for free?"

"Uh-huh, for free!"

Charley's attitude was changing with the mentioning of the Good Book, and he was a bit more comfortable with talking to Bill.

"Could you pray for us in the meantime, just in case we don't make it back?"

"Okay . . . I'll giv 'r a try."

"I mean out loud!"

"Ain't used tuh doin' it that way." Charley's voice was soft, low, and bashful.

"It's just that I need tuh hear what yuhr say'n!" Bill's voice was pleading. The fear of meeting his maker under bad conditions didn't sit well with him.

Charley was silent for a moment; then he said, "Okay, I'll give 'r a try out loud. Just don't close your eyes an fall out o' the tree!"

"I won't."

"Heavenly Father, would yuh keep these two ol' fellas — Bill an' me — safe till we get back home . . . In Jesus' Name. Amen."

"Amen!" added Bill.

Both men sat in silence for the next ten minutes, and then the fast-moving clouds broke and the moonlight came shining through. Charley looked down and he could hardly believe his eyes; about twenty yards away was a wolf. He was soaking wet, looking up at the tree and sniffing the air. He most likely couldn't get any scent on the ground after the rain and was wondering where it was coming from.

There was no hesitation; Charley worked the lever. The clicking of the gun loading caught the wolf's attention; he raised his head and looked up into the tree. Charley slowly brought the gun up to his shoulder. Trying to find the sight was impossible in the dim light. Shaking from the cold, he looked down the rifle barrel, aiming the best that he could, then pulled the trigger.

The gun barked and flame streaked from its muzzle. The wolf yelped, swung around and stumbled back to the junipers, and then it disappeared into the night.

"Yuh hit 'm, Charley, yuh hit 'm . . . .but yuh darn near scared the life out o' me!"

"Listen for a minute!" commanded Charley, his voice low but sharp.

They didn't have to wait very long; from just over the rise of the hill they could hear the snarls and the ruckus.

"Whats going on?" asked Bill.

"Those fellas don't bother tuh shoot their wounded, they just tear 'm apart and eat 'm," answered Charley.

"Good . . . good, that's the best news yet," responded Bill. "I wish you'd wounded a couple more ov them!"

The clouds were breaking and the moonlight was more constant as the two men sat quietly listening to the wolves clean up on their wounded. Half an hour later when everything was quiet again,

Charley got himself down out of the tree.

Bill said, "Charley, I'm stuck!"

"Yuh'r what?"

"I'm stuck!" repeated Bill. Despair was evident in his voice.

"Just how in ol' 'ell can yuh get stuck on a tree limb?" demanded Charley.

"I can't get off it. My legs are numb and the ass ov my pants is stuck to it!"

"Is your ass caught on a knot?"

"No, Charley, I must be sittin' on pine gum. I guess the rain softened the gum some and then the warmth from my ass did the rest. Now I'm stuck!"

"So what duh yuh want me tuh do about it?"

"I don't know, Charley, but maybe yuh could take my gun before I drop it."

"Okay, hand it down, but not the barrel first!"

"There's nothing in the barrel!"

"Don't matter, I ain't takin' any chances!"

Bill handed the gun down to Charley, the stock first just as he asked. Charley took the gun and leaned it against the tree.

"Charley . . . I . . . I think I wet myself!"

"Waddayuh mean, yuh *think*? Yuh either did or yuh didn't!"

"I did!"

"Sure it ain't rainwater?"

"No . . . it was warm, Charley. Yuh know I've be'n up here for hours, and when I had tuh go, I couldn't get down. You must know what it's like, Charley, when yuh have tuh go bad . . . it's either piss or bust!" Bill was humble, but truthful.

"Uh-huh, I think I understand!" said Charley with a bit of a grin.

"Good, so yuh won't laugh at me?"

"Not right now!" said Charley with a smile.

"Can yuh come over here and see if you can help me get down?"

"I ain't standin' below yuh till the drippin' stops!"

"Charley, that's just rainwater!"

"Maybe so . . . but I think I'll wait."

"Charley I can't wait; my legs are already numb!"

"Put yuhr legs back against the tree and push forward."

"I can't, I already told yuh, they've fallen asleep . . . gone numb. They won't work!"

Panic was evident in Bill's voice. He wanted down, but he couldn't help himself.

"Want me tuh reach up and pull yuh down?"

"For God sake's no, Charley, you can't catch me. I'd kill myself!"

Charley muttered half to himself, "No loss!"

"What'd yuh say, Charley? I didn't hear yuh."

"I said yuh'r the boss!" was Charley's response, raising his voice.

"Oh, is that what yuh said? Then why don't yuh listen to me?"

"Listen tuh yuh? And how in ol' 'ell duh yuh think I got here in the first place!"

"What can we do?"

"I could go home and get the chainsaw and cut the tree down." Charley's voice was a little more cheerful as he spoke.

"Charley, this tree is big. Fall it with me in it and I'd get killed!"

"Sounds good tuh me," muttered Charley.

"What'd yuh say?"

"I said, let's try it and see!" responded Charley, talking a little louder.

"I don't think so! Charley, maybe I could take down my suspenders . . . you pull my boots off, and I could pull myself forward and right out of my pants. Leave them right here in the tree, and you could reach up and grab my legs and help me down."

"And you with no pants on? I can tell yuh that ain't gonna happen! . . . And then what? Do you think for a minute that yuh 'r gonna walk out ov here with me in the morning not wearin' any pants? Well, yuh can get that out ov your head . . . and the sooner the better. I'd shoot yuh first!"

"Now, Charley, what would be wrong with that? Nobody will see us early in the mornin'."

"That's just what you think; sure as ol' 'ell there'd be a crowd waitin'!"

"Now, Charley, why would there be a crowd?"

"'Cause in this life that's just the way it works!"

"Then what am I tuh do?"

"Let me see for a minute . . . if I took the laces out of my boots and made a tee out of two sticks, you could put your arms under the limb and hold onto the stick and I could pull yuh forward enough tuh get your back end loose."

"Charley, I'll try anything yuh say!" Bill was subdued and pleading.

Charley picked up a pole that hadn't reached the fire. He tied a stick across the end of it, placed it up under the limb, and Bill grabbed a hold of it. Charley backed up till the pole and Bill was stretched out full length.

As Bill leaned forward, he let out the gas that had built up from sitting all night. Riiippp, ripp, rip.

"Now w'at in ol' 'ell was that?" asked Charley with a grin.

"I think there is something stuck up in there, and it's trying tuh get out."

"Sounds like its makin' pretty good headway!" said Charley, tongue-in-cheek.

"Okay, I'm gonna pull!"

Charley braced his feet and pulled, and in doing so the stick slipped out of Bill's hands. This sent Charley over backwards and to the ground.

"I'm sorry, Charley, my hands slipped — didn't have a very good hold on the stick."

"Okay, then lets try 'r again." Charley got himself up off the ground and again he held the stick up to Bill.

Bill grabbed it.

"Now, when the pole and your arms are out full length, pull hard enough to bend your elbows."

Bill pulled with all his might, grunting and groaning. Then through clenched teeth he said, "I think it's give'n a little!"

"Keep pullin'!"

"It's come'n . . . it's come'n! Okay, I'm loose! Now how do I get down?"

"Let me find another pole and we can make a ladder." Charley picked up his rifle and walked out into the moonlight.

"Duh yuh think they're still around?" asked Bill, sounding a bit uncertain.

"I doubt it, but just in case! And while I'm lookin', try move'n your legs and get the circulation go'n!"

Upon finding another pole, he brought it back to the tree.

"Can yuh reach your boots and pull out the laces?"

"Yah, I think so."

Bill undid his laces and handed them down to Charley. He took the laces and tied two sticks across the long poles, making a ladder.

"Let me lean this against the limb, now see if yuh can get your feet work'n. Swing your leg over and let your feet touch the top rung. Can yuh hold your weight?"

"I think so."

"Okay, now try the next step and I think I can reach yuh."

"Let me take my time and it'll be okay."

Bill slowly dropped one leg to the next rung, then the other.

"All right, now let me get ahold ov yuh.

"Okay ... yuh'r down ... now yuh can quit the hug'n!"

"Charley ... I ain't hugging, I'm just hold'n on. My legs still won't work right!"

Charley held onto Bill and walked him over to the base of the tree.

"Now sit down here by the tree and rub your legs!"

Bill sat down and leaned back against the tree. "Oh, that feels so much better!"

Charley noticed that steam was rising from the remains of what was once a roaring fire. The wet ashes produced an unpleasant odour that Charley didn't care for, but he squatted down by the charred wood and turned over a large piece of pine. Beneath it there were live coals.

He took out his pocket knife, picked up a limb, and peeled off the wet bark. Running his knife down the edge of the limb, he produced dry shavings. After accumulating a small pile, he gently placed them on the coals. Immediately smoke rose from the shavings. Bending down, he blew on the coals, and in a few seconds, flames were coming up through the shavings. Picking up some small twigs that were at the edge of the original fire, he gently placed them on the flames. In a minute, he had a small fire going. The warmth felt good on his hands after being wet and cold. Slowly he added more fuel; it wasn't long till the fire was back to what it had been before the rain put it out.

Both men got as close to the fire as possible, soaking up the heat and drying their clothes as best they could. For a long time they watched the steam rise from their clothes as they slowly dried. Even though they were still damp, the heat had taken away the shivers and goosebumps; things were slowly coming around. Charley noticed that the clouds were gone, and the sun was starting to brighten the eastern sky. The coolness of the night air had slipped away, and it was getting warmer as the day progressed. It was time to move on.

"Do yuh think yuh can walk?" he asked Bill.

"Yah, I think so, if yuh don't go too fast. It's pretty much daylight, and the sooner we get outta here the better!"

Bill struggled to get to his feet, and when he did, Charley burst out laughing. "Wild Bill, yuh should see the back ov your pants; it looks like yuh spent the night in a crow's nest!"

All the dead leaves, dried grass, and pine needles that Bill had sat on were stuck to the pine gum. Bill put his hand around behind and pulled at it.

"Charley, could you get that stuff from off me?" again, Bill was pleading.

"Yuh best be gettin 'r off yuhr self, 'cause I ain't puttin' my hands anywhere near there!" Charley was laughing at Bill's misfortune; he just couldn't help it.

"Oh, Charley, what's wrong with yuh? Can't yuh help a fella out?"

"There are certain times when a man needs tuh learn how tuh help himself, and this is definitely one ov 'm!"

Charley was entertained by Bill's problem, but there was no way that he was about to become a part of it, and that was for certain sure.

"Leave 'r there, it looks pretty good. Yuhr lookin' a lot like the back end ov ol' Bugs Bunny!" laughed Charley.

"That's easy for you tuh say, when you 'r not stuck up with pine gum!"

"Maybe yuh'll be a little more careful from now on as tuh where yuh put your ass down!"

Bill continued to pick at it, but it was no use. It was stuck to the pine gum like it had grown there.

"Get your gun, and let's get movin'!" Charley was eager to be on the move, and when he made it back home again, this time he was certainly going to stay there.

They picked up their guns and walked over to the trail. The brush and trees were still wet, and water droplets were dripping from the leaves. The trail was muddy and dotted with little water puddles after the night's rain. The mud made it slippery, and it would be easy to sit down in a hurry if you didn't watch your step.

After walking for a while, Charley stopped and bent forward. Looking at the wet ground, he placed his hand beside a track in the mud. "Half the size of my palm — must be a big one."

"A big what?" asked Bill.

"Looks like a timber wolf!"

"A w-wolf?" asked Bill, as he squatted down beside Charley.

Bill stood up again and carefully looked behind him, checking to see if perhaps the wolf was still close by.

Then Charley heard a "clickety, click . . . Bang!"

"I got 'm, Charley — I got the wolf!" Bill's voice was high-pitched but Charley could hardly hear what he said from the ringing in his ears caused by the report of the rifle.

Standing up, Charley looked around in time to see a tail doing what looked like a drum beat, then it stretched out and lay still.

"I-I got the wolf, Charley!" Bill's voice was high and excited.

"Yuh did, did yah? Looks more tuh me like yuh just shot Bob Bailey's dog!"

"I-I shot B-Bob B-Bailey's d-dog?" there was panic in Bill's voice.

"Sure as ol' 'ell looks like it!"

"I-I thought it w-was a w-wolf. I-I really did! What'll we do now?"

"We? *You're* the one that shot it!" echoed Charley.

"Oh, lordie! Bob n-never did like me!" Bill's voice sounded like he was in deep distress and in a hopeless situation.

"Uh-huh, and I don't think that shootin' his dog is gonna help any!"

Charley tried to sound serious, but it being a tongue-in-cheek situation, he couldn't hold back the smile that was sneaking across his face.

"I-if we don't s-say anything, m-maybe he'll think th-the wolves got 'm."

"Wolves don't usually go around carryin' guns, and he'd have tuh be deef not tuh hear the report ov the rifle this close tuh home. But I got tuh hand it to yuh, yuh got 'm square between the eyes. He'll definitely know that was no accident!"

"W-what'll we do, Charley?" asked Bill, sounding like he was almost ready to cry.

"I already told yuh, it ain't *we*, it's you! Why don't yuh go an' tell him the truth?"

"Maybe he'll shoot me if I do!"

A smile crossed Charley's face, and he just nodded his head and said nothing.

"Waddayuh think, Charley?" Bill was getting close to the panic mode and Charley certainly wasn't helping any.

"Some things are better left unsaid!" cautioned Charley, smiling from ear to ear. "Anyways, there's nothing more we can do here, so let's get move'n, and besides I'm getting hungry."

"We just gonna leave the dog here?"

"Well . . . Yuh can certainly bring him with yuh, if yuh want to. Yuh thinkin' ov leave 'm on Bailey's doorstep?" Charley was finally getting some joy out of what he had thought to be a wasted night.

"No . . . I don't think so . . . "

"Then let's get movin'."

Charley didn't wait for Bill to think it over; he set out at a fast walk and didn't look back. Bill, not wanting to be left alone, fell in behind him.

In a few minutes they were back at the road. Charley turned

right and kept up the pace. Bill's short legs were working hard, trying to keep up with Charley.

"Could yuh slow down a little? I can't keep up with yuh." Bill was puffing and almost out of breath.

"Oh, I guess I could." Charley wasn't trying to punish Bill, he was just in a hurry and not thinking. As he looked up the road, he could see Bailey's house just ahead of them, and Bob was standing out in front watching them coming. As they got closer, he sauntered on down to the road to greet them.

"You fellas must have been up good and early this morning!"

"Up all night!" Charley informed him, "an' got a good soakin' tuh boot!"

"I see yuh'r carrying rifles. I guess yuh were do'n a little night hunt'n. Get anything?"

"Got tuh spend the night in a pine tree, while a rattlin' good ol' thunderstorm was going on."

"But did yuh see anything?"

"Yah, I shot a wolf that was hang'n around."

"Yuh did? Well, good for you! Is that why yuh were up a tree?"

"Yah, when the rain put the fire out, we figgered that might be the best place tuh be."

Bob noticed the leaves and twigs stuck to Bills pants. "Suppose yuh sat in a crow's nest all night, did yah, Bill?"

"N-no! Why'd yuh say that?"

"Well, it looks like yuh got the most of it stuck tuh the ass ov your pants!" Bob was chuckling as he spoke.

"N-no, I sat on pine gum, and it got s-stuck tuh muh pants, then I s-sat on the grass an' it s-stuck tuh the gum." Bill was on edge, and it showed in his voice.

"Yuh should k-keep an eye on y-your darned ol' dog, or th-the w-wolves might get 'm!"

"When did yuh shoot the wolf?" Bob asked Charley.

"Oh, sometime during the night, just after the rain stopped and the moon came out. He wandered just a little too close, so I took a peck at 'm. Just wounded 'm, but the rest ov 'em tore him tuh pieces as soon as he made it back tuh where they were."

"Yah, they're known tuh do that. I heard another shot just a few minutes ago, down by the trail. Was that you fellas?"

Charley said nothing, just looked away, so Bill spoke up.

"Ch-Charley saw a b-big wolf track, and wh-when I-I looked up, I-I saw the wolf. I-I jacked a sh-shell intu the g-gun and sh-shot yuhr doggone d-dog square between the eyes."

At this point Charley was laughing so hard the tears were running down his face, and he was shaking all over.

Bob, realizing what Bill had just said, burst out laughing as well.

"Well, Wild Bill . . . that's about the best thing that you've ever done in your entire life!"

"Wh-what did yuh say?" asked Bill, not believing his ears.

"I said, thanks, because yuh saved me from doin' it. That was the most useless dog that ever walked on four legs. All he was any good for was runnin' the bush. He'd come home tuh eat, then he'd lay down for a rest, an' take off again. I was going tuh shoot 'm myself, but yuh beat me to it."

"Y-yuhr not mad?"

"Not at all!"

"I thought yuh might shoot me if yuh found out!"

"And yuh were honest enough tuh tell me anyways. Well, Wild Bill, I think I like yuh a little better today than I did yesterday!"

"By how m-much?"

"Not a helluvalot, but a little better!"

"W-well, thanks, because every little bit counts!"

By this time, Charley had wiped the tears from his eyes. "I never seen a man stand up, load a gun, and fire as fast as Bill did. It was all in one motion, and tuh get 'm square between the eyes . . . I'm not sure if it was just plain luck, or if he really is that good."

"I think it w-was just luck; if 'n it had a be'n a wolf I'd a probably missed it!"

"Well," said Bob, "at least now we know that yuhr honest if nothing else!"

"An' yuh like me a little better?" asked Bill, sounding hopeful.

"Yah . . . but very little!" answered Bob with a big smile.

"Well, we best be goin'," said Charley. "I need some dry clothes, some breakfast, and a day in bed. An' if anybody knocks on my door in the next two days, I'm gonna shoot 'em right there on the doorstep!"

"Don't worry, Charley, it won't be me. Not for a long time a-comin'!" was Bill's quick response.

"Good . . . that 'll suit me just fine!"

Bob turned and walked back to the house. He was still smiling and shaking his head as he watched the two men walking down the road with their rifles over their shoulders. The one with a bunny tail stuck to his back end turned his smile into a chuckle.

18

Back at Home after the Hunt

Charley stopped in front of his house, then he turned to Bill and said, "Well, Bill, I guess this is it for today. I finally made it home, and this time I intend tuh stay where I'm at. You have a good day and be sure tuh go tuh church tomorrow, an' I'll see yuh somewhere on down the line. And don't forget tuh pull the grass from off your back end before somebody shoots yuh for a rabbit!"

"Yah . . . an' don't worry, it ain't likely tuh happen. Thanks for comin' with me; too bad it didn't turn out better . . . but sometimes that's just how it goes. Anyways, we made it back alive and so it seems the good Lord answered your prayer, and I guess that's all that matters. Yuh can have another bath now and go to bed."

"Don't think so; got muh clothes washed, plus I had a bath twice last night. That should do for a while, at least till I'm rested again. Okay, we'll see yuh later!"

Charley walked down the pathway to his house, opened the door, and went inside. Bill turned and headed on down the road; in another half hour he'd be home as well.

Charley reached up and placed the rifle back on the wall, closed the door, and unbuttoned his shirt. Taking it off, he hung it behind the stove to dry. Seeing the tub with the water still in it, he opened the back door, pulled the tub over to it and dumped the contents. Then he put the tub back in the shed and closed the door.

He closed the back door and went over and latched the front. After removing his boots and pants, he placed his boots on the reservoir and hung his pants on the wall behind the stove. Taking a towel from the washstand, he went into the bedroom, removed his summer underwear, and dried himself off. He put on a clean pair of underwear, pulled back the covers and rolled into bed. Once he was settled in bed, the last thought that passed through his mind was, "If anybody knocks on the door before I wake up, I will definitely shoot him!"

It was Monday morning, with breakfast over and the dishes put away. Charley decided to walk over to Murphy's store and pick up a few things. Placing his packsack on his back, he went out the door and headed for town.

It took about fifteen minutes to walk to Murphy's from where Charley lived, and the distance was nothing to Charley. It seemed like no time at all till he was there.

Charley stopped at the bottom of the steps and waited for old Bob Walters and his wife to make their way down. They were both carrying groceries.

"Good morning, Charley, and how are yuh?" greeted Bob as he made his way past Charley.

"Well . . ." said Charley, "I'm in pretty good shape . . . consider'n, and how are you doin'?"

"I suppose yuh are . . . yes, I do," answered Bob, "and I'm doing okay; hip bothers me some, yuh know, where the horse kicked me. Guess I'll never get over it!"

"Yuh should ov shot 'r long before that happened!"

"Yah, I know, Charley, I know . . . yuh told me to. But he was a good worker and I hated tuh get rid ov him."

"Well . . . I guess the milk is spilt, no use tuh cry about it now!" said Charley.

"No . . . no, I guess there ain't. Be see'n yuh, Charley."

"You bet, and yuh have a good day now!"

"You, too."

Charley turned, walked up the steps, and entered the store. As he stepped through the door, Murphy looked up.

"Well, would yuh look at who just walked in! Am I glad tuh see you!"

"Uh-huh, are you sure it's not my money that yuhr glad tuh see?"

"Oh, Charley, yuhr not that big a spender — I could never get rich off you."

"Maybe not, but yuh like what yuh get just the same!"

"No, Charley, it's you that I want tuh see!"

"If it ain't money then it must be gossip that you 'r lookin' for!"

"Charley, Charley, I want tuh thank you!"

"Uh-huh, and just what would you ever want tuh thank me for?"

"Well Charley, let me tell you."

"I'm listenin'!"

"It's my brother Bill."

"And what's wrong with him?"

"Nothing's wrong with him!"

"Then what's the problem?"

"There ain't no problem, Charley. Listen to me!"

"An' what duh yuh think I've be'n doin'?"

"Talkin', Charley! Now would yah shut up an' listen?"

"Okay, now tell me what's on your mind; shouldn't take more'n a minute!"

"I want tuh thank yuh for what yuh did for my brother Bill!"

"And what am I getting blamed for now?"

"You ain't getting blamed for anything; I want tuh thank you!"

"I think yuh already said that."

"Oh, Charley, would yuh listen?"

"Uh-huh."

"Bill was out tuh church yesterday mornin'!"

"So why are yuh blamin' me?"

"I ain't blamin' you! I'm thankin' you!"

"For what?"

"For scarin' 'm half tuh death!"

"Now how in the world did I do that?"

"You know, yuh took him huntin' and then there was wolves and a thunderstorm, and such!"

"I didn't take him huntin' — he took me, and I lost another good night's sleep because ov it. And as for scarin' him, don't thank me for that, either. Thank the good Lord for sending a pack ov wolves, a snappin' good ol' thunderstorm, and put'n 'm up a big ol' white pine for the occasion. The only way that I was involved was that I had tuh sit up there with him and put up with it!"

"Anyways, he said you taught him tuh pray."

"I can tell yuh, when the lightnin' was flashin' all around that ol' white pine, it didn't take much teachin'. We both thought we'd be meetin' our maker at any minute!"

"Well, anyways, he went to church, Charley, and I thank yuh."

"Uh-huh, and did he confess that he was huntin' after dark?"

"I don't know if he did or didn't."

"I guess he wasn't all that scared then!"

"Oh, Charley, why won't you let me thank yuh properly!"

"It's like I said, if'n yuh want tuh thank somebody, thank the good Lord, because it was Him that put the fear of God in 'm, not me. Anyways, I'm glad he's go'n tuh church. Now can I get muh shop'n done?"

"Yes, Charley, go spend all your money!"

"See, I told yuh that was all yuh wanted."

"Charley, Charley, you will never change!"

Charley strolled on down the aisle to where Adam was waiting. He was rummaging around through some stuff as if he was looking for something, but he was just putting in time till Charley got free from Murphy, so he could find out what the discussion was all about.

"Well, how is Charley this mornin'?"

"Charley's all right, it's the rest ov the world that's twisted!" came the reply.

"Yah," said Adam with a chuckle, "I believe you got that right!"

"Now, what were you an' Murphy natter'n about?" asked Adam, wanting to get right to it.

"Uh-huh, I figured that was what yuh was waitin' for."

"I couldn't make out exactly what was being said, but it sounded like it might be interesting."

"Uh-huh, yuh could say that. If yuh got a minute, I'll tell yuh all about it."

"You bet," said Adam, nodding his head. "I'll wait all day if yuhr willin' to tell me, because I bet it's gonna be good."

"After I was talk'n tuh yuh at the store the other day, I went home, had muh supper, and took a bath. While I was still in the tub, who should come a knockin' at my door but ol' Wild Bill. He said the full moon would be up in an hour or so, and he wanted tuh go huntin' over at the marsh. Well, I thought some fresh venison would be all right, so I decided tuh go along with him.

"The moon was up by the time we got tuh where the trail leaves the road, and everything was goin' pretty good, till we got tuh where that old white pine stands on top ov the rocky knoll. Yuh know where that is, don't yuh?"

"Yah, I sure do," said Adam, nodding his head.

"Well . . . just as we were passin' it, a darned ol' owl hooted, then took off and flew right over our heads. He let out the worst screech and scream that I've ever heard. It was far worse than a tomcat with his tail caught in a wringer. All the little hairs on the back ov my neck stood up and them darned ol' ten-legged spiders with the cold feet started crawlin' up muh back tuh meet 'em.

"Just about then a cold shudder ran through me. Did yuh ever get the feelin' yuh should be someplace else, rather than where yuhr standin'?"

"Yah . . . a few times I have," admitted Adam with a smile.

"Well, that was exactly how it felt. So I listened for a minute, and then a wolf let out one of those mournful howls just up on the ridge, on the other side ov the lake. I knew ol' Bill was a bit on edge with the owl, but when he heard the wolf, his teeth started tuh chatter, and he stuttered so bad I could hardly understand 'm!"

"Yah, I heard that he doesn't have much use for wolves!"

"I figured that would put an end tuh the hunt, so maybe we should turn around and go home. But just as I was thinkin' about it, another one answered somewhere between us and the road. Well, I can tell yah that put an end tuh that idea; there was no way ol' Bill was goin' back in the dark if there was a wolf between us and the road. The only thing that was left for the take'n was the ol' pine tree.

"While I was listenin', I noticed some clouds moving in from the southeast, and I figured that in about an hour the moon would be covered and we'd be in the dark. In the meantime, a couple more wolves answered the first two down by the marsh, so I figured there was probably six or seven ov them prowlin' around. And if they were timber wolves then I wasn't so sure that I wanted to be out in the dark with them either."

"Oh, for sure. Some ov those fellas are as big as a deer." At this point Adam's smile had vanished.

"Anyways, we went over tuh the pine, gathered some wood, and made a fire. As the clouds got closer, they looked like rain clouds, and that would put the fire out. So it looked like we'd be perchin' on a limb for the night. I guess the owl knew we were comin', that's why he left.

"'Bout a half hour before the clouds covered the moon, Bill decided it was time tuh find a seat. He wasn't takin' no chances ov getting caught in the dark with wolves close by. So he gave me his rifle tuh hold while he climbed the tree. He spied a big limb up high enough that a wolf couldn't jump up and grab him. So he decided tuh go for it. He got halfway there and couldn't reach any higher, so I had tuh let him stand on muh shoulders so he could pull himself up. I told him that he could ov done it himself, but he was short on one end, and he wanted tuh know which end that was. I said it was most likely the one that couldn't reach the limb.

"When he finally got himself up there, he straddled 'r like a pony and let his feet hang down. It was a good-size limb, but yuh don't sit like that too long till everythin' from the waist down goes numb. But the wolves couldn't get him up there, and that was all that mattered tuh Bill.

"I piled some more wood on the fire an' climbed up myself. Found a limb that I could sit on, and there was another one, just a little below me, that I could put my feet on. So it wasn't too bad.

"It wasn't long till the fire caught hold and the smoke and sparks were just a rollin' up round ol' Bill. He started tuh complain that it was getting too hot. I figured that if I'd'a thought of it at the time, I'd'a piled a little more on. Give 'm a good roastin' for trailin' me out there tuh spend the night perched up in some ol' pine tree.

"After I got up in the tree, I could see more clouds comin' in from the southwest, and it looked like they'd both meet right above us. When ol' Bill heard the thunder, he asked if I thought that lightning had ever hit the tree. I asked him how he figgered the dead limbs that we were burnin' managed tuh get to the foot ov it. Then he did get worried. If he stayed in the tree lightnin' might get 'm, and if he went tuh the ground, the wolves might get him. But he stuck with the tree; I guess he was less afraid ov the lightning than he was the wolves.

I told him I couldn't have planned it better if I tried. We're stuck up in a pine tree with one snappin' ol' thunderstorm rolling in, and a pack ov wolves just wait'n below for supper to be served. And if it was a direct hit, supper'd be sure tuh come down hot an' steam'n!"

"What'd he think ov that?" laughed Adam.

"He thought it'd be a lot better if I kept quiet," chuckled Charley.

"Was it a bad storm?"

"I never seen one like it! Wind, cold, and rain, an' there was nothing but fire flyin' all around us. The sky was constantly lit up like it was daytime. I figured at any second we'd be meetin' our maker, but I guess He wasn't ready for us."

"How'd Wild Bill come out ov it?"

"Scared half tuh death!

"Asked me if I'd pray. I said what duh yuh think I've be'n doin'?"

"Oh, oh, oh," laughed Adam, "I guess it must've be'n pretty tough!"

"Let me tell yuh, for about a half hour I thought I'd be kissen 'r all good bye at any second!

"So I asked ol' Bill why he didn't pray for himself. He said he figgered that God didn't like him. I figgered right then and there that God was definitely in with the majority!"

Adam hadn't finished his first burst of laughter when a second bunch of oh, oh, oh's came flying out. He was enjoying Charley's story, and there was no doubt about it.

"I asked him why? And he said it was because he hadn't prayed or be'n tuh church since he was a kid.

"So I explained what the good book said about God forgivin' him if he'd ask Him tuh. I guess that's why Murphy wanted tuh thank me for him coming tuh church Sunday mornin'. But I told him tuh thank the good LORD for a pack ov wolves, a pine tree, and one rattlin' good ol' thunderstorm — 'cause that was what put the fear ov God in him; it certainly wasn't me!"

Adam wiped the tears from his eyes and asked, "What happened next?"

"Well... after the rain stopped, we sat in the tree because yuh couldn't see nothen', and then the clouds broke. And what duh yuh think I saw at the foot ov the tree? A soakin' wet wolf lookin' up at me! I guess he could smell us but didn't know where we were. So I levered the ol' thirty, aimed as best I could. I couldn't see the sights so I had tuh aim down the barrel. I was shake'n pretty bad from being wet and cold, but I let 'r rip anyways. He squealed and staggered over the ridge, and that's when a real ol' ruckus started. I guess the others smelt the blood and tore him all tuh slivers. Wild Bill wanted tuh know what was goin' on, so I told him, those fellas don't shoot their wounded, they eat 'em. That made him the happiest that he'd be'n all night. He was hopin' the whole pack would turn on each other, but I knew there was no way that was gonna happen."

"Wild Bill is a little different, and he was always like that from as far back as I can remember!" offered Adam.

"How him and this fella up front could be brothers is beyond me! But I guess the good Lord made them that way for some purpose, whatever it could be."

"Anyways, what happened next?" asked Adam, anxious to hear the rest of the story.

"Well... after things got quiet, the moon came out in full strength and the clouds disappeared. I got down and stretched my legs. Then Bill said that he was stuck. Now how in ol' 'ell can yuh get stuck sit'n on a tree limb? I asked him if his ass was caught on a knot. He said no, he thought he was sit'n on pine gum. I guess his ol' legs were so numb from straddlin' the branch all night that he couldn't use them to lift himself off it. Then he said he thought that he had pissed himself."

With this, Charley started to chuckle.

"I said what duh yuh mean you *think* yuh did . . . yuh either did or yuh didn't! He said he did. He couldn't get down and he had tuh go. He said it was either piss or bust. Then he said you know what I mean, don't yuh? I said I certainly do, be'n there a few times myself.

"Then he said, will yuh come over and help me down? I said, maybe when the drippin' stops. He said, oh Charley, it's just rainwater. I said, maybe so, but I think I'll wait anyways, just in case.

"So, after a while he said, if you reach up and take my boots off, I'll undo my suspenders. Since it's only my pants that'r stuck, I can crawl out and leave them here. Then I can swing my legs down and you can grab my legs and help me down.

"Uh-huh, and have that ol' thing ov his dangling in my face? I can tell yuh right now that wasn't gonna happen! He'd be sit'n there till the tree rotted down!" Charley couldn't help but laugh as he spoke.

By this time, Adam was laughing so hard the tears were streaming down his face.

"Oh, oh, oh, how in the world do you ever get into so many ov these kind ov messes?"

"Let me tell yuh, it ain't easy," laughed Charley. "I suppose yuh think I stay up half the night plan'n it!"

"No, but I don't know another person that can get in tuh so much trouble, and it doesn't seem tuh matter what yuh do, it just happens! But the best part is when yuh tell about it. I don't know anyone that can tell a story like you can, and you always seem tuh find a funny side to it!"

"I don't like it, but I guess things happen that way!" said Charley, wearing a smile that went from ear to ear.

"Tell me the rest," encouraged Adam.

"He said, oh don't be like that, Charley." Charley was mocking him as he spoke. "Yuh know that beggin' sound he can put in his voice when he's desperate?"

"Yah, I know what yuh mean!"

"I guess he thought I might leave him there. So I said tuh him, if you think that yuhr gonna walk out ov the bush with me in the mornin', and you with no pants on, then yuh better have another thought comin'. Because that ain't gonna happen either!"

Again Adam was shaking with laughter.

"Oh, oh, oh, Charley, I'd sure like tuh have been there to see that happen."

"So he said, and who would ever see us that early in the morn'n?

"I told him not tuh worry, because there would definitely be a crowd waitin'!

"He said, in that whiny voice ov his, why would there be a crowd?

"I told him because that's just the way things happen in this ol' world!

"He said, oh Charley, but yuh have tuh try tuh get me down! I thought, that's what *you* think, but I'll probably be dumb enough tuh do it anyways."

"What did yuh do?"

"I took a pole and a piece ov a limb, and used my bootlace tuh tie it in a tee. Then I held the tee up to him and told him to hold on and I'd pull."

"Did he?"

"Oh, for sure. He held on till I was pullin' for all I was worth, and then he let go! I went arse over tea kettle and hit the ground. But let me tell yuh he wasn't long in saying he was sorry for lettin' go. I guess he figured that I might get mad and go home and leave 'm up there. And that's exactly what I should've done but I stayed and tried 'r again."

"Did it work this time?" Adam still had tears strolling down his cheeks as he spoke.

"Yep, this time he hung on till his ol' arse pulled loose. But when he first bent forward, he let out one ol' 'ell ov a fart; I guess it had built up all night. It was just a rrippp, rippp, rip, so I asked 'm, now what in the world was that? He said there was somethin' in there and it was tryin' tuh get out.

"I said, whatever in ol' 'ell it is, sounds like it's makin' pretty good headway.

"So then I had tuh make a ladder tuh get him down . . . he had a heck ov a time getting his legs over the limb and on tuh the ladder. But he made it. He was kind ov wobbly so I grabbed him and helped him down."

"What would have happened if he didn't have his pants on?" laughed Adam.

"He'd a be'n left there tuh figger it out for himself," Charley said with a chuckle.

"Soon as he got low enough he grabbed hold ov me, so I helped him down. When his feet were on the ground, I told him he could stop the huggin'. He said he wasn't huggin', he was hangin' on 'cause he still couldn't walk. So I waltzed him over tuh the pine tree and set him down with his back tuh the tree and told him tuh try an' get the circulation goin' in his legs. Well, yuh should ov seen the mess when he stood up."

Charley was chuckling as he spoke.

"All the dead grass and the pine needles that he had sat on was stuck tuh the gum. His ol' arse end was all covered with it. So he asked me if I'd pick it off. I told 'm there wasn't the slightest chance that he was ever gonna get my hands up in there."

Again the tears were rolling down Adam's face.

"Oh, oh, oh . . . you get yourself in tuh some ov the darndest messes; if I wrote it in a book they wouldn't believe it!"

"Probably not . . . but it's the truth just the same!" said Charley, laughing as he spoke. "Anyways, I got a fire goin' so we could dry off a little and get warmed up.

"Just before sunup, he figger'd he could walk, so we headed for home. And that was another episode."

"What else could possibly happen?" asked Adam, still chuckling.

"You'd be surprised at what can happen when yuhr with ol' Wild Bill. Well, anyways . . . we didn't get too far till I see this wolf track. And it was a big one. Pretty much the size ov the palm ov muh hand. Again ol' Bill gets excited and begins tuh stutter, just at see'n the tracks. I wonder what would ov happened if he'd ever seen a live one.

"Anyways, we were both squattin' down lookin' at the track when all ov a sudden he straightens up, and as he did, all I hear is clickity-click and then kerbanggo. He said I got 'm, Charley, I got the wolf! I stood up and took a look at what he had shot. I was just in time tuh see the tail ov Bob Bailey's dog do a bit ov a drumbeat and then straighten out.

"He said, I got the wolf. I said, yuh think so? It looks more like yuh just shot Bailey's dog. Then he did get excited. He stuttered so bad I could hardly understand him. He said Bailey never did like him, and he figger'd he'd probably shoot him after kill'n his dog."

"Oh, oh, oh, it just goes from bad to worse!" Adam was shaking his head in disbelief.

"He looked at me and said, what're we gonna do? I said, what do yuh mean *we . . . you* shot the dog! He said, if we don't say anything, maybe he'll think the wolves got 'm!

"I said, uh-huh, and when did the wolves start tuh carry guns? That is definitely a bullet hole between the dog's eyes! And we're close enough to his house that he'll have heard the shot. There's only the two ov us in the bush this time ov the mornin', and I certainly didn't do it, and I ain't about tuh take the blame, either.

"He said tuh me, what'll we do with the dog? Just leave 'm here? I said, yuh can bring 'm with yuh if yuh like, but I'm goin' on home, and he definitely ain't comin' with me!"

"Did he?"

"Did he what?"

"Did he bring the dog?"

"No, he decided against it and left him there. But as we were going past Bailey's house, Bob seen us and walked down tuh the road. He could see that we'd be'n huntin' and asked if we got anything. I said, no, just a good soakin', but I shot a wolf earlier in the mornin'. He said I heard a shot just a little while ago; was that you fellas?

"I couldn't help but smile, so I turned away and said nothin'. Well . . . ol' Bill got all excited and started tuh stutter; 'twas a wonder Bob could understand him. But he managed tuh tell Bob that he thought he saw a wolf, so he up and fired. He said, and I shot yuhr darned ol' dog fair between thu eyes.

"I figger'd the fur would start flyin' at any minute, but Bob started tuh laugh. He said, that was the most useless animal that I'd ever owned, and yuh just saved me from doing it.

"Let me tell yuh, it was a load lifted from ol' Wild Bill's back. He said tuh Bob, yuh ain't mad at me?

"Bob said, no, Bill, that was the best thing that you ever did.

"Ol' Bill's face lit up, and he said, I was sure yuh'd shoot me when yuh found out that I did it!

"Bailey said, Yuh did? And yuh still told me? Well, it's sure good tuh see that yuhr so honest! Why . . . I think I like yuh a little more today than at any other time in your life, but he was smilin' pretty good when he said it.

"So yuh like me a little more, do yuh? said Bill, his face all lit up.

"Bailey said, yes, Bill, a little more, but don't get too excited because it's very little!

"Ol' Bill said let me tell yuh, Bob, when yuhr in my boots, every little bit counts! And I'm pretty sure he was tell'n the truth.

"When we turned to go, Bailey started tuh laugh. He said, what in the world happened tuh yuh 'r back end, Bill? Looks like yuh spent the night in a crow's nest.

"Bill said, yuh don't want tuh know what happened!

"Bob told him, whatever it was, you now remind me ov one ov those cottontailed bunny rabbits.

"Anyways, we made it home and I got tuh bed. 'Twas the best sleep that I'd had for the last three nights."

"Three nights? What happened to the other two?"

"It's a long story. I'll tell yuh another time. Now I better pick up muh stuff and get a move on."

"Okay . . . I hope it's as good as this one," said Adam, still chuckling.

"Better!" said Charley over his shoulder as he moved away.

"Now remember what I told yuh before!" said Charley, "Keep a smile on yuhr face and a dollar in yuhr pocket. Because sooner or later yuh'll be sure tuh meet somebody that will need the one or the other, or maybe both!"

"You bet!" said Adam, smiling as he made his way toward the door.

Charley went about picking up the few things that he needed and placed them on the counter.

"I suppose it was the hunting trip that you two fellas were talkin' about?"

"Could ov be'n," said Charley, trying to skirt the subject.

"I suppose that you and Bill had a pretty good time?"

"Couldn't have be'n better!" said Charley, tongue-in-cheek.

"I suppose you'll be goin' again soon?"

"Not a chance! See the trouble we got intuh by breakin' the rules!"

"What rules?"

"Well... you know, yuh shouldn't be huntin' after sundown!" said Charley, trying not to smile.

"Now, Charley! You know very well that there will be two moons in the sky before you'll ever change!"

"Yuh better go for three if yuh want tuh be real sure!" Charley couldn't hold back the smile any longer.

"Charley, Charley! You will never change. But that's okay because we love yuh just the way you are. Anyways, Charley... I just want tuh say thanks for whatever it was that yuh did for my brother, because I see a little change in him!"

"Uh-huh, and it's most likely to be very little, but I guess every little bit counts."

Charley picked up his change, put it in his pocket, put the bag of groceries in his packsack, and then turned to the door. Over his shoulder he said, "Be seein' yuh!"

"For sure," said Murphy, smiling as he watched Charley close the door. Not another person in this town had caused so many to smile as Charley had. He was different, but in a good way. As the door closed behind him, Charley would again be stepping out into a world of trials and adventure.

But then... what the heck, it was just another day in the life of Charley O' Reilly.

About the Author

In 1945, the author was born on a small farm in the backwoods of Ontario, a place called Bell Rapids. From his youth he dearly loved the country way of life. His spare time was spent hunting and fishing, enjoying the great outdoors. His dog was a constant companion, and he had a love of horses. But at the age of nineteen, the lack of employment moved him to the big city.

This did not diminish his love for the country. Weekends and holidays would always find him back home on the farm. As the saying goes, "you can remove the boy from the country, but you will never remove the country from the boy."

Fifty years later, he retired and moved back to the old homestead. It was then he decided to write about the way of life he had left behind. In writing this book he was able to once again relive those old memories. As the title declares, "Yesterday Is Gone ... but the Memories Live On."